THE FISHER QUEEN'S DYNASTY

Kavita Kané is the best-selling author of four books, all based on Indian mythology: *Karna's Wife* (2013), *Sita's Sister* (2014), *Menaka's Choice* (2015) and *Lanka's Princess* (2016). A senior journalist with a career of over two decades, she quit her job to write books. With a post-graduate degree in English Literature and Journalism and Mass Communication from the University of Pune, the only skill she has, she confesses, is writing.

Born in Mumbai, with a childhood spent largely in Patna and Delhi, she lives in Pune with her mariner husband Prakash, two daughters, Kimaya and Amiya, two dogs, Beau and Chic, and the uncurious cat Cotton.

THE FISHER QUEEN'S DYNASTY

Kavita Kané

Published by
Rupa Publications India Pvt. Ltd 2022
7/16, Ansari Road, Daryaganj
New Delhi 110002

Sales centres:
Allahabad Bengaluru Chennai
Hyderabad Jaipur Kathmandu
Kolkata Mumbai

First published by Westland Publications Private Limited 2017

Copyright © Kavita Kané, 2017, 2022

All rights reserved.

No part of this publication may be reproduced, transmitted,
or stored in a retrieval system, in any form or by any means,
electronic, mechanical, photocopying, recording or otherwise,
without the prior permission of the publisher.

This is a work of fiction. Names, characters,
places and incidents are either the product of the author's imagination
or are used fictitiously and any resemblance to any actual person,
living or dead, events or locales is entirely coincidental.

P-ISBN: 978-93-5520-876-7
E-ISBN: 978-93-5520-877-4

First impression 2022

10 9 8 7 6 5 4 3 2 1

The moral right of the author has been asserted.

Printed in India

This book is sold subject to the condition that it shall not, by way of
trade or otherwise, be lent, resold, hired out, or otherwise circulated,
without the publisher's prior consent, in any form of binding
or cover other than that in which it is published.

To
My sister Asha
Who first introduced Bhishm to me as Devavrat.

To

My sister Anita

Who first introduced [illegible] to me as [illegible]

CONTENTS

PROLOGUE: Bhishm	1
The Birth	4
The Fisher Girl	9
The Sons	21
The Fathers	33
The Crown Prince	43
The King and the Fisher Girl	53
The Dilemma	68
The Oath	84
The Sacrifice	97
The Wedding	111
The Queen	122
The Heirs	136
The Matsyas	150
The Death	163
The Panchals	173
The Regent	189
The Grief	202
The Swayamvar	209
The Three Sisters	223
The Rejection	229
The Waiting	239

The Reprisal	254
The Passing	265
The Widows	280
The Other Son	292
New Hope	303
EPILOGUE: Satyavati	317

PROLOGUE
Bhishm

His life had been one of regrets; and so would his death. Bhishm lay still on his bed of arrows. It was not the arrows that hurt him but the memories piercing his defeated mind. They brought along a tide of remorse, regrets, promises and punishments— nothing of a joyous life, and courage born of faith. He knew he did not have much time to live. Death was upon him ... that is, if he chose to die...

But he had died a long time ago. He did not know when. Was it when he had been twenty, and his life's purpose was snatched away from him—his throne, his identity, his father, his future? Or when Amba, the princess of Kasi, had cursed him to a living death? Was it when Draupadi was dragged by her hair into the very court where once he had defended his step-mother Satyavati's honour, but not the honour of Panchal's princess, the wife of his great grandsons? Or had he died when her words taunted him, reminding him of his worthlessness? Or when the boys died one by one—his half-brothers, Chitrangad and Vichitravirya; his nephew, Pandu; and so many others?

He felt the heat of the tears which refused to fall. What if, by a miracle, the present turned out to be just a terrorizing nightmare, and he was to wake up young again? Would he avoid making the terrible mistakes that ruined so many lives? Would he marry Vatsala? Or agree to marry Amba to save her life and pride? Would he have his own children, and not spend his life looking after his half-brothers? Would he defy Satyavati, and not take his oath? Or not meet her at all?

Satyavati.

My father's wife, the queen-mother, he sighed. He had a terrible longing to die. And a burning desire to live. Not for the sake of living, but to be given a chance to undo what he had done; rather, what he and Satyavati had irrevocably done. But she was long gone, leaving him to his wasted life, and, to face the consequences.

He had longed for his life to be just, righteous and majestic, as the heavens above.

Let me die!

He saw the setting sun; another day gone, another day of the war over, another day of battle won. Like the sinking sun, which does not rise twice during a day, life cannot be brought back; a person can only clutch at what is left of their life, and save it...

But, he had been given his chance to live over and over again; and like Yudhishthir, he had gambled it away, making unforgivable mistakes. No, they were not mistakes, they were misdeeds which cannot be pardoned. He shut his eyes tiredly, waiting for it all to end...

Who was he? He was Prabhas, a Vasu Deva, born as Devavrat to Goddess Ganga, to fulfil Rishi Vasisht's curse. One can never run away from one's own destiny. It will meet them on the path they undertake to avoid it.

He saw how his life had spanned across several generations. And how the sum total of his actions had worked its marvels and miracles. Each of his loved ones had visited him as he lay on the bed of arrows—his Arjun, the rest of the Pandavas, Duryodhan, Karna, Draupadi and Uruvi. To each he had begged for forgiveness, and beseeched them to never repeat his mistakes. To Yudhishthir, his eldest grandson and heir to Hastinapur, he had attempted to teach self-mastery because he wanted him to tell the world what happens when leaders fail in their knowledge and accomplishment, fail to defend and protect, fail to love, and are afraid to lose...

He saw on the wide expanse towards the horizon the sun glittering on the water so dazzlingly that it hurt his eyes to look at it. It was like his truth. He yearned to be that lovely river: *Ma*, always with him but never near. He longed to die—only to die, and nothing more.

He shut his eyes in self-repugnance as he thought about how he had failed all the women in his life: his mother, Ganga; Vatsala, his bride-to-be; Amba, Ambika and Ambalika, the three princesses he had abducted (but most of all, Amba, whom he lost in the fire of love and hate); Kunti, Gandhari and Madri, his grand-daughters-in-law, whom he had used as pawns for political power; Uruvi, Karna's wife, to whom he had promised he would save her husband; and lastly, Draupadi, whom he could not defend at her worst hour in that very hall where he had killed a man who had dared to slander the good name of a Kuru queen, Satyavati.

He had destroyed them all, for her—for that one woman...
Satyavati.

The Birth

The tall, fair man refused to look down at the baby swaddled in the royal blanket. He turned his back and gave the fisherman a hard look.

'The mother gave birth to twins, sire,' said the fisherman, Dasharaj.

'Yes, I know,' replied King Uparichar Vasu, shortly. 'I shall keep the boy with me. You can have the girl.'

Dasharaj looked at the king, aghast. *He was abandoning the girl?*

The king's face softened slightly, seeing the expression on Dasharaj's face. 'I know you have been pining for a child for a long time, Dasharaj. Keep the girl, she is your niece, after all,' he coaxed, but there was a firmness in his voice. It was not a request; it was a royal command.

Dasharaj could barely conceal his joy; he could keep one of the babies. He glanced at the infant girl again. Yes, after all, she was his niece—his dead sister Adrika's daughter. Like Adrika, the baby girl was unusually dark—her smooth ebony skin and her huge black eyes, always alert and watchful. She seemed to be staring at them now as if understanding each word. *Did she know her father, the king of Chedi, was abandoning her*, wondered Dasharaj. Dasharaj felt his heart contract. What the king had said was true: he had been yearning for a child for years, and ever since his wife had died last year he felt bereft like never before. Now Adrika was dead, too... He looked at the girl again. Both of them had nobody in the world.

'Yes, sire, I shall take her with me,' he said quickly, before the king could change his mind. He swiftly picked up the bundle and cradled her in his arms. Overcome by a strong, indecipherable emotion, he felt his heart surge with indescribable joy.

I shall never abandon you, he promised as he saw the dark eyes look up solemnly at him. *I shall give you the love and life you deserve. I could not do much for your mother, but you are born the daughter of a king—shamelessly unacknowledged and deserted—but you shall be my princess. I shall never break your trust. I shall make you the royal princess that you are. And one day, the queen that you deserve to be.*

~

'No! Not again! Please!' he screamed as he saw his young wife about to fling the baby into the deep water of River Ganga.

King Shantanu of Hastinapur rushed to save his newborn son from his wife's hands.

'No, you can't kill another one!' he shouted, snatching the child from her palms. 'You murdered seven of them before! Who are you... a monster or a murderess?'

'I am Ganga, the river nymph,' said the fair lady. 'Your wife. Your queen. But no longer.'

He barely heard her, tears of relief flowing uninhibitedly down his stricken face. He had saved his son, his eighth son from certain death.

His handsome face was contorted with cold fury. 'I never thought I could hate you as much as I do now!' he spat. 'Which mother kills her babies?'

'One who is destined to help them attain salvation,' she said cryptically.

Her unusually cold composure now broke through Shantanu's grief.

'Don't talk in riddles, Ganga!' he snapped. 'Since I fell in love with you, you have always been secretive, an enigma, refusing to tell me anything about yourself. I loved you, and you laid down conditions! But I was desperate enough to marry you in spite of your terms: "Don't ever question my actions or I shall leave you," you warned. All these years, I watched silently as you drowned each of my seven newborn sons. If you want to leave me, Ganga, do so. Don't threaten me anymore. I can't stand the sight of you, you heartless woman! I shall not allow you to kill my eighth son...' he cradled the infant close to his thudding heart.

'No, you cannot keep him. I have to go and so will he,' she said quietly.

Hot anger flooded his face. 'Don't you dare!'

Shantanu was a gentle person and Ganga had never seen her husband so livid before. Nor so devastated. He clutched at the baby as if he was clinging to his last hope of happiness. The baby was his son, the heir to Hastinapur.

'We are cursed, Shantanu,' she stated sadly. 'And so is this child. Today, after asking me this question, you have set me free from my curse, just like I set free seven of your sons from their curses.'

A look of incomprehension crossed his handsome face, replacing the rage for a while. 'What curse are you talking about?' he muttered.

Ganga continued in her soft, sweet voice: 'Not long ago, the eight Vasus—the cosmic attendant deities of Vishnu—visited Rishi Vasisht's ashram with their wives. One of the wives wanted to keep the rishi's famous wish-fulfilling cow, Kamadhenu, for herself. She persuaded her husband, Prabhas, the God of Sky, to steal it. He and his seven brothers were caught in the act of stealing the cow, and all were cursed by the angry rishi to be reincarnated as mortals. The brothers begged for mercy, and the rishi agreed to alleviate the curse. He said they would be liberated from their human birth as soon as they were born. The Vasus implored me to give birth to them and to drown them in my waters as soon as they were born. I managed to release seven, but this child...' she said sadly, looking down at the beautiful, fair-eyed, fair-skinned baby, '...this child is the cursed Prabhas. Had you not stopped me, he, too, could have been delivered from Rishi Vasisht's curse.'

Shantanu looked stunned with horror.

'Probably Prabhas, being the chief culprit, was cursed to endure a longer life on earth,' she reasoned, giving a helpless shrug.

'Why did you not explain all this before to me?' said Shantanu, visibly shaken. 'You could have saved all of us from this tragedy...'

'Because both of us were cursed by Lord Brahma,' said Ganga. 'In your previous birth, you were King Mahabhish, who was privileged to visit Brahma's court. We met there and fell in love. A gush of wind swept my *angavastra* away, and while the gods bashfully kept their heads bowed and their eyes downcast, you could not stop looking at me. I blushed in turn and reciprocated the look of desire for you. Our secret lay exposed. Lord Brahma was furious at this public display of desire. He cursed us both to be born on Earth and suffer the pain of love and separation, like ordinary mortals. I can return only after breaking your heart. And it's all come true, hasn't it?' she raised her eyes, bright with unshed tears. 'I have broken your heart.'

Shantanu stood there, his face ashen, the finality of her words crushing him right in front of her eyes.

'No,' he gave a strangled cry. 'Don't leave me, please. I take all my harsh words back. You know I love you ... Oh, I love you so, Ganga! Don't go, please, no!'

He was crying, holding the baby.

'I have to go,' she said, blinking away her tears, her voice hard. She gently prised the infant from his nerveless arms.

'No,' he whispered hoarsely, grabbing her wrist, his eyes imploring.

'I have to go from where I came. And I have to take this child with me...'

'Why, oh why are you punishing me? You could have killed me instead!' he beseeched her. He looked up and cried out, 'What curse is this, my lord, that I live a life without the woman I love and a son I can never see again!'

He fell to his knees, his broad shoulders shuddering with unrestrained sobs. 'Spare me this sorrow, Ganga, please! Don't curse me to a living death!'

She turned away from his tortured face, squaring her shoulders. 'I have to go, but when the time is right, I shall return your son to you. That is all I can promise.'

It took King Shantanu a moment before Ganga's words sunk in. 'You mean it? I shall have my son back some day?' he said hopefully.

'Yes; not because I want to be kind to you,' she said sorrowfully, 'but because this poor boy is doomed to live a cursed life on earth. As your son, he is born pious, wise and devoted, but will have to endure endless mortal pain and suffering. I name him Devavrat, the one that possesses the piety of the gods. He is your son, but, as his mother, I shall groom him and teach him the wisdom of the maharishis and the craft of warfare from the gods. And then I shall return to you the heir to your kingdom, when he is of the right age.'

Defeated, Shantanu closed his eyes in despair to shut off the sight of his wife leaving him with his newborn son.

'My son,' murmured the distraught father. 'My Devavrat, I shall wait for you...!'

The Fisher Girl

The smell of dirt and decay wafted in the damp air, but the girl sitting alone on the shore seemed unperturbed by it. She had sat down on the rock, burying her face in her hands, her slim body shuddering with silent cries. *Never in my life have I been so deeply insulted... I, well-educated, refined, the daughter of a fisherman-chieftain, suspected of theft by the kingsmen*, she thought. They had ransacked and rummaged through the boat she ferried across the river every day. She had been searched like a common street-walker.

She could not imagine a greater insult, her indignation unmitigated by an oppressive dread. All sorts of absurd ideas came into her mind. *If they can suspect me of theft, then they can arrest me, strip me naked and search me, and then lead me through the streets with an escort of soldiers, cast me into a cold, dark cell with mice and woodlice, exactly like the dungeons in which dethroned kings are imprisoned.* Her heart quickened with such morbid thoughts, all the stories she had heard about atrocities coming back to her. *Who will stand up for me? My poor, old father will probably not have enough money to come and rescue me. If taken to the city, I will be absolutely alone, like a solitary, lost person in a desert, without friends or kin. They can do what they like with me...*

'Kali!'

She instinctively turned in the direction of the voice. Everyone called her that—Kali—an unimaginative reference to her dark skin, dark hair, and dark eyes. Kali straightened herself, her eyes bleak.

'Your father is looking for you. You have a guest!' shouted her neighbour.

She roped the boat to the shore, securing it with an

additional loop of a knot after piling the net neatly in it. That was the only functional one they had. They would have to buy a new one once this season got over. But, as always, they were short of money. The steep taxes were eating into the paltry amount they fetched from trips across the river.

As she walked towards her home, she decided against telling her father about the ignominious episode. She proceeded slowly to the only stone-roof house in the village, an anomaly in the bleak mass of mouldy, thatched huts. All of them seemed the same along the rutty road—decrepit and black with soot and filth, belching black smoke that had yellowed everything into uniform dinginess. There was a sordid, undisciplined feeling about the village which she had got accustomed to, yet loathed. The street was littered with trash and fish scales, groups of men stood around street corners eyeing her as she walked towards her house. *Loafers*, her lips curling in contempt, *they are a sick, seedy looking bunch—dirty, tired and angry. Like me.* Women hurried past like they had something on their minds. She was seized with a sudden temper. *Everything about this place is disgusting. There are no roads any longer*, she thought savagely as she waded through the slush. In summer, the track would be dry and dusty, and during the rains, like now, it was an open gutter, exposing them to disease, stink and discomfort. She detested the way the nobles and royalty lived their lives, while she was cursed to a life of hard work and stench, with no hope of ever bridging the gap.

Even as she ambled down the muddy street, she was aware of how people kept their distance from her. She was young and educated; yet, the fact was that she was a fisher girl, with the vile stench of fish and salt, sweat and grime, as rotten as mouldering fish, forgotten but for the stink they raised. Kali noticed how a passing lady visibly shrank from her, her face twisted in distaste, clamping her nose with her hand as if to keep the odour at bay.

Kali was used to being treated as a pariah, the lowest of the low, only allowed a small vestige of dignity once she turned into the lane of the fisher folk. She was after all, their chieftain's daughter. There was a certain regalness about the girl as she strode briskly with her head held high, her eyes openly contemptuous.

Her father had a visitor, she thought resentfully, *another stomach to feed!*

The visitor was a rishi. A thin, young man with a cadaverous chest and a pronounced limp, immediately lending him an aura of mystery. A lame rishi was an enigma unlike a limping soldier or a crippled prince whose handicap was assumed to be some glorious war injury.

'This is Rishi Parashar, Satyavati...'

Hardly anyone knew her as Satyavati, and only her father called her by that name.

'He is the famous grandson of Rishi Vasisht, a famous rishi himself,' Dasharaj was saying. 'He is currently writing the Vishnu Puran, the first of a series. And he is also an impressive orator, but prefers to call himself a travelling teacher, wandering from one place to another. He was passing through our village.'

Her father was beaming warmly, which was unusual. He had stopped smiling since they lost a dozen boats in a storm some years ago. He was a swarthy, little man with a wiry face and a narrow, bald head with thin hair making him appear much older. Yet, he exuded a charm and strength. 'He will rest with us for a while, and then continue with his journey to attend some yagna. Do drop him to the other shore, whenever he wishes,' he said.

With the morning's incident fresh in her mind, she

shuddered at the thought of going near her boat again to work. But she couldn't say anything, lest she had to explain her reluctance to her father.

'Won't you be having dinner with us?' she asked politely instead.

The rishi was staring at her with his deep, soulful eyes, the single attractive feature on his thin face.

He shook his head. 'I am fasting,' he explained simply.

That is one meal saved, she heaved a sigh of relief. Suddenly a thought struck her and she looked at the rishi with doubt. *Why had such an illustrious rishi deigned to visit an impoverished fisherman?*

'Don't underestimate your father, Matsyagandha,' smiled the rishi, his face transforming magically.

She was amazed at how he had read her mind. She laughed derisively; yet it was an attractive, husky sound. Matsyagandha, the girl with the fish smell, but he made it sound like the girl with a fragrance!

'Your father, as you well know, was once the fisherman–chieftain of a formidable tribe that helped in wars.'

'Was,' she said dismissively. 'As you can see, we have fallen on bad times.'

'Not for long,' murmured Parashar.

'I take that as a blessing and not just a wish,' she continued tartly, pressing her lips and placing a fingertip on the middle of the lower one, her brows furrowed in a frown.

He fixed her with a blank stare. 'I would like to leave before it gets dark. Would you mind helping me across the river, Matsyagandha?'

Again that name, and again he had read her reluctance!

He continued easily, 'I have heard you are one of the most trusted and brave people who ferry boats, come storm, thunder or rain.'

'It is Man who is the most dangerous, not Nature,' she said glibly. 'See how the rich and the powerful treat us, the downtrodden, without the right to live with dignity, to taste all the horrors of poverty and dependence! My father, as you pointed out rightly, was a chieftain, the king's ally, but what is he now but a frail, bankrupt fisherman!'

'It is the war,' said Dasharaj. 'Our guest here was attacked in his ashram. The limp is a reminder, is it not?'

Parashar gave his small smile. 'The war has taken its toll on all.'

'But not on the king,' she snapped.

'Our king is a vassal to King Shantanu and Hastinapur...' explained Dasharaj.

'Our king surrendered to Hastinapur without a whimper,' Kali retorted. 'Yet the Kuru army took over our land and everything we own, with a double tax for both the kingdoms.'

'You seem to know your politics well,' observed Parashar, 'for such a young age.'

'It is not politics, it is injustice,' she replied swiftly. 'I am fifteen, young enough to experience it and old enough to realize it.'

Parashar smiled warmly, and Kali found herself calming down.

They were soon on their way across the River Yamuna, the boat setting off gingerly from the bank.

'You know your way around, don't you?' he murmured.

Kali knew he was not talking about the small boat she was manoeuvring in the choppy waters of the Yamuna. She was to ferry him across, but they were barely halfway there when the skies darkened ominously. If it rained, her task would be more arduous and she would have to return in a storm. She grimaced.

'If you are saying I am good with the boat, yes, I do know

my way around in these waters. And if you are implying I am worldly-wise, yes, I am that, too,' she admitted, gritting her teeth, rowing the boat more strongly against the swirling eddies.

He was sitting awkwardly, accommodating his left leg. She knew he was observing her: her strong, sinewy arms; her lissom body moving against the motion of the rocking boat; the sweat and the spray mingling to add sheen to her dusky, shining skin. Her damp angavastra was clinging to her upper body, straining against the generous swell of her breasts, the heaving movement accentuated by the strain of the exercise. She recognized the gaze. It was a look of lust. She neither resented it nor revelled in it. It was a fact that she was young, lovely and innocent. And she could see it blatantly in his eyes.

She decided to ignore the young man. They were in the middle of the river, and she was surprised to find the waters relatively calmer now, as was the weather. She knew she could pause to rest.

He seemed to read her thoughts again.

'I am not in a hurry,' he said calmly. 'Why don't you rest now?'

She shook her head and continued rowing. She knew what it could lead to if she stopped.

From the corner of her eye, she saw him inching closer.

'Don't move,' she shouted sharply. 'You might upturn the boat.'

He touched her hand, gripping hard at the oars. His touch was fiery. 'Give them rest,' he repeated gently, his voice sounding like a hoarse whisper against the roaring wind.

'If we stop, the boat will toss,' she said shortly, careful not to be rude. She knew the man sitting across was a well-known rishi, no ordinary man, who could wield unnatural and mystical powers. A man of wisdom, whose words could result in either a curse or a blessing. *A powerful man*, she repeated silently to herself, seeing the naked arousal in his eyes.

She felt a knot in her stomach. She looked around her: they were alone in a boat, in the middle of a river. He was a strong, young man, who could easily overpower her despite his crippled leg. But unlike him, she could jump into the water and swim back ashore. But she did not want to. He was an intriguing man. Curiosity and desire held her firmly, waiting for him to make a move.

His intense eyes pinned on her, he put this hand in the waters. The river suddenly stilled.

'Now the boat will not toss. Or turn,' he said with an unsteady voice. He moved closer to her, his breath warm on her face, his hand on her thigh.

'I want you, Matsyagandha.'

It was not a confession; he could not have made his intention clearer. She felt no fear, no apprehension, no uncertain anxiety. Instead, she felt a strange sense of power over him.

'Much gratitude for making it easy for me to row the boat now,' she said casually. 'We will reach faster.'

'Let's go to that island,' he said gently, yet firmly.

'Island? There is no island in the middle of the Yamuna!' she laughed, but her smile died as she saw the silhouette of an approaching land mass. He had created an island in the river with his extraordinary powers!

He remained silent, his burning eyes not leaving her face. She half hoped that by the time they reached ashore, the young rishi would have come to his senses.

The boat hit the sandy bank and glided smoothly to the waterside.

She dropped the oars, her hands placed demurely on her lap, waiting for him to alight and leave. But she knew he would not. He wanted to seduce her; yet, it seemed like it was she who was seducing him. Again, she had mixed feelings—the thrill of anticipation and a reluctant hesitation. *He wants me, but do I want him?* She felt a brief prick of trepidation. She was alone with him; how was she to deal with him?

She eyed him sceptically. What would it be like making love to a mighty rishi? *Menaka had given birth to Shakuntala, after being with the powerful rishi, Vishwamitra,* she thought dazedly, as she watched the young seer get up. *What would this rishi give me?* She shivered in anticipation.

Parashar got up unsteadily, and carefully stepped out of the boat. She expelled a long breath, wondering if he would proceed without looking back. *Had his ardour cooled?* He turned then, and from the one look he gave her, she knew it had not. With a slow, deliberate motion, he took her hand, and gripped her wrist. She could feel the fire within, searing in his eyes, in his touch.

She knew she could not escape him. But was she not repulsed by him—either by his limp or by his desire for her? It was a decisive moment. *I am going to make love to a powerful seer, not some young fisher boy or some callow villager.* Her heart was racing, the thrill of fear and excitement coursing through her, and her blood was pounding rapidly.

'Don't be afraid,' he said softly, pulling her up against his tall, lean frame. Their thighs touched, but she moved her leg adroitly away, tempting him maddeningly.

'Do I have a choice?' she asked steadily, 'to refuse or accept you?'

There was an imperceptible pause, as the question dimmed the smoulder in his eyes.

The Fisher Queen's Dynasty

'Then I beg you, love me, take me!' he whispered thickly, pulling her hard against him. She stiffened.

She had no chance against his strength. His fingers tightened around her waist, his left hand holding her wrists, crushing her into submission. Then aroused by the contact of her slim, half-naked body, he gently pushed her down till she lay sprawled on the sandy surface, half dazed, as he knelt over her.

She placed her hand against his thudding chest, but did not push him away.

'You have magical powers,' she said as she furrowed her brows, thoughtfully. 'I smell of fish. Can you remove it?' she asked. 'People flee from my stink. That is one of the reasons why I have very few admirers,' she said. 'Who wants to make love to a foul-smelling fisher girl?'

'I do,' he urged. 'You shall never regret it.'

She gazed at him, her heart hammering. *Was his power for real? Well ... he did still the waters of the river and created an island in it!*

'Then ... make me fragrant,' she said, more out of curiosity than as a challenge. She knew he was oblivious to her faint stench, and nothing would dissuade him now; yet, she wanted to bide her time.

'Done!' he smiled. He placed his hands on the soles of her feet in the shallow, lapping water, moving his thumbs in a smooth, circular motion. It was strangely erotic. Rubbing them gently, he continued to run a trembling hand slowly from her toes to the slim ankles, up her long, shapely legs, pausing at her waist, then brushing across her breasts, up her long neck to finally cup her face. Suddenly warm now, she smelt a scented glow of sandalwood and roses emanating all around her.

'You, my Matsyagandha, are going to be my one weakness,'

he said, his face buried against the hot skin of her exposed neck. 'That one weakness, I promise, which will make you strong. Can you smell the perfume?' He unpinned her braid, his fingers combing through her loose, long hair, pulling her face closer to his fevered mouth. She was enveloped by the intoxicating scent of musk. 'It's emanating from your body. You will no longer be the stinking fisher girl. Matsyagandha will now be Yojanagandha; your new, musky fragrance will waft for miles together, and shall entice anyone whom you want. No one will dare call you Kali!'

She gave a small shake of her head. 'I am Kali; I don't mind my dark skin,' she said petulantly. 'I don't want to turn fair-skinned. However, what else can you give me, sir?'

'What all mortals crave for: eternal youth and beauty,' he whispered, cleaving her closer, his wiry arms hard around her waist. 'Your fragrance and your eternal beauty will double your charm. And your power,' he murmured. 'That's what you want, don't you? That hot flush of unbridled power ... the way you have control over me right now? I am your slave!'

'And I am a virgin,' she said, without a hint of coyness, pushing him back slightly, her black eyes mocking.

Her restrain inflamed him and he found himself trembling as he reached for her again.

'You won't marry me, since you are a wandering mendicant,' she persisted. 'So how do I go back to the world I come from? And what if I have a child from you?' she questioned shrewdly, thinking again of Menaka and Shakuntala. 'Who will marry *me*?'

'Whomsoever you want! You will remain a virgin,' he chuckled, his lips on her bare shoulder. 'Or rather, the man you will make love to next will not realize that you are *not* a virgin!'

Before she could open her mouth to argue, he pressed it lightly with his. 'You can go back to your world without the child. He will remain with me, brought up as a rishi's child should,' he whispered assuredly against her widening smile. 'The boy will grow up to be a very famous sage, and will bring you great glory.'

'As famous as you?' she laughed softly, parting her lips for him to allow him to taste the sweetness of her mouth.

'No. More famous than me. Possibly more than my grandfather, too,' he promised. 'The world will remember him thousands of years later. Rishi Vishwamitra had given me such a blessing. And you will be known as the mother of this extraordinary child.'

She pulled back her face to look warily at him.

'How can I ever acknowledge this child if it is born out of wedlock, oh wise rishi?' she said, frowning, biting her lower lip. 'I will be an unmarried mother. I neither want to renounce my child nor make him suffer the insult of being illegitimate,' she said fiercely.

Parashar bent his head to caress her smooth cheek with his lips to ease the tension from her face.

'He will be our child, Matsyagandha. He will be so exceptional that no one will dare call him illegitimate,' he said cryptically. 'You are an extraordinary girl yourself. You can never be bound by conventions or be tied down by others. You were born to rule, princess!'

She stiffened pleasurably against him, aroused not by desire but by ambition. *Born to rule*, she murmured to herself.

'That is why I am with you now,' he muttered, pulling gently at her lips. She could feel his heat seeping through her, her strength giving away in his crushing arms. She was being overpowered, trapped under the weight of his body.

'I see,' she said huskily. He was out of his mind with desire. His seeking lips trailed down her neck.

Even though his words made no sense to her, she registered their prophecy. This was her opportunity. He could turn her unprivileged life into an unusual one. He had undone her flimsy bodice, his hands on her full, bare breasts. She glanced up at him with a half-smile, her eyes igniting him to heated urgency. If she had to give, she would take as well.

'We could be spotted from here,' she breathed, her eyes luminous.

'Matsyagandha!' he groaned. As his lips crushed down on hers, she became aware that they had been ensconced in a thick blanket of fog.

'Anything else?' he sighed against the soft swell of her bared breast.

She shook her head as she surrendered, finally and triumphantly, to him. She was dimly aware that he had pulled up her loose *antariya*. She became aware of a sharp stone grinding into her spine, but it was nothing compared to the pain she experienced when he thrust himself into her body violently, with fevered passion. She gasped. It was momentary, but unbeknown, she would feel the ache all through her life. She had lost her innocence to gain freedom.

The Sons

'Do I have to go to my father?'

Ganga heard the faint impatience in her son's deep tenor. His voice had changed, and so had he. Devavrat had grown up; it was not just his voice, he now towered over her. It was not merely a mother's appreciative eyes which acknowledged that her son had grown to be a very fine lad—with his fair, good looks, his deep hazel eyes, thick, curly brown hair, and shy smile. He was no longer a boy, she mused, and no longer could she keep him with her...

It was unlike him to be restive. Devavrat had a mild voice, rarely relaying any emotion. He had asked the same question several times in the past one year, and she had delayed answering him each time.

'Why, are you too happy here?' she asked lightly, but her pale, blue eyes were sceptical.

He shrugged—another sign of discontent, she was quick to observe.

'Have I completed all my training here?' he asked instead, the slight shrug making a swathe of dark hair fall over his broad forehead. She leaned forward to gently push it back.

It was a leading question.

'Yes, almost,' she murmured.

'What is left?' asked Devavrat quickly, a little too quickly, revealing his impatience and eagerness again, that persistent wisp of hair falling over his face.

Nothing, she silently acknowledged, leaning forward again to tuck his hair, but he moved his face away restlessly.

Devavrat had completed his training and had far surpassed everyone's expectations. She had seen to it that he had got the best of teachers in various fields, and he had excelled in each, be it under Rishi Vasisht, Parashuram, Shukracharya or Brihaspati. She had taken him to every prestigious gurukul, crossing realms and reigns. Rishi Markendaya had taught him the complexity of duty and dharma in the *Brahmanas*; from Sanatkumar, the eldest son of Lord Brahma, he mastered the *anvikshiki*, the mental and spiritual sciences; Shukracharya, the guru of the asuras and danavs, taught him political and social sciences with an emphasis on politics; and Brihaspati had concentrated on the various *shastras*.

'I know I have finally mastered all that you had in mind for me, Ma,' he said. 'You have been ambitious for me...'

'Why?' demanded Ganga. 'Because I wanted you to be exceptional; even extraordinary. But what use is it if your skills are not put to use. What has been sown has to be ploughed and reaped. When do you show your skills to the world, Devavrat? You have shown exceptional skill at mastering all the arts and proving yourself in Devlok. But you do not belong here,' she murmured brutally.

His solemn eyes flashed with uncharacteristic fire. 'Why? Give me the chance, Ma.'

She sighed. 'Devavrat, you are not a god, a demigod or a gandharv to be allowed to stay in Indralok! You are a mortal, meant to live on earth!' she said simply. 'You have to return to your father's kingdom.'

It is not as simple as I make it sound, she cried silently. *The world down there is a cruel, ugly place.*

'So now, since I am done here, I have to meet my father whom I have never seen, never known,' said Devavrat, his smooth jaw tense. This time it was not a query or a request, but an assertive statement.

In that devastating moment, Ganga discerned that her responsibility as a mother would soon be over. It was time for the son to be with his father. It was going to be hard on her as it was for him, though he didn't show it; he was being deliberately impassive. *That is why he resents his potential departure. But she would have to convince her on that he had to be with his father too, no matter how much the mother loved him. A child needs both parents,* a sane voice advised her. She herself had experienced a happy childhood, with doting parents and a younger sister. And here she was, reluctant to give her son the time and love of his father. Ganga loathed herself for being selfish, but she hated the thought of separation more. *Separation,* her heart contracted at the emotion that word evoked. *I had to leave Shantanu, too,* she thought, *and it left a void that has never been filled. He too must have been pining for me as well as for his son all these years...*

Ganga knew she was being irrational, but maternal love often made the wisest woman a sentimental person. Her heart was torn, unwilling to let go of her son...

'Ma?' she heard him say, slipping his large hands into her soft ones. 'Do I need to prove myself more to remain here?' he asked hopefully, his tawny eyes eager. 'I have accompanied Lord Indra for most of the wars, and, each time, we have tasted resounding victory.'

She forced a smile. 'You can't boast too well, can you?' she teased. 'I know you were the reason why the devas won most of the time. Indra is uncharacteristically happy, and he admits he is going to miss you once you leave...'

'He didn't seem too happy when Lord Vishnu complimented me on the win over the danavs,' interrupted Devavrat wryly.

'Indra cannot bear competition of any sort, and the fact that a mere fifteen-year-old is winning wars for him must be difficult for his ego!' she lifted her shoulders dismissively. 'He is fond of you or he would not have given you so many of his secret war weapons; that's rare, coming from him! In fact, he is not too keen about you going back to Earth at all. Nor are the Trinity, especially Lord Shiva,' she nodded. 'You are his favoured one.'

'Then I won't!' he responded quickly, squeezing her hand pleadingly. 'But I am your son, too—I am Gangaputra—should I not be with you, too?'

'Not anymore,' she shook her head sadly.

Her heart contracted. Devavrat would *have* to return to Earth one day—the curse lay heavily on his head. But Devavrat was blissfully unaware of it. *Should I tell him? No! But she would have to: there was no other way. He was entitled to know the truth of his birth, his past, his present and now his future.* In calm, crisp words she told him everything. *It will shatter him,* her mind screamed but she hardened her heart and continued.

Ganga was a woman who betrayed no emotions, and it surprised Devavrat as to why his mother was being so insistent, yet clearly reluctant. Now he knew. He was fifteen years old, and till now, he had had no curiosity to meet the man who was his father. His mother was his world, and he wanted to be with her. He studied her with his steady, searching eyes.

'So you left him for me,' he said softly, after an excruciating pause.

She nodded, her throat thick with unshed tears.

'And he lost his all because of me,' he emphasized. 'His wife and his son. Because of this curse I was born with.'

Ganga looked puzzled but nodded slightly.

'Had I been drowned then by you, you would still be with him, is that not so?' he persisted. 'It was because of me, that both of you are not together.'

She had no further words of explanation. The silent

anguish on his mother's face tore at his heart, wordlessly confirming his growing guilt: it was he who had separated his parents.

'Don't you ever feel like going back to him?' he asked quietly.

Ganga was taken aback by the bluntness of his question. He was a fearless fellow, unhesitant to question even the gods—frank, but never rude.

She eyed him, confused. Was that what he wished for: all of them to be together? *But that could never be, that was a mirage...*

'We live in Heaven, and you should know by now that mortals live in a different world,' she said evenly. 'I couldn't have stayed with him forever.'

'Then if I am the son of a mortal, I shall have to go,' said Devavrat slowly, in his most reasonable voice, though she could hear his raw pain .

'You are his wife, yet you stayed away from him all these years, keeping me away as well...'

Ganga felt the first prickle of fear. Did her son resent her for having kept him with her, instead of with Shantanu?

'...because you are a celestial nymph, meant to reside in the Heavens or the Himalayas ... your abode. But I am no longer a child, Ma,' he continued gently, his eyes alit with sudden insight, knowing it was up to him to make the parting as pleasant as possible. He could not bear to see his mother hurting and so anguished. 'What you say is right; my days here are done. I am no longer needed here. As a mother, you have given me love, and guided me all through these years; provided me the best education in the best possible places! Now, it is time for me to learn more from my father.'

The moment he said the quiet words of acceptance, she broke down, desperation flooding her.

'Earth is hell, dear son!' she exploded in a moment of panic. 'There is only grief, violence and disillusionment, unlike the eternal joy here. I shall plead with the lords—Brahma, Shiva and Vishnu—to allow you to live here. I shall fight if I have to!'

There was a frantic tone to her voice, the azure depth of her eyes conveying her frenzied dilemma. Devavrat had never seen his mother so fragile and vulnerable to emotions; he knew he had to be brave for her, too.

'Ma, it is futile to fight a pointless battle,' he smiled sadly. 'And have you not been punished enough that you wish to take on the ire of the gods again?'

He took her hands. 'And I am a mortal, remember,' he reminded her gently, shaking his head with that errant lock of hair, a shy smile tugging at his lips. She instinctively tucked it back. 'I am meant to live and die on Earth.'

His words hit her hard, forcing her to come to her senses. Her son had to go back, live his life on Earth, suffer his spell, and finally die. He would then come back to her...

She turned her face away to hide the warm prick of sudden tears.

'We shall leave,' she said brusquely, as if to end the painful conversation. 'Soon.'

~

Kali never saw Parashar again. They parted ways as if they were strangers, and not lovers; no tears or regrets. The fog had cleared as quickly as it had settled, and, once the boat had reached ashore, he walked away without a single backward glance.

She had transformed: from a young and innocent girl to a woman who was aware of her sexuality, and her power over men.

She was a virgin again; Kali smiled with a curl of her lips, *though not as chaste as social norms dictate*, she thought. She could not care less; she could not help but laugh at how that sheer skin was considered a trophy for men to want and venerate. It had freed her: she had power and control over her life and love.

Suddenly, it was a new Kali that the village saw—one with a sweet fragrance, not the repelling fish odour. Those who had turned their noses at her in the past, now looked at her with frank admiration. Contempt had quickly turned to commendation. People were as shallow as the river shore, never as deep as the river. Beautiful, bold and brazen, Kali knew the effect she was having on the young men of the village. She saw it in their eyes, in their flushed faces when she approached them, and in the quick intake of their breath. She sought and selected her admirers as if she were picking the best fish in the basket: not using her status as the chief's daughter, but her power as a desirable woman. Kali found that she was rediscovering herself, unrepentant and unapologetic about her deeds and her decisions. Desire did not shame her, nor did lust overawe her. After the episode with Parashar, she knew it was her sharpest weapon to cleave and carve a better life for herself.

But Kali also respected the intellect she was born with. She found herself involved in matters of the village, be it resolving a domestic fight or the mending of the fallen school roof, or demanding a fairer share in the fish market from the bigger merchants. She was the voice of the poor and the wretched, a leader most were wary of; even the soldiers dared not intimidate her anymore.

It was several months later, more as an afterthought, that she informed her father about Parashar. He did not look surprised.

'You knew, didn't you?' she realized suddenly.

'My dear, I sent you with the great Rishi Parashar knowing very well that he would bless you in some way or the other,' he said quietly.

'I am going to have his child,' she stated, her voice even.

Dasharaj nodded. 'As planned,' he said cryptically.

'Planned? A sexual favour, you mean, Father?' she raised her brow, but Dasharaj returned her look, unfazed.

'To get, you have to give,' he replied. 'You turned it to your advantage and got what you wanted.'

She twisted her lips into a thin smile. 'I was staving him off with my list of conditions—eternal youth, a rare fragrance all my own, unimpaired virginity...'

'He did not just want you, but also a child from you,' said her father gently.

She frowned, bemused.

'Not just any ordinary baby, but an illustrious son. Mark my words! It was destined to be so! Parashar received a boon from Lord Shiva that his son would be a Brahmarishi, like his grandfather Vasisht,' explained Dasharaj.

He eyed her as she served him some fish and rice. 'Are you worried that the child will be branded illegitimate?' he asked. 'He won't. We can leave this village for a while. I can say that I am unwell and am going to my cousin's home. We can return after you give birth,' he shrugged. 'But are you going to keep it?' he asked carefully.

'No,' she said, nervously tapping a finger on her lower lip. 'It was so decided that he will bring up the child. He honoured my freedom,' her lips twisted. 'It's for the best, for I don't want to be bound by a child now or be an unwed mother,' she said restlessly. 'I want more. I could have demanded marriage, too, but I don't want to be a rishi's wife and live in an ashram. I was born a princess and I shall be queen some day!'

'You are ambitious,' he murmured, chuckling softly.

'Is that bad?' she challenged. 'It was not the only reason. I cannot expose the baby to shame and stigma, or be termed a bastard. That is the least I can do as his mother.'

'I was more worried that he would be forsaken,' he remarked, dryly.

'Like my father forsook me?' she retorted belligerently. 'That's what kings do. I shan't.'

'That is my concern. As is yours, I know,' he added gently, knowing how much it hurt his daughter that she was abandoned. 'You have grown so bitter at so young an age!' he remarked worriedly.

'It's my birthright, is it not?' she asked ironically. 'You may have spun a fine story about me being this gift between King Uparichar Vasu of Chedi and an apsara, Adrika. I remember the story clearly: King Vasu, while hunting, sorely missed his beautiful queen, Girika, and while dreaming about her, was so aroused that he spilled his seed. He wrapped it in a leaf and gave it to a hawk to carry it to his wife. Instead, the hawk was attacked by another hawk and the semen fell into a river, to be swallowed by a fish named Adrika, who was a cursed apsara. After ten months, a fisherman—that's you, dear father—caught the fish and killed it, and when you cut it open, you saw two babies, one male and one female, inside the fish. You gave the babies rightfully to the king. The boy child grew up to become a famous Matsya king, and the daughter was suitably named Matsyagandha, and was destined to be brought up by the childless fisherman. As for their fish-mother, Adrika, she was freed of the curse and went back to Heaven!' Kali laughed mirthlessly. 'What a fairy tale you spun to fool the world, Father! To protect whom? The king? Or me, his deserted daughter? And who was my mother? Adrika, the mythical apsara, or a poor fisherwoman whom King Vasu seduced, impregnated, and abandoned, and who died at childbirth?' she asked scornfully. 'So who was she, Father?' she insisted.

Dasharaj flushed, not out of embarrassment, but unforgotten resentment. 'She was my sister,' he said in a low tone. 'King Vasu took a fancy to her and...' he pursed his lips, releasing an angry sigh.

Kali felt a momentary pang for her unknown mother. *I will not be a wretched victim like her*, she vowed.

'Yes, I get it,' she said harshly, her eyes brittle. 'He didn't marry her. She was what—a passionate moment?'

Dasharaj's face hardened. 'Yes, she was. But she was a fool to hope that a married king would marry her. He was riding by the River Kalindi one day, when he spotted her. She was a lovely girl and he was totally besotted with her, but only for those few hours of passion. She thought it was love,' he gave a sad, short laugh. 'He immediately left for Chedi, never to return. I tried to convince her that he had left her for good, but she kept waiting for him...' Dasharaj sighed at the memory, his eyes distant. 'She was pregnant but she did not lose hope, determined to have his child. She died barely a few hours after giving birth to both of you. Adrika didn't deserve her horrible death!' he said violently. 'She begged me to take the children to the king, wanting them to have a better life than she had...' his voice shook, rough and rasping. 'I obeyed her dying wish. He accepted the son because he was childless at the time; he had five sons later, after he adopted your brother. But he refused to keep you. I returned home with you, and with the fancy story everyone likes to believe about their beloved king and a heavenly apsara. I had a selfish motive too—I wanted to keep you. And I did it for you, too,' he said helplessly.

'I was born a princess,' she said forcefully. 'I am a king's daughter. Just like my twin brother who is now, I hear, the king of Matsya, the new kingdom carved out from Chedi. He roams across the country in his chariot, it's a silk white flag embossed with a shimmering golden fish flying aloft, while I sell fish and ferry people! Why was I denied my right?'

'Because you are a girl,' he conceded. 'Kings need princes, not princesses! If it had been up to him, he would have probably drowned you in the river,' Dasharaj said.

Watching the hurt and distress on her father's face, Kali felt ashamed of herself. 'I am not angry with you, Father,' she said abruptly. 'I owe you my life. But I cannot forget that I was deprived of what I deserved.'

The old man nodded. 'You are a princess, but had to live the life of a commoner. But better alive than dead, right?'

'Alive as what, Father; an underprivileged?' she scorned. 'How can I forget the humiliation heaped on us? Maybe not his name, but he could have offered gold to you to take care of me and save us from this poverty? Look at this hovel we stay in! He couldn't afford either generosity or conscience,' she said bitterly, expelling a long breath. The weight of what had happened with her stayed with her continuously. She felt wronged, and the need to earn her birthright back burned strong within her.

'I—not Fate or God—shall be responsible for my own happiness, my own future. I promise myself, I will not be the victim anymore; nor will my child. His father is famous and respected, so let him live with him. He will gain more respect there than with an unwed fisherwoman.'

Her mouth tightened; her eyes unflinching, she continued, 'It is better I use my ambitions wisely. I would rather make use of a powerful man and get some benefits, as I have done with Rishi Parashar. If it is looks and lust which can seduce a man, weaken him, then I shall employ them as my means; I shall use my charms to get what I want. I cannot afford to have morals like the rich and the royal. The righteous would argue that it is unscrupulous, but I would rather be branded that, than be a forgotten casualty, as my mother was. If men can use women, why can't women get something out of men? Beauty and lust is just that—a means to an end.'

Dasharaj was not shocked by his daughter's words. He recognized in her an astuteness, and a sharp power of judgement. The innocent girl was long gone, and in her place stood a wronged woman. And Dasharaj promised himself that he would see to it that he made it right for her in some way, some day.

The Fathers

Shantanu liked watching the sun set over the Ganga, deriving pleasure from his pain. He still missed Ganga. He had tried to wipe out her memory and his bitterness through several women and liaisons, but it had been futile. Defeated, he had given up all sensual pleasures, and finally channelled his energy on serving his subjects and looking after his neglected kingdom, sprucing up the army and expanding his kingdom into an empire. Yet, he felt lonely and fatigued. The diffused glow of the sinking sun reminded him of the life he was leading: tired and listless, pining for his wife and son.

Suddenly, his thoughts were broken by some disturbance in the river. *Am I imagining it or has the river suddenly gone choppy?* Large waves were rising ominously and crashing over the bank, and he could see small boats bobbing in the water dangerously. The weather looked fine, but the river looked restless. He got up, his eyes searching for the cause, and decided to walk along the bank.

Shantanu had walked almost a mile along the river when he halted abruptly. In front of him was a tall, young boy casually shooting arrows into the waters He would shoot a single one which would split into a swift row of thousands to make an embankment across the river, forcing the waters to be walled in and spill out in turbid eddies. He watched the boy continue his little amusement, often chuckling softly to himself. *Who played around with the mighty Ganga,* wondered Shantanu. *That boy is hurting Ganga,* he realized, and feeling a sudden surge of anger, he decided to confront the boy. Something about the boy made Shantanu approach him warily.

But before he could take another step, Shantanu found himself with an arrow pointing straight at his chest. The boy had swung the bow around so swiftly that it took a moment for the older man to realize that he was unarmed himself.

'Is this a game for you?' Shantanu asked tersely. 'What are you doing, damming the river with arrows?'

'Oh, that? I am playing with my mother!' shrugged the boy.

Was this boy demented, Shantanu thought wrathfully. 'You are hurting the river,' he said icily. 'And you happen to be pointing the arrow at a king!'

The boy's hand remained steady, as did his calm, hazel eyes, unfazed by the whip in Shantanu's voice. Again he shrugged.

'I could arrest you for treason, for attempting to kill a king,' scowled Shantanu at the temerity of the boy.

'Where is your sword, King?' questioned the boy instead.

'I was relaxing here,' snapped Shantanu.

'A king never relaxes, never rests,' reprimanded the boy, but politely. 'Neither for himself nor the public. And he should always be armed for their defence. And his own, too,' he added, slight humour suffusing his solemn eyes. The boy looked around, his eyes searching.

'Where are your guards? Is it not unsafe for you to move around without them? I could have easily killed you right away. In self-defence,' he explained, with roguish charm. When Shantanu looked at him questioningly, the boy clarified, 'You crept up from behind me, King.'

'Stop teasing him, Dev!' said a soft, sweet feminine voice. Before Shantanu could turn to see who the voice belonged to, the boy put aside his bow. 'Greetings, Father,' murmured the boy, his dark head bent low, his hands folded.

If Devavrat had glanced up, he would have witnessed an array of emotions flitting across the older man's face.

'My son?' said Shantanu, as the boy heard the tone of disbelief in his father's faint voice.

'Your son, Devavrat, as I had promised,' interrupted the same melodious voice. It was achingly familiar, he thought dazedly.

Ganga! She looked no different than the day she had left him. Tall, fair and exquisitely delicate; so much so that she seemed ethereal with her dark hair cascading down to her slender waist. Her pale blue eyes were glistening with tears ... or was it unfiltered joy?

Shantanu felt his heart contract; blood pounded in his head. This was not a dream.

Ganga touched him lightly with her fingers, then closing them around his arm in a firm grip as if to hold him together. The boy supported his shoulders.

For the first time, Shantanu looked closely at his son. He was taller than him, much taller, his lean frame not hiding the muscular breadth of his broad shoulders. He was very fair, like his mother, but the high forehead, the dark, flowing hair and soft hazel eyes over a strong, chiselled nose and thin mouth, gave him more the solemn look of a rishi than a soldier. There was nothing boyish about him. Shantanu knew that he must be around sixteen, counting the years that had passed between them, but he resembled a full grown man. It was the tender, raw look in his eyes that gave his age away. There was a shy uncertainty on that finely-boned face when he smiled.

'Stop staring at him so hard; he is our son!' teased Ganga, watching her husband's apparent awe. 'This is our son who is now no longer a child, but a master of all. As I had promised, he has been groomed to be a master at politics, philosophy, religion and warfare. He will follow the code of conduct of a Kshatriya like no other man has ever done, and no other man ever will. He equals Rishi Parashuram in the art of arms...'

'Parashuram?' echoed Shantanu incredulously. 'He is the greatest of all warriors, but he loathes them; then how did he accept Devavrat as his disciple?'

Ganga smiled. 'I pleaded with him,' she said simply, with a slight shake of her lovely head. 'I begged and I entreated and, at last, Parashuram deigned to make our son his student, and teach him the deepest secrets of archery.'

Shantanu could not believe his ears. 'Then our son's expertise must be the unrivalled!'

Ganga nodded, her smile gentle. 'I tried, Shantanu. I tried to bring him up learning from the best. He received his knowledge of the Vedas and the Vedanta under Rishi Vasisht, and the arts and sciences under Shukracharya himself. Take back your son, the finest archer and master state craftsman, for he is destined to bring immortal fame to his father's name and dynasty; the greatest name of the Kuru race.'

'I did what was expected of me, and I promise to continue doing so in the future,' Devavrat said.

Shantanu chuckled with delight. 'His humility is charming!'

Ganga knew it was time for her to leave both of them. She had united the father with his son. With a sinking heart, she looked at her boy for the last time; his eyes crinkling, smiling shyly with that unruly swathe of hair over his forehead. *From Heaven to Earth, or would it be Hell for him,* she thought, not daring to cry, lest her tears dried up the earth. Her son, so reluctant to escape her world, would now be trapped as the prince of an ancient royal house she had lived in and left.

'You take our son back to the palace,' she forced a small

smile, before turning quickly to Devavrat. 'I will not stay longer. Promise me that you will look after this kingdom and your father. Never fail me on both. Your father is old now, but he refuses to believe it,' she laughed shortly.

Devavrat nodded, not trusting himself to speak, the lump in his throat hurting him less than the ache in his heart. She was leaving him. Forever. His emotions at meeting his father had barely filtered through when he was being torn with a larger pain. He clenched his fingers to stop himself from holding his mother one last time. Not because he did not want to display his wavering emotions, but to help her stay strong. He would have his father now, but whom would she have? Heaven was a lovely paradise, but soullessly lonely.

'Meet me whenever I need you, Ma,' he whispered, as he bent down to touch her feet. 'You will come, won't you?'

'Always, Dev,' she nodded, dry-eyed, as she tucked back the fallen lock of hair. He could hear the tears trembling in her voice.

He felt the warm touch of her hands in his, but before he could grasp them, she had slipped and disappeared into the swirling surf of the river, leaving the two men suddenly bereft.

One story had ended, another was about to begin, thought Devavrat as he gently took the hand of his heartbroken father.

~

The baby arrived sooner than expected, heralding its arrival with a loud cry.

It was a boy, as Parashar had said it would be. Kali was filled with a sense of trepidation. She glanced at the baby sleeping blissfully in her arms. He was not fair-skinned like his father, but dark like her; with her ebony hair and large, thick-lashed, sooty eyes. She felt proud. She had already marked her stamp on him. He would be her son, her firstborn. But she would have to let him go.

Rishi Parashar had sent a woman to take the baby to his ashram. As promised, he would bring up his son. And he had given Kali the choice and freedom to meet him any time she wanted. But she wondered if she ever would.

Kali stroked the soft cheek of the sleeping baby. 'Krishna Dwaipayan,' she murmured. 'That is your name. Krishna, because you are dark like me. Dwaipayan, because you were conceived on an island, surrounded by the waters of knowledge, wisdom and prosperity.'

Without further fuss, she handed the baby to the woman, who bowed and walked away as swiftly as she had arrived, the bundle held safely in her arms.

Kali wondered how and why she had met a stranger and had had a child from him. Things happen for a reason, they say. What was the reason that she consummated a fleeting relationship with an omniscient seer like Parashar, who was a guest in her house; and why had she mothered his child and given it back to him, as if it was a gift for keep.

She felt an irrational anger, a frustration that had surely been building up inside her for a long time. She detested her life—the constant ferrying of strangers across the river seemed like a cruel joke. She helped people reach their destinations, but she could not see her own journey's end. Indeed, there seemed to be no journey in her horizon, to travel and be ferried across.

Kali was surprised when she sometimes missed her son. He had hardly been with her for a week, yet the baby was the one person whom she could call her own. He filled her with a sense of family, of identification. She was his mother; he was her very own. Hers, she repeated. Unlike her father.

Who had been this King Vasu, her famous father, who had deserted her, yet kept her twin brother? Why had he given her away so easily?

She shuddered: she had also given away her son; too easily, she thought. But it was better her son remained with his father than with her. He would grow up with dignity, and be groomed with the best education. She had done what she thought was best for him, and it would remain a closed chapter of her life.

Her thoughts kept coming back to her parents. Her mother had lived and died, shrouded forever in obscurity. Would she, too, continue living in this stinking lane, in this derelict house? Or would she be married off to some village boy, or a young fisherman, to live in inconspicuousness? Kali felt a cold fury grip her again. She would not be as helpless as her mother, living a life of seclusion and dying an ignominious, undignified death. She would not allow herself to be used, never again, she promised herself fiercely. Parashar, in his moment of passion, had been as mindless as King Vasu. If one had been a man of power, the other had been a person of knowledge—both privileged and powerful—imposing on the weak and vulnerable. But she was neither weak nor vulnerable now.

'Who was my father really?' she asked Dasharaj directly one day. 'You worked for him, didn't you? Tell me more about him.'

'So that you hate him more or loathe him less?' he asked shrewdly.

Kali nodded. 'I shall try not to judge him too quickly.'

'Your father is an interesting man, he always was. He was the crown prince of the Puru royal line,' Dasharaj said, watching his daughter's face carefully. 'But strangely, he had no affection for land and politics. He wanted to be a rishi, and, at a very young age, he took up meditation. He was so close to becoming an enlightened rishi that Lord Indra was alarmed. In desperation, he offered not an apsara or a woman, as he usually did, but two unusual temptations to the young prince: an eternal world of pleasure, and friendship with the gods. Besides that, he gave him Chedi, the wealthiest kingdom on Earth—with fertile and sacred land, rich in animal wealth, precious stones and mineral wealth, and honest, law-abiding subjects. Lastly, Indra bribed him with a strange, horse-drawn flying chariot, which he had earlier gifted to King Yayati, one of Vasu's famous ancestors. It was the *viman* which every king in the world yearned for. Vasu yielded, and, soon, with his frequent globetrotting travels in the skies, he came to be known as Uparichar Vasu—the upward-going one. He is as famous as he is kind—'

Kali snorted in open derision.

Dasharaj ignored her interruption and continued, 'Uparichar Vasu invaded the Chedi kingdom with Indra's help, and, surprisingly, married not a royal but a lovely mountain girl, Girika, from Kolahala, whom he met whilst building a dam on the river Suktimati. Rumours abound that she was of dubious birth.'

'What! Do you mean she was born out of rape?' asked a startled Kali. 'It could only mean that, couldn't it, Father? Who was it?'

'No one knew, but to squash the ugly rumours, a myth was conveniently encouraged about her birth. Ignoring the ugly talk, King Vasu fell in love with this orphaned girl, and married her.'

'Yet he did not hesitate to seduce my mother?' she lashed out, her face pale.

Dasharaj shook his head wearily. 'Yes, he is a married man, known to be madly in love with his wife, that's why he never accepted Adrika. He succumbed to his one weak moment with my sister. He regretted it, but took in the boy as he needed an heir; but you ... he could afford to give away to me. Who would have accepted an illegitimate daughter? Who would have married such a princess? I really don't know how the royal minds work, but I gladly took you in. You are my blood!'

Her face swiftly softened, as did her voice. 'Because I was the only reminder of Adrika?' she asked sadly. Her heart hurt for this man, who had to witness his younger sister's agony, and her subsequent death.

Kali had always loved her father unconditionally, but for the first time she respected him for his sense of honour and incredible integrity.

'Will history repeat itself with me as well, Father?' she asked with a frightened catch in her voice. Her face was stricken. 'Will my son face the same humiliation and rejection? For what Parashar did to me? Will my past haunt my future? Will my son hate me as I hate my father?' she cried, burying her face in her trembling hands. 'I don't know the answers to my questions; I don't know whom I resent more—my father or Parashar, for their lust, or myself for surrendering to him and the situation!'

'Don't be so harsh on yourself,' said Dasharaj, gently shaking her by the shoulders. 'Your son is with his father. That is what matters; and the fact remains that you have the freedom to continue with your life. You wanted that, didn't you?'

'Yes, but then what was I instrumental for?' she countered angrily.

'For a prodigy to take birth,' said Dasharaj gently. 'I told you, Parashar was so blessed. But he knew he would never marry. In you, he saw the ideal woman who could bear his child; the child he was destined to have.'

'A poor ferry girl he could take advantage of?' she said scornfully.

'No; a woman who did not care for social norms, and one who had the courage to face the consequences. He wanted an unusual child from an unusual woman. That is you, dear. Never forget it. He was aware of your background; he recognized the simmering anger inside you, and that is why he willingly gave you all that you demanded: to empower you further. It was not just an act of seduction and consummation; you became a complete woman. You didn't just give birth to a boy; it was your rebirth, too.'

Kali listened to her father, but she knew she could never let go of the hatred she had developed since early in life: for the royal father whose uncaring decision sealed her fate and future; for what had happened to her mother; for allowing herself to be used; and for the poverty she lived in. Hate was as pervasive as the stench of dead fish that assailed her every day; as strong as the waves which could toss a dingy in the river and drown her in its whirlpool. She was determined not to suffer, but to struggle and survive. She would bide her time.

She shook her head to clear away any wayward thoughts. 'I learnt about the ways of men,' she said tartly. 'I saw the ways of my biological father, then Parashar—both passion-driven, yet emotionally detached. I learnt to love like a man—to love without feelings. And I shall never forget this lesson in my life.'

The Crown Prince

Devavrat made the palace of Hastinapur his home, just as Mount Meru was. He missed his home terribly, as he missed his mother. But he loved his ageing father and understood that he needed him more. While he took his daily stroll with his father, the sun rose, flooding the garden with brilliant light. Foreseeing a long, bright, cheerful day, there stirred in his bosom a joyous, youthful feeling, such as he used to experience in his childhood, running about in the garden of Meru, with his mother. And in a sudden impulse, he affectionately held the frail hand of his father, happy that he was there for him. His father, he knew, was a sad and lonely man, still pining for Ganga. He could never fill the void, but he hoped his presence might bring a smile to his lips. Both of them, emotionally vulnerable, slowly strolled indoors, into the palace, to share more talk over fresh sweetmeats, which again acutely reminded Devavrat of his childhood. The delightful present blended with the impressions of the past that stirred within him; there was a tightness in his chest; yet, he was happy.

Devavrat found, to his surprise, that apart from his father, there was hardly any other family member staying at the palace. There was a stark absence of a personal, feminine touch as there were no women here except for the chirpy Kripi, barely a girl of ten. She and her twin brother, Kripa, had been adopted by his father when he had found them as babies, abandoned in the woods. Which parent could be so heartless as to leave infants in a jungle filled with wild animals? Man *was* more cruel than beasts.

In Indralok, he was surrounded by so many entities—apsaras, gandharvs, devas, rishis and gurus. Vishwakarma,

Vasu, Timburu, Indra, Varun, Agni, Menaka, Rambha and Urvashi—they were all his family, and he missed their presence from time to time.

Like a curious child, Shantanu eagerly wanted to know every small detail of his life with his mother. Was the selective Guru Parashuram as notoriously formidable as was reputed? And was Shukracharya as acerbic? Devavrat found himself patiently answering each of his father's queries. Shantanu could not stop gushing about Ganga, and Devavrat was filled with mixed emotions. He did not want to discuss his mother: he felt her absence more acutely when remembering her. Every time he answered a query about her, he was reminded that he could never have both his parents—he had had to lose one to love and be with the other. The more his father persisted, the more taciturn he became.

'You are so much like her,' mentioned Shantanu several times through the day, every day. 'The way you talk, the gestures—soft yet firm. I wonder how much of me is in you!' he sighed.

'Oh, she used to claim the same,' smiled Devavrat. 'That I am so much like you, especially when I was growing tall rapidly!'

'Yes, we Kurus are very tall,' Shantanu nodded. 'But I am the tallest amongst my brothers, though I am the youngest.'

'You have brothers? I mean, I have uncles?' asked Devavrat, surprised. 'Where are they?'

'You know nothing about our ancient family, do you?' said Shantanu. 'Let me take you to the hall of our ancestors. Hopefully, you will get a fair idea.'

Soon, Devavrat got to learn that he had two uncles: Devapi, an enlightened rishi, and Bahlik, the king of the neighbouring kingdom of Bahl. A Kuru prince, and the eldest son of King Pratip of Hastinapur, Devapi had been very popular with the people and the nobles alike; yet, much to the chagrin of the adoring citizens, an order was put out by the royal council of priests that forbade him to sit on the throne as he was afflicted with leprosy.

'There would have been a civil war between the priests and citizens,' said Shantanu. 'It was ugly politics, started by a wily minister, Ashwavar, and a few priests who were against my elder brother's liberal ideas on religion and rituals. Devapi was dead against customs and rituals that differentiated people on the basis of class and caste. The only way to stem the ensuing public revolt was by publicly renouncing his throne, and leaving for the forests. He soon became a rishi, taking up meditation and yoga at Kalpagram, in the mountains. Hastinapur faced a severe drought then—legend goes that even the gods were angry that the deserving prince was deprived of his throne. It was only when Devapi persuaded both Lord Indra and Lord Agni, that the kingdom was blessed with rain, ending the twelve-year famine.'

'He did what he thought was best for the kingdom,' said Devavrat.

'Was it?' said Shantanu, cynically. 'Devapi would have made a fine king. I was a toddler when he left Hastinapur. But I consider him my hero.'

Devavrat was very impressed.

'And your other brother?' he asked.

'When Devapi was the Crown Prince, my second brother, Bahlik, was handed the post of the army chief. He got busy with war and military campaigns very early,' recounted his father. 'He inherited Bahl, a part of the kingdom from our mother, Queen Sunanda, and was more eager to look after it than Hastinapur. When the crisis arose, Bahlik flatly refused the crown, proclaiming that he would never usurp his brother's rights. My father was dejected as he had lost two able sons; he retired to the forest a very disappointed man. He gave the responsibility of the crown to me when I was barely eight years old. Bahlik helped me look after Hastinapur. He still does!' remarked Shantanu affectionately. 'I don't take any decision without his opinion.'

'Opinion or permission?' asked Devavrat astutely.

'Call it by any name,' his father said, laughingly. 'But his views do matter to me. Even when Ganga left, he didn't allow me to remarry, warning me that, as a father, I should wait for my son. Wait for the warrior, he said. He will be worthy of all those long years. And he was correct!'

Devavrat felt a certain warmth towards his uncle. He was the epitome of loyalty and justice, unhesitatingly giving up his throne for his brother and personal principles.

'I am eager to meet him as well,' he said, strangely reassured that he had a family now. 'Do you meet your brothers often?'

'Devapi is our royal priest, but he visits us only on special occasions!' grinned Shantanu. 'He is old and cannot attend all the court functions, but he is training Kripa, who is still very young,' he explained.

Kripa, and his twin sister, Kripi, were already proficient in the Vedas.

His father continued, '...I hope to make Kripa the royal priest after my brother. But I shall see to it that Devapi will be there during the coronation when you are named the crown prince!'

Devavrat gave his father a steady look. 'I may be your son, Father, but I have yet to prove myself a worthy crown prince.'

Shantanu was taken aback by his son's honesty. Or was it his humility? He smiled, recovering quickly. 'You are

Gangaputra; who better than you to sit on this throne? You have excelled not just in governance and statecraft, but you also know the humane side of kingship. You never humiliate the defeated nor play petty politics, as is the rule,' he said, proudly. It was at moments like these, when he looked at Devavrat that he missed Ganga even more. His son was a reminder of what he had lost, and Shantanu wished he could relive those years with her. Swept with a sudden desolate feeling, he murmured, 'I am old, son; I am tired. I want you to look after everything from now on. That's your so called "test".'

'That's not enough!' exclaimed his son.

'It is more than enough,' chuckled Shantanu. 'You are the greatest disciple of Parashuram and Shukracharya, and have mastered the art of royal politics! You don't shirk from the banalities of court matters and public administration; you excel in warfare and diplomacy. You have toured all over the kingdom, getting to know the country and your people. You *have* proved yourself capable enough; you don't need a heroic deed to be pronounced king, my son!'

'But what do you know of me, Father?' reasoned Devavrat. 'Just now you recounted to me the glory of our family, saying that each member has been extraordinary. I am your son, but please give me a proper chance to prove myself.'

'What do you want, Son, a war to prove your prowess?' laughed Shantanu, mirthlessly. 'Neither I nor the nobles in court doubt your credentials. You have won wars for Indra, and, when the time comes, you will do the same for me and Hastinapur. You do not have to prove that you are worthy enough to be either my son or the crown prince,' sighed the old king. 'You are my only son, Devavrat, and you will be my heir. It is just a matter of time.'

Four years later and Devavrat found what his father had said was true. Administration was more complicated than war—it was a daily, mundane battle. While the end of war meant either defeat or victory, there was no such outcome in looking after the kingdom—because defeat was not a choice. One had to win: for both the people and the state.

Devavrat had just cleared the taxation for merchants entering the city, but could not stop thinking about how to stave off the belligerent Chitramukh, the prince of the neighbouring state of Shalva. Wars were often started to appease royal egos and insatiable greed. Devavrat hated war. It was the people and the state which suffered the most. There was no difference between mortal and heavenly wars. Indra was no worse than the petty prince, both of them threatening to go to war and inflict violence with their privileged whimsicality. War was never an answer; it was always a question of power intrigues, to be dealt with statesmanship and astuteness.

'You are still awake?' Devavrat's thoughts were interrupted by a surprised voice.

It was his father, ambling into his chamber.

'What are you working on at this ungodly hour?' he demanded. 'It's your coronation day tomorrow. You should rest well before the early morning rituals begin. And dawn, my dear son, is barely an hour away!'

Devavrat frowned. 'But why are you awake, Father?'

'Oh me,' shrugged Shantanu. 'It's age catching up. I am too excited to sleep tonight and I decided not to toss in bed and go for a walk instead. Anyway, I don't sleep well.'

'Your walks are getting more frequent and longer,' said Devavrat worriedly. 'The other day I had to send troops in search of you!'

'And what did this search party find? Me sleeping

blissfully under a banyan tree! I am going to be retired soon, Devavrat. Let me enjoy my freedom!'

'If you had gone further, Father, you would have entered the Matsya kingdom,' Devavrat smiled, 'and might have well started a war!'

Shantanu shrugged nonchalantly. 'Matsya is our ally, recently formed by my friend, Vasu, the king of Chedi,' he said airily. 'It was formed to accommodate his son Matsya, who, rumours insist, is of dubious birth!' laughed the old king. 'So much so that he has even named that part of his kingdom after this son!'

'The birth of a child is never dubious; it is a fact. The conception possibly is, but the onus of it falls on the conceivers, not the newborn,' said Devavrat thoughtfully, his lips pursed. His father's flippancy lacked sensitivity, and came across as almost coarse.

Was he, too, of 'dubious birth', a result of consummation between a godly nymph and a mortal king? Was he fit to be a crown prince or was it an entitlement he was born into?

He felt uneasy.

'I am happy you are being coroneted tomorrow,' Shantanu continued. 'The month of *shravan* starts tomorrow. It is an auspicious time, and an auspicious occasion. I have been procrastinating the coronation because of your pointless reluctance to let me work. Both my brothers are cross with me, especially Bahlik, for my laxity in taking the usual amount of responsibilities. He is on his way here and he plans to stay put until he helps you settle down. So get ready to welcome him. He should arrive in a few hours, and the first person he wants to meet is you.'

Each time Devavrat saw his uncle, he pondered over how different the two brothers were. Both were tall men, and handsome. Yet, his father looked surprisingly unimpressive and slight compared to the muscled Bahlik.

The difference was not only restricted to physical stature but the face as well. His father was a handsome man, with classical good looks, but his face lacked the firmness of his uncle's. His father's eyes were more dreamy and the softness in his face was accentuated by a weak chin and full lips that spoke more of sensual pleasure than bravery.

His uncle was fair but sun-flushed, with a stubble of a beard. He had curly grey-black hair and heavy eyebrows that almost met over his thick nose. His ears were small and neat for a man of that size, and his eyes, which had a shrewd glint in them, had a shine close to tears that grey eyes often seem to have.

When he arrived in the morning, he didn't waste any time to greet Devavrat. 'Each time I meet you, you remind me of Ganga! You *are* Gangaputra; you look just like her!' he exclaimed with delighted surprise, spontaneously enveloping the young man in a hearty embrace. He was someone who did not display much emotion, and Devavrat was elated by the gesture, and happy to see his uncle again. 'The few times I met her, I surmised that she was an extraordinary lady who knew how to handle my brother! My brother, well, he succumbs to women too easily!'

His guffaw fading, Bahlik turned serious as he said, 'You have inherited not just her fair beauty but the same maturity of handling situations and people—be it the nobles or the soldiers, the man demanding justice at the court or even your stubborn father. I have been observing you as keenly as you have been watching me these last few years!' he grinned. 'What's troubling you, Son? Are you still uncertain about becoming a king?' he said.

Devavrat was not affronted by his uncle's uncompromising forthrightness; it was admirable, even endearing, the reason why he was so fond of him. Bahlik was a king without any royal hauteur or sweet diplomacy; a shrewd man who said what he believed, however unpleasant or uncomplimentary.

'Careful what you wish for, Son... A reluctant crown prince is not good news. And we don't want the crown going to someone else!' he added tersely. 'It's happened often enough in our family. It's the curse of our dynasty.'

His uncle was not merely referring to his brothers; Devavrat knew his family history well by now. He was talking about King Bharat, the founder of their lineage, the son of King Dushyant and Shakuntala. The disillusioned emperor had disinherited all his nine sons whom he considered unworthy, and had chosen instead Vitath, a relative of Rishi Bharadwaj, as his heir.

From then on, the practice of primogeniture, which was followed by most royal dynasties of the country, ceased to be a mandatory rule for his family. Succession was not a privilege; it had to be earned by worth, not birth. Moved profoundly by his family heritage, it was a legacy Devavrat meant to follow.

'A king, always remember, Son, is chosen for his merit and not because of privilege,' warned Bahlik. 'It's a sacred rule in our family.

'You will be inheriting the throne at a time when the two rival sections of the most ancient families—Kurus and the Panchals—have just about buried the hatchet and agreed to follow a common civil and economic code,' warned his uncle. 'Peace prevails, but temporarily.'

His uncle was referring to an old feud. The neighbouring Panchals, who shared their Puru lineage, were bitter rivals of the Kurus since many generations. It started during the long famine in the land, when the Panchal king, Sudasa, also a descendant of King Yayati, attacked Hastinapur, forcing its King Samvaran into exile in the forest along the River Sindhu. It was his son, Kuru, reinstated by the powerful Rishi Vasisht, who regained the lost land and its glory when he defeated the Panchals to form the Kuru dynasty. This was a story that had often been recounted to him by his mother, to emphasize that while it was through birth that one inherited legacy, it was through worth alone that one sustained it. The burden of that legacy was already getting heavy.

'But neither is war a way out,' gently argued Devavrat. 'We need to have a pact instead.'

'You are sound in political conduct and polity,' murmured Bahlik, visibly impressed. 'Shantanu, you should be proud of your heir. I think he has delighted not just me, the Kurus and you, but, most importantly, the people of his country, too, with his demeanour and devotion. May you live a long life, Son!'

'Let the ceremonies begin,' Shantanu said, and nodded towards his eldest brother. Devapi's benign face had a sharp glow.

'You will be the brightest star of our race, Devavrat,' he said. 'For now, and for ever.'

Devavrat felt small under the weight of such lofty praises, and the rishi's words deepened his misgivings. But he no longer had the luxury of doubt. Before the sun stood high at noon, Devavrat found himself being named the Crown Prince of Hastinapur. He had everything; he just wished his mother had been there too.

The King and the Fisher Girl

'Are you lost, sir?' asked Kali, frostily polite. The man had been following her all the way from the river.

He *looked* lost, his eyes partially glazed. *Was he drunk*, she frowned, *he certainly looked pale under his skin.* He was old, she noticed as she appraised him, noting his splendidly bejewelled attire and silken robes. *Clearly a wealthy man; possibly a nobleman*, she thought. *Hopefully not one of my admirers.* She was weary of lewd, old men.

She repeated her question.

'No,' he said in a pleasant voice, without the haughtiness she often associated with the rich. 'I know my way around here. But I want to go across. Will you please ferry me to the other side?'

She wondered if it was just an excuse to be with her. She gestured for him to climb into the dinghy with a wave of her hand. He stepped in gingerly, and the boat rocked slightly. She hid a smile; she knew most people were not prepared for the sudden motion.

The man settled down and openly stared at her. 'I hope I am not being impolite. I noticed or rather smelled a certain overwhelming fragrance, and I have been following it since...' he looked unsure, struggling to word his obvious discomfiture. 'I thought I had imagined it, but is that fragrance emanating from you?' he sounded incredulous, his eyes riveted on her.

'Yes, it is,' she said wryly. 'A blessing from a rishi.'

His brow rose. 'What did you do to be so blessed?'

She did not respond, her eyes becoming hard and dark.

He gazed at her as she rowed. He felt a rush of blood through his body. Her beauty was arresting. She was very tall and sculpted, with the strength to manoeuvre the wooden boat in the choppy waters. She was dusky and ravishing, with broad shoulders, a provocative bust, a small waist, voluptuous hips and long legs which were taut and tense, swaying with the movement of the boat as the fabric of her short cloth rode up her smooth thighs. Her thick, dark hair rested loosely on her bare shoulders. He took it all in at one glance. She was not classically beautiful: her mouth was too wide, her lips thin, her nose long and too sharp for perfect beauty. But she was the most sensual woman he had ever seen. He felt his stomach clench in swift desire that coursed through his body, his mouth turning dry.

For a long time, they stared at each other, then her lips parted provocatively as she smiled, showing white, even teeth. She looked heavenly.

'That's why some call me Yojanagandha now. But the name Matsyagandha remains,' she murmured, ignoring his question and deliberately not giving any further information. She swept her hair away from her bare shoulders and tied a neat bun before resuming to row.

'Are you a river nymph?' he said, staring at the strange shell anklets adorning her slender ankles.

'Nothing that fancy,' she said dryly. 'I am a working girl who ferries a boat across the river to make ends meet.'

She looked at him closely. Even sitting down, he seemed like a tall man. He was handsome, with a generous sprinkle of grey in his thick hair. He was surely close to her father's age, she guessed. But the man looked fitter, his slim frame without an ounce of flab or sagging muscle. *Must be the result of a rich man's diet*, she thought sourly.

She instinctively gauged what he wanted from her, instantly recognizing the appraising look in his eyes. She moved the oars faster, hoping to reach the shore quickly, wanting to get rid of him.

Suddenly she spotted a brief movement in the water. She stopped rowing, and realizing what it was, picked up the net at her feet and threw it into the water.

'What are you doing?' he asked surprised.

'Catching fish. It's a big one, and shall fetch me a big price.'

Having deftly caught the fish in the net, she started pulling it in, but it was heavier than she had imagined. She pulled harder, feeling a thin film of perspiration form on her forehead, her breath coming in short gasps.

'I'll help you,' the man offered gallantly.

'Don't!' she shouted, staring intently at the furiously thrashing fish. 'You will rock the boat and we may topple into the water! I will manage...' she gasped, as the fish tugged harder at the net, desperate to escape.

She felt the net biting into her hands, the skin breaking and the warmth of her blood trickling between her clutched fingers.

'Hand me your dagger!' she ordered, pointing to the weapon at his waist. He handed it to her silently, fascinated by the show of strength and determination in the girl.

She snatched the dagger and nimbly threw it at the frantically squirming fish, catching it straight at the gills. It lay still and she hauled in the loaded net.

'Got him at last!' Her face was alive and sparkling, chortling over her conquest. 'That's the thing about fishing. Catch it while you can, or they slip away and you never get the chance again,' she explained with a triumphant smile, wiping the blood off her hands.

'You are hurt...!' he frowned.

Kali shrugged, smiling mockingly. 'I had to use my bare hands to catch that fish. Or it would have escaped liked a lost opportunity.'

'You don't allow any opportunity to slip from your fingers?' he asked, impressed with her pragmatic philosophy. 'Even if you get hurt in the process?'

'We work with our hands: they are our sole fortune.'

'Don't you think you were stubborn about catching that fish? You could have got badly injured!'

'Sir, I rely on these hands for my present, my future,' Kali's face twitched in a quick grimace. 'Unlike the fortunate rich who hold their wealth in their hands. And wealth is power.'

'But in your hands lies strength!'

'Labour, you mean! That's why we poor have to work hard,' she said flippantly. 'Strength lies in the mind, in the heart; not just in our hands,' she asserted.

He raised an eyebrow. 'Is it not better to contain only as much as you can hold in your hands?'

'That is so limiting,' she challenged. 'Then the poor remain poor and the rich get smug and lazy,' she said saucily. 'If desire and ambition are to be restricted to our two puny hands, why do we have such small eyes to see the large sky? And two small ears to hear the wildest storms? No, sir, we *can* make our future with our hands!' she laughed. 'And with our minds, we can dream big!'

She resumed rowing smoothly, but the friction of the oars on her bruised palms made them bleed again. She impatiently tore the end of her angavastra and tied strips of the cloth around both her wounded palms.

'I think it will be better if we turn back,' he said, looking at her swaddled hands. 'They need looking after,' he added tenderly.

As she felt the breeze against her face, she was reminded of the long forgotten incident years ago, when she was with Parashar...

She was sure now that this boat trip had been an excuse for this stranger to spend time with her.

'What do you want?' she asked quietly.

'You,' he replied. 'I want you!'

It was an admission of all the emotions churning within him since he had set eyes on her this morning. He had first been assailed by her exotic fragrance. As he inhaled more deeply, he was immediately intoxicated, unable to think. And then he had seen her and stared, unable to take his eyes off her.

Sitting on a dinghy was the most attractive girl he had seen for a long time. Sultry and almost sullen in her beauty, she oozed a raw appeal, a smouldering magnetism that drew him to her like a spider in her web.

Shantanu felt his mind go numb. He remembered how he met Ganga on the riverbank eons ago. This mystery woman—was she real or was he imagining Ganga?

No, she is not Ganga. This one is as dark as Ganga is fair, yet, just as alluring. Who is she?

Shantanu knew he was handsome, and usually that was enough to charm any woman. *Not this one, though*, he thought with some exasperation. He was now sitting close to her, feeling the heat of her body, their feet touching...

'*I want you!*' he had blurted out, the words torn from him, to whistle in the wind.

Did all men seek me only as a quick catch, she sighed, as she continued to row the boat, rapidly heading toward the shore. She was used to flattery and blatant propositions. She was also conscious of the fact that she was attractive, and not to be wasted on all or anyone. She was aware of the impression she had made on this stranger. She instinctively knew when she raised lust in men, and she knew she had stirred his desires. However, she was not sure about herself:

should I reject his advances, or do I have the will to go through this again and wrangle another deal for myself?

She felt the boat hit the sands and she jumped out gracefully, and started to tie the boat, ignoring him and his declaration.

'I said I want you,' he repeated, his shadow falling on her. 'I love you!'

Kali raised a knowing eyebrow. 'You want me as what—a maid?' she smiled, her tone irreverent.

'Don't tease me, please!' he begged. 'I have fallen in love with you, lovely maiden,' he said earnestly. He inched closer, leaning his face forward.

Her eyes widened in mock wonder. 'We just met. I hardly know you!'

'My dear girl, do you know how beautiful you are?' he sighed, taking in her body and face as he inhaled deeply.

As most poor people did, she was attired in rough cotton. She was scantily dressed more out of poverty than to seduce—a tiny *uttariya* barely covered her bodice, the lower *antariya* was short and without the usual *kamarbandh* most ladies wore. It was instead knotted tantalisingly low at her toned waist, hugging her voluptuous hips and half covering her rounded thighs, exposing the bare flesh of her long legs. She was wearing not a single piece of jewellery except for a shell bracelet on her right wrist and its counterpart at the ankles. Yet, she looked as regal and arresting as a queen. It was what had attracted him at the first instance. And she was young, he realized as he felt a rush of hot blood pounding in him. He would have grabbed her and silenced their irrelevant talk, but better sense prevailed and he took in a deep breath. The scent wafted enticingly again. He clenched his fists.

'I know you—you are the girl I am in love with. And I...' he paused, uncertain.

Without a conscious effort, he moved into his regal stance. His expression, schooled by years of experience, was arrogant and alert.

'I am a king,' he declared, more firmly.

Despite her initial shock, Kali was astute enough to notice the slight hesitation. *A king! This man is a king!* Her eyes did not reveal her disbelief, wondering why he had vacillated. Clearly, he did not want his identity to be revealed. It had been his last resort. *He would have preferred a quick, anonymous seduction*, she thought grimly. But for once, she would not be the conquest of a man. It would be she who would conquer and defeat him. *Just this one time*, she swore grimly.

She forced a smile which she knew would make his blood boil, with just the right dose of innocence and reticence. 'But you can't be the king of our region,' she said, her eyes becoming wider. 'Is it a ruse to impress me?' she asked sweetly, arching her breasts at him and lifting her dark eyebrows invitingly.

'I am the king of Hastinapur,' he blurted. 'King Shantanu. I was riding through this village and I noticed you near the River Yamuna. I have been watching you this whole day!'

Kali barely heard his hurried explanation: the king of Hastinapur; one of the most powerful kings of one of the most powerful dynasties. Her heart raced erratically. She was sitting before the king of the land, the cause of her woes but a slave to his desire for her. She took a moment to savour her power over this mighty man.

She bowed her head, elegantly. 'To our king,' she murmured, her mind working furiously. She had not angled for him, yet he was already in her net. *Do I want him*, she asked herself as her eyes shrewdly took in the grey hair, the finely lined face and the dry, shrivelling skin on his hands.

Am I ready to give my girlhood to this old man, and sacrifice my youth for security? I could be a young queen to an old king...

Kali drew in a deep breath, inhaling the salty scent of success. She would not allow ambition be a dirty word. It would cleanse her, empower her and be the cause of her rebirth. She was sick of poverty; it made her ill. She needed a cure; she wanted wealth, which was power. She wanted power, too.

Kali raised her head to look at him again with fresh eyes. He made a distinguished king with his fair, good looks, coupled with his hair greying at the temples, the silk finery and sober display of gems and ornamentation, riding recklessly in the kingdom... Was that how King Vasu had seduced her mother?

Her heart hardened, but in her eyes was a soft glow.

'You are a king—the mighty King Shantanu—and I am but a poor fisher girl,' she said in a low, respectful tone, her eyes suitably downcast.

'No longer,' he said peremptorily, taking a bold step closer. He felt an intense sliver of excitement run through him.

She knew he was yearning to touch her. Her scent grew stronger, and she saw his eyes flare with quick arousal. She felt a heady sense of success: she seemed to attract the most powerful of men—first Parashar, now this king.

'And how does it matter that I am rich and you are poor?' the king murmured. 'You shall live with me!'

Kali ran a tongue over her lips, her eyes luminous. His eyes were riveted on her, taking in her deliberate gesture.

'But I will have to ask my father...' she started, infusing a tinge of helpless confusion in her smoky eyes. Her inviting lips were so dangerously near that he could have kissed her if she had not lowered her head to make him roil in his new passion.

'Later, dear. Later, I shall seek your father,' he muttered impatiently, taking her hands. They were surprisingly soft, despite the hardships they bore each day. She winced, but did not pull them away. She turned her wrist around to display her open palms.

'You want a girl with such calloused hands in your harem?' she asked. She was teasing him and his heart skipped a long beat. Just the way Ganga used to...

'I have no harem,' he said huskily. 'You shall live in my palace at Hastinapur. You, dear maiden, I promise, shall be my special lady.'

'Your queen?' she said innocently, her eyes looking questioningly, full of hope and trust. Kali hoped she had got it right, to make his heart melt. Lust was a quick flare, but what burned longer was unrequited love. She wanted him to fall hopelessly in love with her, and not simply lust for her.

He inhaled sharply, frowning, at a loss for words. At that moment, she snatched her hands away and he felt acutely bereft as if the warmth in his life had slipped away from his grasp.

'I have to go; it is getting late...' she mumbled, raising her large eyes in feigned panic. 'My father will be waiting for me.'

And before he could reach for her, she had capered over the boat and was running along the sandy shore, towards the shrubbery.

'When can I see you again?' he called after her, taking quick steps to follow her.

She darted him a quick smile and vanished among the shrubs. He chased after her, but the slushy marsh slowed him down while she skipped deftly between the thickets.

Perhaps she will come back; I shall wait, he thought, as he abandoned himself to this faint, vain hope which intoxicated him.

Kali watched him from behind the mangroves, hidden by the thick, long grass. She saw him staring listlessly into the distance, lost, confused and annoyed. It had been the right time, the right action when she had broken away from him. He would search for her the whole day and then another. She smiled, pleased at having so easily taken in a man so powerful, and at being the object of such intense passion.

Kali wondered if she should mention this encounter to her father, but decided against it.

As she had hoped, King Shantanu was waiting for her in the pale hours of the early dawn when she went to the river the following day. He took a step forward so as to speak when she cut him off, careful not to be brusque, but firm.

'Good day, sir,' she said brightly, bowing, her smile as inviting as her huge, dark-lashed eyes. 'I cannot stay to chat with you. I have to work and ferry these waiting people to the other side,' she explained, still smiling. With another low bow, Kali ambled away to the waiting motley, knowing his eyes and heart were achingly on her.

He was standing among the tall thicket when she returned late in the evening, a silhouette in the shadowed light of the dusk. The moon was shining. It was still a warm summer night. The stray dogs were howling in the distance. As if in warning...

'Matsyagandha,' he said, the royal command stark in his voice.

Kali turned and smiled, and the anger melted from his face, his eyes turning bleak, almost pleading. Shantanu wanted to cry out loud that he wanted to love, that he was eager for her at all costs. To him, she was not a mere girl but a beautiful body in the moonlight, a luscious shape hiding bashfully in the shadows of the trees, waiting to be devoured.

'For God's sake! I entreat you, don't torment me. Let us go into the mangroves!'

She looked perplexed, but meekly allowed herself to be led into the woods. He grabbed her roughly and before she could utter another word, covered her soft lips with his hungry ones. She allowed it, closing her eyes as if drowning in new-found passion, her hands roaming delicately over his back. She felt him shudder, and softly slipped a moan from her throat—the low, long sound of ecstasy driving him into a new frenzy. Through her half-closed eyes, she could see his lips were moving down her neck to the rounded swell of her breasts. While one hand tugged adroitly at her knotted bodice, the other ran up her silken thighs. *He is an adept lover*, she mused. *Must have done this to all the palace maids*, she sneered silently.

Her bodice was completely undone, and she felt him tremble as he gaped at her half-nakedness. Kali permitted him a long look of her magnificent bare breasts before she stepped back in apparent confusion, coyly pulling up her fallen uttariya to cover herself.

'No, no, I can't do this!' she cried. 'My father will kill me if he gets to know what I have done!'

'What?' he gasped, bewildered, fumbling desperately. 'What are you doing? Come back!' he shouted at her retreating back.

She did not bother to reply but continued to run daintily away, making him rage in kindled fire.

~

She was humming lightly as she opened the door to her house, the fragrance filtering in before she did.

'You sound happy,' remarked Dasharaj, expertly tying knots to mend a torn net. 'Got a prize catch?'

Kali nodded slowly, a small smile playing on her lips. 'Yes, Father. A prize catch. But not the finned variety.'

Dasharaj's hands stopped abruptly.

'King Shantanu,' she said shortly, waiting for the impact of her words.

'You met him?' her father looked incredulous. 'What is he doing in this part of the kingdom?'

'He was out hunting it seems, and I caught his attention. Or he followed my scent,' she said airily.

'Surely he didn't try to seduce you?' he asked, but she could hear the fear in his voice.

'He thinks he did, but it's I who is enticing him,' she shrugged, recalling the brief tussle at the banks. 'I will marry him before I allow him to seduce me. But right now, my absence is slowly making him go wild.'

'Don't believe him. He's not a fool, Satyavati. He's a seasoned womanizer,' he warned. 'It runs in that family. Remember that infamous story of his ancestor, King Dushyant, and how conveniently he forgot his wife, Shakuntala, feigning denial when confronted by her? Though she fought for her right for her son with all her dignity, the king only accepted her because he was childless, and he needed a son for his throne. This man is no better. At the pretext of mourning Ganga, his estranged wife...'

'Estranged?' questioned Kali, curious.

'Yes, King Shantanu met this beautiful girl near the River Ganga, he fell in love with her and married her with his father's blessings. They had seven sons, but the queen seemed to be suffering from some illness. Rumour has it that all seven died. An uglier rumour has it that the mother threw the babies in the river herself. No one knows, but our present Crown Prince is the eighth son of King Shantanu. Ganga took him with her when he was born, and the king is said to have gone quite mad with grief, having lost both wife and son. Whether it was certain madness or simple lust, we don't know, but he is said to have seduced half the maids in the palace and made a harem of the other half. It's only when his son returned to him a few years ago that he came to his senses.'

'He got back his son?' enquired Kali, more intrigued, suddenly filled with a vision of a younger version of the man she had almost made love to.

'Yes, Devavrat is the crown prince. What is going on, Satyavati?' he quizzed sharply.

'To make a long, lusty story short, King Shantanu wants me—'

'Desperate enough to marry you?' he interrupted swiftly.

'I shall make him so,' vowed Kali. 'He claims that he's in love with me,' she chuckled. 'I intend to play along. But not as his mistress in his harem, as he would have preferred; instead, as his wife. His queen. The Queen of Hastinapur,' she smirked, relishing each word.

Dasharaj raised his eyebrows. 'Well planned, yes.'

'Oh, don't doubt me, Father,' she stated. 'I shan't make it a quick affair. Right now, I am playing the poor little girl, living in fear of her righteous father.'

Dasharaj nodded, looking thoughtfully at his daughter. Kali was pulling the net slowly and the king was getting irrevocably enmeshed, thrashing for his life.

The following morning, Kali was not surprised to spot the forlorn king waiting for her.

'Matsyagandha!' he called. When she didn't respond, he called out, 'Kali!'

It was a desperate plea, no longer ringing with royal authority.

She turned around, surprised that he knew her name.

'How do you know my name?'

'I asked about you,' he said testily. 'You are known here as Kali.'

She lifted her chin. 'Yes, because I am dark!' she laughed, a low, husky delicious sound that sent his heart racing.

'And so beautiful!' he breathed. He took the defiant chin in his hand, bending his head to touch her lips with his eager ones. He was like a hungry wolf, ready to devour her, savouring her lips. She permitted the kiss for a long while but before he got more urgent she firmly pushed at his thudding chest.

'No, sir, I told you before, I cannot be your lover,' she raised helpless eyes at him. 'My father will never allow it.'

'But I love you!' he argued.

'I love you, too,' Kali lied earnestly and easily. 'But what about us; our future?'

'I shall take you with me, keep you with me always.'

'As your concubine but not consort?' she asked quietly.

He looked stunned. 'Wife?' he asked bewildered, flushing a brick red.

'Yes, your wife,' she repeated, with all the hope and emotion she could muster.

He stood silent.

'Am I good enough to fall in love with, to make love to, but not good enough to marry?' she asked, her lips trembling with hurt.

He collected his sanity, sparked with a spurt of anger. 'As you said, you are but a fisher girl,' he said in exasperation. 'I cannot marry you!'

Kali uttered a small whimper. 'Why, because I am not of noble birth or a princess?' she choked. 'You can love me enough to ravish me, but then forsake me?' she cried, the tears welling up in her voice as well.

The anguish tore at him.

'I will not forsake you. I shall keep you forever in my

palace,' he reiterated, clasping her by the shoulders. 'Like a queen.'

'But not *as* a queen,' she corrected, looking him full in the face with her big, tear-stained eyes. 'I love you, but I dare not dream of marrying you, is that it?' she asked with the right catch in her voice. 'Am I overreaching, sir?' she continued, with that delightful curling of her soft lips. 'Am I asking for too much?'

He gave a sigh of exasperation.

She did not wait for his reply, but throwing him a last look of utter despair, the tears flowing down her stricken face, she mumbled in a broken voice, 'I shall never forget you, oh king. I bid you farewell!'

She heard him calling after her, but she ignored him, knowing that if she stopped, she would lose her battle. *I am going to win*, she promised herself fiercely. *He will come after me.*

She did not go to work the following day, or the next.

'We are losing money, dear,' admonished Dasharaj.

'We will earn more than money, Father,' she assured him. 'I want respect! I want him to suffer and pine for me!' Kali pressed her lips, tapping a fingertip on the lower one thoughtfully. 'Let him know what it is to not have me. I want him at my doorstep, grovelling for me!'

It was almost after a week that she saw Shantanu again. He was leaning against one of her boats. She stopped short, as if in surprise, and saw his face break into a radiant smile. She began to relax—the fish was nibbling at her bait. As he reached her, he stopped suddenly and grabbed her by her waist. He slid his hands down her long, slender back, over the curve of her hips and pulled her to him, crushing his lips to hers. 'Don't ever leave me!' he whispered frantically, kissing her all over her upturned face. 'I know now I can't live without you! *Yes*, I will marry you; I shall marry you!'

The Dilemma

Kali was assailed by a sustained commotion outside her house. It was not the usual ruckus raised by children playing. She frowned, peering out from the window. She was shocked to see the reason for all the commotion. King Shantanu was walking on foot through the slush on the street, mud sticking to the silken folds of his robes, his sandaled feet grimy. But there was a purpose in each stride that was getting him closer to her hut. He was not alone. An elderly man accompanied him, and, from his attire, she made a quick guess that he might be the king's footman or attendant.

'He has arrived, Father, just as I had said, at our doorstep!' she smirked.

She took a long breath, waiting for the knock on the door. When it came, she took her time, making the king wait for a few moments. As she leisurely opened it, she was greeted by him, his smile tentative.

Shantanu was hit by her fragrance; it seemed to fill the decrepit confines of her house. His eyes strayed over the small hall. He noticed an old man sitting in a corner, mending a fishing net.

Kali waited for him to say something, anything. He seemed unsure, not meeting her eyes. He turned to glance at the growing crowd outside her house, and said, quite abruptly, 'I did not know my son was so popular even here. I have just been talking to them and they want Devavrat, the crown prince, to be anointed king as soon as possible!'

Panic clutched at her throat, her mouth dry. This was not what she had been expecting him to say. *Devavrat will become king*, she thought, with panic rising in her guts. In one wisp, she saw all her dreams of becoming queen turning to ashes, and if she did not think of something fast, she would lose this man and her future. And it would be her fault, her foolishness.

She smiled, hiding her emotions. 'Wonderful. I hear the crown prince is a very worthy boy,' she said politely. 'I thought you had come to ask my father for his permission for our marriage...' she sighed, her eyes clouding with disappointment.

Shantanu hesitated, wondering again if he was doing the right thing. *Why must I live in loneliness? Do I not deserve companionship? As a king, I have delivered all responsibilities towards my people and my kingdom. Do I not deserve love and joy in my later years?*

'Yes, I had come for that, as promised,' said Shantanu hurriedly.

She led him further inside her house, and to his annoyance, the old man did not promptly jump to his feet to greet him. Instead, he threw an enquiring look at him.

'I am the king of Hastinapur: King Shantanu,' he announced briefly. 'And I have come to request you for your daughter's hand in marriage.'

He said it quickly but clearly, making his intention clear, making it sound more like a royal command than a request.

Kali's head shot up, her face flooding with triumph. She was to be his queen! For the first time, Kali gave him a genuine smile, her eyes warmly glistening alternately with unspoken gratitude and the sparkle of victory.

Shantanu returned her smile as if he had already acquired his claim on her. He threw a restless look at her father, as the old fisherman had not spoken a word yet. *Why would this nondescript, stinking fisherman not,* reasoned Shantanu, *be eager to give away his daughter to a king? He should be singing and dancing with joy.*

But the old man did neither, watching him closely with sly, thoughtful eyes. Shantanu felt disconcerted. This was not how he had imagined this situation. The daughter looked giddy with delight, but not the father. He took an immediate dislike to the man with his narrowed eyes and unsmiling, gnarled face.

Kali was feeling a similar sense of dismay. *Why was Father taking so long to reply? We had agreed that marriage would be the sole and only term of condition for the king to have me. The king has come to fetch me, so why is he pondering over it for so long?* She felt a faint knot of uneasiness tightening at the pit of her stomach.

Her father, clearly, had other plans.

'I am honoured, sir, that you have deigned to marry my daughter,' started Dasharaj, his face expressionless, bereft of false gratitude or obsequiousness. 'But you will not have reason to be ashamed of her as a poor ferry girl, the daughter of an impoverished fisherman. She is intelligent and educated, beautiful and young—fit to be your queen in every way,' he added.

The silence was deafening, the unspoken jibe screaming back at the old king. She was young but *the king* was old enough to be her father. Kali was quick to surmise the situation. Her father was making the king feel that *he* was not fit enough to be *her* husband. He might be the king, but she deserved someone better, and, certainly, someone younger.

Shantanu's face grew flushed, and he was speechless with fury.

'Would it not be better if she marries your son, Devavrat, the crown prince, sir?' suggested Dasharaj. 'I hear he is of marriageable age and young, handsome, brave and worthy of my daughter.'

Kali was as visibly shocked as Shantanu. *What is my father doing,* she threw her father a frantic glance. *Is he driving the king away from us or constructing his own masterplan?* She remained silent, lacing her fingers nervously, wondering why her father wanted her to be married off to the crown prince instead.

'But your daughter loves *me*,' insisted the king, with petulant arrogance.

Kali was startled for a moment, but she had made her interest in him clear before. 'And I love her,' he continued. 'Love her enough to marry her,' he said firmly. 'To make her my queen!'

'Yes, she will be your queen when you marry her, but will your children from her be heirs to your throne?' asked Dasharaj. 'Never. They will be one of your many children. The crown prince had been chosen already. And I hear that he is soon to be king.'

She saw immediately where her father's argument was leading. Shantanu was quick to comprehend the words as well, and his face became suffused with colour.

'Devavrat is my only son,' he frowned angrily. 'He is the crown prince. And, yes, he will be the king. The people love him!'

'Exactly,' nodded Dasharaj. 'But what about my daughter's children? They will never be kings, just some princes at the mercy of Devavrat,' he reminded him, his face set.

'I will not disown them!' refuted Shantanu hotly. 'Devavrat will never harm his siblings.'

'But what after your, er, death?' asked Dasharaj delicately. 'You are old, oh King, and my daughter is very young. What happens to her and her children after your death?' he asked bluntly.

Shantanu floundered, bewilderment clouding his handsome face.

Before Shantanu could say anything, Dasharaj continued, 'Either my daughter marries the young crown prince, who is closer to her age. Or she can only marry you if you promise that her children will be the heirs. Either way, she and her children would have an assured place in the kingdom. So, which option do you agree to?'

'Marrying the crown prince is out of the question for your daughter,' said Shantanu hoarsely. '*I* love her!' he whispered painfully.

He paused, drawing a deep breath, his face drained of colour, his voice stronger. 'I love her,' he repeated. '... enough to marry her, but not enough to deprive my son of his right, his throne. *No*,' he said violently. 'You wicked old man, hear me now. By promising to make your daughter my queen, I will not snatch my son's kingship. I refuse your offer! I shall never allow Devavrat to suffer because you are greedy!'

Kali's heart sank. She made a movement, her eyes pleading with her father. He remained unmoved.

'Greedy, I am not,' retorted Dasharaj. 'I want nothing for myself. I am simply securing the rights of my daughter, her future and her children.'

'How dare you question a king's word of honour?' shouted the king.

'I *am* waiting for your word of honour,' said Dasharaj calmly. 'Until you give me a promise, I shall not hand over my daughter to you. You can never see her either,' he added deliberately. 'We shall await your answer, oh King,' he said firmly. 'Then you can take her as your wife and queen.'

Shantanu was stunned, and looked desperately at Kali, waiting for her to say something. But she merely lowered her face. She was confused, but she believed more in her father than the king, however besotted he might be with her. Finally she looked up at the king, her eyes huge and hurt.

'I hope it's not a farewell, King,' she whispered. Tears, more out of frustration than sorrow, pricked her eyes. 'I feel for you with my whole heart, but do understand... I cannot disobey my father's wishes. I will wait for you, oh King!'

Shantanu gave her a tender, hopeless look and held her calloused hands. 'I remember how hard you fought for that fish the other day, even as your hands bled. But I cannot take away what rightfully belongs to my son. What your father is asking for, Matsyagandha, makes my heart bleed, but I shan't allow his ambitions to bleed us white.'

With those final words, he strode out without shutting the door behind him.

Latching the swinging door, Kali turned furiously to face her father. 'We have lost him! He will never come back!' she cried, almost incoherent with rage.

'Calm down, Satya,' assured her father. 'He will come back. Just as you were sure, I am certain, too. He is in love with you.'

'He'll find another young girl, who will be more than willing to share his bed!' she said.

'But not his throne! And are you, like any other girl, ready to do that?' asked Dasharaj. 'I thought you were more ambitious than that.'

Her shoulders sagged. 'It has all gone to waste,' she sighed. 'I wanted to be queen, but you asked for too much.'

Dasharaj shook his head. 'You were obsessed about becoming a queen, not thinking about what would happen afterwards. I do want the best for you. Don't you trust me?'

She nodded, but in weary desolation.

'He is old, and he will die sooner rather than later,' explained Dasharaj patiently. 'Then you will not be his queen, but his widow. And if you have children, what will happen to them? I have heard that Devavrat is a kind boy; he might spare you and your future kids. But it's not uncommon that step-siblings get murdered, imprisoned or are made to disappear. They become an immediate threat to the throne. The bid for the crown, my dear, can get bloody.'

Kali shuddered.

'You were dreaming about the immediate future—as the queen of Hastinapur. Dream for *your* children, too,' warned Dasharaj. 'Dream for *your* heirs, not Devavrat's. If I can extract that promise from Shantanu, then your future will be secured. But the only weapon we have *is* this alliance. Marriage is not a love story, it is a treaty—a political pact, a pledge. And I shan't allow you to go with him unless he gives his promise.'

'I am afraid he won't agree,' she said heavily, after a moment's thought. 'He is right; I can't be queen at the cost of his son's future.'

'Then you are a fool!' remonstrated Dasharaj sharply.

'I was denied my right as a daughter; I can't do the same to Prince Devavrat!' argued Kali vehemently. 'How can I enjoy my happiness at the cost of another's doom?'

'You owe Shantanu and Devavrat nothing, but you do owe your children a future—something my sister and I could not give you,' he reminded her harshly. 'If you want to live in the palace, dear, you have to learn to live by its rules, and they are not always as golden as the palace interiors!' scoffed her father. 'Along with the gems and jewels in the crown, there is intrigue and violence. You can't escape that, but you can survive it by playing your own game. Be a part of it, Satya, or part ways. You have played just one game, and this is only the beginning; but wearing a crown and holding on to it is a quest, not just a contest.'

'I seem to have lost the race before it began,' she said sullenly, pulling at her lower lip. 'You gave the king such tough options that he will never choose me!'

'Always give a person two bad choices; he is bound to choose the one you want him to choose,' chuckled the old man. 'He either has to marry you to the crown prince or marry you himself by disinheriting the crown prince. Both are excellent for us, but only one can work for him. And you know which one it is.'

'Kings are not great with their promises, and he will try to avoid it for sure,' she said miserably, shaking her head in frustration.

'Agreed,' said Dasharaj quietly with a grave face. 'That is why he will have to announce it to his kingdom before he weds you. Remember how King Dashrath conveniently forgot his vow to Kaikeyi's father, King Ashwapati of Kekeya. He had agreed to give his young daughter to the old king of Kosala on one condition: that it will be her son who would be the future king. But you know what happened. He did not keep it, and she had to fight for it, which ultimately alienated her from her family and her son. Kaikeyi lost everything—her husband, her son, her respect, her reputation, and became the most hated woman forever. Do you want that to happen to you as well?'

Kali listened to every word, grappling with the implications. Her father was no greedy fool. He was her father, dear and caring, and he was also a fisherman chieftain and a shrewd businessman. He had that innate instinct of a fisherman in understanding the tide, to grab the opportunity, quickly and firmly. He was doing just that now, for her.

'Don't be sentimental; politics also rules emotions, not just kings and crowns and kingdoms,' advised her father. 'And it is the throne of power that everyone vies to sit on. You don't have to have royal blood to know the game; you simply have to have the courage and shrewdness to play it. Play it well, for it is no indulgent sport: it is a cold-blooded competition, in which not the strongest but the shrewdest will win.'

~

'Where is your father?' asked Bahlik with mounting frustration.

'He has returned, but has not emerged from his chamber since last evening—again,' replied Devavrat with a worried frown.

'Don't worry about him,' his uncle assured him with a heavy pat on the shoulders. 'Does he know about your extraordinary victory? You won your first war without shedding a drop of blood!' beamed Bahlik, enveloping him in a bear hug, much to Devavrat's embarrassment and Kripa's amusement.

'There was some blood, but it was the enemy's,' grinned Kripa.

They were gushing over Devavrat's victory over Chitramukh, the prince of Shalva, who had sent his troops to the border of Hastinapur. Instead of retaliating with war, Devavrat had shrewdly challenged him instead to the outmoded practice of an open duel. Devavrat had won and sent the humiliated prince back to Saubha, Shalva's capital.

'To the crown prince,' proclaimed Bahlik, slipping him a goblet of wine.

'You are all grown up now, Son; you are no more a boy,' said his uncle heartily. 'How old are you? Twenty? You wanted to prove yourself. You have. To all of us. To you, Son. To our future king of Hastinapur!' He cheered loudly.

Devavrat took a tiny sip, allowing the goblet to rest in his hands. He did not need wine to feel happy. He had got what he had wished for so long—to be on the battlefield. He had been there, however briefly, inhaling the scent of the raised dust blending with the thud of racing hooves and the clang of the sword...

Bahlik pinched his moustache, and after a moment's pause, said, 'But a small error on your part... Was it prudent to let that young cad live?'

Devavrat blinked. He had to be honest not just to his uncle, but to himself. He shook his head slowly. 'I realize that,' he rued, his voice strong with self-reproach. 'My gesture seems magnanimous, but my error of judgement is not a small matter.'

'It happens; you will learn,' shrugged his uncle. 'It's better to fight with violence and not mercy, as you so claim. Mercy is often misinterpreted. Possibly the fool's father might be indebted to you, or he might seek vengeance...' he shrugged. 'Where is *your* father? He should be here, celebrating with us,' he threw his nephew a big grin. 'Drink up, Son, take quicker, bigger mouthfuls!'

His uncle sounded too jovial, and he knew it was not just because he was intoxicated with wine.

'You are old enough to sit on a throne, fight a war, drink and get married!' guffawed Bahlik, but his eyes suddenly went serious. 'Have you not thought of it?'

'Thought of what?' asked Devavrat, genuinely surprised, pushing his hair back.

'Marriage, boy!' laughed his uncle. 'Don't you want to marry?'

Devavrat found himself flushing, hating the heat spreading from his neck up to his face.

'Uncle, there's a time for everything,' he murmured, nonchalantly. 'I got the opportunity to fight my first war after so long. The rest, too, will follow.'

'For pampered princes, it is often the other way round!' argued his uncle. 'Women first, then war! You mean you have not been to any *swayamvar* yet? You are almost twenty now, time you started your family!'

He saw his nephew redden, and was amused at his evident embarrassment. 'I have a wife and three sons, Dev, and the succour and satisfaction I derive from them ... no wealth, no war, no crown can compensate! War's over, now for *your* wedding, Son! What is that brother of mine doing?' he exploded. 'His young son, the crown prince, is *the* most eligible man in this land, and he hasn't yet found him a bride!'

There was a slight trace of exasperated annoyance in his uncle's high, jocular octave.

'Or do you have any girl in mind?' persisted Bahlik, eyeing his nephew with bursting pride. He was truly a handsome boy, and he would see to it that he got him the fairest princess.

'Uncle, I don't know of any girl,' said Devavrat, in mock solemnity, his eyes crinkling, 'beside Kripi, my sister!'

'Not even those apsaras of Indralok?' teased the older man. 'What were you doing there? I'll get you a lovely girl, Son. I hear the princess of Kasi is exquisite; I shall talk with her father soon. And she will be your queen.'

'What queen are you talking about?' demanded Shantanu, as he entered the chamber.

'Oh, good, you are here, finally. We are discussing Dev's marriage. I was thinking about approaching King Kasiraj for his daughter, Princess Vatsala, for Dev. What do you say, Shantanu?'

Shantanu looked stupefied. 'I am the father; why did you not discuss this with me first?' he said furiously, not attempting to hide his annoyance.

'That's what I am doing now,' his brother replied calmly. 'Where were you?' he asked curiously. 'Matters of the court and the heart need to be settled fast. I was taking the groom's permission to seek the bride's consent as well. That is what matters. Weddings are not made in heaven, but here in our hands.'

Shantanu winced. 'When is the wedding of my son to be?' he asked sarcastically. 'I shall be the most honoured guest, I presume.'

'If Kasiraj agrees, four months from now should be a good time,' said Bahlik, unfazed.

Shantanu looked sullenly at his brother and son. 'Within a fortnight, it is Devavrat's formal coronation as king. It should all fit in nicely,' he said.

His words still hanging in the air, he walked away, clearly not in a mood to continue the conversation.

Devavrat watched him leave, gruff and sullen. He turned to his uncle, a thoughtful look on his face, wondering if he should voice his doubts. The last few days had been very difficult between him and his father, and he did not know the reason for it. He barely got to see his father these days; the latter either locked himself in his chamber or saw to it that, in the evenings, he retired to bed so early that he would not have to face his son. Devavrat sensed something was hugely amiss. Each time he had tried talking to his father, Shantanu had shown either indifference or dismissed him airily. Just the way he had done now.

'Your coronation and your wedding—that is wonderful!' enthused his uncle. 'Kripa, we need to discuss this with Devapi urgently and select an auspicious day. I shall send a letter to Kasi right away!'

'Wait, Uncle,' said Devavrat urgently. 'Father is clearly unhappy about this. It is strange, is it not?'

'Ignore him, Son,' advised Bahlik. 'It's your time now; you are going to be king, and are to be married soon! Then you can worry about your father. By then, he, too, will cheer up, I assure you!'

'No, there's something more to this,' insisted Devavrat stubbornly. 'Father is behaving very strangely since the day he came back from his hunt near the Yamuna ... all was fine before he left, but since his return, it seems as if he's avoiding me,' he said evenly, not letting his uncle see his bewildered hurt. 'What happened in the forest? Did you find out where he had disappeared to for all those days?' he asked.

Bahlik licked his lips and shook his head. 'He refused to say anything.'

But Devavrat heard the slight hesitation in his uncle's tone.

'Tell me, Uncle, what is it?'

'Son, let me be frank with you,' confessed Bahlik uneasily. 'I know my brother better. He has his moods, especially after his escapades...'

'His escapades?' repeated Devavrat. 'There is some woman?' he guessed.

'Women,' corrected his uncle disparagingly. 'He must be missing them; that's all. Shantanu has his exploits, comes home dejected and his vanity broken, often a little ashamed—if his guilt of betraying Ganga gnaws at him or if he's ever refused. But he usually gets what he wants. After all, who would dare refuse the king? He must have been rebuffed this time. He is just feeling sorry for himself! That's why he is so irritable. With Shantanu, it's always a woman, it's always been about some woman!' he added dismissively.

With an reassuring clap on his shoulder, his uncle considered the matter closed, but Devavrat felt restless, and it had nothing to do with either his impending coronation or the wedding. It was his father... He had to speak with him; he had procrastinated too long.

Later that day, he slowly made his way to his father's chambers.

'Don't ask me anymore about the state's affairs,' said Shantanu wearily, seeing his son entering. 'It's all in your hands. Hastinapur is yours.'

'It is ours,' amended Devavrat. 'It is our responsibility.'

'No more,' sighed his father. 'I am tired, Son. I shall arrange for your coronation to take place next week. The sooner the better.'

'Better for whom?' asked Devavrat shrewdly.

'I want to formally retire,' Shantanu said, with unusual anger. 'It's your time; *you* have to be king!'

Each time he looked at Devavrat, Shantanu saw the woman he had lost because of him. Frustration and rage filled him; the sight of his son was suddenly irksome. He knew he missed his love miserably. The fragrance of Matsyagandha tormented him, the shadow of her presence taunting him all through the days and the sleepless nights. He looked at his son with mixed emotions: *Had it not been for him, I could have had her by my side now...*

He regretted it almost immediately, but the thought could not be wiped away. And as Devavrat continued talking with him in all earnestness, Shantanu felt a flash of unnamed emotion.

'Please stop, Dev, don't argue with me!' he snapped, confused and annoyed.

Seeing the bemusement on his son's face, he tried to soften his tone. 'I am tired,' he amended lamely. 'We can talk later...'

'What is it, Father?' asked Devavrat gently. 'What is troubling you?'

His son's thoughtfulness tore at the old man's heart. He turned away from him.

'It is nothing,' he dismissed listlessly. 'I am simply worried about us, about you...'

'Me?' Devavrat's handsome face creased in a puzzled frown. 'There is nothing wrong with me,' he added with a reassuring grin.

'Having one son, the king is always scared of losing him. Losing the heir,' said Shantanu, and Devavrat noted the hesitant tone. 'The great clan of Kurus needs an additional offspring, for however great a warrior you are, my Devavrat, your death in battle would bring an end to our lineage. According to the nobles and priests, having a single son is like having only one eye. It is a serious handicap. If the only son predeceased the father, the clan would be ruined...'

Devavrat looked perplexed, his clear eyes not revealing the confusion that was building within. *Why is Father scared? Is he scared of his death, or mine? And what is this talk of another heir?*

As if to voice his thoughts, Shantanu continued, 'I heard about that unwarranted skirmish with that rascal Chitramukh! You could have been killed! Then what would have happened to me?' he paused, wondering what to say next. 'And Hastinapur? You are the heir, Devavrat. You can't be so careless. If you had died, this kingdom would have lost its only heir!'

'Then get him married soon,' interrupted Devapi's calm voice. 'Bahlik told me to discuss the dates of the coronation with you. Shantanu, you worry needlessly. Devavrat is a young man, fit to have a throne and father children.'

Shantanu scowled in irritation.

The brothers eyed each other warily. Devapi had entered the room quietly and noticed immediately the unfinished goblet by Shantanu's side: he had always been fond of wine and women. Watching him, Devapi realized his younger brother had been with a woman. The relaxed, satiated expression on the handsome face was enough to confirm his doubt. It did not worry him, it was usual; but that cocky look quickly twisted into a scowl at the sight of him. He was intrigued. His brother now wore a sullen, abject expression, which was new.

'I am serious,' said Devapi, his eyes solemn. 'Devavrat should have been married by now, and you would have had grandchildren instead of brooding about the future,' he added in quiet reprimand.

Shantanu sighed, 'I apologize. Consider my grouchiness a result of the many things on my mind,' he said weakly, but Devavrat noted the emptiness in his words as well as in his tired eyes.

There was one person who could help him out: Manjunath, his father's personal charioteer. He must know where his father had disappeared the past few weeks.

Devavrat pursed his lips in a stubborn line; he knew he would get his answers.

The Oath

Kali heard the resounding echo of thundering hooves in the distance; her heart raced, and she jumped to her feet. *It must be the kingsmen again*, she thought fearfully. She was sure her father's impertinence had enraged Shantanu enough to destroy the entire village and its chief who had dared to defy him.

Kali glanced frantically at her father, who seemed calm. She peeped out of the window cautiously.

'It's the crown prince himself,' she said, her voice low but tense. Had he come along with his father to confront her about their attempt to sabotage his prospects of inheriting the throne?

A small crowd was gathering as news of the crown prince visiting their village spread swiftly.

The prince was with the same swarthy, middle-aged man—the king's charioteer. Kali watched them come in from a corner at the end of the street. She looked at the prince curiously, and her fingers stopped twiddling. He was standing in the doorway with the charioteer just behind him. She saw his face turned at an angle; there was a strange magnetism about him. And as she looked at him, she felt a thickness in her throat.

'Has he come to arrest us, Father?' she whispered.

Kali recalled the humiliation from her last run-in with the kingsmen and her near arrest. *No, if he wanted us arrested, the crown prince would not come here himself. He would have sent his men*, she told herself over and over again, to allay her growing fear.

'Strength, particularly of the powerful, is often misunderstood by the weak, ,' her father said cryptically, as they heard a polite knock on the door.

Dazed, Kali was seized by a strong sensation of déjà vu—the day when Shantanu had come to their very door. But there had been a certain sanguineness then, not this stifling trepidation.

As soon as the crown prince entered the room, he filled it with his presence, unlike his father. Her heart hammering, fighting curiosity and dread, Kali braved herself to look up at him, her chin raised more in unconscious defence than habit.

He was truly Ganga's son, the Gangaputra. He looked like a god, with his good looks, dark hair and penetrating gaze, tall and looming, swathed in royal raiment of silk, pearls and gems. The perfect prince, though the look was slightly flawed by an irreverent lock of hair falling over his wide, intelligent forehead. It humanized him.

He had a pinched face and a very thin, tight mouth. It was not until she encountered the full force that dwelt in his eyes that she realized she was in the presence of a powerful man. He gave her his full attention, keeping a steady gaze on her. She found she was perspiring slightly; she was careful not to stare at him, although she wanted to.

Devavrat had had to quickly rein in his shock on seeing Kali. *Heavens! Is she the one my father is so desperately in love with?* He had been expecting a woman, but the person standing before him was a very young girl: slim, dark and attractive, barely his age, probably younger, he thought noting that her expression was one of an intelligent person, mingled with a certain childish charm. Her figure, though, was nothing girlish, but all womanly, with feminine grace. He swiftly realized why his father had fallen so deeply for her.

He broke his thoughts and turned to the old man who was watching him warily: sour, rumpled and dishevelled.

There was an expression of displeasure on the old man's grey face, as though he were offended by something.

'I apologize for this unexpected visit, sir,' he said, his voice soft and slow, a careful deliberation in every word. 'I am Prince Devavrat of Hastinapur, and I have come here to discuss an urgent matter.'

The old man did not say anything, neither did the girl.

'It concerns my father,' he began tactfully, determined to resolve the puzzle of the mystery woman the king had been visiting. 'He came here and visited you, I hear, but since his return he has not been the same. Clearly, something must have happened here that disturbed him. And I am not aware of what it could have been; please could you help me with this, sir?'

'I am Dasharaj, the chief of the fishermen of this village, and this is my daughter, Satyavati,' said the old man finally. *Crafty eyes, steady and attentive face*, observed Devavrat. 'The issue is simple. Your father wants to marry Satyavati.'

Devavrat did not show his shock. So, it was not a wilful fancy; his father must be seriously in love with this girl to be ready to marry her. He gave the girl a second look: *was she in love with him, too, or was she an opportunist, using the situation to her advantage?* His bland expression did not betray his thoughts.

'What, then, is the problem?' he asked unperturbed.

'The problem is you,' said the old man bluntly.

He saw the girl wince, a finger furtively playing with her lower lip.

'Me?' Devavrat sounded surprised, unable to conceal his astonishment.

The fisherman nodded. 'Yes, you are the reason why your father is not ready to marry my daughter.'

'And how am I concerned with my father's decision?'

Devavrat asked, curious about this man's cunningness. He knew he was being arm-twisted, but with what?

Kali saw the quick flash of contempt in the crown prince's eyes. *He thinks we are shrewd and greedy, particularly me, who made his father fall in love to extract coin and crown, who seduced a king into marriage.* She was strangely piqued by his dismissive glance.

'When you father revealed his desire to marry Satyavati, I, as a concerned father, laid down a condition for the marriage,' explained Dasharaj.

I was right—there had to be a crushing term under which Father was trapped, Devavrat thought. He waited for the man to continue, his face expressionless, his eyes alert.

'That he can marry her only if her children are the heirs to the throne. Not you,' Dasharaj stated. 'If she is fit enough to be his wife, his queen, will her children from your father not be fit enough to be heirs? But your father does not agree with this. He does not want to disinherit *you*, oh Crown Prince.'

An image of his father's sorrowful face and his mother's request pierced his heart. *'Look after your father, Son!'*

The past four years had shown him that his father was essentially an unhappy, lonely man, wrapped in a blanket of despondency. Never had a day gone by when he had not mentioned Ganga, pining and bitter. She was his lost love; a love he sought in other women, earning him the disreputable reputation of a womanizer. It was a harsh assertion, not entirely fair. Shantanu missed Ganga and she would never return to him the way his son had. Devavrat often saw that vacant hope in his father's eyes, wishing it was Ganga who was by his side and not him. So many years ago, had she thrown him into the river, he would have drowned and died and would have been released from his curse. And his mother would have continued to stay with her husband, happily ever after...

But this was not to be, because of me. Mother left Father because of me; she had to return to Heaven to groom me. I cannot bear to see my Father's lonely, empty eyes; they weigh me down, and guilt lays heavily on my heart. Now, Father has found love again, and I am, once again, in the way...

Devavrat blinked as he was brought to the present with a start. He observed the girl again; her father was hovering protectively by her side.

'My being the crown prince should not hinder my father's decision at all. It was foolish on your part to have asked my father for what is mine,' he said, his voice even, his eyes steady. 'My father cannot promise you, sir, or you...' he said, bowing towards Kali, '...or even your grandsons the crown of Hastinapur, because he has already given it to me.'

Kali heard the finality in his voice, and knew what was coming. He *had* come here to fight. She balled her fingers into a tight fist, trying to suppress her fear and frustration. Her father had got it all wrong...

The prince continued in a soft voice. 'It was not his to give. But what is mine, I can give. And I give it to you,' he said, as he again flicked Kali a cursory look before bowing graciously. 'At this very instant, I give up my right over the throne,' he said calmly, and he heard the girl gasp. 'I vow that it will be your daughter's children who will be the heirs; not me. Please, sir, let not this small issue stand in their way to happiness.'

Devavrat felt a sudden load lift off him, making him almost dizzy with light-heartedness. He would no longer be king; his heart filled with relief. He knew with certainty that he had never wished to be king, to have a crown forced on his head merely because he was his father's only son. A father he barely knew; a kingdom that had never been his home.

He noticed the girl staring at him with open disbelief. There was no elation on her face, just plain confusion. Or was it guilt? Even the father looked surprised, slightly discomfited. *Was the allure of the throne so strong that it had become a term of temptation, a deal to bargain*, Devavrat thought with wry amusement. And then he took in his surroundings—the tattered room; the thin, peeling walls; the girl, proud in her shabby clothes; the old man, wasted and tired. For them, possibly, power and wealth were a dream to wake into; an ambition to achieve. Had he got it too easily?

Kali looked down at her twisting fingers, unable to look into the crown prince's frank, open face. She had just wrested the throne from him and grabbed it for herself and her future children. She should be celebrating—the biggest hurdle to her way up had been removed. But this young man had removed it himself, gracefully stepping away to make way for her. His magnanimity made her feel ashamed and small. Her ambition had made her compromise on her values and conduct, violating ethics and moral standards. She alone would have to bear the significant responsibility of her unforgivable transgression.

'If this is what is keeping my father away from his happiness,' he was staring at her now, 'then I promise that I shall never sit on that throne. Mother Satyavati can marry my father with no further delay.'

She felt her heart stop and then hammer rapidly. The new moniker with which she was addressed shook her.

The old fisherman was quick to gather his wits. 'Young Prince, you are the brightest star of the Bharat dynasty. What you have done has never before been done by any royal person until now...'

Devavrat smiled, shaking his head, and Kali was amazed he could smile in a situation like this. 'No, sir, it's been done often in my family!' he said dryly. 'My uncles have refused the throne for my father who was the youngest of the three. And our ancestor, King Bharat, gave his throne, not to his sons, whom he found unworthy of the crown, but to his adopted son, a relative of Rishi Bhardwaj,' he added.

Dasharaj looked suitably chastised, but he continued smoothly, 'Nevertheless you *are* a hero, Prince Devavrat! It's not easy giving up a throne. You have readily relinquished it now. That's very generous of you! History will always remember your sacrifice. But I have one doubt. If your father has no right to make this promise on your behalf, then how come you seem to own the right to make the promise on behalf of your sons? What if your sons go against your word and raise arms against my grandsons for this very throne? Would your future wife and your children agree to this decision? Would they not revolt against it, against their step-brothers and step-mother? How do I know that they will not revoke their rights, as you have done? If they are anything like you, they, too, will be brave, mighty warriors and powerful enough to seize back the throne that is also their birthright. How, then, do I safeguard my daughter and her sons, Prince?'

Devavrat scrutinized the man standing before him, and he felt a strange admiration for him. *This is how a father should be, fighting with all his dignity and conviction for the future of his child.*

He bowed low, and said, 'You are correct, sir! I cannot decide and make promises on behalf of my children. But I can certainly decide something on my own, for myself. To remove any further doubts and fears about the future of your daughter and grandsons, I have decided right now never to marry. The solution is simple, sir. There will be no sons of mine to usurp your daughter's rights,' he continued, rising his right arm to take the oath. 'I vow to you, sir, I shall never marry, and, henceforth, shall dedicate my life to celibacy and unbroken chastity. I swear that I shall never be with a woman, nor father children. May my mother, Ganga, and the devas, be the witnesses to my promise to you—*I, Devavrat, the son of Ganga and Shantanu, pledge never to marry and father children with any woman. I shall remain without a wife and child till my last breath. That is my promise to you!*'

His words stilled the beating of her heart for the longest, excruciating moment. Was there a deafening silence plunging the world into a stillness of horror? It was as if the entire cosmos and every creature inhabiting it had been silenced with the profundity of his words. A strong breeze shattered the silence and whipped inside the house, as if to disintegrate the words uttered in this room and fling them out into the universe for all and the devas to hear. The wind whirled around Devavrat, showering the extraordinary young man with flowers, accepting and appreciating his extraordinary oath.

It was a terrible oath. It was not just an end of him and his future, but he would have none to call his own in life or death—no wife, no children, no throne, no kingdom, no legacy to bequeath; just his soul sealed with this oath for eternity.

'*Bhishm!*' the wind seemed to whistle, rising to a crescendo and into a revered chant.

'Bhishm,' repeated Dasharaj, bowing his head in genuine veneration. 'The devas seem to have given you a new name, Prince. "Bhishm" means a man who takes the most terrible vow.'

Which I made you take, thought Kali with a heavy heart that was tightening painfully. She heard the soldiers outside shouting a chant, a war cry.

'Bhishm!'

The door unexpectedly flew open, not by the howling wind outside, but by his white-faced charioteer.

Manjunath fell at his feet, sobbing. 'What have you done, my prince? Your pledge has disturbed even the cosmos. The clouds are weeping a downpour of heavy rains, and the devas have descended to Earth to shower you, sir, with flowers and blessings. Your words rang out loud, tore through the walls of this room into the open sky and beyond—and see what a tempest it has created! Time has never seen such a terrible oath being taken by anyone, nor will it ever see such a terrible sight. There are tears in the eyes of every soldier standing outside,' he waved a wiry arm towards the narrow lane. 'Princes and kings have been known to slaughter the weak to show off their might and valour. But here you are, the mightiest of kings, giving up everything for the sake of your old father . I don't know if we are blessed or cursed to have seen the most historical moment in time!'

Manjunath paused. 'Had it not been for me, who brought you to this damned place, you would have never met this witch!' he snarled, throwing at Kali such a glare of visceral hate that she felt the physical impact of it. 'I am to blame for letting you meet her and her evil father. You, in your goodness, Prince, and they, in their greed and evil ... all of you cannot foresee the implications of this terrible vow on not just the Kuru clan, but Hastinapur as well! You have said it in your nobleness, sir, and they have happily heard it, but this is doom! Take it back, my dear prince. It will cost all of us dearly!'

The room echoed with the potency of Manjunath's words

and what they would portend. Kali had gone pale; fear clutched at her throat: *First that oath, and now the loyal man's warning. What have I initiated?*

Devavrat looked unfazed. 'My father will be a happier man now,' he said simply.

Kali shuddered, an inaudible 'No!' slipping from her horrified mouth. 'You can't take that vow!'

'Mother,' bowed the Prince. 'It is done.'

Mother—the word sounded horribly foreign to her, crushing her with the burden of its weight. The prince said it with strange detachment; it felt like a stinging slap on her face. By calling her his mother, he was reminding her of who she was: his father's wife. The poor fisher girl who aspired to be queen. The girl who schemed to marry his father. The queen who usurped his throne. The woman who could never be his mother. That word was a profanity, a scornful abuse, a blasphemy to their new relationship.

Had she wanted this? To make her the queen, her father had deprived another of his birthright. With no throne, no crown, no wife, no children, what kind of a life would the prince live?

For the first time in her young life, Kali felt guilty. She had experienced anger and shame and humiliation, but never guilt. It was an unfamiliar emotion: painful, wrenching her heart, making her feel mortified with the searing realization that she had wronged an innocent person. The gravity of her offensive action was so overwhelming, it was drowning her in a tide of remorse and misgiving. She felt that she had lost respect for herself; that she had dishonoured her very being.

'No! Please take back that terrible oath, Prince!' she implored, ignoring Dasharaj's furious glare. 'What my father is asking for is worse than your life; even death would be kinder,' she said, her voice getting firmer with each word. 'What you are doing is an unwarranted sacrifice, surrendering everything to my father's wishes...'

'No,' smiled the prince, his eyes almost mocking. 'It's for *my* father. I am doing this for him.'

Not *you*, he meant to say. He was not getting arm-twisted by her father, but he was willingly relinquishing everything he had for just one man—his father. The gentle correction was like a slap on her face. She, or what she had wrested from him, meant nothing to him. It was as if he was almost laughing at them.

Kali persisted. 'Your father will not agree to this absurd vow,' she said. 'Which father will be happy after sacrificing his son's hope to happiness?'

'It is my vow, Mother; even my father does not have the right to take it from me,' replied Devavrat, his voice quiet but hardened by an inflexible resoluteness.

Kali looked at him in utter amazement. Was he a naive fool? Or an idealist? But what she could gauge in that brief moment was that he was an excessively obdurate young man, having and showing an obstinate determination not to change his attitude, in spite of good reasons to do so. He was unyielding, she quickly realized, unwilling to revise his words and the course of his actions, of his life and future.

The onus of which will fall on me, she thought with a sinking heart. *Neither Shantanu, nor his kingdom, nor the world will ever forgive me.*

'Now that I have taken the oath of celibacy and relinquished the crown, I hope there is nothing more to stop my father from marrying you, Mother. Shall we leave for Hastinapur now?' asked the prince politely, taking in her troubled face. 'That is if your father trusts me with my promise,' he added sardonically.

Kali flushed, ashamed to even glance at her father. Or at

the prince. She would never be able to justify the injustice she had inflicted on him.

'Please could I talk with him before we leave?' she muttered.

Devavrat bowed. 'I shall wait outside,' he said perfunctorily, taking Manjunath by his hand, and leading him out.

No sooner had the door closed behind him, than Kali turned on her father wrathfully. He was prepared for it.

'You are heartless!' she raged. 'But the world will point fingers at *me*, not you, Father, accusing me of being a gold-digger!'

'It is self-preservation,' he replied smoothly. 'As you said, would you rather be known as a vamp than a victim?'

'What you did to the prince is unforgivable, Father,' she said hollowly. 'I shall never be able to look him in the eye. It will lay heavy on my conscience.'

'That is better than to have regrets later! You do not understand the games the royalty play. If you are to marry a king, you need to know the game and that there's always a price for everything,' retorted Dasharaj.

'Take it back, Father, please!' begged Kali.

'He took the oath, not I. How can I force him to take his words back.'

'Do you realize what you have done? You have snatched everything from him, you have destroyed him, taken his present and his future...'

'I know,' said Dasharaj, his voice hard.

Kali shook her head in despair. 'I just wanted to be a queen,' she said simply, her face forlorn. 'But not at this cost.'

'You can and you will!' he said forcefully. 'I couldn't do anything for my sister; I watched her anguish, her heartbreak...' his voice trembled. 'I won't make you suffer her fate. I don't care if someone else has to pay for that wrong. If not the King of Chedi, let it be the young crown prince who gets for you what you lost. So don't undo what I did.'

'If not Shantanu, there will be some other suitor...' she started weakly.

'Some other king who will walk the stinking streets of this village and fall in love with you?' laughed her father mirthlessly. 'Be realistic, child! You started it and I finished it for you. It went perfectly. Don't allow your conscience to hurt you or your future children!'

Kali opened her mouth weakly to protest further, but the door opened and a young soldier entered holding silk robes.

'The prince has sent this for you, my lady,' he declared in a low tone, his eyes downcast.

Kali was not used to such a reverential manner of speaking. She would have to get used to it, she thought irrelevantly, as she accepted the silk raiment: it was a deep purple, fit for a queen. *A queen*, she rolled the word, silently, on her tongue. A sudden elation dispelled the guilt that had pierced her soul.

The Sacrifice

Hastinapur was overwhelming—both in character, and in the welcome that awaited them. As they sailed through the waves of happy faces thronging every street of the walled city, they were greeted with salutes, bows and cheers. Just hours before, Kali had been one of them: an inconsequential face in a mass of humans, lost in the herd.

'Prince Devavrat! Devavrat! Our new king!' they cheered in reverential chorus.

The crowds clearly adored him. *The applause, the love, the veneration is for Devavrat, not for me*, Kali quickly reminded herself. *But one day, they will chant my name in the same breath*, she vowed, pressing a fingertip on her lower lip. *Once I become the queen, they will have to acknowledge me as their sovereign saviour, too...*

'Please respond to them,' Devavrat's curt voice interrupted her reverie, glancing at her with his dark, hooded eyes. 'Or fold your hands in acknowledgement.'

Kali resented his tone, but obeyed him quietly. She was immediately greeted with a loud cheer.

They held each other's gaze for several seconds.

'Only when you give respect, do you get respect,' he said crisply.

Kali bristled, eyeing him mutinously under her thick, sooty eyelashes, her face lowered. There was a certain air about him that made her feel like he was being dismissive.

He suddenly looked straight at her. He had been guarded till now, and, for a fleeting moment, she thought she saw undiluted contempt in his eyes. It was a shock to realize he thought so low of her. But that was to be expected, after what she had done to him. She could not blame him or resent him, but it was a shock all the same. She could see how complicated it was all going to be.

'It is the people who make a king, always,' he went on impassively.

Not a conniving game of crowns, she reckoned, was his sanctimonious insinuation. An angry flush mounted up her neck.

'The people will always bow to a king. Or a queen,' Kali reminded him icily. 'Irrespective of who the king is—a Samaritan or a scoundrel. People are often in awe of the crown; they fear the king, not love him. I know that, Prince. I was one of them,' she added pointedly.

He looked away, staring into the horizon, seemingly amused at her immediate defensiveness, which riled her further.

The palace was so massive that none could miss it even from a considerable distance. Her heart unexpectedly filled, not with animated anticipation, but a flood of dread, as it came into view. Situated almost at the top of a hillock, it resembled a fortress: immense and daunting. *Now she would live here, amongst the rich, the powerful and the privileged,* she forced some enthusiasm. She had yearned for this for years, all through her bleak childhood. But strangely, when it was now in her grasp, the dazzle of it was not so appealing. Could it be because of the people's reception of her in the city or Devavrat's silent hostility? Kali's face twisted in an unconscious grimace: the rich and powerful were anyway harder to deal with than folks further down the social ladder.

Kali had been trained to mask her emotions and expressions, but the grandeur of the palace snatched her wits away. For a girl who had been born and breathed in squalor, the palace was like heaven. The huge domes were what attracted the attention at once, all shaped like large, upturned flower petals. They hung over huge, columned halls, ornate balustrades and carved doorways. From the edge of the high walls, a half-acre of unbridled green grass spread in a gentle slope down towards a serpentine path. The sidewalk and the path were cobbled, both very wide, probably for elephants to amble right in, she mused. The old park, laid out in elaborate style, gloomy and severe, stretched for almost three-quarters of a mile to the river Ganga, and there it ended in a steep, precipitous clay bank, where she could glimpse tall trees growing. The water shone below with an unfriendly gleam, and the birds flew up with a plaintive cry: an unwelcome sound to her ears. But near the palace itself, in the courtyard and orchards, it was all life and gaiety even in this hot weather. Such marvellous roses, lilies, marigolds of all possible shades, from glistening white to deep crimsons—such a wealth of flowers, that she thought it a veritable garden of paradise.

'This is beautiful!' she gushed, the words coming out in involuntary wonder.

'Yes, it is.' For the first time, he allowed himself a small smile, which did not do much to ease the inscrutability on his face. 'I believe everyone should have some hobby,' he shrugged his broad shoulders. 'I love flowers. The place where I grew up was surrounded by flowers. I wanted to keep that bit here with me!' He stopped abruptly, as if he felt he had talked too much.

'You have grown some of the finest flowers I have ever seen,' she smiled indulgently.

Devavrat flushed self-consciously. They pulled up at a well-manicured, circular garden in front of a marbled porch. She was met with a host of maids and manservants, all noiseless and sharp-eyed, looking at her with frank distrust and curiosity.

Devavrat led her through the marbled maze of long corridors and steps. Kali followed with her head high and her heart fluttering, refusing to be daunted by his glacial formidability. She found, to her surprise, that her initial awe was swiftly dwindling—the ornate furniture was ugly and the ubiquitous chandeliers, garish. *Was this how the wealthy lived, in a crass display of their gold and gems?* The palace, heavily ostentatious, was especially cavernous, and the walk to Shantanu's main wing seemed disagreeably long.

Kali soon realized she was being ushered into Shantanu's residential section of the palace. She felt a slight prickle of apprehension: *Would Shantanu be surprised, happy or angry?*

'Father, I have got someone for you,' announced Devavrat softly, as he entered his father's chamber.

He was welcomed by a brooding silence; then Shantanu asked, disinterestedly, 'Who is it?'

'It's me, Matsyagandha,' whispered Kali demurely.

Devavrat masked his surprise well, intrigued by her name. He had noticed the fragrance, of course, and it was intoxicating. She wore it like a jewel—rare and priceless—and flaunted it with a natural hauteur he found faintly annoying.

Shantanu whirled around. *'How?'* he muttered, his voice as incredulous as the expression on his face.

Devavrat watched his father's face flood with unconcealed joy.

'I did what her father wished for, and he agreed to give her hand in marriage to you,' supplied Devavrat briefly. 'I brought her here for you; your new queen. My mother.'

Devavrat saw the elation seep out of his father's frame as quickly as it had suffused it earlier.

'You did *what?*' he whispered hoarsely, his face drained of colour and emotion. He was not gazing at Kali anymore; his eyes bored into his son's.

'Please tell me you did not agree to those terrible terms her father put forward!' Shantanu said hoarsely, his eyes filled with dread.

He swung around to look accusingly at Kali. 'What did *you* make him do?' he cried.

Watching her momentary confusion, Devavrat decided to intervene. 'Father, it was *my* decision. I did it. No one forced me into it,' he clarified quickly.

'No! I can't let you do it!' argued Shantanu, clutching at his son's hand. 'It's your birthright! You are the rightful heir to the throne! I cannot let you sacrifice it! No!'

His guilt was contagious, shooting a sharp dart at her as well. Kali stared at her hands, her head dropping in silent shame. She had thought it would be an easy job to win man and crown; she had not reckoned with the ugliness of it all.

'Father, you were right. Hastinapur needs heirs: a bigger royal family,' said Devavrat, his face soft and smiling. 'There is nothing to get so upset about. It is a time to celebrate. I shall start with the preparations...'

'Stop it, Dev!' said Shantanu forcefully. 'There won't be a wedding! I cannot accept Matsyagandha as my wife over your ruination,' Shantanu was openly overwrought. 'I can't do this to you. I am your father!' he cried, burying his face in his hands.

'And I am your son,' said Devavrat quietly. 'It is my duty to see you happy.' He ignored his father's loud protest, his tone hardening. 'I have taken my oath, and nothing will take it back, not even my death.'

There was a deadly certainty in his words, and Kali, a finger pressed on her lower lip, did not miss the bleak determination in his tone. *Nothing will take it back, not even my death.* She had won, after all, she realized with a delayed sense of triumph.

Devavrat's wilful self-destruction broke Shantanu's remorse.

'You *are* Bhishm!' Shantanu said in an awed whisper. 'I don't deserve you; I don't deserve to be your father!'

The raw grief on his father's face tore at his heart, and Devavrat wondered what he could do to make him feel better. 'But I am your son, Father,' he tried to cajole weakly. 'Can't a son give something to his father: does it always have to be the parents?'

'But I gave you nothing, Son!' cried Shantanu. 'Neither my love, nor my blessings; and now, not even my legacy!'

Shantanu's lips trembled, as Ganga's words reverberated in his mind, *'Our child is cursed!'* It was slowly unfolding before his eyes. And he had unwittingly played his role in his son's destined misfortune.

'No!' he wept, tears of shame and regret flowing down his cheeks. 'Don't make me my son's nemesis, God, please!' he staggered, swaying with the horror of his realization.

Kali made a move to hold Shantanu, but Devavrat reached him before she did. She could not decipher what the king was muttering through his tear-stained voice, but she could see he was a broken man: a defeated, ashamed father who was crumbling under the crushing magnanimity of his son. *Devavrat's oath is going to kill him,* she thought in despair. *Oh, Father, what did you do? What did I do?* The crown was already losing its glitter.

Shantanu gazed searchingly into his son's eyes.

'My son!' he murmured. 'I can give you nothing but this one blessing...' he started wretchedly.

'You are too noble, Devavrat, and the whole world will know you as Bhishm,' he said hollowly. 'All I can do is bless you with *icchamrityu*—the power to choose the time of your own death.'

I have taken everything from you, thought Shantanu bleakly, *but by this boon, may you escape the further cruelty of this world you have been cursed to be born and live in, oh Devavrat. I failed you, Son. I failed you, Ganga,* he cried silently. *Will my blessing release Devavrat from this world; a world in which he is trapped by his birth?* Unburdened of kingdom and marriage through his oath, and endowed with the power to die at will, his cursed son was now free to leave the world. But one look at his strong-willed son told Shantanu that no blessing would help him escape his cruel destiny, and that, somehow, he would once again be cast back into the fetters of love and duty. *I am that fetter, and Hastinapur is his duty.*

Kali was visibly shocked, her eyes travelling quickly between son and father. *Which father wishes for the death of his son and bestows it as a blessing? What had Devavrat received in return for his sacrifice: death at will?*

What Shantanu had bequeathed to Devavrat was a legacy worse than death.

'I *am* blessed, Father. I am your son, and Ganga's,' said Devavrat calmly, watching the stark hopelessness on his father's face. There was more to this blessing, he knew, portending a certain ominousness...

'Is that all you can give your son?' interrupted an angry voice. 'A death wish!'

Devavrat dreaded what was to follow as soon as he heard his uncle's voice.

'What sort of a father are you, Shantanu, that you are willing to live happily at the cost of your son's happiness?' demanded Bahlik, his face mottled red. 'Your son gets a wife for you, when it is you who should have gotten one for him!' he said, throwing Kali a look of disdain.

He reminded her of a vigilant guard, big and muscular, with his beaky, fleshy nose and thin, cruel mouth. His small, watery eyes crawled over her, filled with unadulterated contempt.

Devavrat swiftly realized it was up to him to defuse the situation.

'Uncle, please, it's time to plan a wedding, not argue!' he pleaded.

'It's time to mourn!' snapped Bahlik, his rheumy eyes gleaming. 'I will *not* allow this injustice. This is sheer madness. A chit of a girl aspires to be queen, and snatches your throne to win!' he threw another shrivelling glance at Kali, who was standing proud and defiant in the corner of the long chamber.

'We don't treat our guests so badly,' Kali said softly, through gritted teeth.

Bahlik stared at her with loathing. Her dark complexion, her slim, sensual body, her big, sensuous eyes and her hard mouth reiterated his doubts. 'You are not a guest; you are nothing!' spat Bahlik, a nerve throbbing at his temple. 'If you are hurt by my words, feel free to leave!'

Shantanu made a movement. An incensed Bahlik was quick to notice his reaction.

'See, my brother is more worried about this girl than his son!' lashed Bahlik. 'Shantanu, is that what you are reduced to—an old man seduced by an opportunist, consigning his young son to a living death?'

Shantanu went white. 'You are being irreverent!'

'And you, my dear younger brother, are a selfish fool!' retorted Bahlik, furiously. 'Like our father who set an example, you should have retired and relinquished your crown to your young son. Instead, you got yourself a bride! How could you allow some girl, young enough to be your daughter, to make you lose sense and bearing? You are a king, and a father; but you have failed miserably as both!'

Kali could not believe she was being so brutally insulted. She was seething with anger, but remained quiet; one false move now could undo all that she had earned and gained.

The prince would have to play saviour again, she thought, *as he is the only one whom the enraged old man will listen to at the moment.*

Devavrat rose to his father's defence. 'Uncle, calm down. It's my own decision. Father is not responsible—'

'It has everything to do with him, Son!' interrupted Bahlik. 'Shantanu has brought this upon us.' He shook his head. 'For him to be led on by this...'

Shantanu looked up despairingly, and said, 'I love her, Bahlik. Do not insult her so!'

Bahlik snorted. 'If you could not control your desires, you should have kept her in your harem, Brother. *Your throne* is what she wants; not you, you fool!'

Shantanu looked livid, 'You have gone too far, Bahlik!'

'No, you have, Brother, and now it's too late,' said Bahlik. 'Too late for all of us. You still have no reckoning how deep into the chasm you've fallen, not just because of this damned girl, but your self-pride and self-love as well. You were always a spoilt child, because you were born late to our parents, in their old age. But I never imagined you would turn out to be a debauched character!' roared his brother, derision glittering in his disillusioned eyes. 'Had I suspected it, I would have never handed over Hastinapur to you, Shantanu, just so you could squander it away so carelessly for your lust for a young girl!'

Kali could see a vein throbbing at his temple, and she thought he would explode in an apoplexy of rage.

Bahlik thrust his face close to his ashen-faced younger brother and said, 'How can you be the son of our father, King Pratip? Or do you claim to carry the selfish, decadent blood of our forefathers like Yayati and Dushyant? Cursed with premature old age because of his infidelity to his wife, Devyani, Yayati had the gall to borrow youth from his young son, Puru. Much later, in our same lineage, Dushyant came close to denying his son, Bharat, the right to his name. You are just as shallow as them!' he roared. 'Our Paurav dynasty seems full of such tales where sons are repeatedly asked to make sacrifices to accommodate the whims and fancies of their self-centred fathers. Is that not so, Brother?' he said savagely. 'But yours is an extreme case. Most of those sons eventually regained their birthrights and their throne; but what about Dev? Can you ever give back to him what you have taken?' he demanded. 'You will live in lust, and he in celibacy; how cruel is that? Even Yayati realized his mistake and returned his youth to Puru. You know what he is said to have famously confessed to his son, Shantanu? Yayati is said to have confessed that not all the wine, wealth and women of the world can appease the lust of man. Desire flares with indulgence like fuel to fire. Having found this wisdom at last through his excesses, Yayati, once again, as an old man, renounced his kingdom to spend his remaining days as an ascetic. It was his last days that brought him his salvation, Shantanu, not his full, hedonistic life. But will you ever repent?' he shook his head gravely. 'I cannot stay around and watch the doom of our family.'

He turned to Kali. 'Our family is known for one brother gladly giving up the crown for another. But you twisted it and forced Devavrat to do the same. There is no nobleness or greatness in that deed. It only proves your rottenness. I cannot curse you; for if I do, I shall be bringing ill-will to our family. You have already brought bad luck into our home and my nephew's life. May you live long enough to regret every one of your decisions.'

His burning eyes seared into hers, and she felt the silent curse pervading from him, seeping into her mind and senses. It was a jolt: the pure, vitriolic hatred in the old man's eyes. She trembled, her face pale, in fear and anger.

'I love your brother, sir,' she said demurely.

'But you want his crown more,' taunted the old man, leaning forward. 'You could fool Shantanu and Dev, but not me, girl. You wanted to be queen, and you used my brother and ruined my nephew for it. I hope you believe there is a God, and justice, somewhere, sometime.

'Dev forfeited his all; but do you know what will happen to our family henceforth?' he questioned both father and son, while staring hard at her. 'This girl will be the queen, the grand matriarch of this new dynasty that she will start! Along with yours, it will be *her* bloodline as well from now on.'

Devavrat made a move to stop his uncle. 'You cannot leave Hastinapur, Uncle, with so much anger,' he said imploringly.

He was surprised to see his uncle bow before him. 'You would have been king, Prince Devavrat. I came back to Hastinapur for that, not for my brother,' he said tonelessly. 'I returned for you. So did Devapi. Both of us came to give you our blessing ... to the future king, the crown prince of Hastinapur. But you threw it away so carelessly; without a thought, either for the kingdom or its subjects, both to whom you were morally accountable. Without a thought for the people who love you, have expectations from you and who made you their king. Without a thought to the law and rule of this land, that a king owes allegiance first to the throne, to his subjects, and *not* family.'

Devavrat felt his heart stir with an unfamiliar apprehensiveness: his uncle, his mentor, his teacher was not just angry and displeased; worse, he was disappointed with him.

'Dev, what have you gone and done?' asked his uncle. 'If I have anger for my brother and contempt for this girl, I am deeply saddened by what you have done. You failed me, Dev, and you failed Hastinapur. You would have been a great king; but you threw it all away for the whims of your father. What about your responsibility to the crown?'

'I have not turned away from my responsibilities, Uncle,' Devavrat said in a low voice. 'I have given up the crown, but I shall always be loyal and true to it, and serve it honestly till the last breath in my body,' he said passionately, his voice soft with a strong undercurrent of admirable purposefulness.

'Serve the crown as *what*, Son?' mocked Bahlik. 'As a loyal servant, a minister, a noble or a regent? Now you won't serve the crown, but any wilful person wearing it!' He continued relentlessly, 'You won't serve the kingdom, but you will serve the king. You will be reduced to just a chattel; with no voice, no opinion and no power.'

His eyes as calm as his voice, Devavrat answered equably, 'I shall do that gladly, Uncle. I was born in Hastinapur. I shall live for it, protect it and die for it. That is my promise to you.'

His father had lost pallor; the girl looked uneasy, but she remained silent and motionless.

'Another promise!' exploded Bahlik. 'They are a bane, not a boon, Son. Who gave you the right to give up the crown for this woman and her unborn progeny? Who gave you the right to play with the throne and put it at stake for your irrational love for your father? It was not yours to gamble, Dev; it was the people's. It belonged to this kingdom of Hastinapur. Neither you, nor Shantanu nor this wretched girl are above Hastinapur. You promise to look after Hastinapur all your life, but *you*, Son, destroyed it in one stroke with that oath of yours.'

The harshest words were reserved for him, realized Devavrat, his face anguished. He bowed his head to hide the effect of the heat of his uncle's wrath, the cruel truth of his words.

'You may think now that you helped your father by gambling away your birthright, but you haven't understood the consequences of this decision. You have not only altered your life, but the family lineage. In your bid to make one person happy, you relinquished your promise to the citizens of this kingdom. You are emotional, and for this you will suffer for the rest of your life, Bhishm! What you did was not sublime, but simply an act of misplaced devotion to a man not worthy of it!' Bahlik said with despair, his eyes bleak. 'Indeed, like your new name, Bhishm, between the ideal and reality, falls the shadow. You are a fallen hero, Dev; a leader who fell too early on the way! Your resolve is a wilful act; it is your impotence to see reason! It should not have been a personal, but a political decision,' lashed Bahlik, his eyes fixed on the tormented hazel ones of his young nephew.

Each word was like a welt, and Devavrat took it silently as he had no words to explain his actions. Because he could never forgive himself for separating his father from his mother; he could never tell his uncle his worst guilt. He had tried his all, given his all to bring his father and his newfound love together. Because he, and everyone else, assumed that it was Dev's irrational sense of duty that made him act so. But this was far removed from the truth.

His father looked the pusillanimous man that he was, trembling with indignant rage but unable to mask his fear at Bahlik's ominous words. Was his uncle right? Had his desire to return to his father his lost happiness made him as ineffectual as him?

Kali stood silent. This man was brutal, bleeding both the men with stabbing words. He was the man to watch out for, the one she should be wary of: not Shantanu or Devavrat. Both were—as Bahlik had correctly said—weak-hearted. But not this man, and she was thankful that he was leaving them and the kingdom.

'You, my brother and this woman have started the end of Hastinapur,' Bahlik whispered, his bulky shoulders sagging.

It was a sad, soft, broken voice emitting from such a massive man.

'I am leaving, for I cannot bear to see the doom of my home, my family, my kingdom, *Bhishm*,' he said with emphasis, 'for that is not just *your* name from now on, but also the terrible life you shall lead!'

The silence he left behind was painful.

The Wedding

Kali was in the midst of her wedding preparations. The feel of silk on her skin and the glitter of diamonds on her throat were new to her. *They are like me*, she smiled, *beautiful and seductive, the sparkle never wearing off*. The light reflected off the dazzling stones on her dark face, illuminating it with a strange incandescence, her inky eyes alight. She was going to be married to a king today, and she would be queen; her dream had just begun. However, one glance around her, and she was warned of things to come. Kali had never witnessed such opulence—rich carpets to warm cold marble floors, engraved furniture pieces, exquisite tapestry, an oversized bed. But neither had she witnessed such open hostility. The maids were dutifully helping her dress , but she could feel their resentment, almost palpable in the huge, chandeliered chamber allotted to her. They moved around her, their faces stoic but bodies bristling with antagonism. Kali found herself having to repeat her requests once too often.

'Strangely, the whole palace seems to be afflicted with deafness,' she pronounced with all the hauteur she could muster. 'But I have a cure: hear it loud and clear. Get used to your tasks, and don't make me repeat them. I shall be your queen, and you are bound to serve me,' she said, with a lash in her voice.

The maids did not stare back at her as they did before; their eyes were resentful but their heads were suitably lowered. *You have to be born royal*, she reminded herself bitterly, *or you do not command respect*. That seemed to be the rule of the palace. When she voiced it to Shantanu—the only person whom she could talk to—he shook his head.

'They resent you not because you are a fisher girl,' he

remarked. 'They don't like you because, in their eyes, you are nothing but a...'

'Go on,' she prompted defensively.

'...a common thief who stole Dev's rights, yet roam about in the palace, unpunished. Weren't Bahlik's parting words a hint?'

Shantanu sighed, an expression of unfiltered pain flitting across his lined face. He slipped his hand into hers. 'It is going to be rough,' he cajoled, 'for both of us.'

Much to her shock, after Bahlik's acrimonious words and exit, she had faced hostility from Shantanu, who announced shortly to her that they would have a quiet wedding.

'I am apprehensive about how people will react. I have been informed that they have not taken the news kindly that Dev is no longer their crown prince...' his voice trailed off uncertainly.

Why would a king fear his subjects, she frowned. *They had to bow down before him, not question him.*

She decided it was wise not to show her displeasure. 'Are you ashamed of me; embarrassed to introduce me as your wife?' she asked coyly, masking her disappointment. 'As your queen?' she added more insistently, stroking his raddled cheek.

Warily, he said, 'They loved their queen Ganga so much, she is irreplaceable for them. And they love Dev more. They see you as an intruder—a usurper—who snatched his rights, his crown and his future. They hate you, Matsyagandha, and they will never forgive you,' he paused. 'Nor me. They now despise me, too.'

This was a new experience: she was a leader, popular with the people in her village. *But not always. I had to earn it*, she reminded herself. She would have to work at it here at Hastinapur, too.

Kali threw Shantanu a swift, sharp look. He seemed to have aged years in the last few days, since she had arrived at the palace. She had thought that he would be deliriously happy with her by his side, but he was being torn by an anguish: over the quarrel with his brother as well as Bhishm's vow. If she had been considering that oath a boon, and the quickest way of getting Shantanu and Hastinapur, neither were yet firmly in her grasp. For one, she would have to wean Shantanu off his melancholy.

'No, they don't hate you. You are their king!' she reminded him gently, with a soft smile. 'They love you, and they will do what the king wishes...'

'They are resentful, and an angry public is not good—neither for the king, nor for the kingdom. I don't want to upset them even more. That's why we should have a simple wedding. It is appropriate.'

She nodded slowly, disconcerted that he was unwilling to grant her what she wished for. She had thought he would comply easily.

'Still, it is a royal festive occasion, not a mourning,' she laughed lightly. 'When they see that you are happy, they, too, will be happy,' she said persuasively. 'Don't they also want to see their king smiling after a long time?'

'You are going to be my bride, Matsyagandha, and I am ecstatic that I have you now... But I can't share this moment with them because it was Dev whose wedding they were looking forward to, not mine!' he shook his head agitatedly. 'We have upset too many people, hurt too many...' he muttered, and, after a pause, said, 'Matsyagandha, please understand. You seem to have forgotten you were like them once!'

She gave a tight smile. 'No, I have not,' she said. 'We were used to obeying our king—whatever he said or did. We had to.'

'But this is Hastinapur,' murmured Shantanu. 'Here, the Kuru king bows to his subjects, listens to them and rules his kingdom. Dev was the chosen one; not by privilege but by merit. Besides, he was chosen by the people as well. You—we...' he hurriedly corrected, 'have shocked them and gone against their wishes. They don't like us for what we have done to him.'

Her mouth tightened. 'Agreed, we will have to win them over. But you are still the king!' she said quietly, though her voice was hard. 'A firm hand stills unrest and dissent before it erupts into a revolt. If you comply with your people's wishes too much, you will be known as a weak king,' she said, and Shantanu thought he heard slight scorn in her voice. 'People don't like weakness; they respect authority, and fear it.'

He looked at her for a long time. 'Have you forgotten the sentiments of the common man?'

Flushed, she smiled grimly. 'I say so because *I* know. *I* have suffered.'

'The people are hurt and angry. I have lost my two brothers, and ... the respect my son had for me,' he muttered, his face pale. 'Dev does not show it, but I can feel it. I have lost everyone, Matsyagandha!' he coughed dryly, his voice slowly drowning in a violent paroxysm.

She quickly handed a tumbler of cool water to him.

'Please do not get upset; I understand,' she nodded, with a gentle smile. 'I *was* one of them. And that is why I say—let us have a big wedding, where we invite not just kings and nobles of all the kingdoms, but our citizens as well. People love a festive occasion; we will make them part of the royal revelry. Let our wedding be a public celebration, bringing all of Hastinapur together. Why just this wedding: from now on, let us celebrate our festivals, too, with them. That way, they will forget their animosity and might forgive us.'

Shantanu's frown deepened, and his brows furrowed thoughtfully. Kali allowed him his deep contemplation, not interrupting his thoughts with further words. 'Yes, I think that might please the people and win them over. I shall let Bhishm know,' he said finally.

Kali smiled and nodded.

Shantanu called for Bhishm, and he arrived almost immediately, standing aloof yet expectantly.

'Your father is troubled. He wants a quiet wedding...' Kali said, coming quickly to the point.

'Does he?' he looked surprised. 'But the arrangements have started in full swing.'

Kali winced. The preparations had been for his coronation, not her wedding. They had started even before her arrival at the palace. She looked at the tall, young man with the serene eyes. It should have been his wedding, not hers. He was supposed to have married the princess of Kashi this month. Instead, it was his father's wedding he was attending to. She felt a twinge again: would she never savour a glimmer of happiness; that same share of happiness she had snatched from this man? Would she be as cursed as him?

Shantanu looked vexed. 'We can't have a public wedding! That was what I was telling Matsyagandha now.'

'But...' Bhishm protested.

'We have already upset your uncle,' she started cautiously. 'We don't want to anger the people further ... I suggested to your father that we have a grand affair where we invite the people of Hastinapur into the palace, and include them in the celebrations.'

Bhishm looked surprised, and then, after a long pause, nodded. 'It is an excellent idea.'

He turned to his father. 'Do not worry, Father. You are apprehensive because you think it will upset the people, but I shall see to it that every house in Hastinapur celebrates!'

Seeing Devavrat's eyes glow dulled her triumphant moment, guilt flooding her instead. He was so happy in their happiness; she turned away, hating herself suddenly. Breaking through his armour of cold reserve, she saw him visibly elated for the first time, and could see how much he loved his father and was ready to do anything for him. She twisted her fingers together, her heart stirring uneasily. This was not meant to be her day, a voice taunted her. It should have been his.

Bhishm saw Kali smile tentatively. 'Hopefully, the people will forgive me,' she said. 'I don't want to anger the people further. But nor do I want you to feel guilty on my account.'

'No one is blaming you,' said Shantanu with a weak, reassuring smile.

'I have already turned your brother against you,' she said, and Bhishm was surprised to hear a quiver in her voice. 'The nobles are displeased, too; all because of me...'

'I have dismissed those who were vociferously against you, Matsyagandha,' Shantanu cut her off mid-sentence in his brusquely imperious manner.

'I know! And this wedding should not antagonize anyone, but bring us all together,' she paused, dropping down before Shantanu, and laying her head on his knees. 'I am miserable that I have made you miserable. I can't bear it; I was supposed to make you happy! You are a true, generous, rare man...' she swallowed her tears. 'All you have earned is ridicule and reprimands, because of me!' she went on, the tremble getting stronger in her voice. 'I know that I will be your wife, but never a queen who is loved and respected by everyone. Because I am but a poor, young fisher girl. But what can I do!'

Bhishm saw his father flushing uneasily; his face wore a look of stupid, boyish dismay.

'My darling, you are misunderstanding me,' he muttered helplessly, touching her hair and her shoulders, dragging a soothing smile over his face. 'Forgive me. I was unjust, and I hate myself and all those who hate you! If you want a big wedding, you will have it; and we shall invite the whole city, as you wish!'

She played it well, Bhishm thought, with a mental shrug. *So she does want a grand ceremony*. Bhishm turned away, more defeated than disgusted at the sight of how servile his father was to her, and at the depth of her insincerity.

~

As Matsyagandha had desired, the wedding was a glittering event. The ceremony was performed within the quiet precincts of the family temple, attended by Devavrat and a few nobles only, but the celebrations that followed were open to one and all. Rishi Devapi, the royal head priest, had refused to perform the rites, and his absence was glaring, displaying the depth of resentment simmering against her.

However, the bride looked lovely in her new jewels, and Bhishm almost did not recognize her in her bridal raiment. The ceremony was lavish, and she had appropriately decked herself up: like the royal wife she aspired to be. He admitted, watching her, that she was a very beautiful woman. She glowed with the triumph of a victor. Kali could not contain her happiness, and it shone radiantly on her face, more than the gems on her body.

The palace was richly decorated and the thick scent of jasmine and incense hung heavy in the air. The flaming yellow of marigolds melding perfectly with the soft glimmer of the dancing diyas dotting every corner of the palace. She was led across the hall, out into the sunshine that blazed down on a patio, through arched doorways and along a passage, to the temple which lay in the middle of a huge garden. Six weary looking priests stared at her with indifference.

Rather than a celebration, it looks more like a mourning. But I hope I shall be given a fancier funeral than this, she thought with morbid amusement. *I might lose small battles like these, but I have won my war. I am getting married to the king of Hastinapur, and will soon be crowned as queen... today, Kali will be reborn as Satyavati.*

Bhishm was sitting next to his father, staring into the blazing yagna fire. He looked aloof, detached from the ceremony, even though he had managed the preparations single-handedly.

What is he thinking? Of the princess he was to marry? Of all that he has lost? She felt that unfamiliar emotion again: it afflicted her each time she looked at him. Was it her guilt? Or something else she could not fathom? She frowned, hating that her moment of triumph was being marred by that undefinable feeling.

As she sat down in front of the fire, she glanced at Bhishm, silently asking him to come to her. He went to her and bent down, his ears close to her lips.

'I know no one is happy about this wedding, but could some food be sent to every home in Hastinapur from the palace kitchen for a week?' she murmured. 'And also to the fishing community. They, too, would like to be a part of the celebrations,' she said dryly.

'Yes, of course,' he returned blandly, but she detected a hesitant sliver of warm approval. She glanced at him, feeling her face flush to her neck. She heard him giving instructions to one of the courtiers.

She sighed, and brought her attention back to the rituals. This is what she had wanted. His respect. And the people's blessings too, she hoped fervently. But why was his approval so important to her?

'Don't talk when the mantras are being chanted. They are marriage vows of love and fidelity,' the icy voice of Kripa, one of the priests, filtered through her happy thoughts.

Kripacharya looked frosty, affronted by her whispering to Bhishm in front of the holy fire. He was tall, fair, very young, with a long and thin nose, deep-set and intelligent eyes, and a dome of a forehead, which accentuated the disdainful expression on his handsome face.

Kali flushed, the reproach smarting. She fidgeted in frustration, looking around her.

In this enormous, unfriendly palace, she suddenly felt bereft: alone and lonely. Her father was too unwell to make it to Hastinapur, though Bhishm had been courteous enough to send a special carriage to bring him. But Dasharaj had refused, instead sending her a silver anklet of her mother's as a gift. She was wearing it now: a slender silver coil ending in twin fish heads, graceful and entwined in each other. He had fulfilled the promise he had made to himself: that he would make her a queen one day. But her father wanted her to fend for herself from now on, starting from her wedding day. It seemed more like a battleground. The nobles were coldly courteous, and the palace staff stiff and resentful. Except for Vibha, a girl of sixteen, who had been assigned to her as her personal maid.

Why am I thinking such horrid thoughts? She would see to it that things changed, and changed fast, Kali vowed to herself. She would make these people bow to her!

The day had been trying enough, and then suddenly the wedding night loomed wretchedly over her. Her fingers curled into tight fists as the thought—*I will have to make love to Shantanu tonight. Not furtive kisses and desperate lunges or heavy groping in the mangroves, but as a lover would with her partner; as a wife would with her husband; and as a bride would with her groom.*

Kali knew she was adept at love-making, yet she felt a slight shiver, cold and unsettling. The wasted good looks of Shantanu still lingered on his dissipated face, but she could not forget that he was old and wrinkled... She shuddered as she recalled his parched, rough skin against hers, his wet mouth on hers, his stale breath on her face ... *No!* She couldn't go through with this; not just tonight, but every single day of her life with him henceforth...

But she would have to. She was his queen. It was her duty. Her status as queen would be uncertain till she produced an heir. And for that, she would have to surrender to her king, every day...

She heard the door swing open and Shantanu being escorted inside the bedchamber by Bhishm. Her breath stilled as she took in the sight of the two men. Shantanu looking tired and leaning against his son, intoxicated with wine; and Bhishm, tall, young, handsome, with his shy smile, and the irresistible lock of hair falling over his inscrutable eyes—the eyes that saw more than they revealed. Could he see what she was going through as he bowed low before her? She turned her face away from him, biting her lips. *He* was responsible for this, she screamed silently, unreasonably bitter, as she felt the hot prick of angry tears smarting her eyes. *He* had brought her here to Hastinapur, *he* had fought for her with his father, *he* had seen that he got her married to his father, and *he* was the one who was in her bedchamber, escorting his father to his new bride. *His mother,* she thought savagely.

Kali clenched her eyes shut, feeling a wave of disappointment wash over her. *Why did I meet the king first, and not the prince*, she thought as she saw Bhishm depart, leaving her strangely bereft.

She felt Shantanu's sweaty hand on her shoulder and willed herself to look at him. She shuddered inwardly again. She observed all that she had failed to see before: the fine crowfeet at the corner of his dull eyes, his face lined and slightly fleshy, sagging at the jowls to give him a forlorn look, the soppy downturn of his lips, not just the sign of a spoilt man, but the result of his constant coughing having slackened his cheeks. She had overlooked all this in her greed to have him, have the crown.

She was supposed to be in love with this man. But she was not; she was incapable of falling in love. *One has to stumble to fall in love or otherwise*, she thought grimly, *and I am not one who will ever stumble or fall*. But to own the king, she had to give her all, she reminded herself.

As she felt him lying on top of her, she was overcome by despair, the lingering image of Bhishm, his handsome face smiling, the hazel eyes cold, his beautiful lips mocking her as he whispered, '*Mother!*'

She forced her eyes firmly shut. The final act had to be performed.

The Queen

From that day on, she was no longer Kali; she was Satyavati, the wife of Shantanu. But not yet his queen, honoured with the crown. Satyavati stared up at the gilded ceiling and felt a movement in the soft bed. Shantanu was lying beside her, gazing at her, feeling spent, thinking there was no woman he had ever slept with who could drain him as his bride had.

Satyavati was startled by the sound of an angry roar. She stiffened. Shantanu was already at the window, looking out to check the rude commotion. Would it be another bad day like yesterday, her wedding night? She knew she had made him happy, but she shuddered involuntarily, shutting off the mental picture. There would be many more such nights. She shrugged and straightened against the pillows.

'What is it?' she asked curiously.

'There is a mob outside the palace,' he replied tersely.

'Have your soldiers rounded them up,' she suggested casually, stretching against the silken sheets. She slid off the bed, hugging her shawl, and he watched her sleek, beautiful back; her tight, rounded behind; her long, slim legs as she ambled towards him; and he felt the stir of desire again.

'It's just a commotion. Dev will look into it,' he dismissed, holding her by the waist and edging her back to the huge bed. 'Let's start the morning in a better way,' he said huskily, closing his lips on her surprised ones. He pulled her against him, his hands slid down her back. Pulling away her shawl, his fingers gripped her hips. She closed her eyes. His fingers, gripping her flesh, made her feel sick. She stiffened, pushing slightly at his chest. 'Is it not already late?' she forced a smile. 'It is going to be a long day today as well...'

'Yes, your coronation as queen,' he sighed, releasing her. 'But it'll be a short, simple affair. Not anything like our wedding. It's just a formality.'

She breathed more easily, thankful for the distraction. 'And I think the crowd outside needs looking into as well,' she said with a delicate frown. 'The people are clearly still unhappy.'

And so were the nobles and the courtiers. There was a lot of criticism of King Shantanu from the court, and his subjects, as to why he had removed the crown prince as his heir. Bhishm had to face the crowd and tell the people that it was his decision to step down, and that his father should not be blamed for it. Rishi Devapi was not convinced, and asked him who would be held responsible if the future crown prince was not capable enough. Bhishm then took his second vow: that he would always serve and guide whoever sat on the king's throne. Nobody was pleased. The crowd burst into a cry.

'Bhishm! Bhishm! Our prince, our king!'

The message was crisp and clear: the public wanted only Bhishm.

'How long will they go on?' she asked quietly.

'Until they learn to accept you. Us,' he corrected wearily, his face as tired as his voice. 'Don't let it dampen your happiness.'

He seemed unusually upset. Had he sensed her repugnance a moment ago or that of the previous night? She had tried hard to hide it. Or was it a sign of the day to come, when she would be anointed as queen. Was he already regretting it?

A manservant announced Bhishm's presence. He was said to be the first person Shantanu saw when he woke up in the morning, and today was no exception.

Satyavati left father and son together, and strolled outside. She was surprised to see a teenage girl waiting in her morning chamber.

'I am Kripi,' the girl said sullenly.

'But *who* are you?' Satyavati asked calmly, unperturbed by the announcement. 'Your presence was not announced.'

The girl raised a well-shaped eyebrow. 'I don't need to be announced. I stay here, Queen Daseyi; *you* are new to the palace.'

Satyavati gasped at the open affront. The name 'Daseyi' meant one of the *dasa*—slave, or at the most polite, an aboriginal woman.

'And, you, girl, whoever you are, need to be taught some manners,' retorted Satyavati icily. 'My name is Satyavati.'

Kripi returned a wordless stare, and regarded Satyavati's trim figure with distaste. Satyavati recognized the silent assessment: this impudent girl clearly considered her as the evil temptress who had bewitched the old king.

'I know. As Satyavati, you are the epitome of *satya*,' drawled Kripi, her tone implying otherwise. 'You are well known as Kali, the dark one. But I have heard the king call you Matsyagandha and you make your presence felt sufficiently enough by your ... er ... smell...' she said, as if to imply that the fragrance the new queen emanated was the stench of rot.

'...but I meant no offence when I called you Daseyi. You are the daughter of Dasharaj, that fisherman; are you not?' asked Kripi, with apparent innocence.

'I would prefer Satyavati, though,' the new queen said coldly.

'Are you not your father's daughter, then?' taunted Kripi.

Satyavati bit her lip. She knew she had been cornered.

'Queen Daseyi, you are to be coroneted as queen today,

and I am here to instruct you about the rituals,' explained Kripi, enjoying her obvious displeasure. 'I am your tutor.'

Satyavati could not hide her look of amazement.

'You are a rishi?' she asked in open surprise, knowing she sounded stupid. The girl was so young, barely in her teens.

'I am a rishi's daughter,' corrected Kripi. 'A scholar myself and well-versed in the shastras, besides the daily matters of the royal court. Shall we start?'

While Kripi introduced her to some rituals of the ceremony, all Satyavati could think was how wonderfully confident this girl was. She looked at her closely, guarded in her appraisal.

Kripi was pretty in a sensible way. Her skin was pale and smooth, and her features were sharp and regular. She seemed more intelligent than pretty, even in her manners. Fair, with a sharp, straight nose over thin lips, and an alert pair of light eyes, Kripi was slim and diminutive, but her big ego made up for her lack of height, thought Satyavati with annoyance.

'Are we done for today?' she asked after an hour.

Kripi gave her an almost pitiful look. 'Clearly, Queen Daseyi, since you have never been exposed to any mantras of the Vedas or the Upanishads, I need to familiarize you with them,' she explained smoothly. 'Since you are going to be queen now,' she added pointedly, 'it would be better you start soon. Politics, I am sure, must be one of your stronger subjects, but you need to educate yourself on other things as well. And I have been appointed as your teacher by King Shantanu,' finished Kripi in a voice which brooked no further argument.

Satyavati took in her barb calmly. 'Why not Kripacharya?' asked Satyavati.

And then it struck her, why the girl was vaguely familiar. She had been hovering around the yagna near Kripacharya during the wedding ceremony, chanting the mantras with him. She was Kripacharya's sister!

'He has more important tasks at the court, Queen Daseyi,' said Kripi woodenly.

She marvelled at the girl's malicious juxtaposition of the term 'queen' with the name 'Daseyi'. But Satyavati had always admired spirit, and this was a highly spirited girl in front of her. Kripi was clearly a woman of power in the palace.

~

Kripi, in her brusque manner, saw that Satyavati was suitably attired for the coronation: she had ordered the maids to dress her up in gold and vermillion silk.

'Red would be better. You are still a bride,' said Kripi noncommittally, her face giving nothing away.

Satyavati fumed, but she was pleased at her reflection in the long, gold-gilded mirror. She stood tall and majestic, resplendent in the flaming blood-red silk that hugged her full figure, the richly embroidered gold reflecting against her burnished skin.

'Wear less head jewellery, Queen Daseyi, as you shall soon be wearing the crown,' advised Kripi, her tone crisp. 'It could get heavy.'

Satyavati wondered if she should be charitable enough to retort or discreetly polite, as expected from a queen. She replied swiftly, 'I have carried life's burden so long and so well that I am quite sure the crown would not be that heavy to wear!'

She glimpsed the look of surprise on Kripi's face and decided to follow her suggestion to go easy on the hair ornaments. They were so confusingly varied, displayed on the silver tray, that she wondered at the ingeniousness of the unknown person who created royal jewellery. There was one for each strand of her hair and each part of her body!

Hours later, Satyavati walked up to the court for the first time, taken by the sheer opulence of the hall with its columned aisles on either side. Each column was an exquisite piece of engraved marble, encrusted with gems of all colours. She sucked in her breath, finding it difficult to breathe—this was the grandeur of royalty. It was embossed in every stone, brick and pillar, and she couldn't help comparing it to the filthy street which led to her dilapidated house.

Satyavati squared her shoulders as if to shake off that memory, that burden she did not want to carry any more. She was stepping into a new world: as the wife of the king, and now, the queen of Hastinapur.

She heard the rants outside the palace walls. The sound rang through the high domes of the hall, chinking lightly against the crystals of the chandeliers, reminding her how she was the most hated person in Hastinapur right now.

No one looked happy; not a single person in the assembly hall. She was but an opportunist for them; someone who had dared wrestle away the crown from their prince. But she saw it differently. They were being forced to witness a momentous occasion—a fisher girl had become queen. An abandoned baby had become queen. A misbegotten, unacknowledged orphan had forced the world to acknowledge her as queen. Matsyagandha was now queen. Kali was Queen Satyavati.

She saw Bhishm approach her, bowing. They eyed each other. 'You don't have to make me a stranger,' she said cautiously. 'We shall be seeing a lot of each other; it's best we be civil, if not cordial.' He saw her pressing her lips, pressing a fingertip into the middle of the lower one, her face thoughtful. It was a habit of hers, he had noticed, when she was either worried or was thinking.

His eyes narrowing, he suddenly laughed shortly. It was a harsh sound.

'It is your day, Mother,' he said impassively, as he led her to the throne. 'You will be my father's queen.'

She barely heard Kripacharya formally requesting her to sit on the throne next to the king's. She sat gingerly on it, her heart thudding hard, and experienced a strange but sweet heart-soaring moment when the crown was placed on her head by a sombre Shantanu, with Kripa performing the rituals. Kripi stood nearby, stone-faced. And behind her was Bhishm, carved like a cold, beautiful marble statue. Satyavati's smile slipped, and she quickly looked away; she could not face him, not during this triumphal moment.

Satyavati felt the flow of power sweeping down over her as the crown was placed on her head. Power was often considered insidious, dangerous, operating silently. She knew it; she was using it, experiencing it. And sitting on the throne with a crown resting on her head was a blatant display of that invisible power—it was heady and uplifting.

Satyavati thoughtfully regarded the throne she was sitting on, next to Shantanu. Clearly, the main throne was meant for one—the king, alone. Until now, there had been no queen to accompany the king.

'We need a bigger throne,' she said to Kripacharya, pronouncing it with a practised smile. 'For both of us to sit together,' she said charmingly, the tone carrying a hint of the imperiousness expected from a monarch.

'It shall be done, Queen Daseyi,' said Kripi, with feigned respect.

There was a momentary shocked pause. Shantanu

seemed taken aback, but remained mute. From that moment onwards, everyone started addressing her as Queen Daseyi, reminding her of who she was in the palace.

Bhishm was relieved that his uncles did not have to witness this scene: Bahlik and Devapi had been spared the ignominy. The court was openly sneering at the new queen, despite her pitiful attempts to make her position as a royal accepted.

Bhishm felt an unexpected gush of rage, more at his father than his new wife. Shantanu had just proven himself to be the weak man his brothers had often accused him of being. His son was now witnessing it.

Bhishm could sense Kripi looking at him; perhaps he had felt him tensing up. He knew the world was looking at him, everyone feeling sorry for him. He did not want their pity, he seethed. These days, everyone threw him pitiful looks. He wished he could run away from them, this place, and this endless torture.

He recalled his father's last boon to him. Icchamrityu. He could die when he chose to. Was death the only escape from this new hell? How brave would it be to accept death and escape from the fate he was destined to endure? His vow had not just been to Satyavati's father, but also to the people of Hastinapur whom he had betrayed. He could not accept his boon till he saw Hastinapur in better hands. But having witnessed the spectacle at the coronation this morning, Bhishm felt a cold chill—would his father be an able ruler, intoxicated as he was by his bride?

And he had helped his father to be what he was now. Bhishm could not run away from Bahlik's last reproach: *You failed me, Dev, and you failed Hastinapur. You would have been a great king; but you threw it all away for the whims of your father. What about your responsibility to the crown?*

He had allowed this girl to become his father's wife; he had made her queen. Only he was to blame, and no one else. He had no reason or right to feel fury. He could not afford the luxury of that pointless emotion. He had tried to assuage his guilt and gift his father a new love to replace the pain of his mother leaving him. He had tried to give his father back his lost time, his lost love, his lost joy. *But not at the expense of Hastinapur and the people*, Bahlik's outburst ran through his churning mind.

He had failed them—his parents. Just as they had failed him in some way, some time. He resented his mother for having abandoned him into this world—not as a defenceless baby like his more fortunate drowned brothers—but as a full grown young man to step from her cloistered, loving world into the uncertain world of his father's. He had grappled with it with the grace that was expected of him. He had now come to love the ways of this world—the city, the people, the court and his unknown family. But all had turned away from him—his uncles in displeasure of his father, and his father for this dark beauty: the queen consort. His father had failed him as well, by proving that he was far less important to him than this woman. But, worse, he had failed himself—he was the reason and the cause for his own failure. He sighed as he made to leave the hall as soon as the ceremony was over.

Satyavati saw Bhishm walking away, and she lifted her chin: her head held high and glittering with the crown now snug in her coiffure. Her face was serene, not letting anyone see the heady thrill of triumph running through her, making an effort to contain the dam of joy that was sweeping her. She felt the cold, hard crown upon her head. It was heavy, she found much to her surprise, though it had looked fragile, encrusted with diamonds and pearls, an odd combination.

'It looks good on you, too,' commented Shantanu, trying to make her feel at ease. 'Ganga loved white; she hated loud colours.'

'I am wearing her crown?' she stammered in a shocked whisper.

A borrowed crown for a borrowed queen, taunted her inner voice. *A second queen, a second wife and an interloper.* She was not allowed to forget that.

The happiness dissipated as fast as it had filled just a few moments ago, and she felt a hot flush mounting up to her face. She would be wearing Ganga's crown; she had taken Ganga's husband, Ganga's place, Ganga's role. Even Ganga's son. *Ganga!* She gazed out of the long window into the distance of the glimmering river waters, flowing quietly near the palace: a silent presence in her life from now on. But she, Satyavati, was now the queen, the wife of her husband, King Shantanu, and mother of her son, Bhishm, she reminded herself.

Her blood curdled: how she detested that word. She was *not* his mother! Each time he hailed her so, she withered a little. He was the reminder of her biggest offence. How was she to be a mother to a man more her age, mother to a man whom she had divested everything of—his love, his life, his marriage, children, crown and kingdom? A mother is one who gives selflessly; she had taken everything from him.

Again she looked towards where she had seen Bhishm go, and saw Kripi following the tall figure of Bhishm. A sudden rush of rage swept over her. That girl had branded her as Daseyi: the servant-queen. The insult would reverberate far beyond the palace walls, she knew.

She had believed that if she asked Shantanu to dismiss Kripi from her personal service, he would agree. But he had stoutly refused. He had eagerly obeyed all her earlier requests, and she was taken aback when he refused her request. As far as his association with Kripa and Kripi went, he displayed an obstinacy which was almost irrational.

Clearly, Kripi knew her power over both the king and the prince. This gave her the confidence to be openly hostile. Satyavati made a decision to find out more about her. From what she could gather, Kripi and her twin brother, Kripa, had been adopted by Shantanu after he had found them abandoned on the river bank. They were just babies then. The moment she heard the word 'abandoned', her heart had warmed immediately towards them. *They were like me. But luckier than me, as they did not have to claw their way to the luxuries and power of the palace like I had to*, she reminded herself. Also, unlike her, the twins were inseparable; her twin brother had been crowned the King of Matsya, while she was made to languish in indignity.

'When I saw them lying in the grass by the river bank, I remembered all the babies I had lost...' Shantanu's voice had been infinitely sad when he told her the story. 'I had no child, so I brought them home and raised them as my children. And I was relieved when they welcomed Bhishm so warmly when he came back to me and Hastinapur.'

'They couldn't not do that,' she remarked dryly. 'They might be your adopted children, Shantanu, but they are not your blood. Dev is.'

Shantanu threw her a strange look. 'They love him nevertheless,' he said simply. 'Both are very close to him. Kripi adores him like an older brother, and Kripa is his most loyal friend.'

She did not miss the warning tone in his voice; she had to make amends and accept these people as friends. Bhishm was still his detached, aloof self. She had not yet spoken to Kripa personally, but he did not hide his disdain for her.

For him, she was the woman who had usurped his friend's future and happiness.

'Did you find out who had deserted them?' she asked instead, wondering if they, too, had been disowned by a heartless father.

'Yes, a few years later, I was surprised to see Rishi Sharadwan arrive at the palace. He claimed the twins were his, from the apsara Janapadi, who had been sent by Indra to seduce him. Angered at her deception, he had retreated to the forest to continue with his meditation. Years later, he came to know that she had abandoned the twins. He then came to Hastinapur searching for them. He wanted them back, but the children refused...'

'I don't blame them,' she commented wryly.

Shantanu shrugged. 'Lord Indra had sent many apsaras to break Sharadwan's meditation, but he remained undeterred, till Janapadi broke his concentration. According to rumours, his fallen semen split a weed into two halves. From it were born two children: a boy and a girl, respectively...'

He was interrupted by Satyavati's short laugh. 'Really, you believe that rubbish? This "divine" tale sounds more like a cover-up for an illicit relationship between the rishi and the apsara!' she said scornfully, contempt curling her lips.

It was achingly similar to hers: the tale of a king and a fisher girl masqueraded as a celestial romance.

'These are smart stories to camouflage dirty secrets,' she remarked tartly.

Shantanu frowned, puzzled. 'Why do you feel so strongly about the twins?'

'I was moved by their story of abandonment,' she said with a tight smile.

'They were not! I took them in, and their father, Sharadwan, became their guru!'

Unlike my father, who preferred to throw me out of his life and palace. How would I react if I ever met my father, Satyavati wondered. *Would I forgive him as easily as these twins did their father?*

'He was their teacher?' she asked curiously.

'Sharadwan was dejected with his children's refusal to come away with him. I suggested that he remain in the palace as their guru, teaching his children the mastery of war and weapons, so he could be close to them.'

'But shouldn't a rishi be teaching the Vedas and the Upanishads?'

'That, too, but Sharadwan was exceptional,' explained Shantanu. 'He was the grandson of Rishi Gautam, and a prodigy. Legend goes that he was born with arrows! He grew up to be the best master archer ... the reason why Indra felt threatened. I decided to use his knowledge; it was too precious to let go. By imparting the secret of the martial arts to his children, he would be helping out Hastinapur.'

'That's why you made his son, Kripa, the royal head priest,' she interposed shrewdly. 'Also, as the acharya, he would impart the knowledge inherited from his father to the princes of Hastinapur ... to the future scions?'

'Yes,' nodded Shantanu. 'Kripa is no ordinary rishi. Don't go by his skinny frame and studious looks. He is also a trained kshatriya, superior even to his father. He is so good that he can single-handedly fight a battalion. He is often compared to Kartikey, the God of War, who famously defeated the asuras. Kripa and Dev make a formidable pair on the battlefield. But he is no match to my Dev. No one is!' beamed Shantanu, his voice suddenly tender. 'Dev did not need a Sharadwan; he has been groomed by legends like Parashuram, Shukracharya and Vasisht. My Dev is the best!'

She heard the raw pride in his voice.

'And so now Kripacharya will be the guru of our children?' she smiled suggestively.

Shantanu's face brightened immediately, catching her by her wrist. 'Certainly! I am waiting eagerly for that day!'

And so was she. As Shantanu pulled her down on the bed, she gave a victorious smile. She felt his dry lips touch hers, his hands urgently tugging at the silk folds of her antariya, as if to complete a big task. She knew what it was. She was now queen, and she had to produce heirs for her kingdom.

The Heirs

She felt a cold thrill, looking down at her newborn son. Satyavati could recall Bahlik's warning before he had flounced out from the palace a year ago.

'This girl will be the queen, the grand matriarch of this new dynasty that she will start! Along with yours, it will be her bloodline as well from now on.'

His portentous words had been similar to her father's hopes. *This infant is the heir to the Kuru throne*, she smiled victoriously. But she had another one, too; no one knew she had another son. What would Shantanu say to *that* if he ever got to know? He need not know. Ignorance would be his bliss, and a blessing for her. She might divulge that secret if the occasion demanded, and when she was in a position to proclaim it. He was her firstborn, and she was not ashamed of having him. But now was not the time...

With a single encounter with Parashar, she had managed to turn her whole life around. She had got rid of the stench of her past, and, like her fragrance, she had made her life pleasant.

Satyavati realized the power of love and making love—a means to an end. First Parashar, then Shantanu; she had got what she wanted from both men. Some would deem it immoral, but virtue was a quality invented by men to suit their needs. If men could use women, why couldn't it be the other way round? Sex and beauty were the weapons of seduction that she could, and had, wielded in conflict and contest.

The end results of using these weapons were what she had in her arms right now. Or her other son. Both would be masters of their fate and future—one a king and the other a rishi—with the blood of their fishmonger mother flowing in their veins.

Satyavati remembered cradling her first son, Krishna Dwaipayan, in her arms. *Where was he now? Wandering with Parashar, his father, or mastering the Vedas from him and his great-grandfather, Rishi Vasisht?* The boy had been endowed with the legacy of famous scholars, and she was sure he would further it beyond compare.

In her vulnerable moments, she gave in to the guilt of giving him away so easily to his father. Would he bear the same resentment she bore for her own father? It was her worst fear. He had barely been with her for a week—a dark, wrinkled and quiet baby. Unlike this fair son, whom she pressed fiercely to her bosom, promising herself she would never let go of him, come what may. She looked at him affectionately. Her son was every inch the prince he was—all fire and fury; his light, pale skin mottled crimson in an indignant, lustful cry. He was already showing signs of being wilful, furious at having his slumber broken by the unruly holler beyond the palace walls.

Satyavati felt a surge of annoyance. Today, again, she and her baby had been awoken by the angry shouts of the mob at the royal gate. It had been over a year, yet the animosity towards her continued to simmer within and outside the palace walls.

She had tried to win them over several times, but was rebuffed unkindly each time. The ringing slogans from outside were a reminder of their displeasure. They orchestrated it on every special occasion in her life—her wedding day, on her coronation, at the birth of her son, and now, on the day of his christening ceremony. They openly loathed her. She looked towards the open window from where the harsh shouts wafted in with the soft breeze. She had underestimated the resentment roiling in the people of Hastinapur.

'When do you intend to stop this open show of hostility?' she asked her husband.

Shantanu coughed harshly, reminding her he was a sick man. 'There was a promise made to them; we did not fulfil it, Matsyagandha,' said Shantanu weakly. 'They still hanker for Bhishm, and they have neither forgiven you nor me for what we did to him...' his voice trailed away, his eyes distant.

She had to snap Shantanu out of his melancholy. 'Today is the christening ceremony of our son,' she interposed brightly. 'Bhishm has personally selected clothes for you and the baby; the palace is decked like never before, and the street minstrels have been singing new ballads in the name of the Kuru kings since the day our son was born... Get up, Shantanu; it is a new day, a new beginning!'

'I am well aware!' he sighed weakly, lapsing again into his self-willed lugubriousness. 'I have become a father again, but I have proved in the past that I am not a good father, and it will go down in history!' he muttered wildly. 'You have given me a son, the prince, the heir your father so wished,' he added bitterly. 'Dasharaj must surely be happy now.'

She looked back at him with a stiff smile; she noted his thin, shrivelled body and dark-circled, weary eyes and wondered how quickly Shantanu had dissipated into gloom.

'My father is happy being a grandfather, and he doesn't hide it,' she said shortly. 'What is so annoying about that?'

'I have never liked him. He is too interfering!' retorted Shantanu, his face darkening.

'What is it that annoys you?' she continued calmly. 'That he is staying here in the palace, or the fact that he is a representative of the fisher community in your court? You agreed to this arrangement because you, too, realized that marginalizing the fishing community was not wise.'

'Yes, you made me realize that,' replied Shantanu, slightly mollified. 'You saw to them very well—the children's education, healthcare and employment. Your father got houses built for them, too. As you told me to, I have done everything for your people.'

'Because it was needed,' she argued with a smile. 'They are your citizens, too. Make them feel that they belong, and they will serve you loyally. I know them. Treat them with the dignity they deserve. They are not pariahs that they should struggle with stigma and poverty, and be made to settle on the outskirts of the city, in ghettos.'

Shantanu looked peeved. 'I agreed to everything that you said, Matsyagandha, but did you? I told you not to bring your father to the palace, but you did not listen. I am your king, not just your husband, and I expect you to comply with my commands!'

'I am your wife, your queen,' she said evenly. 'I sit with you on the throne, sharing space and thought...'

'And power...?' added Shantanu in an ironic tone.

'Power, prestige and position,' she agreed. 'Power is craved for the pleasure it brings.'

'Which you already seem to be misusing,' he accused.

She was stunned by his accusation. 'Because I brought my father here?' she asked incredulously. 'I just did what a daughter's duty entails. He is unwell, and needs to be nursed.

'Your "ill" father seems to be managing well enough at his new job and position at the court.'

'He is working in spite of his illness,' she said heatedly, her eyes narrowed, her chin up.

He interrupted her harshly. 'I speak as a king! You have already antagonized the people, and getting your father here furthers their argument of favouritism. The racket outside is their voice against you.'

Shantanu leaned his head against the pillows, exhausted. 'It's up to you and Dev to take it up. I am too weak to handle them,' he said wearily, with a deep sigh, before being wracked by another bout of coughing.

Satyavati frowned. 'I shall call the doctor,' she said shortly, now worried more about the ailing man lying on the bed than the disturbance outside. She would have to personally tend to both.

'Don't worry about those people outside; they won't listen to you,' he hacked hoarsely. 'I shall tell Dev to handle them. Summon for him, please.'

Bhishm again. Shantanu could not function without that man, she sighed, pressing her finger abstractedly on her lower lip, thinking hard.

But she called for Bhishm regardless, and as always, felt secretly better when she did. His presence was soothing, and his voice slow and soft, as if he were speaking to a child. Previously, she had misunderstood it as condescending, but, with time, she had realized that he spoke like that with everyone, even the mercurial Kripi.

'Is father's health worse?' he asked immediately, watching Shantanu's inert sleeping form.

'Yes. More because of these shouts we have woken up to today. The public is voicing their love for their king,' she gave a dry smile. 'And I am still their wicked queen. So, what do I do now?' she asked, good-humouredly. 'At the coronation, I had invited some of their representatives. They paid obeisance to the king, but not their new queen,' she recalled, a finger tapping impatiently on her full, lower lip all the time.

She grimaced. 'The insult was noted. What I cannot understand is that I am one of them; yet, they don't accept me!'

The Fisher Queen's Dynasty

Bhishm noticed a light stiffness in her voice. It sounded like something she said a little too often, a little too routinely.

He remained silent, out of habit; Bhishm kept his opinions to himself unless persistently asked.

'What do I do?' she repeated. She frowned in thought. 'There is only one thing left to be done... You had personally talked to them, too, but in vain. Both of us tried in our own ways. Now let's do something together, please?' she added as a polite afterthought.

Bhishm hesitated. Last time she had spoken to the crowd, they had been unkind to her; some women had even pelted her with abuses, but she had braved their wrath. For what it was worth, she had tried her best, but her efforts had proved inefficacious. Each of her gestures—be it sending food to the town, giving alms at the temple, personally distributing coins to the people—all seemed to be looked upon with open distrust and hostility. They loathed her, and Bhishm almost felt sorry for her. She was trying to win their hearts, but it was a losing battle.

'What do you propose?' he asked reluctantly.

'Let's talk to them right away?'

Bhishm baulked at the suggestion. The sight of her, the queen mother, with the infant prince, could incite them further, and she would expose herself and the prince to uncalled for danger.

'Don't; it's not safe!' he said.

'It is,' she said swiftly. 'I will have you with me.'

He was taken aback at the trust she placed so implicitly upon him. But he was unwilling to accept it. He wanted nothing from her.

He shook his head absently, deep in thought.

'Please, for your father,' she said.

He hesitated. 'I shall, for his sake, but there's more to it, don't you see, Mother?' he said. 'I can't have them arrested if they misbehave, if that is what you want. That would surely worsen matters. It would anger them further.'

'But this has to stop!' she said peremptorily.

'It won't stop till you appease them in some way,' he suggested.

He looked at her steadily in the eyes, cold and expressionless. She was sure that he was accustomed to intimidating people with that flat stare of his. But it did not work on her. She simply returned his gaze, keeping her chin up.

She grimaced. 'I can't throw my father out just to appease them!'

Bhishm looked at her dispassionately. 'Exactly. You could have avoided this crisis if you had listened to Kripa's suggestion to provide your sick father with a house and servants. But you brought him to the palace...'

'I want to personally nurse my father, like I am doing yours, Dev!' she snapped. 'They are the two people most precious to me. I am what I am because of my father—' she came to an abrupt stop, recalling that Bhishm knew nothing about her birth and her childhood.

'I know,' Bhishm agreed, a faint irony in his voice.

She looked away then, and began to turn the ruby ring around on her finger. He realized that she was suddenly uneasy.

'Neither have I indulged in any nepotism, as accused, nor shall I betray my people,' she said finally, bestowing on him that ingratiating smile of a queen which he had got accustomed to. 'The fisher folk have as much of right to live with dignity, as the other citizens of your state. They, too, are your people, Dev!'

Bhishm heard her out, his head slightly bowed, his eyes

shuttered. He knew she had done a lot for her people, but it had been regarded as preferential treatment by the other citizens, rather than good work.

He could not but commend her defiance, her open resistance to the system, her bold disobedience of the royal order; and her determination to help her community and her father. She was the son her father never had; she was the leader of her people. She was proud to be known as Kali by them. But in the palace, she had reserved more unkind monikers. The name Daseyi had stuck, and it was sniggered at her behind her back.

It was with a defensive hauteur that Satyavati treated the people of the palace, including him, much to everyone's affront and his amusement. She regarded him as she would an obsequious minister, because she felt guilty for stealing the throne from him. He was given orders and asked questions, but she thought it unseemly to say more to him than was usually said to people of a lower order. He knew she pretended to be favourably disposed to him all the same, because of his father. She feared his popularity. But he suspected she behaved the way she did because if anyone in the palace could be humiliated easily, it was she.

However, at times when she was sending him on some official errand or explaining to him the things she wanted done her way, her face would soften, and she would look him in the eye. At such moments, he always fancied she remembered with grudging grace how he had allowed her to be in the position she was in now. Was it gratitude or guilt? Right now, though, her dark eyes had a brittle hardness as she watched him warily.

'You don't like me very much, do you?' she asked bluntly.

'Does anybody?' he riposted with his usual equanimity.

She burst out laughing, her eyes crinkling in genuine amusement.

'You are honest. So am I,' she said in good humour. 'Can we not help each other?'

An angry shout cut through their conversation. She cast him a last despairing look and then, deciding to take matters in her own hands, she strode out of the chamber, down the marbled steps, across the sprawling garden, towards the huge, barricaded gate.

His brooding eyes followed her.

'Open the gates,' she ordered, taking the guards by surprise.

The previous time she had summoned the protestors inside, but today she would face them outside the palace, on their ground, she swore defiantly. They had showered her with abuses, but she had to get through to them once and for all, she decided grimly. They did not know her; neither the people in the palace nor beyond it.

The waiting crowd were taken by surprise as the palace gates opened unexpectedly. Shouting abuses at their queen was their way to show collective displeasure. Their prince had requested them to stop, passionately arguing that no injustice had been inflicted on him, as assumed. But they had countered him by saying they were fighting not just for him, but for themselves as well.

Their surprise turned to shock when they saw the queen herself approaching them. Tall, dark and graceful, there was a purpose in her long strides, but there was no trace of anger or even annoyance on her face.

She folded her hands, bowing to them.

Most bowed out of habit, some stopping short to show their belligerence.

'I invite you all for the naming ceremony,' she said humbly, her voice soft, yet her eyes, straight and clear.

'The prince has already sent the invitation to us, Queen Daseyi,' said one of them rudely. 'But we refuse.'

The Fisher Queen's Dynasty

'You would rather show your affection by shouting outside the palace?' she asked with a faint smile.

He flushed. 'The affection we reserve is for the prince.'

'Not the king?' she asked. 'Is that not treason?' she said, her voice low.

'Are you threatening us?' he snapped.

'No, I am letting you know that you could well be arrested if you were in any other kingdom but Hastinapur,' she replied. 'But the king refrains from doing so because he loves his subjects.'

'He clearly loves the new queen more than us and our prince,' he retorted angrily. 'That may be his personal decision but it affects us, the citizens. We want the prince as our king. He sacrificed it for you!' he spat. 'We cannot forgive him for that!'

Satyavati took in his stubborn expression, knowing she had to give in; but not too much, nor too little.

'What are you achieving by shouting slogans against me?' she took on an imploring tone, her face earnest. 'I can see you are showing your displeasure well, but I *am* one of you, not just your queen.'

He shook his head violently.

'You are *not* our queen. You *were* one of us, but what have you done for our good?' he sneered. 'Except helped your father and your own people. You are *not* a queen by birth. Or by worth. You took what was our prince's, and now you have the temerity to invite us for the naming ceremony of the very person who will be sitting on the throne meant for our prince!'

There was a short silence.

'If I were a queen by birth, would you have dared to speak with me like you are now?' she flicked each of them a steady stare.

'No, but you are not a queen by merit, just by marriage,' he argued, throwing caution to the wind. 'What have you done for us, or for Hastinapur, to make us want you to be our queen? You married the king by extortion!'

Matters were getting volatile, and, as he stood watching the scene from the palace terrace, Bhishm wondered if he should intercede. All he had to do was to speak out, but he knew the conflict would be delayed, not defused.

He glanced at Satyavati worriedly. She looked every inch the queen, glittering in gems from her tiara to her toe-rings; but the glitter in her hard eyes was fiercer. She wanted a confrontation; she did not want to run away from her opponents. She would get her closure today.

'I agree I *am* a queen by marriage to the king,' she pronounced with a calm dignity that forced them to look up to her. It was not arrogance of manner, but an honest confession proclaimed with elegance. 'I have yet not had an opportunity to serve you...'

'You served your fisher folk well!' shouted a voice boisterously.

She nodded. 'I did. Because they gave me a chance to help them. I ask for an opportunity to serve you, too. Today, I am a mother of the son of your king...'

'We already have a prince; we don't want another from you. Give us our prince back; give him his throne back! You took it from him!'

An angry chorus echoed his sentiments.

Bhishm made a movement, but Kripi, who had joined him on the terrace, gripped his arm.

'It's now or never for her,' she warned. 'She started it; let her end it.'

'No,' he said, his brow furrowed. 'I made that pledge, not she. It was Father who chased her, not she.'

'She made you take that awful oath, do you not see it? They were your words, but it was her wish.'

'And I granted it to her,' he replied evenly. 'It was my decision.'

He was interrupted by the clear, ringing voice of Satyavati addressing the crowd below.

'The throne is not mine to give, it is the king's. And I am the king's wife, and now the mother of his child,' she announced, firmly. 'I am the mother of your prince as well.'

'She is using you for emotional exaction!' gasped Kripi, giving Bhishm a questioning look. 'You are right here, Dev, but she is speaking for you! You can never go against her in public, she knows that. She is cunning!'

The mention of Bhishm had the desired effect, as the people looked visibly mollified. Satyavati gauged the change in mood quickly.

'Bhishm shall be the one naming my son, and I leave my son under his care from this day on,' she bowed. 'I vow to you, my people, that my son shall be the pupil of Bhishm,' she paused, raising her head. 'Bhishm will ensure that his oath will not prevent his loyal service to the kingdom. He loves his king, his father, and the oath proves that. He loves his new brother, too. It is again his wish, his own will, that he shall serve the king sitting on the throne with utmost love and loyalty.'

Bhishm regarded her, startled. He could see that she was a woman of great strength, and he felt a surge of admiration for her run through him. He was completely convinced that she meant what she was saying.

'But you were to be king,' hissed Kripi angrily. 'Oh, Dev, what did you *do*?' she cried. 'It was not about you relinquishing your right as a crown prince, as some of your ancestors did. Yati did it for his younger brother,

Yayati, to become an ascetic, as did both your uncles. But you made the ultimate, incredible sacrifice demanded from any man: that of celibacy! Even rishis are not celibates and they marry; yet, you took on the worst punishment for yourself. Lifelong celibacy does not ever help anyone receive salvation. Brahmacharya is supposed to be a phase in a man's life, not a life-long pledge. That is what makes your oath so terrible, *Bhishm*!'

When Bhishm remained silent, a scornful frown clouded her face. 'You did it to sub serve your father's infatuation for a fisher girl! And here this girl has the gall to proclaim you as her son's mentor to appease the public. She has left you impotent, Dev, with nothing. Not even your pride!'

Kripi's pale cheeks were flushed, but it was grief at his helplessness that made her lash out.

'Surely you can rise above such pettiness?' said Bhishm, shrugging and walking away from the terrace. 'If it bothers you so much, then take no notice of her, and then she won't anger you. And you won't need to make a regular tragedy out of a trifle.'

Kripi threw him a searching look. 'Is that how you handle it? How you comfort yourself?' she grimaced. 'I teach Daseyi every day. She is smart and intelligent. But I am scared to teach her more, never knowing when she will use all that knowledge against me one day. As she has done to you, Dev. She has defeated you, the king, and all of us.'

Bhishm looked down at the scene below—the queen and her people. He saw how she had won, going straight into the battlefield but not shedding a drop of blood. She had shrewdly aligned herself with him, understanding and diverting the interest of the mob.

'I have you with me,' she had said. Now he knew what she meant.

He had to be with her, too, and not just with his father, whether he liked it or not. He was to be her aide and her shield—protecting her from everything, be it the people's ire against her or the rebuffs she received daily at the palace. This was her warning, her truce, her final victory.

'She wooed and won, our Queen Daseyi,' spat Kripi.

'She already had,' he remarked quietly. 'You might have nicknamed her Daseyi, but who is serving who? She is the queen, remember. Now, she is queen of the people as well,' he said, as he saw Satyavati leading the way for the crowd through the palace.

She owed him but he did not own her; no one did.

The Matsyas

He named his infant brother Chitrangad. As he held the wriggling baby in his hands, whispering his name in his ear, Bhishm knew he was a slave of this tiny being for the rest of his life. A strong, strange, undecipherable emotion filled his hollow heart with a warmth he had never known. He gazed at the small, smiling face with shining eyes—this wee little boy had given him a new vigour and purpose in life.

Bhishm glanced at the boy's parents. His father looked pale and drawn, his haggard look a permanent feature these days. He was unwell again, the rasping cough getting worse with each passing week. The queen mother looked beatific, like a queen who had conquered all the three worlds. She had, after all; she had everything she had aspired for.

She was deferentially hovering by his father's side, and Bhishm watched as she inappropriately sunk down onto the rug at his father's feet. He could see she was worried from her subtle, anxious movements.

As his father sat in his easy-chair, she, like an efficient and alert nurse, handed him his dose of medicine.

'May I get you some water?' she asked, smiling softly. The adoring look his father returned nettled Bhishm. 'Are you fine now?' she enquired, deftly removing the full wine glass from the table.

'You are always drinking while reading...' she rebuked affectionately. 'Do you know, Shantanu, what is one of the secrets of your success? You are very well read. What book have you there?'

Shantanu laughingly answered. A silence stretched, and Bhishm, standing stiff in their presence in the sun room, watched them as he played with his brother.

'There is something I wanted to tell you,' she said. 'Shall I? Very likely you'll laugh and say that I flatter myself. You know I hope that you will allow the unemployed into our infrastructural services. It would help hugely, wouldn't it?' she asked, driving in her point. 'I know most of them are not natives, and they have always been on the social periphery,' she continued, before Shantanu could protest. 'But now, since they have become subjects of the sovereign state—of course, under stipulated conditions—they need to be productive. If the king is their protector, I think, as their queen, I, too, can grant them certain benefits?'

She was empowering the poor migrant community, and it had already riled many at the court and in the city. Bhishm secretly agreed with her, but was more amazed at how, with a pretty smile and honeyed words, she could get the toughest task done where the wisest ministers had failed with the king.

She did not wait for his reply and continued. 'Why have you not gone for your hunt? Is it for my sake and the baby that you feel obliged to stay back?' She threw her husband a reassuring smile. 'Do go with Dev for the game—you need to be with him, too!' she said. 'Both of you will be happy in each other's company. Besides, you need some fresh air.'

'Yes,' said Bhishm, laconically. 'Happy is the man who thinks not just of what *is*, but of what is *not*.'

'That was a long sentence which I did not quite understand,' she riposted with a grin, but Bhishm knew she understood every single word. 'You mean happy people live in the real world, and not in their imagination? Yes, possibly. Let us talk of our life, of our future,' she pouted dreamily. 'I keep making plans for our life, all sorts of plans and ideas! Shantanu, may I ask you a question? When are you going to give up your crown?'

Bhishm was startled, as was Shantanu.

'I still *am* the king,' he said weakly.

'But you are so ill these days, dear. How about making Dev the regent to look after the court and the kingdom? Till Chitrangad becomes old enough to handle the throne, of course!' she hastened to add, pressing her forefinger on her lower lip. 'It would relieve you of all the responsibilities and duties. Your health is suffering even more because of the constant pressure of managing the kingdom. I know how it worries you so.'

Shantanu's thick brows furrowed in swift thought, as he pondered what she had said for a moment. Then, he nodded, brightening slowly.

'That's a sensible thought,' he agreed.

Bhishm was neither impressed nor impervious to her ways. 'Chitrangad is barely six months old; he cannot be appointed as the heir so soon...'

'But you are there, Dev, to look after him and the throne,' Satyavati interrupted smoothly. 'That's why I requested the king to make you regent.'

Soon after, Bhishm was appointed as the regent of the throne, on behalf of a sick king and the infant prince. That day, his father looked pleased, but somewhat disconcerted with the deluge of guests invited for the official ceremony.

'It seems like all the kings of Bharatvarsh are attending this show!' Shantanu laughed hoarsely, a laugh that quickly descended into a long, dry bout of coughing.

His father could not have been more succinct. *This show. It is. Right now, the palace of Hastinapur is hosting more than a hundred kings in the country, a thousand nobles and courtiers from various royal houses. Except for Uncle*, he thought sadly. King Bahlik had sent his son, Somadatt, instead, with rich gifts for him, but not a single one for the queen mother. Bahlik would never forgive her.

The palace was as resplendent as the queen. She looked every bit like royalty, with her gems and attire. She was, after all, the mother of the heir to the throne. She played the courteous hostess, mingling with guests, attending to them, greeting them all with that ingratiating smile she reserved for such occasions.

Bhishm felt a tap on his shoulder. He turned around to see his father with Prince Matsya, along with his own father, King Uparichar Vasu, of Chedi. Bhishm was meeting them both for the first time, and he was struck by the startling resemblance between father and son. They looked so much alike—tall, fair, light-eyed, with narrow faces, jutting jaws and a prominent, hooked nose.

But while King Uparichar Vasu was a hearty man with a hearty laugh, the young prince looked stiff.

'How was the journey?' Bhishm began politely.

'Quick!' laughed the older king. 'Thanks to my viman, which I have inherited from our ancestor, King Yayati. He deigned to gift it to me, favouring us rather than your branch of the family, Shantanu!'

Bhishm was familiar with the family story. He also knew that the king always travelled in his air-borne chariot. His stories were as flamboyant as the man himself.

'This is a big event to commemorate the new crown prince,' Vasu commented, eyeing the decorated palace. 'Shantanu, congratulations on your new son,' he added perfunctorily.

Shantanu nodded slightly.

'She is a fisher girl, is she?' asked Vasu jauntily.

Bhishm saw his father wince. The king of Chedi was being crudely curious.

'Yes, Matsyagandha comes from the fisher community,' answered Shantanu, tersely. 'But why have you named *your* son Matsya? He has no connection with that community, does he?' he asked innocently.

Vasu gave a thin smile. 'As you well know, Matsya is my special son from Adrika, an apsara, unlike the five sons I have with my queen, Girika. Adrika abandoned him, as apsaras often do, and he was found by a fisherman. I named him after the community who saved the poor boy's life. Matsya respects that, and that's why the name of the new kingdom I created for him has the same name—Matsya— and the royal emblem is the fish.'

Bhishm's fingers curled into a fist, as he involuntarily felt the need to defend the queen. She did not deserve this man's contempt merely on the basis of her birth. Before he could say anything though, his father spoke up.

'Strange, you give a lot of credit to a mere fisherman,' said Shantanu. 'I guess I went a step further. I married one and made her my queen.'

Bhishm threw him a surprised look, as his father was rarely rude to his guests. Not that his father was ashamed that his queen came from the fisher community, but he never defended her so bluntly.

'Her father, Dashraj, is the chieftain of the community,' added Shantanu, as if that would redeem her dignity in the jaundiced eyes of the king of Chedi.

To his astonishment, Bhishm noticed the colour drain from the king's fair skin, making him look deathly pale. Vasu pursed his lips thinly and turned to look up at Satyavati, who was at the top of a marbled staircase. As he gazed at her, several expressions swept across his face.

She was in conversation with the king of Surasen, courteous and attentive, her brows knitted in a slight frown as she listened to him. She was no silly queen; she was not absurd nor foolish; she did not show a lack of common sense or judgement. Instead, she was fast proving herself to be an astute woman, without the submissiveness usually associated with being a king's wife.

If the world condemned her as a crafty woman, little did they know that right then, using the occasion as a pretext, she had managed to negotiate a pact with the wily king of Surasen. Bhishm had warned her about him but she had airily hinted that she would convince him with words, not war. She had made her move and she had won, as always. They were both smiling at having reached an agreement when she caught sight of Shantanu and Bhishm in the hall below.

'Do you want to meet the queen, King Vasu?' asked Bhishm politely.

As if on cue, she looked down towards them and their eyes met. Bhishm saw her gaze trail to the two men standing next to him and recognition seemed to flood her eyes. Bhishm found it hard to hide his surprise. *She knew them!* He frowned *But she has never met either the king of Chedi or his son Matsya till now, though, of course, she knew they had been invited for the occasion.* He saw her face freeze, the smile slipping from her face; her dark eyes dulled with a sudden emotion.

When Satyavati saw her father for the first time, she became numb with shock. She had imagined this meeting a thousand times through the years. How would she react if she ever met the famous King Vasu of Chedi; the man who had thrown her out of his life as if she were a piece of trash? And then she knew why. One look at the two men, and she knew why her father had not wanted to acknowledge her as his daughter. Prince Matsya might be her twin, but he was so unlike her. While her skin was a dark, deep olive, and she had lush raven hair and ebony eyes, Matsya had pale skin and sharp hazel eyes, and was handsome, like her father. She had clearly taken after her mother, a reminder that King Vasu had not wanted around. Was she a physical aberration, and therefore a departure from the respectable, her dark skin unsuitable to the fair-skinned royalty of Chedi?'

Did she want to meet him? She could turn around and walk away from him, like he had done many years ago. Or did she want to watch him wilt with embarrassment?

Satyavati could see the king's face already mottled red with acute self-consciousness. Or was it awkwardness, shame? Plain mortification? She realized that he knew who she was; and he could not face her.

Unknowingly, she started moving towards them. The decision was made for her.

Her brother was talking to his young wife, Rekatwati, and glanced at her with blatant curiosity as she walked down the stairs. He probably didn't know about their father's deception, and was kept in the dark about his sister. She bestowed them with a small smile. It was neither friendly nor hostile; she smiled like a hostess welcoming a stranger in her home—no more, no less.

King Vasu stood rooted, pretending an unconcern for what may happen or be said, but his hazel eyes were dilated. Bhishm's quick, keen glance noted this shift, and also how Vasu had suddenly gone quiet. There was something very amiss, and Bhishm could feel the tension, palatable and thick with every step that drew Satyavati closer to them...

She still had time. She felt her heart racing, her hands suddenly clammy. And then, suddenly, she did not want to meet her father or her brother. It was a swift, instinctive decision. She could not face them. They—wealthy and powerful, like the others in the hall—no longer held any interest or even curiosity for her. She was like them, too: rich, beautiful and powerful.

Satyavati tried to recall the passionate hatred she had felt for her father since the time she had known who she was. She urged herself to bring out at least some trace of that former emotion, but failed. Her father's aged, crinkled face doused the burning embers of resentment, and brought out nothing but cold indifference. Perhaps she found it difficult to strike a flint against a crumbling stone. The cold glitter of his crown made her realize the transitory nature of everything—power, prestige, even pain.

She continued to converse with the king of Surasen, who was still by her side, walking down the marbled steps, and turned her face away deliberately from the king of Chedi. *She does not want to meet them, And the king of Chedi does not want to meet her*, Bhishm realized, noticing that Vasu was still pale under his fair skin.

Shantanu had not noticed any of this; conversing as he was with Prince Matsya and his bride. She passed by them—her head turned away, her eyes glacial—with regal hauteur.

'If a treaty doesn't work, an army does,' the king of Surasen was saying with a loud guffaw.

Suddenly sick of the luxury surrounding her, she wanted to flee from all of it. There was a big crowd still pouring in—every woman wore diamonds and embroidered silks—the uniform of the rich. Some of them looked at her with interest, their curious eyes lighting up with malice, staring at her in that contemptuous way only the rich can at the impecunious. Others gaped at her long enough to satisfy their curiosity, before they went back into their collective coma. There was an odd, mundane routine to the whole event. Everyone trying to prove themselves better than the other, playing the same game; they even looked the same. Suddenly, the vast hall felt claustrophobic. She excused herself from the king's company, pretending that she needed to check on her son.

For a moment she paused to look around, noting that the guards looked young, aggressive and alert as they stood by the king and the sleeping newborn in his enormous and elaborate cradle. She walked across the ornate hall, towards the nearest exit. She needed to be alone for some time to recover her flailing composure. She wanted to rush to the quiet precincts of her own chamber, but she knew that there would be guards there and everywhere; she had no private space in this vast palace.

Finally, she found a quiet alcove, and tried to recover her breath and composure. She was filled with self-contempt: how could she not face her offender when she had the chance? Was it cowardice or procrastination? Or a weakness she refused to admit? Or a wound she had allowed to fester too long? Would it ever heal?

All she could think was that she could not bear to see the man whom she had grown to detest all her life. It was making her feel queasy at the pit of her stomach. And he was in her palace, her home, her haven. That hatred which failed her in the hall when she had laid her eyes on the old king, took possession of her now. She wanted to rush to him and throw him out, along with all his memories and all the associations she never had. She wanted to fling curses at him—some coarse words of abuse.

'Yes, I am angry; *angry!*' she repeated, and tears of fury glistened in her eyes. She pressed her hands on her temples, and went on wildly, 'I hate him! How much more can I hate him!'

She began crying, the tears gushing out. The rage inside her swirled with thoughts of what could have been and of what was; of what she had endured and suffered; of what she had done to get what she had achieved; and she cried violently.

Were these the only memories she was going to inherit from her father? The hate, the anger and the aggression ... were they a part of her? Is this what made her hate the world and the people around her? Her father was a monster, as far as she was concerned. She had nothing to fear from this frail, old man. In fact, he deserved to feel her rage. Why then could she not face him?

She felt herself shudder at the thought, and took in a long breath, trembling in the quiet sanctum the empty portico temporarily provided. She did not know how long she stood there, motionless as within her churned the unforgotten, familiar emotions: hatred, anger, pain and humiliation.

In a corner of the portico, Bhishm stood, having entered the area silently some minutes back. His sense of apprehension deepened. This was not the Satyavati he knew, always so sure and ruthless, having no pity or compassion for others, or even for herself. The resigned stoop of her shoulders, the bowed head as she leaned against a column, the bent curve of her slender neck revealed a strange surrender. To what? He stood watching her, allowing the silence and her ragged breathing to speak.

She suddenly swivelled around, as if sensing his presence, her face drenched with sweat and tears. He reeled at the grief he saw lying bare in her eyes, stark and livid. He had never seen her crying before; in fact, he had never seen anyone crying so disconsolately before. It reminded him of a dying doe, hurt, mangled and gasping for its last breath.

She blinked desperately, hoping to stop the tears. He saw not apprehension, but a flash of embarrassment in her dark eyes, as if she had forgotten where she was, and who she was. He had found her in an unenviable, vulnerable state.

She quickly covered it up with her characteristic smile and straightened herself up. Yet she could not quite gather that composed aura he suspected she used as a mask. She still looked like that dying, wounded deer, her eyes huge and haunted, as he gazed into her face.

He was standing close to her, and though she stood tall, she seemed small and fragile, as if cowering from a fact she did not want to confront.

It had to do with the King of Chedi, he was sure, *but what? What was it about that man that had disconcerted her so profoundly?* He frowned. *King Vasu had looked equally uncomfortable, if not more so. But not the prince; he had not been aware of the tension.* And suddenly, Bhishm knew what it was; it came to him like a lightning bolt through a dark cloud.

As they stood in thick silence, she avoided his eyes. This was his chance to break her—from the inside. But, strangely, he felt consumed by her sadness. It had left her looking bereft and defenceless—the warrior without her weapons.

His mere presence, so close and warm, was unnerving. She stopped twisting her fingers together.

'King Vasu...?' he asked abruptly, but the tone was not demanding; it was so tender that she thought her heart would burst and she would shatter again into a thousand tears.

The blood seeped out of her face and rushed back, and she could feel the heat of it. *How did he guess,* she thought wildly. *There is nothing he knows about me; I have not told a soul about it, and yet he knows ... how?* The best defence was, of course, denial. But one glance at his even, steady gaze crumbled her from within. Her voice died in her throat. Her answer did not matter: he knew the truth. *Her* truth.

She opened her mouth to protest, but she heard no sound; the words were buried in choked-back tears. He saw the swift look of pain and fear flaring in her eyes. She was clearly scared that he knew her truth. He wanted to hasten to assure her that she need not fear him, but before he could say anything, she shook her head violently.

'Don't, *no*...!' she whispered, her voice quivered and broke. She was evidently trying to restrain her tears, desperately stifling her sobs.

'Don't what: pry further with words, or reveal her secret to his father? It was hard for him to see her in this state. Her truth had exposed her and made her vulnerable. Gone was the anger and arrogance of this woman who was destined to bring him down in every way. Now, he had the power to overthrow her, to turn the tide against her and drown her in the depths of despair as she had done to him. He suspected it was more rage than grief that filled her: the anger of a deserted daughter. To be recognized as one had been her single hope, which turned into a tale of desire and determination.

Through her broken sobs, Bhishm saw who Satyavati was—a child who could have been a princess, but was rejected and forgotten. Now he knew where the burning desire and ambition came from. Her ruthlessness had been her sole weapon of survival, of fighting back. No means would be too despicable, no method too deplorable. Why should she owe anything to him or his father or Hastinapur or the society at large to live and conform to their wishes? He could also understand why Dashraj had behaved the way he did: he was ensuring history would not repeat itself.

He was afraid to touch her, to console her with word or gesture He knew that any words of consolation would be received with hostility. She hated him now for knowing her truth.

They looked at each other again, and he quickly shifted his gaze. He knew what he had to do; the only thing he could do. Pity and sympathy and an irrational helplessness seemed to have robbed him of all words. He pursed his mouth, bowed his head slightly, and turned on his heel, quietly leaving the room, giving her the respite and release she wanted.

She turned her head to stare at Bhishm's retreating back through glazed eyes. She could hear her heart hammering. He had left, but his unsaid words floated back to her. How could she ever allow herself to forget that he now knew her truth? Fresh tears spilled onto her saree, staining it with memories.

The anguish broke something inside her. She felt like she had been reborn out of the shell of hatred, anger, revenge and humiliation. She remembered her shanty house, her old father and neighbours and friends, and her first thought was how she had long past overcome her inadequacies without ever realizing it. She only knew one thing—that before King Vasu's visit, her position as a queen had a meaning; it now appeared absurd to her.

She felt her hatred and sadness dry up as fast as the tears dried on her face. She was ready to embrace and include in her life every possibility open to her. She was free: to let go of her anger and bitterness, and, at the same time, to be happy. Life was crass and brutal, and she would battle it. The crown, somehow, seemed lighter now.

The Death

They were arguing again. It seemed to Satyavati that Shantanu had little strength, and the little he had, he reserved to fight her.

'You took the crown, the kingdom, Dev's rights ... you have two sons now, and your father is a minister at court...' Shantanu was saying. 'Yet, you are insecure. Or is it simply greed?' he muttered tiredly.

It was a strong accusation, but she was used to it. It was his way of attempting to alleviating his own guilt.

'I am not insecure about Dev, if that's what you are insinuating,' she said calmly. 'He loves my sons as his own; he's like a father to them, and he has taken over the responsibility of their upbringing completely.'

'This was his kingdom to rule. He should have been fathering his own children, not looking after his stepbrothers!' said Shantanu unhappily. He moved restlessly in his bed. He was bedridden since their second son was born, six months ago. 'Both are still babies, Matsyagandha! Chitrangad cannot be anointed heir, as you are requesting. He has to be of age; he is barely five!' coughed Shantanu angrily. 'Till he comes of age, Dev is regent. How can I make a child the crown prince when the most capable of all, my Bhishm, is on the throne!'

She quietly wiped his damp brow. 'Dev will always be there. He has promised loyalty to the throne and whoever sits on it—be it his father or his brother,' she said quietly, reminding her delusional husband of the reality he desperately wanted to escape from.

'Dev is the king, no one else,' he muttered stubbornly. 'The people will not accept it.'

'The people have accepted me now, as well as our sons...'

She heard her husband snort derisively. 'Never as much as Dev!'

She hugged the baby closer, as if to reassure herself that she now had two sons—her two heirs.

'I *want* to make him king!' confessed Shantanu with a loud sigh. 'But even if I want to ... you won't allow it, and Bhishm will never agree...' he lapsed into a dejected silence.

'He won't break his vow. Ever,' she said confidently.

Shantanu threw her a scathing look. 'You know him so well, don't you?' he charged, his eyes flaring with sudden fury.

Her heart stopped, thudding wildly. *What did Shantanu know?*

'You know he will never turn against you or the boys,' he said, and she breathed more easily. 'He is too loyal; and worse, he will tolerate you and your wickedness only because you are my wife and they are my sons, and thus his brothers by blood!' he seethed. 'The people of Hastinapur and I will have to suffer the oath you made him take!' he accused, his eyes glazed with grief.

'I did not make him do anything. He took it, Shantanu, for you,' she interposed evenly.

Shantanu went berserk. 'His kindness lies too heavily upon me; it is too cruel. I would rather endure his unkindness any day ... oh my Dev, what have I done!' he wept uninhibitedly.

Satyavati watched her husband cry; her heart contracted at the misery on her husband's lined face, and the pain he was inflicting on himself. He could never forgive himself for what he had wreaked on his son. Nor could he forgive her. In his grief and guilt, he saw her as the culprit; he barely endured her now. Love had soured to bitter loathing.

'Why do you keep going over it?' she pleaded. 'Don't be so harsh on yourself; you are making your health worse. You are killing yourself!'

He pushed her hand away. 'I would rather die than live with what I have to ... *you*. Oh I wish I had never met you!'

'If you can't live with your shame, don't blame me for it,' she replied, hurt.

'Don't you, for even a moment, feel remorse?' he cried. 'You shall pay for this; you shall have to answer for your sins!' he closed his eyes but not before she saw hatred and sorrow in them.

Shantanu saw her in his fermenting mind; she was abhorrent. He opened his eyes and they were clouded with disgust. Moving his gaze over her body—young, lithe and strong—he thought, *I met a woman and she lit a carnal response in me. I could think of nothing else but her: not my Ganga, not my grown-up son, not my throne, not my kingdom. I thought there was no one like her in this world. And then something happened ... and it was all over. Finished.* She meant less to him now than a used glass of wine after a good drink. How little was that? How little had he been...?

'A debauched moralist telling *me* about my sins?' she smiled sadly, standing up wearily. 'You men are so selfish, it's revolting! I have heard enough stories about you, my dear husband. And they are not all flattering. Had I not demanded marriage, I would have been your whore, not your wife, and never a queen!' she sneered. 'I don't know how you can pretend to be so grand and noble when you are the one who started and ended it all,' she paused, looking at the deathly pale face of her husband, his eyes glittering with loathing. 'Of course, you are right, Shantanu,' she said, bending over to gently wipe his mouth. 'It makes me miserable to see you so miserable,' she added sardonically.

'But remember, dear, it was *you* who chased me, *you* who wanted to marry me despite my conditions. I never fooled you, Shantanu; you fooled yourself, your son and your people!' she said, her lips curling in a mirthless smile. '*You* made me queen just as you dethroned your son. It was *you*, Shantanu, who took all the decisions. It was *your* choice; never my decisions.'

Shantanu could not help marvelling at her cold logic. But she was right. He had undone himself, his son and the fate of Hastinapur. He found it despicable, just as he found her despicable. How could he have fallen for such a cold woman? She was the most alluring woman he had ever seen, even though she had been nothing like Ganga. She was her opposite: dark, beautiful with big, marvellous eyes and a body that he could not keep his hands off. Even now, with two children, she was still heavy-breasted, with a slim waist, flaring hips and long, tapering legs, which she had the habit of wrapping around him when they made love. He clenched his jaw, desire rushing through him at the very thought. How could he hate her yet lust for her still? He had been besotted by her, putting at stake everything for her. He was now sure she had never loved him.

Besides his brother's furious words, their wedding night should have warned him. There was no passion, no love. She had given of herself, and he was hopeful that he could rouse her if he was patient, but he never could. He then discovered that her only obsession was power; all she wanted was to be queen. He had been so hopelessly smitten with her that he let her do all that she wanted. *I allowed her to expropriate even my son's rights*, an inner voice reminded him. He could never rid himself of that guilt. He sensed he was walking on the edge of a familiar abyss, the one he had been peering into for the last couple of months. It had become wider and deeper, waiting for him to jump into it someday. How much longer, he wondered, could he evade its deadly pull?

He had loved her, trying hard to please her in every way. And she was devoted to him, patiently nursing him in his sickness, but he always had the feeling that she was not his. She did everything efficiently, even made love to him, coming into his arms and bed dutifully. But he had not been able to touch her soul. Or even her cold heart.

'How beautifully you cover up your evil by coating it with my inadequacies, my weaknesses,' he said, his voice trembling.

'You fooled me, and you fooled Dev, making both of us think that you loved me. Dev did it for *me*!' he spluttered with renewed rage.

She nodded. 'And what did *you* do for *him*?'

Shantanu flushed. 'I gave him nothing but grief,' he said tonelessly. 'But you haven't fooled anyone, Matsyagandha. The people still hate you, they see through you. They may call me a weak king, but they call you the wicked queen! For all your pretence and subterfuge, you used me, Matsyagandha. You know that and so does the world!'

'You are my world, Shantanu,' she said bitterly. 'And the world is one which we create. I created my own, Shantanu, with you, in this palace, this city, this kingdom, far away from the squalor I was born in.'

'Through me, through my unsuspecting son!' he roared, which made him collapse in a bout of dry, violent coughing.

She gently pushed him back against the pillows. He thrust her hand away as if her touch contaminated him.

'You may call yourself Matsyagandha, dear, but the stink will never leave you!' he spat. 'The stench of your past, your wickedness, shall smother you one day. You stink, Daseyi,' he mouthed maliciously. 'And, I fear, it will pervade my family, my Hastinapur!' he closed his eyes, defeated and surrendering to a fate he could see in his mind's eye. This woman. And that woman whom he could never forget, who left him adrift ... *Ganga*.

He recalled how he had met Ganga on the river banks, just as he had met Matsyagandha. Were both river nymphs? One he had found near the Ganga, the other near the Yamuna, the sister rivers; one plentiful and generous, the other dark and dry. Both had remained a mystery to him. Who had they been? They had seemed like goddesses to him, without any flaws. Ganga *was* a goddess, but not Matsyagandha. She was just a fragrant fisher girl, and she had ensnared him. Or had it been his lust for her? Shantanu felt a wave of shame flood over him.

He was ranting, venting his fury on her, but it was he who had brought this day about, this fate upon his son and his kingdom. Bahlik's words rang louder and clearer in his churning mind. Dev did not need a Vasu's curse to live his life on earth; his father had been the curse. He was his son's worst enemy. Shantanu's shrunken body shuddered with sobs, the tears flowing unchecked, in despair about what was to come.

He whimpered. 'I am still the king; I can throw you out ... if not from this palace then from this chamber. I can't bear to look at you!'

'We keep going around this every day. The reality is that you made a mistake, and you won't acknowledge it,' she said. 'You prefer blaming me for your foolishness, your guilt. You put me on a pedestal, and it has turned out that I am a most ordinary woman, not fit to be in your court, palace or room!' she twisted her lips in bitter contempt. 'I symbolize all that is rotten for you; a world in which you lived once, but now find revolting in its triviality and emptiness. Recognize it and be just: don't be angry with me, but with yourself, as it is your mistake, and not mine.'

'I wish I had never met you!' he said venomously.

'Really? You wanted me, you got me but it is not what *you* wanted from me, is it?' she asked pityingly. 'For you, now it is all tears, wailing, cursing. You are wretched, and you make me wretched.'

Shantanu pressed his head against the pillows. 'I wish I could leave you and get back what I lost—my son, my kingdom, and oh, my peace!' he cried in an agonized whisper.

She smiled thinly. 'Yes, dear; except, you would come out worse, having first dethroned your son and then thrown out your wife and two infants,' she said, sarcastically. 'Ever heard of a brave, virtuous king committing such a dastardly act? Especially one from your famed dynasty?' she added, placing the cup of medicine against his mouth. He refused to open his lips.

'Have it, please,' she implored. 'Don't hate yourself so. Live to hate me instead.'

'I know you would rather have me dead! Because I have served my purpose—you are queen and I have given you the heirs you wanted. I am of no use to you now!' he tried to shout but his voice came out as a gurgled hiss.

'I would still prefer to be queen, rather than queen mother,' she retorted dryly.

'I am dying,' he said simply, shutting his eyes. That abyss beckoned him but each time he saw his son, at the crest, restraining him. 'I *want* to die. But not without your forgiveness, my son. Please!' he buried his face in his shaking hands.

'He has already forgiven you, Shantanu; you need to forgive yourself,' she said sadly. 'Can you do that?' She pulled up the sheets, tucking him in more comfortably.

He did not answer, holding his breath and turning suddenly ashen. Finally his eyes closed. She looked at the deathly wan face, her own face thoughtful. He had lapsed into an uneasy sleep again. The medicine had worked; the seeds of the herb were soporific, inducing sleep, however fitful.

She could scarcely think, so consumed was she with anger. She felt miserable, bitter, as she listened to her husband's heavy breathing. She tried to think of the most offensive, biting and venomous word she could hurl at her husband, and at the same time she was fully aware that nothing could penetrate the deep sleep he was in. What did he care for her wretched words? Her most bitter enemy could not have contrived for her a more helpless position. She was her own enemy; she had created her own battlefield.

Taking a deep breath to calm down, she began to nurse the baby. He was pale and thin, sickly from the time he had been born, unlike Chitrangad, who was tall and strapping for a five-year-old, she thought as she watched her elder son practicing the mace with Bhishm on the terrace below. Bhishm had started his training early, and she had been sceptical; but Kripacharya had assured her that her son was in the best hands. She knew that. She knew Dev ... she could not think of him as Bhishm ever...

She watched them from above. Dev was bare-chested as he held out a small mace for the boy to use. His usual hard, cold mask slipped and she glimpsed another man— smiling and loving, his fine-boned, handsome face softened in tender lines, his lock of hair falling over his eyes as he sharply instructed her son, diminutive yet fighting furiously. He loved him; there was no doubt about it. *He is like a father to him, just as I am his mother*, a voice pierced her. She was their mother, *his*, and her two sons', she told herself, her lips twisting, a sharp pain tugging at her heart.

The reminder jolted her back to her senses. She felt her mouth go dry, her hands sweaty, closed into tight fists, her nails biting into her skin. She pulled her eyes away from him, but she could not remove the image of his stunned face, so tender and troubled, when he had guessed the truth of her parentage. His eyes had held a strange softness and uncharacteristic concern, not the usual glacial look he reserved for her. He had tried to console her, his beautifully shaped full lips moving, but not a word slipped through them, his molten eyes as helpless as the hand which had stretched out to comfort her. He had stopped. As had her hammering heart. She felt herself flush, still feeling the heat of that moment, and it warmed her with a certain reassurance, with a sense of belonging and connectedness that now linked the two of them in an undecipherable churn of emotions.

Her eyes had glazed over, the two figures now blurs, and yet she was thinking of them. She felt the slight weight of the sleeping baby. Dev had named the younger one Virya. *More likely Vichitravirya*, she grimaced, worried about the baby's chronic sickliness. She sighed and gently put him back into the cradle. Would she need to have another child to strengthen the bloodline? The thought made her shudder, recalling each night spent with Shantanu. She thought of Dev instead...

She glanced at her husband. He was motionless, in deep sleep. There was something amiss, she thought, frowning. His skin appeared more sallow, the hollow of his cheeks caving in and his jaw slack, dropping at a grotesque angle. Her breath caught in her throat, a flicker of fear unfurling within her. She quickly touched his forehead. It was ice cold. She checked his pulse, but felt nothing. *He is dead!* her mind screamed in a silent whisper.

She stared down at him for a long time, recollecting their time together. It had been brief but momentous, almost fateful from the day he had seen her at the river banks. He had come to her as a saviour, lifting her from destitution and insignificance, giving her the life she had always dreamed of. As his wife. As his queen. As the mother of his heirs. And now he was dead ... the king was dead.

The Panchals

As he stared into the still waters of the Ganga, Bhishm recalled it was that very spot where he had met his father for the first time. His father was dead, then why was he still in Hastinapur? He had no further wish to be in this city. What was it to him now?

He walked slowly towards the River Ganga, his mother. He sat on the banks, on a rock, his hands resting slackly on his lap. He was alone. He thought of all the years ahead of him. What would he do with the kingdom anyway? It was not his. It only meant long years of slavery. He couldn't go back there. He wanted to live decently.

He was a prince without a crown, with nothing left here now—not his home, his land, his father. Bhishm had not allowed himself to bow down to excessive, self-absorbed sorrow, but today he felt bereft, an orphan, as if the cloak of family and belongingness had been ripped off from him. All he had left now was the terrible vow he had to live with. And the self-desired death wish, his father's gift. He could use it right here, right now, and die in the arms of his mother—in her warm, welcoming waters—and go back to her.

It was this cowardice that made him angry with himself. The dispassionate face of Satyavati floated before his wide, open eyes, taunting him of his pusillanimity. Her soundless laugh followed the guffaw of the two small boys, their faces turned up to him in open adoration, their eyes bright with trust.

Bhishm turned away from the dying embers of the funeral pyre, but not from the ashes of reality. He had nowhere to run; he had to stay here, in Hastinapur, in the palace, bound by the chains of obedience and obligation. Not that *she* needed him. Satyavati had taken his father's death stoically. No tears, no histrionics, just a quiet acceptance. He never ceased to wonder at her calmness. No situation ever seemed to throw her off her stride. Not even the death of her husband. He knew he could not leave the two young boys in good hands but ...

But I can't let Hastinapur down, whispered a voice within him. *I can't forsake the widow and those two small boys now. I can't let my father down either. He will never forgive me if I turned away now. No, I have to go back.* He put his hands on his head and groaned. *My people trust me. She trusts me. If I run away, I will no longer be a man of truth.* He lifted his heavy shoulders in a despairing shrug, mounted his chariot, and drove back towards the palace.

The flames of the pyre had barely died down when an unexpected conflagration flared up in the court of Hastinapur. Bhishm had not expected the nobles to start pushing him to accept the throne.

'How does this issue even arise?' he said, his voice dangerously restrained. 'I have been appointed the regent, and so I shall be,' he added curtly, his tone warning that he would brook no further argument.

'The Crown Prince is too young, and with you around, how can we think of another king but you?' argued Kripa. 'Your vow is no excuse. Your uncle was right. You need to see to the throne first ... not your family, not your father. The kingdom is especially vulnerable now that the king is dead, you know that.'

'And I am here to protect it; I don't need to be crowned the king to do that,' said Bhishm briefly, laconically.

He noticed the restlessness in his friend's silence. 'You are like my brother, Kripa; what I do now is especially important,' he said, his tone softening slightly to alleviate the reproof. 'There is a young widow with two young sons; one of them is heir to the throne. My duty is to protect them. If I do otherwise, I shall forever carry the stigma of a traitor. The world is watching us. Especially me.'

'You were always so bothered about what the world thinks of you,' snapped Kripi, her tone sharp. 'You were the perfect prince, the perfect son; now you will rule as what? The perfect regent and the perfect brother?'

Bhishm smiled at her indulgently, his eyes weary.

'That is the way of the world now; call it politics. But I say it is conscience. How can I act against a widow and her sons? What you are suggesting is treason, Kripa ... a coup, a posthumous defiance against my father.'

Something in his tone made Kripi give him a second look. They had not given Bhishm the space and time to grieve for his father.

'My father died a bitter man,' he sighed. 'Let him rest in peace now; he trusted me to look after his family. I can never betray that trust, Kripa.'

'Your uncle won't leave Hastinapur till you are king,' Kripa reminded him.

'Then he need never leave Hastinapur,' smiled Bhishm mirthlessly.

'Agreed,' interposed a voice.

Bhishm turned and saw a mountain of a man sitting in the shadow of the heavy curtains. His uncle was getting on in years, but he was still in good physical shape, he thought; there was not much fat on him. His thinning grey hair was swept up away from his forehead, making him look distinguished; but his face was still massive, leathery and brutal. He rested two enormous hairy hands on the arms of his chair and glared at his nephew.

It had been six years since he had visited Hastinapur.

He had stuck to his word that he would never return, but his brother's death led him to break his pledge. He looked pallid under his tanned skin, his face drawn with grief, but masked by a brisk demeanour. Bhishm knew better, though.

'The funeral is over and many attending kings are returning today,' cut in Kripa brusquely. 'Bhishm, I think you should attend to that for now. The king of Panchal is especially impatient to meet you.'

'King Ugrayudh Paurav is itching for war, nothing else,' shrugged Bhishm. 'He wants to invade the Kuru kingdom. Matters have never been good with the Panchals since their King Sudas overthrew our King Samvarn. It was King Kuru who recovered all our land and honour back from the Panchals.'

'But Ugrayudh himself is a usurper,' Bahlik said to his nephew. 'I have also been told that he wants to meet you urgently. Or rather the queen,' he paused with a scowl. 'He has a proposal that you will want to hear, he claims.'

Bhishm was surprised. 'The queen?' he frowned. 'He came for the funeral, and now he may leave. I have nothing to say to or hear from him.'

'Be careful of the man,' warned his uncle. 'He is young, ambitious and ferocious, a Paurav king from another family branch—the Dvimidhas. He has already killed the king of Uttar Panchal, but the young heir, Prishat, managed to flee to Kampilya, the capital of South Panchal. Enraged, Ugrayudh attacked South Panchal and killed Janmejaya Dushtabuddhi, a tyrant best disposed of. Prishat is missing but Ugrayudh is still searching for him. He has now turned his eyes on us, the Kurus. So do meet him and hear what he has to say.'

Bhishm nodded thoughtfully. 'Agreed, Uncle, but this king wants a fight. Talks won't help. He considers us vulnerable when we are in mourning. Keep the army standing,' he announced. 'But I shall try to handle him myself, face-to-face. It shall save blood and breath!'

'That's always been your policy,' remarked Bahlik. 'Somewhat old-fashioned, but practical.'

'You would be surprised how many men want to wriggle out from an open confrontation. Most prefer their army to fight their wars,' smiled Bhishm, his eyes unamused. 'Call him in. Let's see what the rogue has to say. He certainly seems to live up to his name!'

'Ugrayudh is a nickname,' supplied Kripa with a grin. 'He is a war-thirsty hound.'

Half an hour later, Ugrayudh entered the assembly hall with as much élan as his reputation. Bhishm was slightly taken aback when he saw him. He was a very short, tiny, wiry man, with dark skin and sharp, shifty eyes; he had an impetuous air about him. His face was battered—with scars and welts all over it. The expression on it seemed to say that he had nothing to fear, but everyone feared him. His long hair was tied in a loose knot at the nape of his neck, and one ear, Bhishm noticed, was without the lobe.

He bowed slightly. 'Where is the king?' he asked irreverently. 'In the crib with his mother?'

He is a rascal, decided Bhishm.

'I am the regent, talking on his behalf. Pray, what is it that you wanted to express?'

'My condolences, of course, on your father's death,' said Ugrayudh quickly. 'Died a little prematurely; too soon after his marriage to that fisher girl. But he had two sons quickly, I must say.'

Kripi gave a low gasp. The insinuation was crass, and Bhishm realized the man was out to provoke him.

'May I meet the queen? I would like to talk to her and offer my condolences to her as well,' said Ugrayudh.

Bhishm merely shook his head briefly. 'She is resting.'

'That is an insult,' said Ugrayudh. 'I need to speak with her. I have something of importance to tell her.'

'I presumed you wanted to speak to me,' said Bhishm. 'Kripi can convey the message to the queen.'

'I prefer to speak with her confidentially,' argued Ugrayudh.

'You may not,' retorted Bhishm. 'You know the protocol well, King!'

'She may be queen, Bhishm, but she is a widow in mourning. She has to meet with all the visitors. And I *am* your guest,' he reminded him suavely.

Bhishm hesitated, but Ugrayudh looked poised to get into a pointless argument. Bhishm imperceptibly motioned to Kripi with his eyes to fetch Satyavati and saw her quietly slip away. Bhishm felt a strong sense of unease. This man was not to be trusted.

'Your message is being conveyed,' he said. 'If the queen mother wishes to meet you, she shall.'

'That is discourteous,' Ugrayudh commented dryly.

Bhishm stared back, unsmiling. 'Meanwhile, please do disclose the proposal you wanted to discuss.'

'I had but a marriage proposal in mind...'

Bhishm could not hide his shock.

'For your *mother*,' Ugrayudh drawled out the word insultingly. 'Of course, for taking your queen, I shall compensate the Kurus with considerable wealth. That's what I wanted to speak to her about,' he grinned. 'Do you deign to convey something as personal as *that* to her, Gangaputra?' he said scornfully. 'You call yourself the loyal servant, but you are nothing but a lackey!'

Bhishm could barely contain his wrath, and his big hands balled into tight fists. 'You dare to walk up here to our palace and talk of marriage with the widowed queen,' he said, managing to speak evenly. 'Ugrayudh, it's disheartening to see you have no manners or sense of protocol. But then, you are not a king, but a thief, stealing what is not yours.'

Ugrayudh flushed a dull red, but his eyes were bright and bold.

'What is the problem, Bhishm? I am politely asking for Queen Satyavati's hand in marriage. I wanted to ask her myself but you did not permit me. Why don't you let her give me the answer? Surely, if she could marry an old man like your father, how ineligible would I be?' he jeered, baring his teeth. 'I am young, wealthy and powerful—everything that she wants.'

Bhishm clenched and unclenched his fingers, restraining the urge to smash his fist into the leering face of the man in front of him.

'The proposal is rejected. Please leave,' he said calmly, the breath coming through gritted teeth.

'Who are you, Bhishm, to answer for her? Or are you a lackey *and* her procurer as well?'

There was a collective gasp of horror in the assembly hall, and Bhishm saw his uncle take a step forward. Bhishm swiftly stepped before him. *If this man wants a fight*, he swore grimly, *he will fight me, not Bahlik*. A faint feminine fragrance wafted in, which Bhishm was quick to notice. *She was here!*

'Can't blame you, young man,' continued Ugrayudh impudently. 'I have heard she is so enchanting that no one can keep away from her. What is that the world calls her? Yes, from Matsyagandha to Yojanagandha! Aha, the scent of that woman! It would drive any man crazy,' he paused, chortling roguishly. 'Did it affect you, too, eh Bhishm? Did she turn you from Devavrat to Bhishm and back to

Devavrat again, damn the vow of celibacy?' he cackled in malicious glee which echoed in the stunned silence of the hall. Bhishm stood very still. The muscles of his face rippled under his grey-white skin. His eyes narrowed and his mouth turned into a white, thin line. He clasped his sword in a tight grip, the knuckles growing white with rage. He could see the king was deliberately goading him, encouraging him to strike.

Ugrayudh paused, a little surprised that the Kuru prince had not yet challenged him. He would gladly rip that inscrutable mask off that handsome face. 'Do you think I am a fool, or is it you who is fooling the people, Bhishm?' Ugrayudh continued slyly.

Bhishm stood motionless, his heart now thumping, a cold wave of blood crawling up his spine. He eyed the small man.

'There's you and there's this lonely, beautiful widow...!' Ugrayudh sniggered, staring at Bhishm, whose eyes flared gold in fury.

Bhishm's lips trembled as he bit back the words that jumped to his tongue. With an effort, he took a deep breath and said quietly, 'Mind what you say, King!'

'Mind what *you* do, Prince. The world is watching and talking about the two of you,' Ugrayudh leered. 'It's but natural; I quite understand. Both of you are young and beautiful ... but be bold, Bhishm, for once!' taunted Ugrayudh, his expression changing to animal viciousness. 'Like me. I want her, I want to marry her and I am not ashamed to tell the world. Unlike *you; b*e a man and have her!'

His words ended in a gurgle of blood. Ugrayudh shrieked in pain, his hands reaching instinctively to his mouth, terror-stricken at the warm taste of his own blood in his mouth. His eyes widened in horror as he realized what had happened. He tried to speak but no sound came out but for a grunt. He tried again, but the hoarse sounds curdled with his blood. He looked down at his hands—he was holding his tongue in his palm. Bhishm had cut off his tongue!

He felt dizzy: he thought he would faint with pain and the humiliation. He wanted to scream at the cold, handsome face of Bhishm, but all he could hear was his own undignified groans.

'From henceforth, you won't have a loose tongue to utter filthy words from your foul mouth!' pronounced Bhishm, his voice a harsh rasp. He realized he was shaking, his head pounding with fury. 'I refuse to waste my words on a guttersnipe like you.'

He turned away, disgustedly.

'*Dev*!' he heard her warning cry and a soft swish behind him.

Bhishm swivelled around, his hand still at his dripping dagger. Ugrayudh had his famous discus out. Staggering, with his mouth agape and blood trickling down his chin, he threw the discus at Bhishm.

Bhishm ducked, and the discus crashed against the pillar behind him. He swung his dagger shoulder high like a scythe and sank it straight into Ugrayudh's heart. The king swayed unsteadily, his bloodied hands clutching at the hilt of the dagger, and slowly crashed to the white marbled floor. The silence was shattering, broken only by the rasping sound of the man's last breaths. Bhishm walked slowly towards the prostrate figure, the spreading pool of blood, a stark crimson against the white floor.

'You are dying quite a pathetic death,' he said, staring down at the dying king's face, twisted in agony and hate. He watched dispassionately as the last breath left the king's convulsing body. 'No one insults a Kuru, especially a Kuru woman.'

Ugrayudh gasped, his legs twitched. Then he lay still.

Bhishm heard a movement. It was Satyavati.

She glittered as she stood there, the royal widow; her face was pale, and in her white silk she looked wan, but her dark eyes glinted as hard as the diamonds she was wearing.

'This piece of shit thought I would marry him?' she barked, her lips curled in contempt.

'Queen Daseyi!' Kripi looked as aghast as the others at the display of such colourful language.

'Yes, queens don't curse,' she muttered. 'My real opinion is a little too intimate for expression. My apologies. Not that I am sorry that this cad is dead!'

Bahlik eyed her with reserved approval. 'He thought he was invincible because of his heavenly discus. Possibly the discus lost its power because he lusted after another's wife,' he said, glancing warily at Bhishm and her.

Colour flamed her cheeks. 'The discus lost its power because it confronted Bhishm.'

Bahlik's nodded grimly. 'Ugrayudh wanted to marry you to take over the Kuru kingdom. Wooing is easier than war.'

'Women are easier than war,' she scoffed. 'Or that's what men like to believe.'

'Men like Ugrayudh,' corrected Bhishm and swung around to look squarely at her. 'I had sent Kripi specifically for you *not* to come here.'

Kripi bristled. 'When does *she* ever listen to me? When does *she* obey anyone?'

'I am the queen. I don't obey, I order!' Satyavati's voice dripped ice.

She looked up at Bhishm, her lips pursed. 'I came *because* you did not want me to be here! I demand to know all!'

Her voice had lifted slightly, her chin raised, her eyes flashing dangerously. The air was rife with sudden tension. On cue, Kripa led his reluctant sister away and Bahlik joined them after a moment's hesitation. The other nobles and ministers followed suit to become quiet shadows that drifted soundlessly across the floor through the doorway.

'Don't *ever* talk to me in that tone!' she fumed, her voice shaking.

'Yes, Mother,' he mocked, enraging her further. 'Clearly you seemed to have enjoyed the blood bath. Did you feel bad that you missed the show right from the beginning?' he said silkily.

'I was here from the time he called you a lackey!' she retorted, her cheeks reddening. 'He clearly came here to pick a fight. His insults, his filthy innuendos...' she suddenly looked flustered, her face hot and flushed. She sat down suddenly, lowering her lashes to hide her confusion. 'Is that what the people are saying about me now?' she said, her voice low. Ugrayudh's vicious words were still screaming in her mind. Her face coloured in deep mortification; she bowed her head to conceal the blush, her thudding heart so loud that she was scared he could hear it.

Bhishm's hard eyes softened for a moment as they probed her lowered face and wringing hands. 'You are not just any widow; you are the widowed queen of the Kuru kingdom,' he started, his voice suddenly gentle. 'There will be no shortage of suitors. But do keep your suitors in hope,' he said, his voice teasing, 'for as long as you want. You could keep our enemies friendly that way! You will always be hounded by ambitious kings—Kamboja, Kasayas, Srinjayas...' he paused to suck in a dramatic breath, his eyes crinkling. 'The Kekayas, the Pandyas...'

'Enough!' she burst into a giggle, holding up her hands,

the tension easing. 'I neither want to wed nor go to war with them!'

His smile widened into a chuckle and, for a few moments, the sound of their joined laughter filled the hall.

'But seriously, how is it that small kingdoms are rearing up their heads and becoming powerful?' Her grin slipped and her fine eyebrows knitted in a slight frown.

'Quite unlike King Bharat's notion of an empire, you mean,' shrugged Bhishm. 'He did not wish to "own" or rule a single homogeneous empire where all bowed down to him or surrendered to his suzerainty. His idea of a nation was a heterogeneous empire based on plurality, with each kingdom having independent rulers. Then there were also the rishis...'

'Rishis?' she frowned. 'Why, did they become warriors?'

'No, they had other weapons—knowledge and wisdom. They united the country through their words and works. They travelled all over, from one country to another, spreading the same message of knowledge, wisdom and spirituality, crossing borders; they were not stopped but welcomed by each king in every country.'

For a fleeting moment, Satyavati thought of Parashar who called himself a travelling teacher. Her son, Krishna Dwaipayan, would be doing the same with him...

She blinked. 'So rishis and kings, the two most powerful people in society, in the country, unifying the nation in their own way,' she murmured. She recalled how Parashar had injured his leg in a war. 'But even rishis can't stop wars.'

'War never serves any purpose except to assuage the greed and ego of the king,' he said. 'It takes just one person to upset the balance.'

'And who is it right now?' she prompted.

'You can say no one, or you can say everyone. All are

prepared, but it takes one small step for a stampede. Like Ugrayudh. He had to be killed to save the peace.'

'So by killing him in this hall, you averted a war?' she said, her eyes thoughtful, her forefinger pressed to her lower lip. 'Won't anyone challenge you?'

Bhishm tilted his head, a small smile playing on his lips. 'I'm afraid not. He was more hated than I am,' he drawled. 'But it can change the delicate balance right now.'

'Who is it that we need to guard against most?' she asked.

His eyes grew solemn again. 'Most powerful right now is King Vasu of Chedi.' He paused, noticing her flinch. 'He calls himself an emperor now, and is spreading his tentacles through all his sons. Matsya is already the king of his new kingdom. Vrihadrath, his oldest son from Queen Girika, is now the king of Magadh. His other sons—Pratyagrah, Kusamva and Mavella—are also governors at various places. But they are not a threat only because ... well, my father and he were friends,' he said wryly.

'In politics, there are no friends; only allies,' retorted Satyavati. 'Why wouldn't King Vasu attack the Kurus?'

'Because you are his daughter, and you are now a Kuru queen,' said Bhishm bluntly.

She felt the floor swim, his words throwing her off balance. It was the first time he had voiced her secret. She was shaking inside, but kept her voice firm.

'Unacknowledged,' she said softly.

'Yet, still his daughter. The fact that he will not touch Hastinapur is acknowledgment of this,' returned Bhishm equably, his face inscrutable. 'Marriages and children are reasons enough to form political and economic alliances. We need never fear him. He is...'

'Family?' she asked nimbly.

'Yes,' he nodded slowly. 'King Vasu has also instructed the same to all his sons.'

'My brothers! Suddenly half the royal houses are my family now,' she laughed self-deprecatingly. She paused, and then said, 'It was not that I was ashamed or fearful of telling Shantanu the truth about my parentage...' She looked honestly into his eyes. 'I was wary of Shantanu's reaction. King Vasu was his friend, and I did not want to upset their relation or the political ties.'

Bhishm nodded thoughtfully, impressed with her political acuity. 'Your trade treaty with the king of Surasen worked wonderfully. Both of you agreed to squeeze out the common enemy—the king of Kasi—through a food grain sanction,' he said, tactfully changing the subject. 'Now, with Ugrayudh dead, both North and South Panchal will be our allies. We shall reinstate young Prishat in Panchal; he's hiding in Bhardwaj's ashram, or so my spies say. That leaves Gandhar and Kamboj in the north, but Uncle Bahlik has handled that and they are *his* allies. So is Sindhu. And in the east, it's Kosala and the Angas...'

'Both are under King Vrihadrath of Magadh, who is my half-brother. It is Kasi I wanted squashed!' she said virulently. 'That's why I had asked the king of Surasen if he would comply. He was shocked initially, but the idea quickly grew on him, and he was ready to sign the treaty that very day! We trapped Kasi that way.'

'Kasi is our enemy and always will be...' Bhishm faltered.

She nodded, pressing her lips and placing a fingertip on the middle of the lower one. The Kasi king had not forgiven Bhishm for breaking the marriage alliance with his daughter. 'We could draw Videha into new talks. Invite them over. Let them know that our spies have information that Kasi is stockpiling weapons against them for a future attack on their mightiest neighbour,' she recommended dryly.

Bhishm raised his brows in frank admiration.

'Videha becomes our new ally and a cornered Kasi is reined in,' she said and shrugged one elegant shoulder.

He felt much more relaxed. The more he listened to her explain the plan, the more confident he became of success.

'But you yourself are in a vulnerable position now,' he cautioned. 'You will be wooed by other mighty kings, more interested in the crown than you,' he stated brutally. 'As Uncle said, it's a bloodless double coup—the enemy gets the crown and the queen.'

'I shall never remarry,' she said unequivocally. 'I know that if I remarry, it will be dangerous. I will not gain a husband but lose Hastinapur to some king,' she said wryly. 'It is convenient to believe that a queen needs a husband to fight wars and make political decisions for her—that she is incapable of taking any of her own.'

'I serve you instead, Mother,' he murmured, mockery in his voice.

Was he laughing at her or being ironic, as always? With seeming nonchalance, she continued, 'All that is expected of the queen is to provide male heirs to further the royal bloodline.'

Bhishm looked grave. 'But heirs have been murdered, too! We avoided one battle today, but, right now, our nation has a pack of hungry kings roaming, searching. This is just the beginning. Each one of us, every powerful royal dynasty, is trying to take over, to terrorize its own country and the world with their armies. Any powerful king can now send his army and start a war. Ugrayudh tried it today through you, but this will go on, get worse till one day we will be killing each other on some huge battlefield...'

'Can't it be averted?' she whispered in a shocked undertone. 'How can war be heroic; why bestow it with grandeur when all it leaves behind is a trail of blood, carnage and suffering?' she mulled. 'A war leaves widows, not dead heroes on the battlefield. An entire generation of people and society get subjected to its endless horror, killing not just warriors but women and children, old and young, scholars and statesmen, thinkers and workers. All that is left is a ravaged country full of weeping women, children and crippled men!'

She had always hated violence, and war was a flagrant justification of it. Ugrayudh had been defiant and died for it. She had seen Bhishm putting down a man in cold blood, without remorse or restraint. War and violence, war and women; the lines blurred in her mind, convincing her, providing her now with a valid, deeper reason for her reluctance to remarry—the idea was preposterous and had never occurred to her. She had to keep her crown and throne safe for her sons. She would not lose all that she had gained. She would not lose her powers to some man, some king.

Her biggest fear was that the throne would slip from her hands. She would never lose her own independence and her sovereignty as queen, she swore to herself. She would not allow any man, marriage or motherhood to erode her power. She had to decide her priorities as she sat on the throne. And she was far too intelligent to compromise herself.

'I am married to Hastinapur. I need no king, *I* will be its queen,' she said slowly to the man she knew would protect Hastinapur and her all his life. She needed no king. She had Bhishm.

The Regent

Bhishm was restrained by the fear of appearing sentimental and ridiculous. When he wanted to be affectionate or to say anything tender, he did not know how to express himself naturally. And it was that fear, together with lack of practice, that prevented him from being able to express with perfect clarity what was passing in his mind, his heart, all this time, all these years.

He allowed a sigh to escape his lips. He had never ordinary feelings for Satyavati. He had seen her in all her shades—deceitful and despairing, loving and bitter, pained and proud—but when he saw her with her boys, Bhishm knew that was when she felt most fulfilled. There was youth, freshness and joyousness in the way she loved her sons unconditionally.

As he did, too. Five years had passed since his father had died. Circumstances had changed. He was no longer afraid of coming across as sentimental, and gave himself up entirely to the fatherly, or rather idolatrous, feeling roused in him by the two little boys. His thirst for normal, ordinary life became stronger and more acute as time went on, but it was cut short by the princes, and he found what he needed with them. He adored the two boys; he could go on living in those twin pairs of crinkled dark eyes, their silky, curly hair, and those dimpled pink hands which stroked his face so lovingly and clung around his neck.

He gave a start. He realized that he was even dreaming about being back with them once he finished his work. It was late morning, and he was quietly listing out the daily chores of the court, but he could not but help look out of the window to catch a glimpse of Satyavati chatting with the boys. He saw how her impatience died down as she tolerantly tended to each of them—the precocious and fair Chitrangad, and the dark, sickly, six-year-old Virya. She fed them with her own hands, never assigning the task to any maid. She gave them their baths, put them to bed, and never took her eyes off them for nights together. She was devoted to them.

The world had gotten kinder to her now. He supposed it was more to do with her personal efforts to win the people over than her being the widow of his father. The people now acknowledged her as Queen Satyavati and not Daseyi, as she had been disparagingly called for so long. Again, it was not that the moniker had died with her father, Dashraj, who had passed away soon after his own father, but because today she was more Satyavati than Daseyi. She was the Kuru queen, mother of the heirs and champion of the people. It had been a trying task, with the public and the nobles both casting aspersions and accusations on her intentions and integrity, but she had eventually won them all over.

But behind her charm was a ruthless efficiency that had brought about a miracle in the palace and the kingdom.

She tolerated no slackness, nor lazy service. She had made this palace the best in the country, and she was determined that it would remain the best. She left the running of the palace to highly trusted experts, but she supervised them all, correcting and making suggestions.

Each morning, she left her chamber and visited every room, hall and court of the palace, smiling, but constantly checking for possible faults. She began with the royal wash house, exchanging a nice word with the chambermaids who adored her; then she would go to the cellar to inspect the wine and the victuals, after which she visited the three kitchens, and discussed the day's meals with the royal head cook.

The morning's rituals took time, after which, she would come into the court and speak, with her earthy accent and unpretentious attitude, to the nobles and the ministers who were sufficiently charmed.

She actively looked into the matters of the court since his father's death, a decision precipitated by the Ugrayudh incident and the determination to never be used as a political pawn again.

Finally, she would settle the young princes and join him to discuss the court matters of the day. It was with shock that he had realized that he looked forward to her inputs. He was often taken aback by her sharp mind; her brilliance dazzled him, but he preferred not to let her know. As they worked, sometimes until late in the evening, her mind often ran on excessive energy and excitement, always eager, curious yet cautious.

He inhaled the faint smell of musk and knew she had arrived in the room.

'How is it today?' she frowned, with a tilt of her head, pursing her lips and absently tapping a fingertip on the lower lip. For the first time, he noticed, she was wearing pearls and not gold. He suddenly realized he was noticing things about her that were new to him: like her string of pearls, the way she arranged the angavastra on her shoulder, how the grey-white sari complemented her skin, or how her calm, intelligent eyes flashed when provoked.

Her eyes widened as she pored over the information supplied by his spies posted in every village of the kingdom.

'Each one of them hopes to invade Hastinapur,' she grimaced. 'They want to, but they can't, as your reputation as a warrior is getting more fearsome by the day, Dev! Yet you claim to hate wars.'

'I attack only when provoked,' he explained laconically.

'Defence, never offence,' she smiled. 'We win, Dev, yet we win.'

The 'we' added a strange ring of togetherness, belongingness and agreement, a new cordiality and confidence in each other. They did everything together. There was a camaraderie between them, a fondness and a fellowship neither denied.

'And, yes, there's this person, Dron. I wanted to talk to you about him,' she remarked, a frown pleating her smooth forehead. 'Who is he and what is he doing here at our palace for the past one week?'

Bhishm was used to her forthright manner of speaking. It sounded imperious to some, and plain arrogant to most. But he never found it off-putting, as she often did not mean it; she was simply blunt and had no time to waste.

'Dron is the son of Rishi Bhardwaj and the apsara Ghritachi...'

'Another story of romance and quick lust? What did he do? Leave her with child?' she interrupted, warily.

'She left him,' he corrected her. 'With the son to keep.'

As I left Vyas with Parashar, Satyavati flushed instinctively.

Bhishm noticed her face tightening with sudden tension. *She is hiding something*, he was quick to perceive, but had no intention to prod further. *Is it another secret she hopes I will not find out? She will tell me one day when the time is right; I am sure of it.*

'In fact, he got his name because of his birth,' he continued smoothly. 'It is quite a dramatic story, as dramatic as his name. It seems when Bhardwaj caught a glimpse of Ghritachi, who had come to bathe at the river, he forgot to perform his morning ablutions and er...' he paused, wondering how to explain further discreetly.

She grinned. 'Don't say that he ejaculated and kept the

semen in what ... a dron ... a vessel made of leaves, and thus that name!' she said with her incorrigible candour that made Bhishm smile.

He nodded and then his eyes narrowed at her brooding expression.

'It sounds similar to my story!' she scoffed.

It came off easily now with him, without shame or pain, anger or aggression. She could tell him everything.

'The same story but a different apsara...' she added harshly.

'That's how his story goes,' Bhishm shrugged. 'He remained with his father, who got him to master the art of war weaponry and martial arts, especially archery.'

'That's unusual,' she stated. 'A rishi knowing warfare. Like Rishi Sharadwan, Kripa's father.'

'Dron is considered something of a genius. He is a student of Parashuram...'

'Like you, which means he, too, must be exceptional,' she said swiftly, without hesitation.

Bhishm's eyebrows went up. 'Praise?' he murmured. 'No, he was not groomed entirely by Guru Parashuram. When Dron came to know that Parashuram was distributing his possessions to the Brahmins, Dron approached him but arrived too late. Parashuram was left with just his weapons and he offered them to Dron, the weapons as well as the knowledge of how to use them. Gleaning this rare knowledge and all his weapons, Dron thus received the title of *acharya*,' remarked Bhishm.

'But why is he at our court to train Chitrangad and Virya?' she queried, slightly puzzled. 'They are being taught by Kripacharya...'

'No, Dronacharya is in Hastinapur not to teach, but to wed Kripi,' he said shortly.

She glanced at him incredulously. One look at his sure, stern expression, and she knew the decision had been made.

'And you agreed?' she demanded. 'You think he is good enough for her?'

'Yes,' he drew in a long breath. 'He is supposed to be cleverer than Kripa, and that's something.'

'But is he as smart as Kripi? That's more important!'

'She likes him,' he shrugged.

'Well, that's more important than anything else,' she agreed. 'I am surprised that she said "yes" to this man. She has refused so many proposals previously,' she started hesitantly, not wanting to vex Bhishm.

He was excessively defensive about Kripi, though the feisty girl needed no protection whatsoever. She looked after herself well enough with her sharp tongue.

'Where did they meet?'

'At Rishi Bhardwaj's ashram,' supplied Bhishm.

Satyavati was surprised. 'As early as that? She was a child then,' she said.

'Kripi continued to visit the ashram even later, as a teacher, and that's how she got to know him better. As she got to know Prince Drupad, too. The three are said to be very close.'

Satyavati quickly surmised the situation. 'Drupad is the Panchal prince, King Prishat's son, isn't he? When you killed Ugrayudh Paurav, Drupad's father got back his throne. They owe us,' she said, a defiant glint in her eyes. 'And now this friendship of these three bodes well for us, too.'

Bhishm nodded, the lock of hair falling forward. 'Yes, Panchal is a peaceful neighbour now.'

'But that's unusual—a friendship between a rishi and a prince,' she commented. 'It makes for good politics, though. I presume Dron will be the royal rishi with the Panchals soon?'

'I doubt that,' Bhishm shook his head. 'Dron's father, Rishi Bhardwaj, is the royal *purohit* of Kasi since the times of King Divodas. But King Prishat and Rishi Bhardwaj were great friends. Rumours are that he took refuge in his ashram when he was hounded by Ugrayudh. Their fathers being friends, Drupad used to go to Bhardwaj's ashram to play with him.'

'So Dron is now without any royal patronage?' she asked shrewdly.

'But, pray, why are you asking so many questions?' Bhishm's eyes narrowed in sudden suspicion.

'To be aware of the changing relations between kings and their rishis!' she replied lightly.

'No ... you are checking whether he is truly eligible for our Kripi,' he retorted with a knowing smile. 'But whatever he does, or wherever he goes, Kripi is determined to marry him,' he sighed, betraying his anxiety. He *was* upset about the news—not because Dron would be an unsuitable suitor, but because he was inordinately fond of Kripi.

'It's time she did; she's already well past marriageable age. Most girls her age have children by now,' he said, forcing a small laugh.

'But you had ambitions for her, didn't you?' she guessed shrewdly.

'Yes, she is a bright girl, destined to be a scholar,' he nodded. 'I thought she would pursue her studies and start her own ashram one day, especially for women, like Gargi once did. Marriage, I am afraid, may kill that dream.'

'It was *your* dream for her, Dev, not hers,' she pointed out mildly. 'She wants to marry. It's her choice.'

'Hmm,' he murmured resignedly.

'And she could still do that after marriage,' she said dubiously.

One glance at Dron when he arrived at court reaffirmed her doubts.

'He is ... he is ... so *poor*!' Satyavati whispered, aghast at the young rishi's appearance.

Bhishm raised an eyebrow. 'He is a rishi, not a king! He is meant to wear clothes of bark, not silk,' he said, but she could hear the smile in his voice. He was laughing at her again, but he could not understand what was troubling her.

She tightened her lips in impatience, scrutinizing the young man standing before them. He was a man of few words, saturnine and lean, of average height, probably as tall as Kripi, a disconcerting intensity emanating from his flashing eyes. As if they were perpetually angry with the world.

'Compliments and good wishes, Kripi. But you never told me you had a man in mind to marry!' she teased when Kripi visited her in her chamber that evening. 'What a huge secret!'

The hard lines of Kripi's mouth melted into a soft smile and she blushed. 'I was waiting for Dron to complete his studies,' she said.

Satyavati frowned. 'He is still studying? Does he not want to settle down, now that he is going to marry?'

'I don't mind,' replied Kripi tersely, resenting the peremptory tone. 'I have waited long enough for him.'

'But he needs to work to earn money!' exclaimed Satyavati.

'He intends to start his own ashram where he will teach,' returned Kripi, her eyes turning stormy.

Satyavati threw Kripi a worried look, wondering whether she should voice her doubts to the woman she knew would not take kindly to what she had to say. But she said it nevertheless.

'Will you be able to live as he does?' she said. 'He is poor, Kripi, and you have lived all your life in this palace...'

'Not as a princess,' snapped Kripi.

She ignored the girl's rudeness. 'You were regarded and respected as a reputed scholar at court, a priestess of royal position,' she reminded her gently. 'Dron might be an intellectual and learned rishi, but he is a man of no means. I am not questioning him, but are you prepared to live a life of poverty henceforth?' she asked bluntly.

Kripi resented the words more than her tone. 'I shan't be marrying for money,' she scowled, '...or fame or status, but love. I don't want to be a queen, but a wife,' she added with a jeer. 'But I don't expect you to understand because, let me be frank like you, *you* did not marry for love, did you?'

'It's not me we are talking about, but *you*, Kripi,' she said, placating. 'I am genuinely worried, and not disrespectful towards your decision. I am sorry if I have overstepped the bounds of acceptable protocol. I speak as your friend, not as your queen,' she said.

She saw Kripi smile sardonically. 'But you were never my friend, Queen Daseyi. For me you will always be that, though, for the world now, you are Queen Satyavati. I was appointed to help you, educate you and groom you. I did just that. We were never *friends*,' she finished with cold candour.

'But I consider you mine, and it is my duty to warn you,' she said. 'It will not be easy marrying a poor person. I know what poverty is, Kripi.'

'Is that why you married King Shantanu?' sneered Kripi.

'Why does it come down to me, dear?' smiled Satyavati. 'I have lived my life; it's yours which is going to start afresh. If you want to marry into poverty, so be it. But I will still say that following one's heart does not always end in happiness.'

'Yes, you have lived your life by depriving Bhishm!' returned Kripi scathingly.

Satyavati was disturbed at the raw rage glittering in the

girl's eyes. Kripi had always been hostile to her, but she had underestimated the depth of her hatred. For once, Satyavati found herself floundering for words. She decided to remain quiet, and not aggravate the situation.

Kripi was more enraged at her silence. *This was the woman who had ruined her brother; how had he forgiven her so easily?* She had noticed the friendship between them, and she resented them both for it. With renewed anger, Kripi remembered what this woman had done to him: She had destroyed him, and yet she still had him. A familiar flame of fury burst alive. Kripi scrutinized Satyavati closely, that dark, haughty face gloating, smiling...

'You think you have it all, don't you, Daseyi?' Kripi's voice turned vicious, making Satyavati glance at her with surprise. 'The crown without the burden of your king, the kingdom, the people who give you the respect and love you yearned for, Dev eating out of your hands, your two sons—the heirs of Hastinapur... But for how long, dear?' Kripi had the pleasure of seeing Satyavati's face redden. 'I shall go from here, but I can never wish you well, Daseyi. You could never charm me; never!' she spat. 'Don't push your good luck too far, too long. It might turn against you. The universe gives you answers in strange ways.'

With a silent sigh, Satyavati decided to confront the accusations.

'We are not friends, agreed,' said Satyavati. 'But that is what makes it easier perhaps to be frank with each other. I do care for you, Kripi, though you don't believe me. I care for you because you are so precious to Dev,' she continued tonelessly. 'As you were to Shantanu.'

'You mention King Shantanu as if he is an afterthought,' retorted Kripi. 'In fact, you rarely mention him these days. After all, you were married to him!'

Satyavati looked at her, a strange expression on her face. 'Kripi, don't think I didn't pay for that mistake.'

Kripi was surprised at her outspokenness. Satyavati continued, 'A girl has to live. And it isn't always as easy as it looks. A girl can make a mistake, marry the wrong man, looking for something that is not there—security or whatever it is,' she shrugged.

'You are talking about yourself or advising me?' laughed Kripi, sneeringly. 'But you did not need any love to marry!'

'Don't be so cynical, so early and so young, Kripi. You will be surprised at how many girls marry to find a decent home, a simple roof over their heads. Especially girls whose arms are tired of fending off unwanted leers, fighting off poverty and the groping optimists that they pass by on the streets and dark alleys. You wouldn't understand, Kripi.'

'You had a home, yet you intruded on Dev's home!' argued Kripi, refusing to melt.

'I settled for whatever I could get. I thought it would be better than what I had.'

Kripi threw her a knowing look. 'You *are* clever, Daseyi. And you are tough and wise. I suppose when you married King Shantanu, you thought you could get your hands on wealth and prestige ... you were so right!' she said, her eyes glittering with dislike. 'You are a smart, ruthless woman who wrapped first King Shantanu and now Dev around your pretty finger! Why do you call him Dev when it was *you* who turned him into Bhishm? What right do you have over him? You are his *mother* by marriage, by deceit!'

'I simply don't dare to call him by the name the world now knows him by and calls out with such reverence. He got it because of me, and it's like a taunting reminder of what he was made to do. I know you hate me for what I did to Dev, and I can never forgive myself either,' she paused.

'I live each day but I cannot forget that I am living on *his* borrowed rights and *his* borrowed throne. I never thought I could loathe myself—but I do. Each time I see *him*...' her voice trembled as she tried to collect her emotions. 'I can't tell this to him or to anyone else; no matter how much I beg for forgiveness, it will be inadequate,' she muttered under her breath, wanting to ease the crushing weight by her admission, hoping to relieve herself of some guilt.

Kripi was too stunned to speak. For a moment, she could not believe her ears or her eyes, and was immediately suspicious of the other woman's motives. Was she fooling her to soften her up? Her cautious distrust of Satyavati came rushing back, but as she slowly assimilated what she had heard and seen, all that her shocked eyes could register was the sight of a woman without her mask of pride. How many were brave enough to say it in words? Satyavati had thrown open her veil of ten years and more.

Kripi gave a start. She could not but recollect all that she had noticed but preferred to ignore. She recalled that swift glow of delight that often dawned on Satyavati's otherwise haughty face whenever Dev entered the room, or when she heard his voice and his footsteps. Or those moments when Kripi noticed him, patiently waiting at the door of Satyavati's chambers, ready to accompany her to the court every morning. Or when he stood watching her as she tended to the young princes. Or when he courteously held out her shawl for her by the hall staircase, adjusting it neatly while she rested her hand on his shoulder, her eyes lowered, hoping to hide...

Kripi forced herself to ask the one question she had avoided—was their closeness the reason for her resentment towards Satyavati? With a startled realization, she knew the answer was 'yes'.

Kripi often wondered if Dev ever longed to be in love, to have a wife and child of his own. But though she was one of those closest to him, someone he could bare his heart to, Kripi had never had the courage to ask him. *Did he ever dream of what he could have had, and all that he lost forever, as he lies awake at night, gathering them all as his, tenderly cherishing them in his dreams, loving them and begging them of destiny?* she had wondered many times.

Kripi knew that Bhishm could never dare to hope or think of love. In his quiet way, he considered Satyavati as significant to him, just as he was important for her.

Both of them had long realized that, for ruins like them, happiness was only to be reserved for their dreams.

The Grief

'You are too easy on your sons,' Bhishm accused Satyavati with exasperation. Chitrangad had just thrown a violent tantrum, which Satyavati had endured quietly. It was the cold whiplash in Bhishm's voice that had brought the young boy to his senses.

'You are not a child, Prince. You will be king soon,' Bhishm warned the young lad in front of him, his voice dangerously soft.

Satyavati knew Bhishm's terse voice was worse than his roar, and she did not intervene. Only Dev could handle this boy. 'And if you do not learn to rein in your temper and temperament, Prince, I still have the power to see to it that you don't sit on the throne!'

Chitrangad threw his mother a belligerent glare but quickly lowered his eyes. 'The first step is to be polite, then kind, helpful and humble. Do *I* need to teach you that too now?'

Chitrangad was a good warrior, and he had quickly learnt war and warfare from his brother. But the boy had a vicious temper, and was yet to master the craft of administration and the art of diplomacy. *That temper*, Bhishm was certain, *would prove more dangerous and damaging for himself than others. Few ill-tempered people realized that temper often corrodes one's own reason. Rage was a parasite, feeding in and on the person it inhabited. And his mother seemed to encourage it by her overindulgence.* Bhishm had often admonished her, but she had shrugged it off as a family trait. She had a temper, too, she reasoned.

He had tried to make Chitrangad as capable as a king should be. Chitrangad fought with him in numerous battles and was a brilliant warrior, helping Bhishm expand the kingdom and defeat the enemy at the gates and in the battlefield.

Chitrangad, however, still relied heavily on his elder brother. The real reins of rule and power would remain with Bhishm till he thought the scion was a capable successor, able to take decisions as efficiently as expected from a benevolent king. And after that, Bhishm planned to leave Hastinapur, knowing that it would be in safe hands.

But Satyavati had other plans.

'I wanted to discuss Chitrangad's marriage with you,' she started, stubbornly.

'No,' he said as strongly. 'He is just sixteen; he is too young.'

'He is old enough to be a king, so why can he not have a wife?' she returned hotly.

'You just want him to have heirs,' he sighed.

'Don't dismiss it as some illogical whim of mine. It is necessary.'

He heard the worry in her voice.

'What is it?' he asked perceptively, his eyes thoughtful, his tone softer.

'Chitrangad is young and strong, unlike Virya,' she started uncertainly. 'Virya is so ill most of the time that he has been nicknamed Vichitravirya. I am not too sure he can ever have children; that's why I would like to have Chitrangad married off. If we start looking now, he can get married by the end of this year.'

'And you can be a grandmother by next year!' he quipped.

But he understood what she was implying, and grudgingly concurred—Kurus would be stronger, in every way, with the lineage of Chitrangad rather than Virya, the weaker of the two.

He nodded slowly, as was often his habit. 'You may be right,' he conceded. 'I shall have a list of eligible princesses ready for you within this week.'

'Eligible in the political context, too,' she reiterated, throwing him a hard look. 'I don't want just a pretty face. She should have enough political clout to consolidate the Kurus as the most influential empire.'

But three days later, Chitrangad was killed in duel with a gandharv.

Bhishm was not in Hastinapur at that time, and when he got the news, he started back immediately.

Never before had Bhishm been so shaken; not even when his mother had left him or when his father had died. He was used to war and violence, death and despair, but he had never considered that he would have to witness the death of his beloved boy. Bhishm blinked hard at his unshed tears. An image of the handsome boy flashed in his weeping mind: tall and slim, the fair, chiselled face with long, wavy hair, and easy laugh.

Rage grabbed at his throat, and he could not console himself. *How has Satyavati reacted to her son's death?* The thought sent a chill of cold fear and worry down his spine. He knew she would be devastated.

Bhishm was barely aware of the journey back to Hastinapur. It was silent, as still as the palace, which was shrouded in darkness and gloom. He raced to her chamber. One look at her and he knew she was broken. He approached her with concern.

Satyavati stood motionless as he drew near, her face ashen, and her eyes pleading. And then she slapped him hard, his head jerking back, the imprint of her fingers and fury raw on his cheek.

'Where were *you* when we needed you the most?' she cried, her voice dissolving in her tears.

The slap did not surprise him. Had he been here in Hastinapur, he could have saved the king, saved his brother from the needless death he had brought upon himself, Bhishm kept telling himself.

It was just the week before that he had to leave Hastinapur to visit a troubled outpost at the border of the kingdom. As regent, it seemed more appropriate for him to go rather than the king himself, and he was to return within a few days. But a gandharv chose that opportune moment to challenge the king. *And for what*, thought Bhishm. *A name?* Chitrangad was said to be such a great warrior and so successful that the king of the gandharvs, Chitrangad, challenged him to fight at Kurukshetra as he claimed that two kings with the same name could not exist at the same time. And so they had fought their absurd duel. It had lasted for two days, before Hastinapur's king died on the battlefield.

Satyavati began to weep quietly. 'When the gandharv threw the challenge, Chitrangad was wary, but he agreed only because the brute was threatening to destroy the city,' she recounted, her voice toneless in numbed grief. 'Like a true Kuru king—and your true protégé that he was—Chitrangad did not want any unnecessary carnage. He opted to fight the gandharv single-handedly, confident that he could defeat him. But that gandharv managed to kill him with deceit!' she choked, but then her voice rose. 'He killed my son, Dev! He took away my everything—my son, my hopes, all my dreams!'

She broke into sobs and his heart jumped into his throat, seeing her so broken, the anguish raw in her eyes. Chitrangad had been her fier one weakness.

He had not seen her shed a single tear when his father died. Not even at her own father's funeral. The last time she had cried was when King Vasu had visited them, but those had been tears of anger and humiliation. This was pure, undiluted grief.

'This is my punishment, Dev,' she muttered. She kept shaking her head, which she was holding in her hands. 'This is what I get for what I did to *you*! My son had to suffer for my sins!'

'Stop it!' he said, shocked. She stared back, her face glistening with tears and a sheen of sweat, her icy, black eyes almost opaque in their intensity, which terrified him. That haunting look seared into his soul.

He sat there for a moment, struggling against his own tears. Finally, he gently patted her hand and waited till she fell into a fitful sleep. He got up, staring down at her tear-soaked face, and made his way out of her chambers.

It was an endless torture watching her suffer. When she sat up night after night, awake yet empty and dry-eyed, staring at the doorway, hoping to see Chitrangad walk through it, or when she shuddered and turned pale when she saw his armour, Bhishm suffered with her.

This was not the Satyavati he knew.

Her hair was loose, not tied in an elaborate bun as it used to be. She wore the same robes for days. Her face was drawn and wan. As he studied her, he realized with a start that she actually looked her age now. She was as old as he was, but she had always appeared younger, because of how animated and engaged she was. There was not a single strand of grey in her raven mane. Now, her anguish had aged her. She would just lie on her bed, wishing for bad things to happen in her life, and cursing herself and her past.

Bhishm was frightened for her, wondering if she would ever make her way back from the pain the loss of her son had caused her, swerving fragilely on the precipice of sanity. Even the presence of Virya did not seem to help. This was quite unlike her.

He would have to lance this festering wound as quickly as possible; but how was it to be done?

Every day, Bhishm tried a new way to wean her out from the abyss of darkness. He talked to her and told her anecdotes of his family, hoping to provoke her into a reaction. Nothing worked.

Her behaviour became erratic, leaving him bemused. Some days she refused to dress up, but on other days she would order expensive silks for herself. On some days, she could not resist glancing into a looking glass if she passed one and neatened her hair; on other days she would walk without looking anywhere. While on some days she would eat a feast, on other days she would not swallow a morsel.

Five months had already passed since the tragedy, but she did not seem to notice the passage of time.

'So be it, then,' she murmured woodenly when she was informed of Virya's ill-health, bedridden this time with high fever and a relentless cough. 'He, too, might die; he is consumptive.'

Until five months ago, she was the only dependable aspect in his life. He had learnt to trust her, her abilities, her motives and intentions. But seeing her condition, he feared that he was going to lose her as well.

It was more than that—he missed her. Daunted as he was by her quicksilver mind, he needed her—her presence, her counsel, her friendship.

One day, he found himself sitting beside her as she cried.

'Shall I call in the doctor again?' he asked gently.

'No, there's no need; it's nothing, just a headache!' she said, and she looked up at him, her face tear-stained.

He offered her some fruit to eat.

Pale and worn, with her head propped up by pillows, she ate tentatively. Raising her eyebrows, she kept looking guiltily, first at her maid, Vibha, and then at him. When she finished what was on her plate, she appeared livelier.

'You look thin, Dev,' she murmured, as she tilted her head in her usual manner, and looked at him with concern.

He had missed that caring look.

He looked away, not wanting to think about it, feeling relieved that she had eaten well and spoken one long sentence to him after many days.

'And how is Virya now?' she said abruptly, sitting up straight.

'Better,' he said. 'The doctor is with him constantly.'

'He should be,' she retorted sharply, pressing her lips and tapping an impatient finger on the lower one. 'He has to nurse the heir to the kingdom back to robust health. Dev, when do we start training him as the new king?'

That's when Bhishm knew she was all right and suitably recovered.

The Swayamvar

'The king of Kasi is holding a swayamvar for his three daughters,' began Satyavati.

Bhishm at once registered the tone of her voice.

'He has not sent an invitation to Hastinapur,' she persisted belligerently.

Bhishm patiently put down his quill. 'You know why,' he said quietly.

She gave an exasperated snort, tapping her finger furiously on her lip. 'Because you could not marry his sister,' she said candidly.

She saw him tightening his jaw. 'I don't expect him to invite us.'

'I don't want to be a guest,' she said, her eyes flashing. 'Virya should have been invited as a suitor.'

Bhishm raised his eyebrows. 'Virya is barely sixteen!' he said, reprovingly.

'You had the same argument for Chitrangad. I shouldn't have listened to you!' she gave a decisive shake of her head. 'Had he gotten married then, he could have had a child before he got killed.'

'An heir,' said Bhishm grimly, wondering again if her son's death had made her cold-hearted. Was she regretting the absence of an heir from Chitrangad, or mourning the loss of her son? Be it because of her initial hardships or her innate nature, Bhishm had long realized that Satyavati was unrelenting, especially when it came to asserting her authority. Essentially unsentimental, she was someone who could plan ahead dispassionately, while setting her grief aside.

He remembered something that had happened soon

after Chitrangad's death. The priest of a local temple had stopped the daily worship when his young daughter died unexpectedly. Satyavati, when she came to hear of the complaints, personally rode out to his hut and, while offering her condolences, offered some advice as well. The priest, utterly overawed by the bereaved queen mother, had promptly opened the doors of the temple that very day.

'A queen needs to be more sensible than just sensitive,' she said in brief explanation.

But had her unbridled grief trampled upon the compassion she was capable of? She looked older, her eyes were harder and her lips seemed to have forgotten how to smile.

'I have mourned enough for him,' she said harshly, reading his thoughts. 'But we cannot escape our responsibility to secure an heir for the throne. We didn't act on time for Chitrangad, and I don't want to repeat the mistake this time with Virya. He is of age, he is the king, and the king needs his queen. Or queens,' she emphasized. Immediately after Chitrangad's death, Bhishm had taken it upon himself to groom the young Virya as the next king. It helped Bhishm recover from his grief. Virya was a bright boy and, despite his poor health, quickly picked up administration of the kingdom; and with his amiable nature and fluency in languages, he turned out to be a good diplomat, besides mastering weapons and warfare under Bhishm's stern tutelage.

Two months ago, he had been anointed as the new king, but the reins of power were shared by Satyavati and Bhishm.

'None of the three princesses is going to marry Virya,' he said dryly. 'It is a swayamvar. The princesses get to choose their own grooms.'

'A swayamvar for which we were not invited,' she said. 'Kasi will have to pay dearly for this insult!'

'This is not just about affairs of the heart; it's also the affairs of the state,' warned Bhishm. 'You can't wage war against Kasi because the father of the brides did not invite your son!'

'You make it sound petty and personal, Dev,' said Satyavati calmly. 'But it is an open affront to us. He has called all the kings of the country but us. Is that not humiliating for Hastinapur? For the Kurus?' she taunted.

'Yes, but it *is* personal,' he admitted in a toneless voice. 'I have hurt the king of Kasi once, by not marrying his sister, when it was promised and arranged.'

Bhishm struggled to keep his face straight, his eyes flat and cold, but a storm raged within him, remembering the untold distress he had bestowed on the unfortunate girl and her family. 'I am guilty as accused; I *am* the offender.'

Satyavati bit her lip. Bhishm avoided talking about his past, and his wedding was a forbidden subject; yet, she had to bring it up again.

'What happened to her?' she asked softly, her dark eyes probing.

He shrugged, his broad shoulders slumped in sudden dejection. 'She got married later to the king of Vidarbha,' he said ambivalently.

'All's well that ends well. So, why does the father hold a grudge against you? '

'Bruised honour,' corrected Bhishm. 'If they have not sent an invitation, it is their right, their choice.'

His expression grew taut and severe, as if to end the topic of conversation.

Satyavati felt the atmosphere suddenly thicken with tension, but she cut through it.

'But this time it's not about you, it's about Virya,' she said, her face hardening. 'Virya is an eligible suitor...'

'He is *not* eligible,' said Bhishm strongly. 'Neither as a king nor as a husband! He is consumptive and has started drinking, too. We need to curb that...'

Satyavati was shocked, then angry. 'What are you talking about? You have trained him yourself!'

'That doesn't mean he is an able king,' he said succinctly. 'You forced him on the throne, in spite of my misgivings. I am talking about his health. You should know better. He is a sickly boy. You have nursed him so devotedly all these years,' he continued, his voice more gentle. 'Frankly, his ill health does not permit him to be on the throne. I told you earlier. So did Kripa...'

'How does mere illness prevent a rightful heir to sit on the throne?' she said.

Bhishm expelled an exasperated sigh. 'It has happened before. Uncle Devapi, though an exemplary prince, was not allowed on the throne because he had leprosy...'

'My son is ill, not diseased!' she shot back furiously. 'And even if he were, no one, not even *you*, Dev, would have stopped me from crowning Virya as the king. It is *his* right, he is Shantanu's son!'

So was Dev, the taunt swirled in her mind. *He was the rightful heir, never my sons.*

Bhishm lapsed into an abrupt silence, pursing his lips thinly as if to stop a retort. She knew what he could have said—it never stopped echoing in her head.

She raised her chin in defiance. 'I shall send Virya with an army to get all the three girls and marry them here in Hastinapur,' she said curtly, her hands raised as if to end their argument.

He raised his hooded eyes, giving her a look that scared many people. She returned his stare, her eyes as cold and impersonal.

'Virya is not fit enough to battle,' he repeated, after a long pause. 'Just as Chitrangad wasn't up to handling the gandharv alone,' he added deliberately, watching the colour recede from her face. 'Virya need not go; I shall go to Kasi instead.'

She knew what he was implying—that her sons were helpless without him, Hastinapur was defenceless without him. Bhishm was the protector and the destroyer.

'You will get the three princesses?' she said.

It was not a doubt or a request. It was a command.

'Yes,' he replied impassively, but a nerve twitched at his temple. 'I shall go uninvited and take them away uninvited from their swayamvar—I couldn't be more unchivalrous!' he said with some difficulty.

She nodded.

He persisted. 'Would *you* have liked it?' he asked. 'It is force!'

He looked visibly disgusted.

She shook her head and said, 'It is an accepted form of marriage, Dev.'

'That is why it's called the rakshas marriage,' he said. 'You are using not just your under-aged son but three innocent girls to fulfil your mad wish. If you want a bride for Virya, surely there are others. We could send forth a formal proposal to any princess he—or more importantly—you wish for!'

'Right now, there are none more eligible than the princesses of Kasi,' she pronounced, her expression impatient. 'Besides, I want Kasi. We tried many ways to subdue them. By marrying all three of them into Hastinapur, Kasi will be solely ours. If the three princesses marry three different suitors, we will be in conflict with them all our lives. This is politics, as you said, Dev, you should know better. We have to seek alliances, not just brides.'

'You *are* a cold-hearted woman,' he rued.

She shrugged. Her face was hard and her eyes were bleak and indifferent. He knew he had no power to hurt her. Her past life had armoured her against contempt.

'Do you think I care about what you say about me? Or the others? Don't forget who I am,' she reminded him. 'I *am* your queen, Regent! I command you and you obey me!' she said arrogantly.

His handsome face showed amused cynicism.

'Yes, I know well who you are, Mother,' he said. 'I am trying to address the mother ... to convince the woman, not the queen. I ask again, would you have liked to be forced to marry someone?' he repeated, his voice insistent.

A memory arose from the depths of her mind—she in that boat with Parashar; she making love to Shantanu. She suppressed a sigh. She had enjoyed neither experience, yet it had been consensual. It was for a purpose, not pleasure.

'What you are contemplating is horrifying,' he continued, his face drawn. 'It is a crime! It's abduction, snatching them away without their consent.'

'Then let there be a duel to win the brides,' she said airily. 'After all, of the eight types of marriages practised by the royals, there is the practice of veershulkaa, when the suitor proves himself valorous and virtuous by carrying away the bride after defeating the other suitors. You can easily defeat all of them, Dev, and win the brides, not snatch them away, as you say.'

She saw him hesitate. 'Or are you too scared to confront the king of Kasi?'

'Don't seek to justify your intentions with my inclinations,' he returned placidly.

Had she gone too far? She had wanted to rile him into action, rouse him from the stand he had stubbornly taken.

In the end, she did succeed. Bhishm continued contemptuously, 'I offered to save Virya, for his life and as my duty as regent. Not my honour, Mother. He will be killed the moment he enters Kasi. It is better I get the princesses.'

~

Bhishm had never visited Kasi before. It rested by the calm waters of the Ganga. He stopped and got down from his chariot and bowed to the river.

'I don't expect your blessings, Ma, for I know that what I am going to do is unforgivable,' he murmured, agony burning in his heart. The waters remained still, not deigning to respond.

He stood motionless for a long time, looking at the silver waters of the river, washed with the tender rays of the rising sun in the horizon.

'If your heart so bleeds, why are you doing it?' the breeze seemed to whisper around him. He could hear his mother speaking to him.

He closed his eyes, his lips pursed, his head bowed.

'For Hastinapur,' he said hoarsely. 'I have given my all to it, and today I give my conscience and my soul.'

'You don't need to,' she said softly, her voice coaxing. 'Come with me, Son. Walk into the waters and end your misery.'

He jerked his head. 'You are telling me to give up my life? And what about my life's goal?' he asked wretchedly.

'I am stopping you from committing a crime,' answered Ganga serenely. 'Your father blessed you with the icchamrityu for a reason—when you realize that your deeds on this earth are over and death is the next step forward. Your work is done here, Son. You have inflicted grave pain on yourself till now, but now, under the burden of your loyalty to the throne of the Kurus, you might wreak injustice on others without even realizing it. You did what you could for your father, your kingdom, your vow. But not anymore,' she said.

'I cannot *not* protect the crown. Who is there after Virya?' he muttered, but he did not sound convincing even to himself. 'He has no heirs. I have to find a suitable wife for him.'

'Is abduction the answer?'

'The princesses may agree. Or I shall win them,' he argued, his voice earnest; but again, he feared he was giving himself false assurances.

'Hopefully,' she whispered; and then he knew she was gone. But her warning kept ringing in his heart even as he entered the palace of Kasi, unhindered, the guards intimidated by his very presence.

King Senabindu appeared visibly shaken at the sight of Bhishm sauntering into the assembly hall, his long, lazy stride purposeful. So were the other princes and suitors; they were all struck speechless with horror. He heard his daughters gasp in dismay. Rage gripped his heart. He straightened his shoulders, narrowing his eyes into fiery slits.

His expression was cold and hostile. 'What are *you* doing here, Bhishm?' he asked. 'When did you start attending swayamvars?' he taunted. 'Especially ones to which you have not been invited!'

Before Bhishm could reply, the court broke into a nervous titter. The two men eyed each other, both recalling the reason for their hostility.

'Has the beauty of these princesses caused you to break your famous vow of celibacy?' asked a voice sarcastically.

Bhishm turned to see young Prince Shalva. He was as arrogant as his father, Bhishm thought grimly, recalling that hostile encounter with Prince Chitramukh years ago.

The hall burst into rude laughter.

'Prince Bhishm, don't you think you are too old to marry now?' sneered a suitor in the crowd.

Chuckled another, 'He is getting old, *that* is why he wants to wed!'

'Like father, like son,' chorused a few.

Bhishm shot them a frosty glance, his eyes on each one of them cutting short the irreverent jocularity.

'If I am old, will anyone dare to fight me right here, right now?' he asked casually, naked derision flaring in his pale, hazel eyes.

He received a long silence in reply. He bowed to the king instead. 'Kasi has always been married to Hastinapur since the time of King Bharat,' he began. 'He married Sunanda, the daughter of Sarvasen, the king of Kasi. Recently, our cousin King Vrihadrath, the king of Magadh, married the twin daughters of your cousin—'

'And *you*, when you were the crown prince, Bhishm, were to marry my sister,' reminded Senabindu, his voice dangerously soft. 'I have not forgotten the recent past.'

Bhishm remained calm, not a muscle moving on his face. He nodded and said, 'It is too late, but I apologize,' he said. 'Deeply, with all my heart...'

'You have no heart, you cad!' shouted the king. 'You broke my sister's heart!'

Bhishm's hands clenched as he looked into the hate-filled eyes of the king, whose face was contorted with rage.

Then he folded his hands and bowed his head. 'I have come to ask for the hands of the three princesses in marriage...'

He heard one of the girls gasp in bewilderment.

'*Not* for myself, but for my brother, Virya, the king of Hastinapur,' Bhishm rectified curtly.

Senabindu laughed openly. 'Virya? Vichitravirya, you mean? That's how the world knows him—a sickly boy who has been made king by his excessively self-assertive and ambitious mother!' he said scathingly. '*That* woman for whom you gave up my sister, Bhishm! And now you dare come here to ask for my daughters in marriage?' he thundered. 'Kasi does not permit marriage by proxy, and Kasi does not recognize the Kurus. Your brother might have given you the authority to represent him, but I do not! My daughters would prefer to meet and choose the man they want to marry for themselves. You do not decide for them as you clearly do for your brother, that puppet king!' he sneered. 'He is nothing but your toy, a weakling, and a coward. Besides, why would I marry off my daughters to my enemy?' he rasped, his eyes glittering with fury.

There was a momentary flicker of remorse in Bhishm's otherwise expressionless eyes. He knew, though, that contrite words might assuage his own guilt, but would not douse that anger of the king, the embers of which still smouldered.

He took a step forward. 'I come here with my apologies and my blessings,' he said persuasively, his voice softening perceptibly. 'I have no desire for a fight or war. I simply ask for the hands of the princesses.'

There was a movement. One of the princesses looked restless, noticed Bhishm.

He turned to them, bowing, 'I repeat the entreaty to you as well. I wish to take you all to Hastinapur as brides for my brother, King Virya.'

He saw the restless princess open her mouth to say something, but she was interrupted by Shalva.

'This is a swayamvar, Bhishm, which involves a choice, and not a contest where the princesses are trophies to be won,' he said testily.

'I repeat, I want no fight. It is a request,' said Bhishm mildly.

'We well know your requests are often camouflaged threats,' remarked Shalva. 'That is how you win your wars, don't you? But you can't win women and wives that way, Bhishm! You arrive with an army and threaten the king with a demand to surrender. The king concedes from fear of you and your barbarism! But not this time, Bhishm. I am ready to challenge you. You cannot take away the princesses without a fight!'

Bhishm felt a flicker of annoyance at the young man's brashness. He had wanted to avoid any sort of confrontation, but Shalva was as belligerent as his father who had challenged him to a duel a long time ago. The son was repeating history. Bhishm sighed; he had no choice but to fight him.

There was a lusty cheer in the court, all eager for the duel, baying for blood.

Bhishm nodded slowly. Gripping the hilt of his sword, he approached the centre of the hall. Shalva did likewise, with his sword drawn. Both bowed to King Senabindu. He looked pale, as worried as the tall princess near him, her dark eyes troubled. The other two princesses appeared faintly excited, their lovely faces lit up with animation at the sudden action in their swayamvar.

The duel started. With each stroke of the sword, Bhishm realized the father had taught his son well. Shalva was not committing the mistakes of his father, whom Bhishm had trounced so heavily decades ago.

Shalva persisted, but soon it was clear that the young prince was getting tired and was seriously outmatched; yet, he refused to give up. Desperate fury etched starkly on his face. He charged towards Bhishm over and over again, but each time, Bhishm met him blow for blow. Each thrust of the sword didn't seem to hurt him as much as it did his ego. Driven to apoplectic rage, Shalva came back again, bleeding profusely from his hands, but Bhishm knew they were flesh wounds, not deep or lethal. He had no wish to kill this young boy and turn the swayamvar into a battlefield. The other kings cheered for the flailing Shalva as Senabindu looked on, his face twitching with excitement. As the father of the princesses and a king, he could have forbidden the fight; but he had no wish to. He wanted to see Bhishm dead. But with rising apprehension he saw that the duel was not going the way he wanted.

Bhishm realized that if he did not strike decisively now, the fight would get bloodier and uglier. He glanced at Shalva, who looked insane with rage. That was in his favour. As he rushed, Bhishm fell forward and, diving in neatly, struck straight at Shalva's chest, piercing him high above the heart. Shalva collapsed in a fast-spreading pool of his own blood. Bhishm heard an anguished shriek from a girl, but he was not sure who had screamed in the ensuing pandemonium. The other kings quickly stepped back, hesitant and fearful.

'Anyone else?' asked Bhishm, twitching his bloody sword towards them.

None stepped forward, and with a last look at Senabindu, he grabbed the princesses by their hands and dragged them out of the hall. He felt a tug on his right hand. He turned back impatiently. It was the princess who had appeared restless.

'No! Please, no! I...' she said, her words garbled with fear and fury.

But he barely registered what she was saying as he heard an angry rush of feet behind him. Senabindu had ordered the other kings and his men to chase Bhishm.

'Don't let him get away!' he roared.

Bhishm reached his chariot and pushed the girls quickly onto it, commanding Manjunath, his charioteer, to drive away. He threw down his sword and picked up his bow and arrow. The other kings were chasing behind him, firing arrows at him furiously. But he handled each of them, leaving them either hurt or far behind. The crowd slowly fell back, unable to keep up with the pace and violence of his arrows.

Bhishm kept a lookout for further attack as they raced towards Hastinapur; Kasi had been left far behind. Finally he drew in a long, tired breath, and became suddenly aware of the three terrified girls.

'My apologies,' he muttered, wiping the blood off his arms and chest. 'I meant no harm or disrespect.'

Two of them nodded mutely, fear visible in their rounded eyes. He felt sorry for them that they had to witness such bloody violence on the day of their wedding. It was a day every girl wished to be perfect, a dream coming true. He was exhausted, and no further words would reassure them, he might even frighten them more, so he chose to remain quiet for the rest of the journey back home. However, he kept glancing back now and then to check if they were being followed.

He noticed that the tall princess was looking frantically around her; her face was drawn, and her eyes mutinous. He saw her eyeing the dagger at his hip.

He shook his head.

Her eyes were full of fury, but he saw a flash of pain lurking in their depths. She turned her face, brushing away her angry tears. 'You turned my swayamvar into a battlefield!' she choked. 'You killed him, murderer, I hate you!' she muttered venomously, her lips trembling. 'I don't want to go to Hastinapur.'

He looked at her wordlessly. And for some reason, he had that empty feeling of having miscounted the trumps. He had won the battle, won the princesses, but... Maybe it was the cold determination of Shalva. No whimper, no bluster, just the twisted grimace, the light voice, and the angry princess's unforgiving eyes.

He looked at her closely: she was clearly furious; her oval face flushed, her black eyes blazing fire, her red mouth turned in a mutinous pout.

'Shalva is not dead,' assured Bhishm, his face grim. 'I hurt him just enough to stop him. It's a deep flesh wound; he is unconscious, not dead.'

She stared at him unbelievingly. 'He's ... alive?' she stammered, her face flooding with joy.

'He should be,' he said dryly. 'I did not want him dead.' He stared at her in puzzlement, unease stirring again in his heart.

She threw him a grateful glance, her face breaking into a radiant smile.

Politely, he asked, 'What are you called, princess?'

'Amba.'

The Three Sisters

The moment Bhishm ushered the three princesses into her chamber, Satyavati's face broke into a rare smile. *Bhishm had done the impossible. Again. Three princesses for my son*, her heart surged, singing wildly. After a long time, she felt truly happy.

But she was quick to note that Bhishm did not seem to share her euphoria; there was a frown nestled in his furrowed brows.

'The princesses of Kasi, Mother,' he said carefully.

The three princesses bowed, their hands folded in salutation, and each came forward to introduce herself.

'I am Amba,' announced the tallest of the three, and Satyavati was quick to notice the confidence in her tone.

All three girls were fair and tall, and had a staggering likeness to each other. But Amba had a fire that was absent in the other two. Her eyes flashed and she seemed to simmer, as if coming to a boil. For what, wondered Satyavati.

'Ambika,' announced the second girl, firmly. There was a sulky air to her, and her prettiness appeared to be because of the rich clothes and gems she was elegantly wearing. She had broad hips but was otherwise slim, so slim that the sharp bones of her shoulders were prominent. Her eyes, wide and open, dark and intelligent, had an intent gaze, as though looking for something.

'Ambalika is my name,' nodded the third timidly, a voluptuous girl with a nervous smile. She was pretty in a vapid, colourless way. She had large, brown eyes, a pretty nose and an attractive mouth, her chin rounding in a charming way to define the heart-shaped, lovely face.

Even the names sound alike, Satyavati observed with some

amusement. 'Welcome to Hastinapur, your new home,' she said, her tone gracious, her eyes tender, hoping she was according the three girls a better welcome than the one she had received years ago. 'Oh princesses of Kasi, soon you will be the future queens of Hastinapur...'

She was interrupted by a restive movement. It was Amba, fidgeting, trying to attract her attention. 'My Queen, please ... I wish to speak with you!' Amba stepped forward, her tone urgent. She looked as if she had somehow gathered the courage to speak.

'Yes, what is it, dear?' Satyavati prompted gently, taking in the girl's anxious face.

'I wish this question had been asked before, and I would have said earlier what I am going to tell you now,' said Amba spiritedly, throwing Bhishm a pointed look. She continued, her tone stronger, 'I cannot be the queen of Hastinapur. Nor can I marry King Virya,' she announced, her voice low, but firm.

There was a dazed silence as Satyavati took in her words. She noticed that the two sisters did not appear surprised at Amba's announcement. She looked questioningly at Bhishm. He showed slight surprise, but pursed his lips, wordless and still.

Amba cast a troubled glance at the towering Bhishm. His reputation, Satyavati thought grimly, was as formidable as his name. People were supposed to shiver in fear, and this princess was but a young girl. She appeared intimidated by him but not enough to stop her from speaking out.

'Don't hesitate, girl, say what you have to say,' Satyavati said, her tone encouraging and soft. 'I assure you that you can be honest; speak up without any fear or hesitation.'

Amba looked straight into her eyes and nodded gratefully.

'I cannot marry your son because I love another man,'

she confessed, lifting her chin defiantly. 'I love King Shalva of Sauba...'

Satyavati stood still in shock, her confused eyes meeting Bhishm's hooded ones, but he looked stunned.

The girl continued, her tone hurried. 'I was going to garland him at my swayamvar when *he* interrupted us...' She cast Bhishm another hostile look, and Satyavati felt strangely chagrined at the girl's temerity.

She said curtly, 'Bhishm was sent to Kasi on my request. So, you wish not to marry my son as you love someone else?'

The girl nodded mutely.

This would soon escalate into a crisis, but Satyavati nodded. 'So be it. I shall not force you. Hastinapur will not have a reluctant queen.' She turned to the other two girls. 'Do you agree to marry the king of Hastinapur?' she asked formally.

Both nodded vigorously, as if to compensate for their sister's decision.

A thought struck her. 'Why did you not let Bhishm know earlier?' she asked sharply. 'He is chivalrous enough to not have dragged you here against your wishes.'

Amba gave her an incredulous look. 'It all happened so suddenly...' She floundered, in slight bewilderment, before continuing accusingly, 'And we were not asked! There was none to hear what I wanted to say!'

'I would have not got you here had I known. Why didn't you protest and stop me, Princess?' intervened Bhishm.

'Did I get the time and opportunity to put in a word, sir?' she asked angrily. 'You were fighting Shalva...' she trailed off helplessly and, for the first time, seemed entirely defenceless. For all her feistiness, she was as vulnerable as her sisters.

'You kept quiet because of your father, wasn't it?' guessed

Satyavati shrewdly. 'You did not want your father to know till you garlanded King Shalva; was that it?'

Amba had the grace to look embarrassed as she mutely nodded.

'Yes, I dared not divulge the truth in front of the entire court,' she admitted softly.

'It would have prevented this huge misunderstanding from taking place,' said Satyavati.

Bhishm sighed. How had he overlooked taking the princesses' permission before he got them here? *I was challenged by Shalva*, he recalled, *and all was forgotten in the resulting skirmish*.

He cursed himself silently, wondering how he was going to rectify the damage he had irrevocably wrought upon the eldest princess of Kasi.

'My words will not be enough to convey my sincere apologies,' he said slowly, bowing to the girl. Amba looked faintly taken aback. 'If I had known, I would not have done what I did,' he sighed, shaking his head.

There was no point in interrogating Amba now and dissecting the matter. He should have paid attention to her and her sisters instead of the war of words between him, King Senabindu and Shalva. If only he had asked then...

Furious with himself, he spoke more brusquely than he had intended. 'Let's not waste time discussing this further,' he said tersely. 'I shall return you to Shalva with full honour and finery. Like a bride,' he added. 'This is my duty; the rectification of my error.'

Satyavati wanted to clarify that it was not his fault; it had been hers. Had she not been adamant, he would not have blindly obeyed her orders. She was shocked at the sudden turn of events, but she showed no emotion. She felt a faint chill of unease that matters were not going as she had wished. She would have to take control again; she could not allow this small hiccup to upset her. But the knot of dread in her heart was tight.

She glanced at the girl again. Amba looked deliriously happy at Bhishm's words and seemed all set to rush to her lover's land. But Satyavati was assailed with a doubt that kept getting stronger every moment: *would Shalva accept the return of his lover? And if he did not, what then?*

'Wait!' she said sharply, hoping to halt the girl and her own troubled thoughts. 'She can go tomorrow. Let her rest. She should attend her sisters' weddings.'

Amba opened her mouth to protest, but Bhishm countered more quickly. 'No, it's already too late, and she needs to go back as soon as possible. Had I known, I would not have got her here, or hurt Shalva,' he said with a worried frown. He was unsure how Shalva would react. He must have hurt his ego more than that wound on his body. Hopefully, the sight of Amba, returned to him, would appease the king's pride.

This girl clearly needed to go back as early as possible, either to her father or her lover. Her father, Bhishm was certain, would not take back a daughter abducted at her swayamvar. It was now up to him.

Satyavati nodded slowly, holding her breath, pressing her lips, a finger tapping thoughtfully. Amba was looking at Bhishm with luminous eyes. *She is half in love with him,* thought Satyavati, *and sees him as her saviour. She must be thinking how magnanimous he is to send her back in his royal chariot so that she can marry the man she loves. It is to salve his guilt ... to save himself, not you, foolish girl.*

But she bit her lip and forced a stiff smile. 'Yes, I bid you well, Amba. May you live as happily as your sisters will here, from now on.'

Turning to Bhishm, her smile broadening, Satyavati gave him an imperceptible nod. 'All the arrangements have been made. The auspicious time for Virya's wedding has been fixed for early morning tomorrow.'

As Bhishm saw the princess out, he observed what his worried mind had missed when he had arrived—the palace was shimmering with oil lamps and flowers, the fragrance mingling with glowing incense sticks. The preparations were perfect, as Satyavati had meticulously looked into all the details. *It will be a lavish wedding; she will see to that ... even though the parents of the brides won't be there to give their blessings,* he shook his head in quiet agitation.

He shaded his eyes, watching his chariot take Amba away in a whirl of dust.

I hope the dust will settle quietly, he thought, wishing for the best and dreading the worst.

The Rejection

Even as the ceremony of Virya's wedding was underway, Bhishm's ears strained for the sound of his chariot returning from Sauba. He could not thrust away the princess from his mind and conscience. He had got her and her sisters without their consent. That had been an unforgivable crime for which he could not pardon himself. His eyes searched the blurred horizon of the distant hills silhouetted against the sinking sun, willing his chariot to return to the palace fast. The future of Amba was still uncertain till he heard it from his charioteer.

He was alerted by the sound of wheels crunching outside on the gravel. Bhishm rushed out, yearning to hear the assurance from Manjunath, but the sight that met his eyes stopped him in his tracks. Manjunath was not alone. Amba was with him; but this was a very different Amba from the one who had left the palace.

It was clear that she had been crying. Her eyes were dull with grief, and her lips were white and trembling. She was helped down by Manjunath, who was looking at her with concerned eyes.

'She is barely conscious, sir,' said Manjunath. 'Since the time I was ordered by Prince Shalva to get her back here, she has not spoken a word, but has simply kept sobbing her heart out...' his voice trailed away in distracted worry. 'Look after her, sir, she is going to collapse!'

So he has thrown her out, the coward, Bhishm swore silently. 'Yes, call for the royal doctor,' he ordered.

Amba stared up at him vacuously. 'He doesn't want me...' she whispered hoarsely, her large eyes glistening with anguish. 'What do I do now?'

It was a cry from a broken heart.

She buried her face in her hands, swaying fragilely.

He heard a sound behind him. Satyavati was standing at the top of the marbled steps of the porch.

'She is in shock,' she said tersely. 'Bring her upstairs, Dev.'

Bhishm lifted the girl in his arms and strode up the steps to a chamber. He could feel her trembling, shuddering in silent pain, her face buried in the crook of his arm, hidden by a swathe of hair falling loosely on her upturned face.

He laid her gently on the bed as Satyavati briskly straightened the pillows so she could lie comfortably.

Satyavati thrust a tumbler of cool lemon juice towards her mouth.

'Drink it up,' she said kindly. 'You need to have some strength.'

'For what?' whispered the girl tearfully. 'I want to die!'

'Don't ever say that!' reproached Satyavati sharply. 'No one is worth dying for. Your life is more precious than the tears wasted on men like Shalva!'

Amba straightened her shoulders. 'I don't blame him really. I was foolish to expect him to accept me...'

'Wrong again,' retorted Satyavati. 'Blame him, not yourself, dear. Your fault was to love him. *He* did not love you enough,' she said, her lips curling contemptuously. 'He loved his pride and reputation more.'

Amba stared at her, uncomprehendingly. 'He is a broken man,' she defended. 'Defeated and humiliated...'

'And what about you?' said Satyavati grimly. 'Has he not broken you? He said he loved you, and he was to marry you. You were taken away; you did not run away. Why can't he marry you now? Does it hurt his ego or his pride? Does it not hurt his conscience to turn away the girl he said he loved? You did not betray him; *he* has betrayed your love, your trust. He deserted you in the face of his defeat. He is a coward, Amba, not worthy of the love you still reserve for him!'

Amba shook her head through her sobs.

'Oh why did *you* come for my swayamvar?' cried Amba, looking at Bhishm accusingly. 'You were not invited. You are an invader who came and took us. Why did you take me away? And then, you trounced Shalva in public. He can never forgive you; he cannot forgive himself, and he cannot forgive me. Who will forgive you for what you have done? You have ruined my life!'

Love is not just blind, it is deaf to reason, too, thought Satyavati, hearing Amba's words of defence for her weak lover.

'Agreed, you are angry with Dev, but he did it not out of ignorance; he was obeying my orders,' she intervened stoutly. 'Your lover, dear, did it out of selfish ego. He loves himself more than you! Then why are you not angry with *him*?'

Amba's face suddenly looked deflated. 'Why would I be angry with him?' she said helplessly, leaning her head tiredly against the pillows. 'I can't make him love me; I can't make him marry me. He is not what he was; he is not what I thought him to be...' her lips trembled. 'I ... I ... I hate him!' she said violently, her voice low and cold. 'I hate him for what he did to me; I hate him for what he is. But I hate myself more for not knowing what he was!'

'Don't blame yourself,' interrupted Bhishm, his voice infinitely gentle.

Satyavati looked at him quickly. His face was tender as never before; his eyes soft, the lock of hair falling endearingly on his worried brow.

'You are right; *I* am to be blamed for this mess,' he conceded guiltily. 'I should not have got you here without your consent. I should not have sent you to Shalva alone. I should have gone with you...'

'No, you did what no one would have done; you sent her back with the accorded respect! If you had accompanied her, it would have made matters worse,' refuted Satyavati strongly. 'He would have been more incensed at the sight of you with his lost bride!'

Bhishm wore the stubborn look Satyavati dreaded. 'This time I shall go myself and beg him for forgiveness. Why should Amba suffer for my mistake?'

Satyavati shook her head impatiently. 'Dev, he won't listen. He just threw the girl out; why will he listen to what *you* say? He loathes you; he thinks you have ruined him in every way.'

'Exactly,' said Bhishm calmly. 'That is why I shall entreat him to marry Amba. He hates me, and I shall bear the brunt of it, not Amba. He can't forsake her, punish her for my mistake.'

And with those words still ringing in the room, he strode out and rushed towards his chariot to go to Sauba.

~

'How dare you enter my palace?' shouted Shalva, staggering up from his chair. His chest carried the angry welts and scars of the skirmish. 'What do you want now?'

The wounds seem to be healing, but certainly not his injured pride, Bhishm thought. 'Your forgiveness,' he said simply. 'And some kindness for the girl you love.'

Shalva laughed aloud in fake astonishment. 'Truly? After what you did to me, I can't face the world. Do you realize that? I lost everything—my dignity, my love,' he muttered through clenched teeth, his face a cold mask of fury. 'I hate myself more than I hate you!'

'You were a brave man, Shalva; you fought for the woman you loved till the very end,' said Bhishm. 'So why didn't you marry her when she came back to you? The duel was a mistake. I did not know she loved you. Had I known, I would not have taken her away. I would have personally brought her to you, like I am doing now. Please take Amba back,' he beseeched, his voice pleading, his hands folded in a rare gesture.

His words seem to enrage the king further. 'Who are you to bring her back to me?' he roared. 'You are a plunderer, a savage who took away what was not yours! Now you decide to return her on some generous whim!'

'It's not generosity; it was an error on my part for which the girl is being punished, Shalva! Please, I beg you!' he repeated, imploringly. 'I took the three princesses of Kasi for Virya, my brother. At that time, I did not know that Princess Amba loved you. The moment she told me, I sent her back to you. She is innocent. Why make her a pawn in our pointless fight? She loves you, Shalva; please marry her!'

Shalva looked coldly at Bhishm. 'I, too, loved her, and I fought for her. But I lost her ... to you. So she becomes yours, does she not?'

'She is not a trophy to be tossed around, to win, or lose,' said Bhishm quietly.

'Is she not? You certainly made her one! Why else did you come for her swayamvar?' he taunted. 'To win her, to abduct her, to defeat her other suitors—was it not? She was going to garland me, when you thundered into the court unannounced. You are nothing but a barbarian, Bhishm, a bully who uses strength and power to intimidate others. I battled you for her and I lost. I am a defeated man, Bhishm; don't throw accusations at me!'

Bhishm saw the wretchedness on the unhappy man's face. 'Is your pride more important than your love?' he asked, mouthing Satyavati's words.

Shalva went white. 'Yes, I am an honourable man, Bhishm. My honour and my respect are more important than my love for Amba. It caused my downfall. I lost her in a fair fight. I can't accept what I lost. What sort of a man do you think I am?'

'Definitely not an honourable one, if you don't accept her,' Bhishm said. 'You brood about yourself; but what about Amba? You have abandoned her! Do you not wonder what will become of her?'

'I have, and I hate myself more than I hate you!' exploded Shalva. 'You destroyed us, our love, our future! But why are you so earnest now? You should have thought of this before you charged uninvited into her swayamvar,' returned Shalva bitterly. 'You were seeking her for your brother, weren't you? Why does your brother not marry her?'

'Because she loves *you*, fool!'

Bhishm saw Shalva's lips tighten in a thin, unpleasant line. That pursed mouth made him realize that no matter how much he pleaded with Shalva, he was not going to change his mind.

Frustrated, he turned to go.

Halfway down the hall, he heard Shalva call after him. 'If you are so concerned about Amba, why don't *you* marry her, Bhishm?'

The remark mocked him in the high-domed hall and echoed in his mind all the way back home to Hastinapur, screaming at him, laughing and leering. He reined in his horses, bringing the chariot to a standstill, breathing hard. He could not break his vow; he could never marry her. *But he should*, a voice taunted him. He had brought upon her this crisis. *No!* He could not; he could never.

But would Virya agree to marry Amba? Bhishm thought over Shalva's other suggestion, and the more he brooded over it, the more it seemed like the only solution.

As soon as he pulled in at the palace gates, Bhishm rushed to meet Virya.

'Why do you want to meet him?' he heard Satyavati asking him. 'He is with his brides. He is a newly-married groom, Dev; leave him be!'

Bhishm turned around, his face flushed. 'If it was not urgent, I would not interrupt him, would I?'

They had reached Virya's chamber and Bhishm went in unannounced.

'Virya!' he shouted.

'He is king, Dev!' muttered Satyavati. 'There is a protocol!'

'Let him know that it's important,' Bhishm replied curtly.

Virya came out of his chamber, bare-chested, his hair dishevelled.

'What is it?' he bowed politely, a look of worry crossing his face. 'Is anything wrong? What brings you here, dear brother, at this hour?'

It was then that Bhishm realized that the day had still not broken into dawn, the twilight hour still dark, waiting for the sun to rise.

Bhishm quickly explained the situation to Virya. He listened, cocking his head to one side, and then finally asked, 'So, now what?'

'I want you to marry Amba!' said Bhishm.

'No!' replied Virya immediately.

Seeing the look on Bhishm's face, he retracted slightly. 'I cannot marry her, Brother,' he shrugged helplessly. 'She loves someone else!'

'But she was brought here for you!' argued Bhishm. 'You were supposed to be her groom as you are now of her sisters.'

'You brought her; I did not!' retorted Virya.

'Virya!' reprimanded Satyavati.

'But I am being honest!' he snapped. 'Both of you decided this. It is unto you, not me! I would have gladly wedded her had she agreed. But she preferred Shalva to me,' he said almost sulkily.

'It is a question of the girl's future, not about ego and honour, Virya,' said Bhishm softly, but desperately.

Looking slightly mollified, Virya tried to rectify his quick refusal. 'No, Brother, it is not correct!' he repeated, pleadingly.

'But Shalva has refused to marry her, and she has nowhere to go! Please, Virya, marry her, at least for the sake of our family honour,' entreated Bhishm. 'For my sake.'

Satyavati was amazed to hear the beseeching tone in Bhishm's voice. *Had the girl affected him that greatly?*

Virya folded his hands in quiet salutation, bowing his head low. 'Please don't plead with me... You are my elder brother. You are like a father to me. I have always obeyed you, but not this time. I have to refuse. She is not mine to marry!' he repeated more strongly now. 'I know you brought Amba here for me ... but she considers Shalva her husband! How can I marry her then? It is *not* right!'

Bhishm pleaded with his brother more, almost grovelling, sounding more desperate each time, till Satyavati could bear it no more.

'Stop it, Dev! It doesn't become you!' she said abruptly. 'We can't do anything more on this!' She turned on Virya furiously. 'You can marry her for the sake of keeping her honour, can you not, Virya, as an honourable man? It's not about love anymore; it's a simple consideration. This is all a horrible twist of mistakes and misunderstandings, but only you can make things better now, Virya. If you do not have the decency to obey Bhishm's pleadings, then I, your mother, order you to marry her!'

'You can't, Ma!' said Virya, a glint in his eyes. 'I am the king. I choose my bride and I do not want Amba, who loves another man.'

'The girl has nowhere to go!' Bhishm said passionately.

Satyavati spread her hands helplessly. 'Take her back to her father...'

'You know he won't accept her, just as Shalva didn't!' said Bhishm explosively, crashing one fist into his palm.

'Try,' she persuaded. 'If he doesn't, then...'

'He will not accept her; I know him. We will have to keep her here.'

'Here?' repeated Satyavati incredulously.

'Yes, she can stay here with her sisters,' he said.

'As what?' she argued hotly. 'Dev, you are being unreasonable!'

'Then *what* do we do?' he asked desperately, his eyes so tortured that Satyavati's heart skipped a beat. '*Where* will she go?'

'Are you talking about me?' asked Amba tonelessly.

All of them whirled around, more embarrassed than shocked at her presence. Satyavati wondered how long she had been standing there, overhearing their conversation. Amba appeared calm, but her eyes were listless. She had heard it all—both the rejections—and Satyavati wondered how much more the young girl could take.

'Shalva does not want me, nor does the king,' she said absently, bowing to Virya. 'Greetings, my brother-in-law!'

Virya flushed, a dull red suffusing his face.

Amba ignored him, and turned to Bhishm.

He looked at her sorrowfully. 'I pleaded with Shalva, but he refused...' he muttered as if ashamed to say anything further.

'I know,' she said. She took in a deep breath and looked expectantly at him, her face not betraying the agony she was suffering. Her expression wasn't pleasant to see. She seemed to have grown older just in the past few moments.

'And that leaves no alternative but for *you* to marry me!'

The Waiting

The echo of Bhishm's refusal to Amba had been hanging ominously in the palace for the last six years, and yet she continued to wait for him...

Satyavati sighed as she stood by her window, watching the stately figure of Amba stride purposefully towards Bhishm's palace. It was her daily practice, a pattern, and her sole purpose. She was going to confront him again. Yet again, she would beg him, curse him, rant and rave and beseech him to marry her. Each time he would refuse her, pleading with her instead to ask him anything apart from that one impossible task. He had suggested that he would take her back to Shalva, and that had enraged Amba further, driving her into an impotent frenzy.

'I want *you*, not him, not anyone else!' she screamed in despair.

The vow was as terrible as him. He was now Bhishm in word and worse. Had it hardened him into a monster, cruel and insensitive? By following his promise blindly, could he not see the mad grief in the girl's eyes? Was he protecting or hiding himself from commitment?

But Satyavati knew this was not so. He was as tormented as the girl. Every word of Amba's pierced him deep, bleeding him white, drowning him in his own guilt and sorrow. But while each time he refused her, the girl was crushed under despair and disrepute, it lifted him to further heights of exalted loftiness: he remained a man still revered, not reviled. But no one saw his inner turmoil. Watching Bhishm suffer made her suffer, for had it not been for her, he would not have taken that horrible oath of lifetime celibacy. It was testing him, Amba as well as her.

'The girl loves you; do you realize it?' she had confronted him one day, unable to see his agony. She saw him stiffen, his face carved in marble, but a muscle twitched at his jaw. He turned away abruptly.

'I cannot comply with her wishes,' he said stiltedly.

Satyavati stared at his broad back, stiff and straight with obdurate resolve. She did not know whether to be exasperated or relieved. In her heart, she did not want him to marry Amba. She did not want to see them together—talking or laughing or arguing—she did not want that wretched girl in the palace anymore...

A memory quickly seared through her mind: Amba, in the alcove of Bhishm's palace, walking and stumbling, almost swaying, and Bhishm instinctively catching her by her waist. She had seen the girl's eyes widen in sudden pleasure and she spread a hand against his chest, as the other gripped his strong neck. She had relaxed and let her head go back and her scarlet lips open a little.

'I think it's the fever,' she had said softly, leaning her weight on his arm. Her head went back now, pulling him down, her beautiful eyes drooping, fluttering a bit, and her lips were parted and smiling. She pressed him closer, her breasts against his chest. She had heard Amba letting out a long, easy sigh, *'Make me feel better; I am going mad with your love...'*

Bhishm had almost violently thrown her off, firmly holding her by her trembling shoulders. 'No, Amba, I can never be yours!' he muttered, his eyes burning wild and tortured. Satyavati had shrunk back in the shadows and hurried away. *Was the girl besotted or desperate?*

She felt the taste of bile even now in her mouth as she was talking to Bhishm. She blinked, gathering her scattered thoughts.

'Amba loves you, and you won't marry her,' she sighed. 'Could it get worse?'

Scanning his stiff back turned against her, Satyavati decided she would have to try another means of talking it out with him. 'She worries me, Dev. She is beside herself with this mad hatred-love she has for you! She is losing her mind, I think,' she started hesitantly, unsure of how Bhishm would take it. She saw him regarding her with pain in his eyes. 'Six long years in Hastinapur, receiving only your rejection each time, is undoing her. You can see that, can't you? She sees her two sisters so happy. She loves you but I think she hates you more. She blames you for her misfortunes. She would have lived as happily as her sisters, had it not been for you. Loose tongues are not being kind to her, Dev, and such ugly talk will not bode well for her, you or us.'

'But where else can she go?' he said dully.

'Does that mean you should make her suffer here—seeing you, loving you, waiting for you every day?' asked Satyavati in an exasperated tone, tapping an impatient finger against her lips. She would have liked to throw the girl out of the palace and out of the kingdom, but Bhishm would never allow it.

He flushed under his fair skin, his mask slipping, his brittle eyes darkening in anguish. 'What should I do?' he said helplessly. 'I can't leave her, and I can't accept her!'

She flinched at the torment in his voice. 'Dev, you have to let her go—for your good and for her betterment,' she said gently. 'I have seen that look on Amba's face from the very day you got her here. You defeated her lover in a fair fight; you showed him to be a weakling, not man enough to marry her. You were her new prince in shining armour, her saviour; and now she looks up to you for everything,

Dev!' she said. But his face was again stony, and his jaw was clenched.

She continued after a pause, her voice persuasive. 'That is why I did not want her to stay here. You can't marry her, and she can't stop hoping that you will. It is cruel on both of you. She sees you, talks to you, and you are one of the only people whom she shares a laugh with!'

He gave her a strange look. 'She is our guest, and she can stay as long as she wants. That's the least I can do for her,' he said woodenly.

'Not anymore! She's being called Virya's concubine, Dev; have pity!'

'I *can't* marry her, you know that!' he exploded, his voice breaking, his eyes tortured. 'I *can't*...' he muttered to himself, his breath hoarse. 'I can't save her, please!'

'Then release her!' she shouted back.

It was as if he was speaking to Amba. Satyavati again felt a red hot flush of jealousy—it was an unfamiliar feeling, burning through her, searing her with its very intensity.

She had never shared him with anyone. He had been with her since the very first day she arrived at Hastinapur. Nothing had come between them—not his oath, her guilt, Shantanu, Kripi, her sons, the throne, and not even Hastinapur—nothing, except this girl. Amba was slowly driving a wedge between them. She had felt him distancing himself from her, more concerned about Amba, worried sick about her, silent and staring at her with his bleak, guilty eyes. Amba had some strange power over him. Was he in love with her? Or was she mistaking his heightened sense of guilt for love, the burden of which he carried so heavily upon himself? Again, she felt pierced by that hot stab of jealousy burning right through her soul. *Does he love Amba?* She did not dare ask him that question. It would not just rile him; it would also defile him, and his capacity to keep the oath would be desecrated.

Satyavati drew in a deep breath. He rarely lost his temper, or rather, he rarely showed it. This fit of rage was unusual; he was breaking from the inside as well.

'I *know* you can never wed her, so let her go,' she pleaded. 'I have tried to explain to her, too, but she hates me even more for suggesting it!' she remarked. 'She's right. It was because of me that you had to take that vow. She resents me for that!'

She saw him look out of the window, towards the distant river, a sparkling Ganga in the horizon. She stared at him, and thought, *No wonder that girl is in love with him. Tall and fair, with that careless lock over his chiselled, handsome face, tanned from his campaigns, winning wars, brilliant and brave, gentle and gracious, kind even to his prisoners—but not kind enough to that girl to break his oath and marry her...*

She felt a prick of alarm. Her own worst fears were being brought back.

He would *not* marry Amba, she was certain; but, sometimes, seeing Amba's persistence, she wondered if Bhishm would break one day. That small fear grew larger each day as Amba continued to remain in the palace, corroding her confidence and conscience. *Amba as his wife. No! It must never come true*, she thought with panic. *I have to somehow get the girl out of here.*

She heard raised voices, breaking her thoughts. Amba was creating a scene again, she was certain. It grew worse each day. It was Amba who was earning a bad name; some were even ridiculing her, including her sisters. But Amba was past caring.

Her sisters were not indifferent to their sister's anguish. But Ambika and Ambalika lived in their own world, with

Virya. Six years down, neither had produced an heir. Was it because of Virya? He had always been a sickly child, and recently she had noticed that his cough sounded nasty and persistent, reminding her of Shantanu's; she felt faintly uneasy. Virya was like Shantanu in many other ways, too—his luxurious self-indulgence, his over-fondness for wine and women, though he mercifully restricted himself to his two pretty wives. Lately, though, it was these three who worried Satyavati more than the presence of Amba.

A pale Ambalika rushed into the chamber, interrupting her thoughts. She walked with a hurried step, her face ashen.

'Mother, it's Amba!' she mumbled in fright.

Her heart hammering, Satyavati followed Ambalika.

It was a sight that did not surprise Satyavati. Bhishm was standing near the window, taking in Amba's angry words, her voice hoarse, tears streaming from her eyes, her face grey, her hair dishevelled, the tendrils damp at her flushed forehead. She was still lovely, in a cold, hard way; the beauty drained by a vicious temper and thought. Amba stopped the torrent of words as they entered the chamber.

Her expression was something that Satyavati hoped never to see on a woman's face again. There was pain, anger, frustration and bitter jealousy that had turned Amba's face into a mask of despair.

Amba stood glaring at her sister. 'Why have you got *her* here?' choked Amba, her eyes on Satyavati. '*You* are the one behind all this; you are the reason for my ruin!' she spat, her eyes wild. 'You told him to get me here for your son, did you not? You claim to be a queen but you are still that fisherwoman, reserving the first catch for the king! Was I that catch for your son?' she taunted, ignoring the gasp of horror from her sister.

'Amba, please, come to your senses!' cried Ambika. 'Either you leave this palace which is your only home now, or behave yourself!'

The words stung like a slap, and Amba looked momentarily hurt, her eyes widening in disbelief.

Then she recovered. 'My dear sisters,' she sneered in vicious fury. 'So happy in their conjugal bliss, forever in the arms of their dear husband! You call yourself lucky?' she suddenly grabbed Ambika's wrist with surprising strength, digging her nails into her skin. 'What has become of you? You are as decadent as that drunken husband of yours. You follow his each whim, his every fancy. He calls himself king but it is that closed bedchamber, not the court, which is his favourite place, locking himself in that room and in your arms. Or is it our little, luscious Ambalika he prefers over you?' her laugh turned into an ugly giggle. 'He has made you his slaves, his sluts!' she finished viciously. 'I am relieved I escaped such a depraved life!'

Satyavati felt a cold, creeping dread. Amba, in her madness, was speaking the truth. Marriage had quickly made Virya succumb to erotic profligacy, overindulging in sensual pleasures with his two queens.

Amba was now talking to her, her fingers still clutching her sister's arm. 'Is that why you did not send your debauched son for the swayamvar but sent the invincible Bhishm instead?'

Amba rounded on him, her eyes livid. 'You reject me for that damned oath you took for this conniving woman?' she rasped viciously, her face suddenly unpleasant, almost ugly. 'She fooled you just as you fooled me!'

Satyavati felt oddly detached from Amba's anger and abuses; it was the unravelling of the girl that she found more distressing. The last six years had been unkind to

Amba, breaking her in every way, turning her beauty into a bitter mask of disillusionment. The two rejections from Shalva and Virya haunted her, but it was Bhishm's refusal which had unhinged her.

She remembered Amba as she had been when she first arrived: a fair girl with warm, brown eyes; angry and frightened, yet brave, hoping courageously that all would work out fine for her. And now, she was a woman who never smiled, only perhaps sometimes at Bhishm. But the last few months, she was slowly getting undone, her patience curdling, her despair deepening into hate. Hate for all of them but more for that one person whom she loved and hated with equal passion. Amba had found a prey her hate could feed on—Bhishm. She blamed him for everything: for her dashed hopes, her scorned love, and her hopeless future.

Bhishm's silence seemed to incense her further, her demented mind not recognizing that in his silence lay his gnawing guilt.

Amba leaned closer to him, her eyes wild and agonized, her face white, her breath, love and fury mingled, fanning his face. 'You are as noble as the world says you are. You turned my wedding day into a battlefield, defeated and disgraced my lover, and took me away against my will. *You* did it, Bhishm, only you. You abducted three women against their wishes and you can't marry one? You say you are bound by your vow to be a celibate. Then you should not be here in this palace, in the royal court, but in the forest, meditating. What are you doing here, meddling with politics, power and progenies of this self-styled queen?' she spewed out her scorn.

She clutched at his arm, pulling him closer to her. 'You say you did your best, but your best is not enough. I want more. I want *you*!' she raged, her breath coming in gasps, her eyes glittering in her pale, damp face. 'You made my lover disown me. You showed me how shallow the man was; you made me turn my love for him into contempt. You got me here for a brother who refused me. *You* did it, Bhishm; you left me with no one but myself and my hopes on you. You were kind to me but unkind to my plight, giving yet not committing. What sort of a man are you? You made me fall in love with you! I begged for that love...!' she choked in a pathetic whimper. 'I raged, I ranted, I raved, I made it known to the court, to the world, I made a fool of myself—which girl says that; which girl does that?' she swallowed convulsively. 'But nothing matters to you other than your cursed oath! Is it more important than my life that you destroyed, or my love that you spurned?' demanded Amba.

Bhishm stood stiff and stared vacantly back at her, his hazel eyes searching for solace in her frenzied ones.

'How noble is that?' wept Amba, shaking him. 'Who are you loyal to? Where is your sense of fairness? Is life not more important than principle? Would you allow your soldier to die in the battlefield because you are helpless to carry him? That is what I am, Bhishm, that wounded soldier, your victim ... *you* owe me, Bhishm, you owe me my life, my future, my happiness that you trampled upon!'

Amba stood trembling before Bhishm, her face twisted with the agony of hate; yet, there was vulnerable, wistful hope. Satyavati wanted to shake him herself to make him utter a word in defence, but he had only wordless silence to give. He looked stricken, his face haggard, crowded with lines of pain and guilt.

Satyavati, overwhelmed and drained, knew she could not remain in this oppressive chamber a moment longer. She made a move to leave.

The movement attracted Amba's attention. 'Don't leave, Mother dear. Don't you want to see the fruits of your deed?' she jeered with an unpleasant smile.

She walked slowly away from Bhishm. 'I demand that Bhishm marry me. Our marriage will be his penance, his punishment for the crime he has committed on me. He cannot escape in the name of his vow that he pronounced for himself. His oath does not concern me, his accountability does. He is responsible not to that damned promise, but to *me*!'

She paused, waiting for him to react, but he just lowered his eyes and shook his head.

'Forgive me, Amba, if you can,' he muttered at last, his eyes tormented, his voice ragged, a hoarse cry of anguish. 'Forgive me, please, for I *am* your sinner. I cannot go against my pledge, but by doing so I am committing a worse, unpardonable crime. I cannot marry you, and I cannot forgive myself.'

'I don't want to forgive, I want justice!' Amba shouted, her fists clenched, as if to stop herself from hitting him.

'You don't want justice, Amba. Bhishm tried to give it to you in every way he could,' said Satyavati, her voice icy.

'For me, justice means revenge! I want to avenge the humiliation and suffering I've undergone all these years. He started it but I shall end it!' she spluttered in fury, her eyes glistening.

'Revenge will destroy you, too, Amba. What will you gain?' Satyavati implored, hoping that an emotional appeal would reach the girl.

'I have lost everything...'

'So has he! Bhishm lost everything because of me!' Satyavati shot back, trembling. 'He could have finished me and my young sons when my husband died... He could have had his revenge on me, but here I am and so is he, standing before you. He is not your offender! He is a good man, Amba. Look at him. What does he have except that oath which traps him more than anyone else? He is a prisoner in his own cage, chained by the shackles of that damned vow. Look around you; you are not the only one suffering. You are demanding justice, but life is not fair; the world is not fair,' she cried. 'We are women, Amba; through justice we demand answers. We don't get them, we live through them. Live, Amba, live, but not with hatred,' she said passionately. 'This is your pain talking; you need someone to hate, and you chose Bhishm. That hatred will destroy you, Amba; it cannot destroy him, for he has nothing to lose, nothing to gain...'

'I shall call upon every king in the country to fight for me,' said Amba through clenched teeth. 'There will be someone who will help out a wronged woman!'

'There will be none to help you, Amba,' warned Satyavati. 'No king will oppose Bhishm, as all fear him. And why do you keep harking on about being this wronged woman?' she demanded, with suppressed anger. 'You have been grossly wronged, yes, but that does not give you the right to wrong other people. You have lost reason! Is hatred easier than fighting back? Do you hate Shalva who deserted you in your hour of need, and who is married now? Do you hate your father for not taking you back as a father should? Do you hate Virya for turning you down because you loved someone else?' she asked unhappily. 'Then why do you hate Bhishm? He did what he did because I told him so!'

'I detest both of you,' replied Amba tonelessly. 'You string up people and play with them as if they are your puppets in a show.'

'I am sorry; I truly am,' said Satyavati, folding her hands

in earnest appeal. 'Bhishm was against interfering in your swayamvar, but I forced him into it,' she confessed, sinking slowly to her knees. '*I* did it, Amba, not him.'

Everyone, even Amba, was taken aback. She had never seen the queen so stripped of pride and poise. Bhishm took a step towards her, unable to bear the sight. The queen of Hastinapur was grovelling. Satyavati, who would not bow to any man, or admit her mistakes and misdeeds, was prostrating herself in abject surrender. Bhishm knew she was trying to obtain both forgiveness and favour from Amba for his sake. He swallowed convulsively, yet he could not find words to defend himself.

Amba recovered, more incensed. 'Don't protect him, Queen Mother. You are as guilty as him, but he is the one who won me like a trophy, a gift for his brother. So, he is accountable to me. Only *him*!' she muttered through white lips.

'Amba, let me tell you something more about myself. I, too, lived in hate. Hatred for everyone and everything. I am an illegitimate daughter of a king,' she started, and there was a swift stillness in the room. Bhishm made a move towards her, but she stretched out her arm. She would do anything to make this demented girl see sense. Even if it meant exposing her past, baring herself.

'I was born an unwanted princess, to live a life of a common fisher girl. I allowed myself to be seduced by an enlightened rishi, because it would serve some purpose. I had a son from him whom I could not keep...'

She heard a gasp. It was Ambika. Behind her, Bhishm looked ashen, his eyes suddenly brittle.

She continued unflinchingly, '...as I had to live ... to survive. But I didn't want to just survive in this wretched world, I wanted to rule it ... to have power, position and prestige,' she said softly, looking into the wild eyes of Amba. 'For that I had to have a crown, a kingdom. I met Shantanu and I married him, but not before securing my position here in this palace for myself and my future children. I dethroned the crown prince to carve out my place,' she paused, expelling a tired breath, feeling Bhishm's eyes boring into her. 'Amba, you talk about justice and revenge. Was I just to Bhishm? Was my royal father just to me? Was I just to my first son? I still don't have answers, Amba, but I have realized that neither hatred nor vengeance is one of them.'

Pin-drop silence echoed in the room. Her words were not just revelations, but the confession of a queen.

Amba's crazed chortle broke the silence. 'But I am not *you*, Queen Mother. You gained everything, I lost all! I lost even my dignity,' Amba whispered harshly. 'I have thrown my love at him but he does not want it; so all I have with me is hatred.'

'Because it makes you feel validated?' said Satyavati, the edge back in her voice, her eyes flinty. She stood up, regal again, her voice indicating that she would not be tolerant of any further nonsense. 'Like you, I was rejected by my father, and I hated him for a very long time because of it. But when I got my chance to confront him, I was met with another truth—that he meant *nothing* to me! I could not waste my hatred on him; I sought no revenge. I am me, on my own, with or without him. I refuse to be victimized; but you, Amba ... you feel like a victim. It makes you more comfortable in your bitterness. Fight injustice with justice, for yourself, Amba. Have mercy on yourself. Is there no option but vengeance? You are a princess...'

'I *was* a princess, I am a beggar now ... at your mercy!' corrected Amba.

Satyavati shook her head. 'You are still a princess. Could you have not done anything better than hope for an impossible marriage to Bhishm?' she asked, sadly. 'Was there no one else but him or Shalva? Does the world end and begin with Bhishm? Is that your only succour?'

'You are a fine one to preach, Queen Mother,' Amba gave her a twisted grin. '*You* married an old man to be queen! And you made sure Bhishm never married, even a desperate girl like me. I know you don't want me here; you don't want me to marry the man you own, you possess, you...'

'Stop it,' thundered Bhishm, his face wretched. 'Amba, please, don't...'

'Don't what? You speak at last, for *her*!' she scoffed. She looked at Satyavati and said, 'Just as you wanted the throne through marriage, I want Bhishm through marriage! For the crown, you destroyed Bhishm. For my revenge, I shall obliterate him!'

Satyavati felt the blood drain from her face and then rush back.

Amba turned to look at him, her eyes burning into his. 'You are kind, Bhishm, but you are as hard as stone!' Her voice suddenly dipping, her face close to his, her whisper hot on his cold face, she continued, 'And I *hate* you for it. I hate you, Bhishm, much more than I ever loved you!' A choked sob caught in her throat. 'You did not heed my love, but you will pay for my hatred. You will be *mine;* it's your vow against my vengeance!' she said, her voice hoarse. 'If you forced me out of my swayamvar hall, I shall force you out of this very palace to fight me. *I* shall challenge you; I shall be the death of you!' she shrieked, her voice dripping venom.

Drawing in a quick breath, Amba threw him a parting look, piercing him and his shattered conscience with her flashing eyes, spitting such hatred and intensity that it sent a cold chill down Satyavati's spine. Amba smiled at him then, a tight, spine-chilling grimace, and flounced out of the chamber, out of the palace. *And hopefully out of our lives*, thought Satyavati as she stared after Amba. The demented look had seared into her soul, her curse hung in the air, filling her heart with unknown terror—this girl was going to be his nemesis. *Their* inescapable nemesis.

The Reprisal

Bhishm could never forget Amba. She had made sure he would not, thought Satyavati, as she heard the latest news of the girl from one of her spies. The first person she had sought help from was her maternal grandfather, King Hotravahan. Her mother, Queen Swargavdhini, had visited Hastinapur several times earlier to persuade Amba to give up her obstinate demand but had failed, as all others had. Her grandfather, too, implored her to give up, but the princess remained adamant. She wanted him to challenge Bhishm for her sake. He reluctantly refused. She was now a woman with a mission—to vanquish Bhishm. Counting on her powerful grandfather's support and then losing it made Amba realize soon enough that none of her friends or family members was going to help her. She needed some other powerful king. And she set out in search of that king who would be willing to fight for her, travelling across the country, imploring princes and kings to challenge Bhishm for her. But none dared; none would, Satyavati thought wryly. Lost to the mortals, Amba turned to the gods for help, particularly Kartikey, the God of War.

Satyavati sighed. *The girl is obstinate! ... But I have worse matters to worry about,* she thought, as she strode into her son's room. The moment she entered, she was assailed by the stench of alcohol fumes. Her heart sank as she realized that he was drinking in the middle of the day again, as he did often. She wished she could talk to him but wondered if he would be in a state to even hear her. *How can I force him to produce an heir,* she thought despairingly. She had spoken to both her daughters-in-law and they had shrugged helplessly. Her son had laughed it off. Like he was doing now.

'If I can't give one, we can always adopt!' he guffawed, more in inebriation, less in humour. 'It's been done before in our family!'

'When Emperor Bharat did it, it was because his sons were incompetent,' she said harshly. 'Do you want me to do the same?'

'Are you threatening me, Ma?' Virya gave a weak grin, but his eyes were sharp.

'You *are* incompetent,' she replied, her gaze even. 'You can barely walk to the court, let alone attend it!'

'Yes,' he agreed with a candid smirk. 'But are *you* willing to give me up, give up the throne and reinstate another? Do you have that moral courage?' he asked maliciously, his smile wicked. 'You *can't*, Ma, never. You are too attached to the crown!' he added scornfully with a half-supressed laugh.

She found she had no words, not even anger; only disappointment. Clenching her fists, she screamed silently, frustrated at her powerlessness. *Is this the heir I have produced to sit on the throne meant for Bhishm*, mocked a small voice within.

'You were wilful enough to remove my stepbrother from his throne, but do you have the strength to put him back or anyone else?' taunted her son, sipping his wine, his hands unsteady.

For all his drunken senselessness, he was talking sense to her.

He finished half of the goblet's contents at once, and then wiped his lips. 'You are not as tough as you like to pretend, Ma,' he rasped, reaching for the goblet again and emptying it this time. You only take, you don't give. What do you want from me but an heir! I have no other purpose for you. You have been living too long with people like us who are scared of you. Wait till you meet up with some nasty shock that Fate is sure to deal you...'

'I have had my share, and you, Virya, are one of them!' she said expressionlessly. 'Bhishm *is* virtually the king of Hastinapur, thanks to you,' she countered coldly.

'Hah, only by duty, not by right. You took that away from him!'

Ignoring the accusation, she continued relentlessly. 'It is *he* who looks after the kingdom, not you. It is *he* whom the people love and respect, not you!' she said cruelly, her lips drawn in a thin line, hoping to provoke him.

'And whom do *you* love, Ma?' returned her son, his silly grin plastered on his face, pouring himself another goblet. He drank from it, shuddered violently, and all at once his eyes seemed to get sane and cunning, bringing him a certain balanced moment of reality. She never knew when it would come or how long it would last.

'Not me, not Bhishm, not my father, not anyone but your goddamned throne!' he said violently, pouring out more wine and gulping it down too fast. 'And I love it that I can't give you what you want most—a bloody heir!' She paled at his viciousness. 'What are you going to do now, Ma?' he chortled, his peals of insane laughter quickly dissolving into a fit of coughing. The goblet he held in his shaking hand slid on to the bed, and wine slopped all over.

'I did what no one else could do, not even our great Bhishm! I defeated you, Ma, *I* did!' he sobbed through his coughs. He threw himself forward, purple in the face now. 'I ... I can never give you a grandchild.'

'Stop it, Son!' she pleaded, rushing to his side. 'Stop drinking, and you will get better! Just get fine, that's all I want!' she said gently, swallowing her tears, brushing the damp hair from his perspiring forehead. He let out a strangled sigh and drew in a shuddering breath. His face had lost pallor, and his chin quavered. Was this her once good-looking son, wasted to disease, drinking and debauchery? The arguments she had had with Bhishm came rushing back, when he'd rebuked her for her overindulgence and pampering of her son, and how she was responsible for his feckless dissoluteness.

'I am sorry,' he wept, tears sliding hopelessly down his gaunt cheeks.

'No, Son, don't; I love you!' she cried.

'And I was wrong; you *did* love that one person in your way...' he whispered, his words slurring. 'You adored Chitrangad, and you died a little when he died. And you do love me, much less than him, but still that mad, blind love you reserved for your sons. And you love Bhishm,' he said flatly. 'It's there ... I have seen it, I have sensed it, and it's strange. You destroyed him, Ma, and you loathe yourself for it. And you can't do without him. He loves us, too, so unselfishly, so unswervingly. I hate what we did to him...' his voice trailed off, his eyes closing in a descending stupor. 'I never could bask in borrowed power like you could. It's probably your sins catching up...' he mumbled, distinctly enough to sear her soul.

She stared down at him, insensible, his face buried in the pillows, his mouth open grotesquely.

She sat hunched forward, staring at her open palms. She absently wondered whether she had managed to outwit Fate. She had prided herself that she had chartered her own destiny, despite the setbacks in her life. It was she who had a sole role in shaping her life. She had been responsible for her happiness and her unhappiness, both, she thought bleakly.

She was aware of a presence in the room. She looked up. It was Ambalika, frail and fair, her eyes huge and worried, shifting from the unconscious form of her husband to the queen mother sitting next to him. Ambika, who had also entered, moved forward wordlessly and straightened him up against the pillows, pulling the silk coverlet high so he would be comfortable.

Satyavati made a move to quietly leave the chamber.

'It's about Amba, Mother,' said Ambalika urgently.

A tired sigh escaped Satyavati. She waited, allowing her daughter-in-law to tell her some dramatic tale about her sister.

'Lord Kartikey has given her a garland of ever-fresh flowers. Whosoever wears it is supposed to destroy Bhishm,' started Ambalika, her tone breathless. She usually talked a great deal, often a cheerful chatter, more often to hide her diffidence.

'How could he bless her when she was praying for revenge?' Satyavati questioned harshly. 'Penance is supposed to be atonement, a meditation.'

'Probably to make her understand that none, even with the Lord's blessing, can help her,' answered Ambika quietly. 'She has gone all over the country, visited every kingdom, but none of the kings have responded to her entreaties. Amba even approached King Drupad of Panchal.'

'He will never help her; he is a close friend of Dronacharya, Kripi's husband, and Kripi is from our family,' dismissed Satyavati confidently. 'Besides, Panchal is our ally.'

Ambalika look worried. 'The last the spies heard was that, frustrated at King Drupad's refusal, Amba flung the garland at his palace gate and it hangs untouched while Amba is back wandering in the forests...'

'Amba was always a stubborn girl, but she met her match here,' interrupted Ambika bitterly. A few years ago, she was pretty; but now the edges of her face had hardened and her mouth had begun to turn downward.

Satyavati looked surprised. 'Why the rancour, or are you suffering from your older sister's affliction?'

'All of us are suffering, aren't we?' replied Ambika, belligerence in her voice. 'We are only slightly better off than our sister.'

Ambalika interjected faintly. 'I am happy,' she said timidly.

'You would be,' retorted her sister, with a sneer. 'Virya adores you! What am I supposed to be happy about? Being married to a drunk, debauched king?' Her laugh was unpleasant. 'He likes you more because you are so delicious and docile, and you spoil him! Had he been checked in time, perhaps he would not have become so debased, and our lives would not be wasted! But then, we get to console ourselves that we are queens,' her smile remained mocking. 'The lesser queens!' she added, staring pointedly at Satyavati.

'Every queen wears her crown, but not without her share of conflict, concession and compromise,' returned Satyavati.

'Yes, we heard!' scoffed Ambika. 'For you, Ma, everything is a deal, with terms and transactions. But, mostly, it is you who lays out the conditions and we are to follow—all of us here in this palace! For how long, Ma, and how much more?' her voice cracked, her hand flying to her mouth, breaking into a small sob.

Satyavati glanced at Ambalika and said coldly, 'Ambalika, though you are the youngest, you seem to be the most sensible of your sisters. Look after this one and try to knock some of your good sense into her. Let her know how fortunate you are, considering your older sister's fate—roaming the woods, thirsting for revenge and all that she lost!'

'We have nothing in this damned palace but a drunk, impotent husband and no children!' muttered Ambika, under her breath, her voice notches lower so that Satyavati could not hear.

But she had, and, with those words, her old fear resurfaced. Where was Hastinapur's heir? Satyavati could not still the panic in her heart, and Virya's persistent cough reminded her constantly of some unspecified dread.

It came sooner than expected.

'Are you going to war?' Satyavati looked surprised as she saw Bhishm collecting his bow and arrow, his sword and dagger hanging at his trim waist. He didn't bother to answer. He nodded wordlessly, with his steady look that may or may not have disguised his thoughts, depending on whether he had any he wanted to conceal.

'That's unexpected! With whom?' she persisted.

'Rishi Parashuram,' he replied briefly.

Fear gripped her heart. Parashuram! *The man who had massacred generations of royal warriors to appease the murder of his father. No one could defeat him, not even the gods, then why Bhishm,* she thought wildly. *Why was he confronting his own guru?*

'Why?' she whispered through white, stiff lips.

Bhishm gave her his serene stare. 'He is fighting for Amba,' he said.

Stark fear flickered in her eyes as she stared at Bhishm. *That wretched girl; she would be the death of them, of him...*

'You won't fight your teacher, will you? You never would...' she said, trying to stem the terror spiralling inside her.

He stood wordless, but his silence spoke volumes.

'You are planning to fight him knowing you are going to lose your life!' she accused, her voice shaking in fear. 'You are preparing not to go to war, but to your death; isn't it, Dev?' she asked, her mind hammering, her pulse racing.

She moved her eyes over his inscrutable face. They stared

at each other, a deadly stillness between them, speaking of an unspoken terror. She had gone pale, drained of colour and courage. He stood silent, tightening his bow.

'You are, aren't you?' she said through clenched teeth. 'You are going to ask for your death, your icchamrityu, while fighting your teacher! You would rather die than defeat him, is that not so?' she whispered and she reached out for him, clutching at his arm, her fingers digging hard.

She stared at him piteously and said nothing, her eyes speaking to him, full of fear and entreaty.

'I have to fight him. It's an open challenge,' he said at last, regarding her.

'Go, then; I shall not stop you,' she said, her voice low. 'But you fight, Dev, you fight him like the warrior you are! Not his protégé, not his inferior, not a coward, who wants to die rather than face defeat. You will *not* surrender; you will come back to me! You will fight for the reputation that woman has tainted, for the infamy of her accusations. You will return a hero!' she said fiercely. Her hands gripped his. 'You will not die, Dev, you will *not!* You will fight and win and come back to *me!* For me.'

The words would stay in his mind, imprinted on his heart forever.

A ferocious light shone in her eyes. 'Promise me!'

A shout interrupted them.

'Come on out, Bhishm!' Rishi Parashuram bellowed from outside the palace gates.

Satyavati peered through the wide palace window.

'Get your weapons!' he shouted, brandishing the arrow ready in his powerful fist. 'We shall fight!'

And fight they did. Hours melted into a day and the day slipped into night, dawning into another day and the next and another. Two women watched them—Amba and

Satyavati—each with a fire in their heart and bated breaths. Their duel raged for a fortnight, as glorious as it was gory. Whatever Parashuram came up with, Bhishm trumped, even as Parashuram countered each of Bhishm's moves. The student bested his teacher, and the teacher never lost...

He will win, he will, he will, chanted Satyavati, *and he will come back to me.* She stared down at Amba, hating her as she had never hated anyone before, not even her father. Satyavati had prided herself that she was not petty, or mean, be it with people or emotions; but for Amba. If Amba hated Bhishm, she loathed Amba as much and more...

Satyavati was like a wounded animal struck by an arrow. She was in pain; she couldn't move, she couldn't concentrate ... all she could think about was Bhishm battling his teacher. *What was happening to him,* she kept asking herself. *Would he win? Was he dying?* She stood rooted at the window, looking fearfully, longing to stop the bloody duel...

It was the twenty-third day of their battle, neither winning, yet both lost in their war. Bhishm could feel the stinging warmth of his own blood on his body, the wounds oozing, draining him slowly, his life sapping away. Her words kept drumming in his exhausted mind. He could not die; he would not die. He blinked; it was not tears, but blood, falling in a steady trickle from his wounds, obstructing his view of the bulky figure of his guru. His guru, who he had to kill; or get killed by him. He had to make his decision now or never. And as he saw his teacher raise his arm to strike him with his famous *parshu* weapon; Bhishm knew he was left with no choice.

He closed his eyes, the peace of surrendering to death beckoned him, almost bewitched him. In the scarlet haze, he saw Amba's triumphant face, gleaming with a hatred he wished he could quench. And he saw the sad, sorrowful eyes of his teacher, contorted in pain. He turned his head towards the palace, where he knew she was watching him, watching over him. *'Come back to me the hero that you are!'*

Each word pierced him like an arrow and he raised himself, murmuring the most dreaded words. The Brahmastra—that horrific weapon of complete obliteration.

Parashuram roared, his face twisted in disbelief. Bhishm wouldn't use *that* weapon of destruction, he shouldn't! Like a prayer, he saw the gods descending to stop the duel. It couldn't go on further or it would be annihilation for all. Though he was ready to take out his Brahmandastra to counter it, Parashuram stopped. He knew he had been defeated.

'I would rather lose against my student than use this weapon,' he declared, bowing to Bhishm, as his final gesture of defeat.

Bhishm bowed his head. 'I do not desire your defeat, sir. I want to win back the respect that I lost in your eyes.'

Parashuram gave a tired sigh. 'You never lost it, Son. I had to be gallant for this girl, and fight even a righteous person like you. I was the offender, never you!'

Satyavati thought her heart would burst. She was not sure if it was relief or joy that flooded her heart. As ecstatic tears filled her eyes, she heard a shrill cry.

An ashen-faced Amba stood distraught and demented, the scream wrenched out of her revealing her frustration, her hatred.

'I am not a beggar, I do not want your pity!' she shrieked, her voice harsh. Her face had suddenly become pinched-looking and her glittering eyes seemed to have sunk into their sockets. 'Whatever the world may claim,' she paused contemptuously, 'or your guru may claim, *you* are the culprit, Bhishm! And you will pay for it; if not today, then some other day!'

Amba had lost; she was defeated and disappointed in love and life, trounced in her war of hatred and revenge. Watching her as she stood motionless, Satyavati saw a resigned, hopeless expression cross her death-like face.

Bhishm's next words revived her. 'If my death can liberate you of your hatred and me of my sins, pray, kill me, here and now,' implored Bhishm, dropping wearily to his knees, removing his dagger and offering it to her on his bloodied palm. 'All I can do for you, Amba, is die willingly.'

Amba took a step back, her hands trembling, her wild eyes running over his torn, handsome face. Satyavati's breath caught in her throat, her lips moving in prayer, her hands clenched to her beating heart. *No, please, no, don't let her kill him!* It was the longest moment in her life.

Amba's lips drew back in a snarl. 'If killing you was so easy, I would have already done so!' she snarled through her clenched teeth, her voice dipping to a deadly softness. 'But I want *my* life back, Bhishm, and if no one can help me get it from you, I would rather die! But even in my death, I shall seek my vengeance, Bhishm. I shall come back for you again and again!'

The Passing

She had never thought she would be heartless enough to rejoice at someone's death. But Satyavati had to admit that she could not have been more relieved, and, strangely reassured, when she got to know that Amba had committed suicide. Her thoughts immediately flew to Bhishm. *How had he taken Amba's death?*

Two years ago, after the bloody episode at the palace gates, Amba had stormed away to renew her attempts to wreak vengeance against Bhishm. As a last resort, she took to praying to Lord Shiva, still seeking her justice. Shiva, though impressed by her devotion, had turned her down with the cryptic words, 'I cannot help you kill a person in your hate. But you will be reborn to repay.'

The poor girl, deranged by her fury and desire for revenge, was ready to die, and without any further thought, immolated herself by jumping into a self-made pyre. It did not take long for the rumour mills to start working furiously, all across the kingdoms. One of the strongest being that Amba would be reborn to King Drupad of Panchal, as it was at his garden gate that the faded garland of flowers still hung, waiting for the person destined to kill Bhishm.

Satyavati dismissed the rumour, thinking that royal houses often made their own myths. Besides, the young Drupad would never go against them. He owed them allegiance, and was a friend of Dron.

Ambika and Ambalika had taken their sister's death poorly, as expected. But what was disconcerting was the growing hostility of Ambika towards her, as she held Satyavati responsible for Amba's death.

Both were weeping, as she entered their chamber. Ambika was trying to console her younger sister.

'Amba would have been a different person, leading a different life, had she gotten married to Shalva that day,' Ambalika was muttering.

'Amba died, she escaped our fate,' returned Ambika fiercely.

Satyavati went cold, stopping herself at the doorway, her whole body stiff and erect, formal and disapproving.

'If you have finished mourning for your sister, would one of you kindly attend to your sick husband?' she cut in coldly. 'As expected from a queen?'

Ambalika hastily left the chamber and her sister followed suit, but not without returning Satyavati a blistering glare.

'*We* are born princesses, raised to be queens,' said Ambika mockingly. *Unlike you*, the impudent girl meant.

Satyavati couldn't care less. If opinions were likely to be based on fact and knowledge, judgements were often formed on emotions. What she was now bothered about was Virya, his failing health and the looming reality that there would be no heir. The thought consumed her even as his cough worsened by the hour. He had been spitting blood since the last week. Bedridden for the past six months, he was sinking fast. Satyavati had learnt to take premonitions seriously. Virya, her hammering heart told her, was going to die, like his father.

Bhishm was by his side, through the long days and longer nights. She had not seen him so desperately sad before, enveloped with a dread of hopelessness and challenging death to dare take Virya from him. She would find him praying, a sight rarely witnessed. Amba's violent death also lay heavily upon him.

'Will praying save Virya?' she asked cynically, but not without compassion. 'The best doctors are with him,' she said gently. 'We are doing our best.'

Bhishm turned, surprised. His eyes were weary from lack of sleep and strain. 'What are you doing in this temple? You don't believe in God. Only yourself,' his lips twisted in a grimace.

His terseness hurt her.

'God, Fate, Destiny,' she said, shaking her head, her finger moving restlessly on her lower lip. 'They are just consoling words, descriptions of man's weakness. Fate can be conquered. You need to have control of your life and decisions first. Blaming everything and everyone for one's mistakes, for one's situation, for one's unhappiness in the name of Fate is escapism. *Everything* is our own responsibility,' she reiterated. 'You have to be your own God, carve out your Destiny, make your own Fate. If they make us behave as we do, then what about the choices we make? It is our actions that defines us, our lives.'

Bhishm looked listlessly at the shimmering river in the distance. *He is thinking of his mother. It is his way of self-reproach. Is Ganga watching us and counting our sins,* Satyavati wondered. Ganga was supposed to be so pure and holy, that a dip in her waters could wash one's sins away and lead to salvation.

His eyes still riveted on the glistening horizon, he murmured, 'You are arrogant in your self-belief...'

'And you are a fatalist, Bhishm!'

'Be your own God?' he repeated her words. 'Can you save your son now?' he asked hollowly.

'I lost him when he took to wine and women,' she said slowly, her breath ragged.

'Whose fault is that?' demanded Bhishm angrily.

'You are blaming me again for spoiling him,' she said, a thoughtful frown on her face.

Bhishm did not reply, but the contempt in his silence was clear.

'Are you making me eat my own words?' she said quietly. 'When I say that we are responsible for our own Fate, when I say there is always a cause for everything, and that cause is always created by us, you are insinuating in your characteristic way, that it was *my* decisions that were the cause for all that has happened.'

'Not just your decisions...' he sighed.

'Both of us have been doing what we have always done, which is looking after the kingdom. Virya knew that we were more than capable of dealing with the matters of the state, and the people of the kingdom never complained,' she said. 'Seven years have gone by, yet Virya never took the crown seriously. He went to waste instead, and the excesses have taken their toll.'

'He got a throne and wives too early,' Bhishm said. 'Was it your haste to have an heir?'

He was voicing her deep-founded fear. Seven impatient years down, her son was going to die childless, leave the throne without an heir.

The raw pain in Bhishm's voice cut through her stifling thoughts.

'Virya is dying! I can't bear to see him go!' He moved his head in abject misery. 'Why!' he cried. 'First Chitrangad, now him...'

'He is carrying his father's genes—the unhealthy ones,' she replied tonelessly, her face frozen.

He stared at her. This time, she was quite unlike when Chitrangad had died. Now she seemed a moving, ghostly figure of her original self: cold and perfunctory, ice flowing in her veins.

A cry tore through the palace walls. Both of them heard the wails renting through the stillness. Her heart plunged. *Virya is dead*, she knew without conscious thought. She watched a white-faced Bhishm rush down the steps of the temple, his stride breaking into a run.

She stood still, gazing at the idol in the temple, so exquisite and ornate in gold, but as hard and cold. Was that Bhishm's God? Her face crumpled in grief, unshed tears scalding her eyes and, in a haze of pain, she turned to look accusingly at the idol. Bhishm's prayers had not worked. Her second son, too, was dead.

~

She could not show the world how battered she was, not even Bhishm. But she knew that, like her, his heart must be weeping dry tears. As she attended to the last guests at the funeral, she felt that the visiting kings resembled hungry vultures, waiting with bated breath for their quick fall. They reminded her of Ugrayudh at Shantanu's funeral, eyeing the vacant throne while mouthing platitudes.

She sensed something was wrong because of her innate alertness, and her spy confirmed her suspicions: some of her guests were hatching a plot. She needed to inform Bhishm. She sat alone in her room for a long moment, looking down at the procession of mourners. A sobbing Ambalika could barely stand on her feet, while Ambika stood tense, holding her close. Virya was gone but he had left behind a void, an heirless legacy, and worse, a political stalemate.

The need of the hour was not to mourn, but to manage with whatever means and measure. Satyavati was doing what queens should. She was shattered within, but she would not allow her Hastinapur to break into fragments. A kingdom without an announced heir was like a rudderless boat, thrown adrift in a tossing river.

She had to continue to rule: without her son, without the scion, without the king, without the regent. Bhishm was like a broken arrow, prostrate with despair. She glanced emptily at her daughters-in-law, feeling helpless at their grief, unable to console or comfort. She had been counting the hours, hoping each time she looked at the two widows: would either one of them be carrying an heir in her womb? But just this morning she had got to know that Ambika, too, had menstruated, like her sister a week before. So there was no hope—there would be no child, no successor.

Would the dynasty die, burnt to ashes at Virya's burning pyre? Satyavati shut her eyes in frustration, the tears refusing to roll down. She would not allow herself to sink into hopelessness; and prayers were of no use. Her God had long died, and she had faith solely in herself. She gripped her hands together; *No*, she vowed fiercely, *I will not surrender, I will not be defeated. I have to find a way.*

She found her answer, and he was approaching her right now with his usual long strides—Bhishm. She had to convince him to break his word to keep another.

'Have you eaten?' he demanded the moment he glimpsed her wan face, her shrunken figure huddled behind the regal facade she employed to conceal the reality. He came to her side and gently took her hands in his. He was surprised to find them trembling.

She shook her head, her hands clutching his in a gesture of urgency. 'You were right—I shouldn't have forced you to kidnap the princesses, Dev,' she started in a slow whisper, the skin stretched on her pinched face. 'It was all for nothing. Matters got worse. The girls are widows, Amba died...' she paused. 'There have been too many deaths. Shantanu died, Chitrangad was killed, and now Virya. I lost all of them,' she said, a slight quiver in her voice. 'But I am a survivor, am I not, a maker of my own decisions ... even if they are wrong?' she sounded ironic. 'I can confront the ugliest of truths. But the death of my young sons—first Chitrangad, then Virya? What does it mean?' she whispered. '*They* paid for my sins. This is *my* punishment. You know why?' she looked up at him, allowing him to glimpse the anguish in her eyes. 'Because I stole what was not mine,' she enunciated slowly. 'I stole your throne, Dev, your rights as a son. That is why I lost both my sons, lost all that I had usurped from you.'

Bhishm made an impatient movement. 'You are torturing yourself needlessly!'

He knew she was mourning, ripped from within yet striving to make a brave attempt to prove otherwise. Often, in these past few days, he had seen her submerged in the darkness, leaning her head on the arm of a sofa, refusing to break into tears even in the privacy of her chamber. But he saw how her head and shoulders were quivering, defenceless in defeat.

'No, one can't build palaces over others' graves. I snatched from you all that's been snatched from me now!' she murmured, gripping his wrist urgently, her fingers biting into his fair skin.

'Don't!' admonished Bhishm, a muscle jumping at his cheek. 'You are stronger than this—don't allow yourself to wallow in self-pity.'

'It is self-realization,' she said in a low voice. 'I have to face a truth and so do you, Dev. The kingdom was always yours; the crown, too. It was never mine to have. It *is* yours, Dev. You talk about God and Fate, and both are telling you the same thing—you were meant to have the throne, never my sons. That's why they died. The throne was never theirs. It was always yours. Take it! '

'*What* are you saying!' he muttered furiously, dropping her hands.

'Take back your throne, marry and have heirs!' she said quickly, her eyes darkening in silent appeal.

He gave her a strange look. 'What is this? Some ploy? Do you think I am a pawn to be played with?' he said through clenched teeth. 'I don't want the throne, and nor will I marry!'

'Because of that same wretched oath of yours? You took it for whom, Dev?' she demanded. 'For your father? He is dead! On my father's insistence? He, too, is dead! For my sons? They are both dead, Dev. *All* are dead! The purpose of this vow is over; there is no successor from me who is likely to contest your progeny for the throne. What remains is an empty vow, and the empty throne which was yours, Dev. Please take it back; take back that damned vow!'

'No, I can't; I won't! Amba died!' he shot back, his eyes flashing in his white face. 'She died for it, burning in her fire of hatred till her last breath, cursing me...' he stopped, choking, and turned his face away.

He is mourning for Amba! Satyavati held her breath, feeling more than a cold pit of fear uncoiling within her, as if her life was going to change forever. *Is it Amba's curse working on my family, this palace, on Hastinapur? No!*

She straightened her shoulders and forced him to look her straight in the eye. 'Is your oath more important than the future of this kingdom you owe your allegiance to? Is that not your duty, your dharma, too?'

Bhishm felt a slow anger build within him. He detected a shift in her mood and tone. She was no longer the bereaved queen mother of two dead sons. She was back to her assertive self, like the queen of Hastinapur that she was.

'I won't break my vow!' he seethed, through gritted teeth, his eyes bloodshot, his face tense. 'I will *not* marry. You know that.'

'Not to strangers, Dev, but to Ambika and Ambalika!' She did not pause, hurrying on firmly. 'As their brother-in-law, you have a right of *niyog* over them. Break your vow and marry your brother's wives!'

The colour drained from his face and rushed back, flushing his fair skin all over.

'They are like my daughters! Virya was like a son to me!' he shouted, horror and disgust clouding his eyes. 'You are sick! You were never yourself after Chitrangad's death, but the death of Virya has unhinged you!'

'No, I am not insane. I am being sensible,' she said sharply. 'Men and women handle their grief differently. Women can fall apart completely. They let all their feelings out. And then just get on with things and life. I am doing that. I can't afford to grieve for Virya; it is Hastinapur I worry about...' she sighed, scrutinizing him closely. 'Some men are not used to handling any intense emotions, grief particularly. They lose their mind as they can never get to express the feelings of their heart...'

Bhishm stood up, abruptly turning away.

'Don't run away from your emotions, Bhishm. That's what you have been doing in the name of loyalty and duty!' she said. 'Each time you felt it—anger and hatred for me, disappointment and betrayal about your parents, your hapless guilt for Amba—'

'Stop!' he cautioned, his jaw clenched, his hands balled into fists, an indecipherable emotion glimmering in his eyes.

He got up abruptly and moved away to the window, closing his eyes to shut out the pain. He could still see Amba, her eyes looking up at him with hope, love, eagerness and undiluted hatred. That ebony hair cascading down, framing her lovely heart-shaped face, sometimes beseeching, sometimes sobbing, hurt, raging. Or, she leaning her head on his arm, weeping bitterly, her shoulders quivering. Or her hair, escaping from her combs, covering her neck, her face, and her pale arms.

Her sobs still racked his mind. It tormented him. She was dead. But he could hear her tinkle of uncertain laughter, the loathing in her voice when she had cursed him, the hurt in her eyes each time he refused her, the rage and frustration glistening in her falling tears.

He found his heart beating furiously. *Will I ever forget her? Will I ever rid myself of the clawing guilt tearing me apart bit by bit, day after day? Was it guilt, or just simple, unadulterated love I will not allow myself to feel?*

He knew that if he had ever loved her, he could have never dared to hope for the miracle of having her. Every day of the six years she had been in the palace were stamped in his memory. As he worked in the morning, practising with his weapons, he would sense her watching him from her chamber, and his skin had prickled with anticipation. He would wait with a thrill in his heart for the moment when he could hear her voice and her footsteps. To stand watching her as she listlessly gazed at him with her bared love, to hold her away, struggling with her, against her, as she wept, her head surrendering against his hammering chest, to hear the tinkle of her anklets on her slender ankles, the same tinkling as her rare giggle, the scorching heat each time she rested her hand on his shoulder, her face flushed, warm and rosy, shining with a thin film of perspiration, her eyes flooding with joy at the sight of him—if only she had known how much all that meant to him!

The anguish had been more exquisite when he realized that she returned his love: that reflection had driven him to guilt. It killed him each time she had implored him, her eyes full of hope, her soft cheeks drenched with spent tears. He suffered with her. He had realized a long time ago that, for a ruin like him, hope and happiness were forbidden forever. Even now, each time she came in his dreams, he saw her clutching his hands, begging him, screaming at him as she jumped into the fire, her wail echoing in his numbed mind when he lay awake at night.

He had wished a thousand times he could save her. He dreamed of it even now, as he gathered the memories, tenderly cherishing them in his dreams and loving them.

Satyavati's harsh words reminded him of the darkness and the fire that he was living in.

'You felt each of these emotions every time, but each time you denied it,' she was saying. 'The only time you have displayed any feelings is when the boys died, and you wept like a child! So, you *are* capable of pain and tears, aren't you? Yet, you use your oath as a shield, covering you from any onslaught! I won't allow it anymore. Throw it away!'

'You *are* mad!' he exclaimed, breathing heavily, desperately collecting his scattered thoughts together. 'In your obsession for successors, you destroyed three girls and your son; how much lower can you stoop?'

She felt the heat of his words. 'If you can find fault in my slavish commitment to get an heir for Hastinapur, you, Dev, the living institution of sacrifice and ethics, have caused more harm! All for your unreasonable devotion to your pledge! How long will you allow it to destroy people, the kingdom and you?' she cried. 'It was because of me you took it; and now I am begging you to take it back!'

It was like screaming into the universe. Obduracy was a trait Bhishm had developed as his defence. Not even that obstinate girl could break him. Amba—clever, beautiful, fiery, demented and damaged—had gone hoarse demanding the exact same thing from Bhishm that she was asking of him now. But he had resisted her for full, six tempestuous years. The chances that she would succeed where Amba had failed, seemed bleak.

Bhishm was pacing, consumed by a raging fire within him as he tried to stem the rush of thoughts her words had caused. What Satyavati was suggesting was outrageous; it was contrary to reason and conscience. Even coming from her, it was the last thing he had expected. Numb with shock, deprived of emotions and unable to think anymore, Bhishm wondered, in that one small moment, whether he abhorred or admired the woman before him. She had put aside her grief, and placed this absurd suggestion out of worry and love for Hastinapur, because she was desperate to give it the heir it did not have. An effective queen must remain unemotional when the kingdom and the people are vulnerable. She had displayed her *sangfroid* often enough, but today she had surpassed her passionless self.

She would never give up. But neither would he, he promised himself grimly, shutting his eyes briefly and thinking of all that he had lost in that one swift decision of his.

'I did it not for you but for my father. And promises are meant to be taken for oneself, not others,' he retorted dully.

'You have been left with just your empty promise to yourself! All are long gone!' she said, incensed. 'Your integrity and morality are the standards for the era. Yet you keep quiet in the face of tragedy and crisis. You pride yourself in being just, but being silent is not being fair, Dev, it is being evasive; you are closing your eyes to reality. You have never taken a decision that you think will make you fall short of your high standards. You protect yourself with that armour in the name of that darned pledge *you* made to appease your irrational love and guilt for your father. And that same irrational commitment to your pledge is your sole goal now; it is consuming you!'

Each word thrown at him was true, and they pierced him. Slow anger flickered in his hazel eyes. 'Who made me do that?' he prompted, his voice low and hard. '*You*; my father's mad love for you and my mad love for my father. You used me then, as you are using me now by asking me to produce your precious heirs this time! I am not some bloody weapon to be used in your wars and discarded in peace!'

She threw up her hands in despair. 'Don't blame me. *Your* one spontaneous emotional promise that came out of love for your father will annihilate Hastinapur. What is more crucial—self-imposed ethics or the future of a kingdom?' she shouted back.

He gave the woman who started it all a look of unmitigated disdain. 'And I ask you, was my vow more precious to me than the life of a person? Can I ever forget what I did to Amba?' his voice was abnormally even, flat yet vicious. He threw her a scornful look. 'Can I ever forget that I fought with my guru for the sake of that very oath? How easily you ask for something I cannot give, after all that I lost...' he swallowed, his voice quickly hardening. 'You expect me to break a promise just because you find it convenient now? Not me, it's that empty throne that you are imploring to!'

He was ruthless. 'Why are you asking so much from me—to assuage your guilt or to whip your ambition further?' he sneered.

She had never known him to be cruel before, but now she was making him face his demons. As was she facing her own. It was their day of judgement, the time for retribution.

'My ambition is lost, Dev; all my hopes reduced to nothing! Just like our family is now threatened with extinction, leaving the kingdom at stake,' she replied dispiritedly. 'We *cannot* forsake it. Can't you see that we're in real trouble already?' she beseeched.

His icy voice scraped at her like claws. 'The things you made me do! I have committed the worst crimes!' he blazed, his face white in cold fury. 'I snatched three princesses from their swayamvar, against their wishes to win brides for my under-aged, sick, alcoholic brother. As a celibate, I should not have stepped inside the swayamvar hall at all! Perhaps Ambika and Ambalika could have got a better husband than Virya, but they did not have a choice. I took it from them by getting them here. I broke Amba's hopes, her heart, and pushed her to a certain death...' he drew in a tattered breath, his face bathed in anguish. 'I broke all Kshatriya laws for you, tarnishing the reputation of even our family name by that needless abduction. And now you have the temerity to make me commit a more heinous crime—marry my brother's widows!' he spat, his face livid. 'For *your* ambition...'

'No!' she said, her face white. 'Not for me, Dev; for Hastinapur.'

'For the throne, you mean, oh Mother of mine, for which you forsook your scruples, your conscience, even your sons!'

'Then what do I do?' she cried. 'Hide from my responsibilities like you do? You think I like doing this?'

He expelled a long breath. 'All I could do was watch and submit each time because of that same vow which binds me ... binds me to obey the throne, to obey the crown, to obey *you*!' he hissed.

'Then do it for Hastinapur!' she pleaded. 'It needs you right now!'

He shook his handsome head.

'*You* took that oath, Dev. *You* said those words, and only *you* can take them back as there is none and nothing left,' she prayed, suddenly defeated, stunned and shattered by his obstinacy, watching him prowl in the chamber, restless and raging. 'Or is it easier for you to condemn me instead? Does it make you feel more noble?'

'You made me a monster; one that is hated and feared by all, and worse, one that I hate the most!'

'No, that vow did you in!' she cried. 'That's why I beg you to relinquish it. It is malignant, destroying you and everyone, and Hastinapur!'

He walked up so close to her that she had to look up at him. 'Don't throw Hastinapur at me! Understand this once and for all, I shall not say it again and you will never ask me *ever* again!' he said, his jaw clenched. 'The Ganga might run dry, the sun may stop rising, the clouds may not rain, but I shall *not* give up my oath. I lost everything for it. And it is all I have now. It is my truth, my reality, and I shall not relinquish it.' He turned away from her abruptly, and strode out of her chamber.

She felt a cold chill, her skin prickling at the echoing icy silkiness of his voice. His outburst had been as sudden as rare. The calm that now followed was as uneasy and unsettling. What was she to do now?

The Widows

'*What do we do?*'

Satyavati repeated the question to Bhishm the following day—the one for which she had no answer, and which he did not want to provide. By walking away from the chamber, Bhishm could not walk away from the crisis. The following day, for the whole day, he stayed away from her, unheeding further requests or commands. It was towards evening when she called for him again, and he surprised her by showing up in the very same chamber where they had argued.

She was markedly changed since the previous day. There were no traces of tears on her pale, terribly sunken face, and her expression was different. Was it because he saw her differently, or was it that their relationship was different now? Or perhaps intense grief had finally set its mark upon her; though she was as elegant and as well-dressed as before, she struck him as being shrunken, her figure smaller. There was an abruptness and excessive nervousness about her, as though she was in a hurry.

She caught him regarding her closely and she noticed that he looked more tired than usual. In spite of their concern for each other, she was aware of a hostile and uneasy atmosphere in the chamber.

'Dev, what shall we do?' she repeated, her voice flat, splintering the awkwardness between them. 'After Virya, who is to be king of Hastinapur?' she asked, her tone efficient.

'We can adopt a worthy successor,' he returned equably. 'It has been done before.'

'Yes, I know, but who?'

'Uncle Bahlik's son, Somadatt, would make a good king,' he said.

She frowned. 'He is an able general, but his recent clash with Prince Sini over Princess Devaki of Mathura at her swayamvar has changed the political situation drastically. Sini, as you know, was fighting on behalf of his cousin, Vasudev, the Surasen king, and carried her away from her swayamvar. Devaki, too, is in love with Vasudev. But Somadatt, one of her suitors, challenged Sini and was defeated,' she stopped abruptly. The story was strangely similar to Amba's swayamvar.

Women were political trophies, she conceded with a slight shake of her head. She continued, seemingly unperturbed, 'Sini is said to have dragged Somadatt by his hair, pushed him to the ground with his foot on his chest, put a sword to his throat, humiliating him publicly. Typically, Somadatt is now bloodthirsty for revenge and this feud between the two royal houses has triggered a fresh diplomatic impasse. If we make him king, we will be earning more enemies and fighting his pointless wars.'

'He is the next kin, an heir presumptive. But knowing Uncle, who gave up his claim for father, he won't allow Somadatt to accept the throne of Hastinapur anyway,' Bhishm said indifferently, shrugging. 'We will have to search for someone else.'

'There is no one,' she said, frustrated. 'The current scenario is too delicate, too precarious. All are watching Hastinapur; every king is aspiring to capture it. But till you are there, no one will dare covet it. Dev, you are the only hope...' her voice softened into a plea, trying again to reason with him. 'Please, Dev, take over the reign.'

'I am anyway doing so, am I not?' he said. 'As the regent, I am looking after it. Both of us are. We shall, till our last breath...' he said stoutly.

'But after us, who?' she asked urgently, and waited with bated breath.

Observing his silent stance, she hardened her voice, and her eyes turned brittle. She announced, 'If you do not have the courage to break your vow and accept your throne and life back, I am left with no choice but to choose niyog, for which I will search for someone else for the widows of Virya.'

'Niyog!' spat Bhishm disgustedly. It was his turn to stare. 'That is a right only a husband has over his wife, where he requests her to have a child through another man. You can't do it; you are their mother-in-law!' he insisted, his lips set in a grim line.

Her mouth took on an obstinate pout. 'I can; I am the queen. They will have to obey me for the sake of the crown. They are queens, too, and it is their royal duty to secure the future of the throne by providing heirs.'

Bhishm expelled a long breath, tightening his fists. 'What more are you going to impose upon those poor girls?' he hissed. 'You are a ruthless manipulator: without pity, compassion or conscience!'

She twisted her head to look up at him. 'Easy to put the blame on me, is it not, Dev? Why have you not taken on the responsibility, instead?' she challenged. 'That is why I asked you to be the king and marry them. Only *you* can help them now,' she added, her eyes mocking him.

He moved uneasily. It always agitated him that she could probe into his most secret thoughts. His handsome face twisted in a grimace.

'I can't even help myself,' he said bitterly. 'But I wish I could help them! You have me trapped, as always, but don't trap them. Don't, please, I implore you. Don't make them go through niyog. We forcibly took them from their swayamvar; now you want to coerce them to be with some stranger to have an heir... It is wicked!' he swore, his eyes blazing in outrage.

'It is duty!' she retorted. 'As queens, it is their moral and legal obligation, a familial responsibility. Niyog was never meant to be a means to derive pleasure, but to beget a child.'

He leaned back, running his fingers through his hair, surveying her with a half angry, half defeated expression, 'What all will you make me witness?'

Hurt, she gazed out of the window; his words had cut her to the quick. They reminded her of Shantanu's accusations as he lay dying. Both father and son tended to place their decisions and drawbacks on her, ignoring the fact that they were the ones who had started it all.

All the images of the past and all her misty thoughts, for some reason, blended into one distinct, overpowering thought—everything was irrevocably over for him and for her. She had crossed the line. The cold, inky sky outside the window contained a prophecy. She began to feel as though they had been together for a long time; that for ages they had been suffering, and that for ages she had had him at her side; but no longer.

'I have not concocted this practice, Dev,' she said quietly. 'It is an accepted thing. Is it not common, though often done furtively, in most palaces?'

'Your innate contempt for royalty and all things royal notwithstanding, there happens to be a more valid reason for niyog; it's political,' he said. 'When Rishi Parashuram started his internecine vengeance, he killed not just the Haiyaya king, Kartaviryarjun, who had murdered his father, but all the existing royal warriors and kings. He is said to have annihilated twenty-one generations of them. Soon, kingdoms were left without king or heirs and it was then that the widowed queens approached learned men and rishis. It quickly became an accepted custom for the queens to have children with sages, and that custom continues even now...' he took a breath, jutting out his jaw, '...by queen mothers like you, who want their bloodline to flourish!'

She smiled, unfazed by his scorn. 'I see it differently. I think the royal women defeated Parashuram's purpose beautifully. By going to rishis and Brahmins, they were still the creators of their progeny, a new race. And through niyog, I am giving the same powers to my daughters-in-law. It is not the men who are important, Dev, it is the women who give birth and create a new life, a new hope, by perpetuating their family line, their dynasty, their clan, their race. Though men claim it to be theirs, in the name of patriarchy.'

Bhishm tilted his head, regarding her thoughtfully. 'You are doing the same in your irrational quest for a male heir,' he accused.

'Yes, because a queen is always the king's wife; the ruler is always the king,' she rued. 'A princess is never born to be queen, as a prince is to become king. I want an heir, Dev; be it a girl or a boy. If so destined, a daughter might rule Hastinapur. But there has to be a scion in the family.'

'There are good kings and allies ...' began Bhishm.

'No,' she said vehemently. 'Such a man, if chosen to father the children, might grasp a position at the Kuru court by force, jeopardizing the political equation. He will simply make himself more powerful, and the Kurus weaker.'

Bhishm sighed dispiritedly. 'It is a suggestion that I do not approve of myself, but it is my duty to let you know,' he added curtly, getting up, his manner stiff. 'I shall inform Kripacharya, and ask him if he knows of a revered rishi for this noble purpose. Or do you know of any?'

It did not take a fraction of a second to decide—there was only one name she could think of.

Without further ado, she told him briefly about Rishi Parashar and their son.

'Krishna Dwaipayan is your son?' asked Bhishm, placing his powerful hands on the table and leaning forward to stare at her. He had been stunned when she had first mentioned this unknown son before marriage, but that the famous rishi was that son, left him speechless.

For once, Bhishm could not hide the incredulity in his voice. He gazed at the woman before him. She was an enigma. *She was baring her soul, telling him her deepest secret, darker than that of her own birth? She was a bravely honest woman even when it came to herself.* What she had just divulged must have been difficult for her—as it had been when she confessed everything to Amba, in the presence of everyone—but she had said it all with a poise and dignity only she could muster. She sat there, calm and collected, sounding slightly urgent, but neither apologetic nor ashamed. No regrets, no recriminations, no rancour. For her, it was a fact.

He understood and believed her—he saw that from her sudden pallor, and from the way her hands lay loosely in her lap. In one instant, all that had happened of late flashed through his mind. He reflected, and with pitiless clarity he saw the whole truth—her abandoned child; her quest for prestige through power; her fear of losing it all; her drive and determination, stemming from her basic instinct for self-preservation. Her zeal for heirs for her dynasty was not about ambition; she was beyond that.

'What do you say?' she interrupted his thoughts, her voice quiet, but firm. 'He is known as Ved Vyas now, the compiler of the four Vedas, trained under the four Kumaras, Narad and Lord Brahma himself.'

He detected a faint surge of pride in her voice. He was

her son, the only one remaining, and she was unrepentantly proud to be his mother.

He nodded, his tone now reverential. 'Yes, he is a great scholar. The division of the Vedas was a feat in itself, making it easier for people to understand the divine knowledge that lies within.'

'Vyas, it seems, means to split and differentiate, or describe,' she said thoughtfully, a finger pressed against her lips. 'He forsook the name I had given him.'

'Just as you forsook him,' he reminded her. 'You should not expect anything from him; you gave him nothing but birth.'

They were silent. She took in his anger and held his eyes for a couple of moments, her face wearing the same haughty expression.

She said bluntly, 'You are angry with me? That your father was not the first man I had?'

She waited with bated breath for his reply, as his disapproval still mattered.

'Nothing you do shocks me,' he said indifferently.

It was a reprimand; he was still angry with her.

'You want to say that you despise my past, and you are right,' she said, deeply stirred. 'You belong to a special class of men who cannot be judged by ordinary standards. Your moral requirements are exceptionally rigorous, and I understand you can't forgive things,' she said ironically. 'I understand you, and if sometimes I say the opposite, it doesn't mean that I look at things differently from you. We speak the same language, which is our common love for Hastinapur,' she said proudly. 'But I don't despise my past, or Parashar or my son. But there never was love there either. It's an absurd emotion,' she said, going to the window and looking down at the river. 'All this love does, is muddle the conscience and the mind. The meaning of life is in the struggle, the fighting. To trample and to crush it! *That* is what we have in common; that is what keeps us together, Dev. Our life, our throne, our battlefield is Hastinapur.'

'But that does not give us the right to rule others' lives,' he said shortly.

'It does, sadly; and I am not happy about it, as you seem to think,' she remarked bitterly.

From her unhappy eyes and face, he saw that she was miserable, and that the conversation would lead to no good, but he went on impetuously.

'Though you suffered it once yourself with that rishi, you are willing to inflict the same on those two helpless girls. How can you? Have you no conscience, no consideration?' he muttered under his breath.

'Conscience often has to give way to consciousness of duty, however unsavoury,' she remarked, her smile dry. 'I did it then, and I will do it now,' she said, inhaling deeply. Do you give me a choice, Dev? As I said once, if it comes to being either fair or firm, I would rather be firm,' she said mildly. 'Being firm means you *have to* take a decision, good or bad. I am ready to take that bad decision, for there is no good one to choose, is there?' she goaded. 'You would rather be fair, sheltered by a cloak of righteousness, whereas I bare myself to censure and criticism.' She took in the hard lines on his unforgiving face. 'When Ved Vyas arrives, I would like you, too, to meet him,' she added, dismissively.

Bhishm nodded perfunctorily. 'Yes, of course. But I repeat, I do not concur, and I never will,' he said cautiously. 'Please prepare the girls. Let them know what they are in for. They are too young...' his voice dragged into a weary sigh.

She replied tartly, 'As always, I will do the dirty deed.

I shan't allow anything, oh noble Bhishm, to tarnish your spotless image.'

~

His words were echoing in her mind as Satyavati hurried to the other wing of the palace, but she did not give them the power to hurt her. It was upon her to do this task; wicked or wise, only time would tell. It was best that it was Vyas, more importantly, *her* son, who was going to perform niyog with her daughters-in-law, not some roaming rishi or unscrupulous king. It had not been just caution or discretion that prompted her to take this decision. It would be her blood that would inherit the throne. *It would be the same*, she thought rationally, *as Chitrangad's or Virya's son occupying the throne. All three are my sons.*

The two young queens were still in mourning, and she could hear them sobbing when she entered their chamber. Satyavati knew her two daughters-in-law well. From their birth, they had been spoilt. At their swayamvar, they had been curious and eager, but with enough intelligence to realize that the various young princes who swarmed around them had a calculating eye on the riches and kingdom that would eventually be theirs. She, Satyavati, had ruined their plans, their dreams, and had them whisked away by Bhishm straight into the arms of an eager Virya. In spite of having everything that wealth could buy, they had led a life of unadulterated merrymaking with Virya. They were not just his queens, but also his lovers, his constant companions in a promiscuous pursuit of wanton pleasures. But now he was dead, leaving them bereft. They had no one but each other.

Her son's cloying affection had pampered them, and without it now, they were wilting like flowers under a hot sun. She was that hot sun. Satyavati had quickly realized this, soon after Virya's death. They regarded her as the reason for their unhappiness and misfortune.

Satyavati had tried her best to understand them, or rather, make them like her. But her eager interest in everything they did or planned only infuriated them. Her suggestions on ways that they could relieve their ennui were received with scorn. Her attempts to make them escape their sorrow had made matters worse between them. She did what she thought was best for the two girls, but she did not see that she was spoiling them by showering everything on them, whether they wanted it or not. She had become to them an officious meddler. She knew they sneered at her behind her back, and offered her nothing in return.

But now they will have to, she promised herself fiercely. *It is time they gave something to Hastinapur.*

Instructing their handmaid, Parishrami, to leave the chamber, Satyavati approached both the girls. Ambalika got up swiftly as soon as she entered the chamber, but Ambika, lying listless in bed, only reluctantly sat up.

'I have an urgent matter to discuss,' informed Satyavati, nodding to her elder daughter-in-law to sit and listen. And in swift, succinct words, she explained her intention. The girls looked at her with mounting horror, their eyes round and alarmed.

'No!' whispered Ambalika, her face bleached white from horror.

'Never!' hissed Ambika vehemently, her tears drying up in surging anger. 'How can you give us away to some stranger?'

'He is your brother-in-law, not a stranger,' replied Satyavati briefly.

Ambika gaped. 'But...' she turned to look uncomprehendingly at her younger sister.

Ambalika looked as dazed.

'We are not courtesans, to be presented to a stranger for one night,' persisted Ambika fiercely.

'You are queens, and one of your duties is to provide heirs,' retorted Satyavati, cutting short Ambika's protests. Her voice became cold and firm. 'You will have your child, if not from my son, then from another!'

Ambika inhaled harshly. 'Don't you ever feel fear or pain or compassion, Mother?' she raged. 'All these days, I haven't seen you shed a tear, or mourn for your son...' her voice broke. 'All you can think of is Hastinapur and its heirs?' she sneered through her thick tears—not sad, but bitter, angry tears. 'You ruined Amba's life, and now it's our turn. What gives you that right?' she fumed, her steady brown eyes livid.

Satyavati threw Ambika a hard look. 'You say you were born a princess, so you should know the royal rules well by now, dear. You are now a queen, a widowed queen, and you know your royal responsibilities well.'

Her tone softened. 'Please, just this one time, for this one night tonight,' she pleaded. 'The future of this family, of this kingdom, lies in your hands.'

'Both of us?' croaked Ambalika, in a stricken whisper.

'Ideally, yes,' said Satyavati. 'We need to have two princes, at least.'

Ambalika steadied herself. She looked at her sister, and nodded numbly. Ambika drew in a quick, startled breath. She remained very still, staring at her younger sister, whose pallor was as white as the silk she was wearing, courage and colour drained from her.

They would have to agree; their consent did not matter.

'Then who would be the heir?' asked Ambika, in a stilted tone.

'Yours; the older one from the older queen,' returned Satyavati with a reassuring smile.

Ambika felt a strange sense of jubilation. For once, she would win. She threw her younger sister a sidelong look of envious resentment. Virya had always favoured the soft-spoken, voluptuous Ambalika. *Now it will be my turn to preen*, she thought elatedly, a flare of hope kindling within her.

She noticed the gold pot her mother-in-law had placed on a table.

'What is that?' she asked curiously, her fears deferred for a short second.

'Ghee,' said the older woman. 'In niyog, the bodies are to be covered with ghee, so that there is no lust or desire in the minds of the participants; only the facilitating of the actual act to make way for conception.'

Ambalika shuddered, close to tears.

'The act is seen primarily as a duty,' continued Satyavati, her voice soft and reassuring. 'And while doing so, the appointed man and the woman will have only duty on their minds, and not passion or lust. The man does it to help the woman in the name of obligation, whereas the woman accepts it only to bear the child for herself and her husband and family. Think of it as an allegiance you owe to the throne of Hastinapur, which lies vacant without a king.'

'It is cold-blooded!' muttered Ambika. But there was a glint in her eyes. She squeezed her fingers into small fists. She was ready for anything to give Hastinapur the heir. *Her* son, the first born, would be heir...

The Other Son

'There is a young rishi waiting for you, Queen Mother,' declared Vibha. 'Should I lead him inside?'

Satyavati nodded.

He was as she had expected him to be—a dark, thin, young man, with matted locks, his face largely obscured by a long, shaggy beard and overgrown moustache. *My son*, the words stuck in her throat. He was a square-shouldered man of medium height, a definitive jaw and a straight narrow nose. But she looked into his dark brown eyes and she saw the man within—a gentle soul with passionate eyes, alight with the glow of knowledge. Parashar had groomed him to be a revered rishi, as promised, while she had erased him as a momentary episode in her unstoppable life, and moved on.

She stood gazing at him wordlessly for a long time, drinking in the sight of him. He had never been hers, and this was the first time she had felt a sense of possessiveness for him. Vyas was *her* son, after all.

He smiled slowly, the same glorious smile of his father. Her heart somersaulted.

'It must be for some urgent matter that you called for me; not because of a surge of maternal love,' he smiled. 'It had been promised to you by my father, Ma. Whenever you think of me, I shall be there.'

She detected the taunt in his soft voice. She did not give herself time to feel more anxious, but began immediately to tell him everything—about herself, Hastinapur, and what she wanted out of him, for the sake of the throne. He sat pale, with a grave, almost stern face, his lips compressed. He did not even bat an eyelash, but simply sat listening to her keenly. His attitude, and his fixed, expressionless gaze reminded her of Parashar and their incredibly intimate, icy-cold memories.

When she had finished, Vyas looked at her gravely, without a trace of judgement or the condemnation she had been secretly dreading.

'Do you know what you are doing?' he said eventually, his voice soft. 'Such decisions don't augur well. Adopt a child, as Bhishm suggested.'

'Whose?' she shrugged. 'And what assurance do I have that it won't lead to torn loyalties?'

'You can assure yourself of nothing, Ma. Even gods can't control their future!' he smiled. 'But these children you so desire from me won't be of the royal Kuru bloodline,' he warned.

'The world will recognize them as such,' she replied evenly. 'They will be known as Kurus because their mothers married into the Kuru clan. The children thus born will always be considered as the children of the mothers and their husband's family, and not that of the appointed man. And I am sure that even you would not seek any paternal relationship or attachment to these children in the future.'

'No, I shan't; just as you did not. But which my father did,' he said pointedly.

Satyavati bit her lip.

'How is your father?' she asked hesitantly.

'He passed away recently,' said Vyas, his face remote. 'He was walking through a forest when he and his students were attacked by wolves. He was unable to get away in his old age with his limp,' he paused, and she noticed his hands had balled into fists. 'They say that when a rishi dies, he merges back into nature. My father left this world, merging into those very wolves.'

She felt a lump in her throat, and swallowed hard. She touched his hand fearfully, trying to connect with the son she was meeting for the first time.

When she sat like that, with their hands tightly clasped, sympathetic and mournful, Vyas felt as if they were not strangers. Both were bound by blood, both had been abandoned in the course of life.

'Do the queens know of me?' he asked finally, breaking the awkward silence. 'They are princesses who were married to a young, handsome king. How would they respond to me in this state?' he said, looking down at his rough bark clothes and his matted appearance. 'I have come straight from the forests, cut short my meditation for you. I am dirty and dishevelled, not fit to be in the presence of any royalty. The queens will be repulsed... Should we wait...'

'No, it has to be done tonight, as quickly as possible,' she cut in curtly.

Vyas immediately knew why. She wanted to hasten the heirs into the world as early as possible, for them to be known as Vichitravirya's sons.

'I thought you were not scared of what society has to say,' he said softly. 'But you did desert me for society...'

'I did not. Your father wanted you for himself; what I wanted did not matter,' she interrupted quietly.

Vyas shook his head. 'Why did you not fight for me? My father wanted me; you didn't,' he accused.

'Yes,' she admitted. 'I did not. Why would I? I was a child myself, too confused about all that had happened! Why can a woman not choose motherhood?'

She paused abruptly: ironically, she was forcing her daughters-in-law into motherhood as well.

She continued harshly, 'Yes, I confess you did not stir in me the maternal emotions expected out of me. That's why it was so easy to give you up to your father. As you rightly said, he loved you more and was more a father than I was a mother. He wanted a child and it happened to be through me; I was in no position to refuse or choose,' she pursed her lips, feeling a constriction in her throat. 'Was I to explain that you were born out of my acquiescence to the advances of a famous rishi?'

Vyas flushed under his dark skin.

She continued grimly, 'I tried to make the most of a bad situation. Does that make me capricious? Conniving?' She gave a slight shake of her head. 'A girl often has to endure what is forced on her: be it man, marriage or motherhood.'

'I am talking about myself,' he said with a sad smile. 'You did not want me until now. Yet, you are unafraid to use your forgotten son for your great royal plan. Who *am* I to you, Ma?'

His gentle voice almost broke her.

'I am not ashamed of you. Never!' she said fiercely. 'Nor am I ashamed of what I did, if that is what you are insinuating. Parashar and you are gifts in my life; I was blessed. I have acknowledged you to the world, Son. You have been received in this palace as one, and have been accorded all the respect due to you. You are Rishi Vyas, and I am proud to be your mother. I bow to you, Son. But now I wish to employ you for a more political reason, rather than personal,' she gave a twisted smile.

'Ah, yes, you are the queen mother,' he nodded knowingly. 'One who commands all.'

'But I am not commanding you; it's a request. I am begging you,' she said simply. 'I can see no other way.'

'The way of the world is often misleading, taking us down a path we should actually avoid,' he said cryptically. He stood up. 'I am ready. But are the queens?'

She nodded. 'My maid, Vibha, will lead you to their chambers.'

She saw him leave the hall. She stood still, staring bleakly at the doorway as she listened to his heavy tread disappearing down the corridor. She stepped out on the terrace; a light evening breeze was blowing. She spotted Bhishm immediately, walking up and down in his garden below, amidst his beloved flowers. Even from a distance, she could detect the agitation in his stride, the suppressed frustration in his hunched shoulders. She gazed at him, feeling the familiar sense of belongingness. She forced herself to tear her eyes away from him and looked instead for a long time at the Ganga. There was not one sail on the horizon. On the silhouetted banks, in the lilac-coloured mist, there were mountains, gardens, towers and houses, and the sun was sparkling over them all. Yet, it all seemed alien to her; an incomprehensible tangle against the echo of a boatman's song.

~

Satyavati practically rushed into Ambika's bedchamber; her anxiety making her gait unsteady. She stopped abruptly when she heard voices. The sisters were in deep conversation, oblivious of her presence.

'Whom are we fooling but ourselves, Ambalika? We lived with our husband for years and never had a child; neither of us! Did no one suspect?'

'Virya was so ill, Ambika,' her sister replied weakly, but Satyavati detected the hesitancy in her voice.

'He was impotent!' wept Ambika in anger. 'Dead or alive, I guess we would have had to endure this torture and bear a child through niyog!' she gave an off-key, short laugh.

'But we might get to have a child after all these years of waiting,' said Ambalika, hope in her voice.

'For a child, are you ready to suffer this indignity?' demanded her sister.

'I don't know,' said Ambalika feebly. 'But I *do* want a child—I have waited for years! Don't you too? What is left for us anyway?'

Satyavati walked in at that moment, with heavy footsteps so she would be heard. The girls looked up guiltily.

One look at her hard face and the older girl burst out in a rush of words.

'I couldn't bear that man! I kept my eyes tightly shut!' whispered Ambika with a visible shudder.

Satyavati absently wiped her perspiring face. It was a hot morning, but she realized she was sweating more than she usually did. She was aware of an uncomfortable feeling in the pit of her stomach, a feeling of fear. *Was the child conceived well*, was her frantic, first thought.

'Tell me what happened,' she ordered.

Colour flamed Ambika's fair face, more out of anger than embarrassment. 'No, I shan't! Allow me some privacy, please!' she scowled. 'All I can say is that it was a nightmare, and the man you sent was a revolting monster! I couldn't bear to look at him!'

Her sister's words had made Ambalika shiver. 'It is my turn tonight,' she stammered, her face ashen as she turned piteous eyes towards her mother-in-law.

Satyavati pursed her lips, placing a fingertip on the middle of the lower one, trying to seem calm while she was raging inside, dread mingling with wrath. The foolish girl had somehow ruined it.

Looked at the frightened Ambalika, she placed a reassuring hand on her shoulder, and smiled.

'Under no circumstances, dear, should you shut your eyes,' she warned. 'Vyas told me what *you* did, Ambika,' she said nodding towards the older sister. 'He says that this does not portend anything good...' she frowned.

'How will it be good when I was forced into it!' cried Ambika fiercely. 'And, moreover, he wasn't whom I was expecting...' she stopped abruptly, her face flaming.

Satyavati looked puzzled. She noticed Ambika bite her lower lip and the usually outspoken girl was unusually wordless. The girl seemed to think hard for a long moment. She studied Satyavati's face, as if making up her mind. Then her words came with a burst, 'He was not whom I was told to receive!' she accused, her voice sharp.

Satyavati was taken aback, her confusion deepening.

Ambalika's distressed voice broke in. 'Ma, you had told us that it would be our brother-in-law who would be visiting our chamber, and we assumed it would be...' she stopped, acutely embarrassed, her face coloured a bright pink.

It dawned quickly upon her. They had been expecting Bhishm in their chamber!

The sheer ludicrousness of the thought made her want to giggle, but seeing the red, tense faces of the two girls, and knowing the gravity of the moment, Satyavati shook her head in dismay.

Ambika's eyes glittered with the flare of disappointed rage. Her mother-in-law had tricked her into believing that her handsome brother-in-law would be coming to her that night. She had been excited, though nervous, and had urged her maid to dress her up splendidly, after a luxurious bath. She had waited for him in her chamber at the appointed hour; the father of her future child, the heir-to-be. But instead, in the dimness of her chamber, she saw a dark, dirty monster with flowing dreadlocks, an ash-covered body and glowing eyes. She shuddered at the memory. Unprepared and aghast, stunned into speechlessness, she had closed her eyes in horror, as his rough body had descended upon her.

'Who was that man you sent?' she asked tremulously, her voice now shaking more with fury than fear.

'His name is Vyas. He is a rishi,' Satyavati said tersely. 'And your brother-in-law.'

Both the girls gave a start, staring at her in open disbelief.

'I had him before I married King Shantanu,' she said, her face as wooden as her voice. 'I, too, was once in a situation like you girls are in now, but I think I handled it better than you!' She felt a spark of renewed anger. 'Could you not have been more accommodating, considering you are a princess who knows the royal demands from a queen?' she said, her voice sharpening as she glared balefully at Ambika.

Ambika did not miss the reprimand in the older woman's voice. She bristled, recovering her breath and spirit. 'That is because we are pampered princesses, as you rightly pointed out,' she said maliciously. 'If we were tough, like fisherwomen, I accede we would have taken it well.'

Satyavati's eyes narrowed at the girl's impertinence. 'You act like a wilting touch-me-not!' she snapped. 'When, for seven years, you enjoyed a royal wanton romp with my son!'

Ambika stiffened, coming to her feet with a lunge, her face white with unconcealed fury, her lips drawn in an angry retort.

'Stop it, please!' interrupted a breathless Ambalika. She turned a petrified face to her mother-in-law. 'Please, I can't do this...!' she gulped.

Satyavati turned to her fiercely. 'Don't you dare spoil things further! You girls were told to do this one thing; I don't want the situation getting worse! You do it right this time, unlike your spoilt, selfish sister!'

Watching the colour drain from the girl's face, Satyavati stopped herself. She knew she was being harsh, but Vyas's warning words had left her anxious and high-strung.

'Your daughter-in-law shut her eyes at the sight of me, Ma,' he had said after her persistent questioning.

'She is young, a princess, sheltered in her upbringing,' she had defended, annoyed that Ambika had fumbled.

Vyas had nodded gravely. 'Yes, and I am not the most attractive man to be with,' he had smiled wryly. 'Especially in my present state.'

She gave him a quick, cursory glance. His hair was matted, his dark skin swarthy and dry from his wanderings in the sun, his hard hands looked calloused, the nails dirty, as were his feet.

'Have a bath before you go to Ambalika tonight,' she advised shortly.

'I need more than a bath, Ma. I am worse than an animal in a jungle. The princess was revolted as I had predicted ... how do you expect a good end to this bad beginning? I had told you that it would be better if we had waited and postponed this ... er, task.'

His warning ringing in her ears and the cold fright in Ambalika's eyes brought Satyavati to her senses. She had to reassure this girl; if the stronger-minded Ambika had been revolted, her timid sister would surely faint at the very sight of Vyas.

Satyavati forced a light smile and gently patted the girl's hands. 'I am sorry, but I am worried,' she said softly. 'Vyas, like his father, is not an ordinary man. He is a famed rishi, and to be with him is said to be an honour. Don't waste your chance, dear; your child will be great if you allow it to so happen.'

Ambalika stared back at her, her eyes questioning, but she smiled wanly, nodding. 'Like yours was?' she whispered knowingly.

'Yes,' replied Satyavati. 'You, too, will have a child as

famous as him. Just bear with me—and him—for one night, please!'

Ambika felt a flash of jealousy sear through her and thought again of the child she might have. *He will be the heir, not Ambalika's, however much she impresses that ugly man. I will give Hastinapur the heir mother-in-law so desperately wants.*

'And what if it is a girl?' said Ambika, her smile spiteful.

'She would be heir, too,' replied Satyavati calmly. 'First she, then her husband, and then her children will rule Hastinapur.'

'That man is awful, whatever you may say,' sulked Ambika petulantly, lifting her shoulders, knowing her words would frighten her sister further. 'He smells, he is bristly, filthy, rough and fiery, I couldn't bear the mad intensity in his eyes, and...'

Satyavati caught the flare of fear in Ambalika's eyes.

Her voice dripped ice when she said, 'Ambika, don't scare her further. It is a calm, strong mind of a queen that is needed now, not the selfishness of a pampered princess!' She turned to Ambalika and took her trembling hands in hers. 'Listen, dear, I know it's hard, but try not to think of the worst. See it differently; not as a duty, not as coercion, not as a victim, but a victory—that you will be able to have a baby. By going to Vyas, and not Virya, you are still the mother of your child, the creator of progeny, new hope to this family. See it as a power, a *choice*, to have a child. It is not the man who is important, dear, it is you, the woman, who has the power to create a new life. Would you not like to have a child, a child to love?'

Ambalika nodded wistfully, the tears slowly drying on her pale cheeks.

Satyavati saw to it that she remained with Ambalika the rest of the day, so Ambika would have no opportunity to frighten or influence her younger sister further. It was only when she knew Vyas was about to knock on the door of her daughter-in-law that she left her to him.

'Do *not* shut your eyes,' she reminded her in a warning murmur.

It would be another long night. Satyavati shut the door of her own chamber and went to her bed. She sat on it, her hands balled into fists, gripped tightly between her knees. She listened to the faint sounds that came through the panels of Ambika's door. Finally, as these sounds became more out of control, she got to her feet. She stood, hesitating. There was no way to stop what she had started. She heard Ambalika stifle a cry and that decided her: she was doing the right thing. She sat motionless in the hot night, while she listened to the high-pitched silence of the stillness, her face frozen, staring blankly out of the window towards the silver river glistening in the moonlit night. It was an interminable wait, but finally she heard her son leave Ambalika's chamber. She wanted to rush out and meet him, but she would have to wait a little longer; at least until the first light of the morning.

'How was it?' she urgently asked her younger daughter-in-law at the crack of daybreak.

'I did not close my eyes,' Ambalika replied meekly.

Satyavati heaved a brief sigh of relief. Her words had knocked sense into the girl. She smiled gloriously; it would be all right. She just had to wait another nine months...

New Hope

It was a warm, winter morning. Vibha handed her the angavastra and the news that Ambika was in labour. Satyavati felt her heart race, then contract. The time had come. Hastinapur would have its heir. She could not hide the blinding joy that assailed her. She dressed hastily, almost fainting with anticipation, and hurried to Ambika's chamber.

In the heavily curtained room, she found a doctor, a midwife, and Parishrami, the efficient, pretty maid of Ambika. There was a smell of *kapur* and herbs in the room. She had scarcely crossed the threshold when, from the adjoining room, Satyavati heard a low, plaintive moan.

'Queen Ambalika, too, is in labour,' informed Parishrami.

'You attend to her; I shall see to Ambika,' she ordered.

The cry of the newborn broke the tumult in her mind. The baby was here! The heir had been born. The infant's wail carried with it a breath of fresh hope and memories of what had been: Shantanu and her, the evening of Dev's oath, her wedding, Chitrangad and Virya being born, the drifting rains as Chitrangad lay lifeless, the fire in Amba's eyes as she cursed Bhishm, that cold morning sky, and Bhishm's despair as he cried over the cold body of Virya.

Satyavati blinked. All was over. Now it was another beginning. She rushed to see Ambika, feeling as though she were the father of the child. Ambika was lying down, drowsy and pale, her hair drenched with sweat. She had a look of childlike helplessness—not her usual cold indifference. She appeared not to have heard Satyavati come in, or perhaps did not pay attention. She continued to look towards the large baby that the nurse was holding, as she waited for him to be placed in her arms.

The nurse was white-faced, and Satyavati immediately realized something was horribly amiss.

When the baby was given to Ambika, her face contorted with pain. She gazed up at the carved ceiling, as though wondering what was happening to her. There was a look of loathing on her face.

'It is horrible!' she whispered. 'He is blind!'

Satyavati froze; she was dumbstruck. Her shocked eyes moved from Ambika, to the maid, down to the swaddled baby. She could not speak, cold with fear, her eyes blinded by sudden tears. Her heart was beating erratically as she sank to her knees, her arms open to embrace the swaddled baby.

He was handsome and huge, with a prominent nose and a pointed chin. His eyes were not shut, but open; he was staring at her with accusing, opaque-white eyes. Her breath caught in her throat and burst out into a sob. *No!*

'He is your heir, Ma!' Ambika muttered softly. 'A blind heir, a blind king!' she cried bitterly, burying her face in a pillow.

For Satyavati, that one statement crystallized the great truth. The heir of Hastinapur was blind!

Satyavati stumbled into her own chamber and sank to the floor in stunned disbelief. Her dreams crumpled before her eyes like leaves scorched by the sun's heat. She felt like she was in a tossing boat with no command over Fate or Future. Was Fate laughing at her? There never had been any affinity between them: she had been either running away from it or trying to chase it away. She was no more to Fate than a cobweb to be flicked away, hanging precariously, to be torn away by the wind. She stared fixedly at the great river looping the palace: *Was Ganga taunting her for all that Satyavati had taken away from her son, and everything that she was losing, over and over again.* The sun had sunk over it, enveloping everything in a blanket of darkness, the stars sparkling overhead, but it was all an indifferent, incomprehensible tangle she could not unravel.

That is how Bhishm found her in the early hours of dawn—sitting on a low chair, huddled up, her face hidden in her hands, her long, unbrushed hair falling around her. It was an impression of exquisite anguish, and the last traces of any animosity he had for her left him; his heart ached. And as he looked at her, it occurred to him that, all these years, he had played and was still playing a strange, symbiotic part in the life of this woman; and that it was beyond his power to alter it. He knew now that he wanted to live only for her and Hastinapur. He had not seen her for days together since their disagreement, she had been avoiding him, and he knew why: she always pushed him away when she was most hurt. And he *had* hurt her. Ironically, the colder and harder her face grew, and the more distant she became, the nearer she was to him, and the more intensely and painfully he felt their kinship. Never mind her light, careless tone; never mind her silent, cold treatment; never mind the ruthlessness she displayed to safeguard her vulnerability.

Bhishm stood there a little while, then went away, without letting her know that a boy had been born to Ambalika as well—as pale as a ghost, as white with fright as his mother had been when he had been conceived.

When Satyavati came to know from a sombre Vibha of the second son and his unusual ivory pallor, she said, wearily, 'I need Vyas again. Tell Bhishm to send for him.'

Vyas, when he arrived, found his mother inconsolable and more stubborn.

'Both the infant princes are not healthy enough to be the heirs. One is blind and the other is an albino! Vyas, what did you give me?' she cried.

'The queens were not prepared, nor was it the right time,' he responded gravely. 'I tried to warn you that coercion always leads to undesired results.'

Her mind was a white flame of vicious fury. 'What fools these girls are!'

A thought struck her, which she voiced immediately to her son. 'In niyog, is not the man allowed a maximum of three times in his lifetime to be appointed in such a way?'

Vyas nodded, knowing what his mother was insinuating. 'It was to avoid misuse, Ma. Now you are being avaricious for heirs,' he warned softly.

'Not avaricious, simply cautious,' she returned imperiously. 'The third one should be perfectly healthy! Three princes for this vast kingdom which Bhishm and I have expanded over the years.'

'It was always his, Ma, and it still is,' he gave her a strange smile. 'You would not have to commit such impropriety had it been otherwise.'

She was beyond rebuke or reason.

'I want you to use your third chance, too,' she said bluntly, her eyes desperately appealing to him.

'And if I refuse?'

'You cannot refuse your mother,' she argued.

'You refused me, Ma,' he said, his voice hard.

'Never your existence!' she broke in. 'I need you, Son!'

He sighed. 'I shall do this last favour for you for the good deed of you having given birth to me; no more, no less! I leave tomorrow.'

Having barely managed to convince her reluctant son, Satyavati knew it would be another uphill task to convince Ambika to acquiesce.

'Again?' Ambika gave a small scream of horror. 'But why? You already have your heir, Ma.' She handed the month-old

Dhritrashtra to Satyavati, who immediately stopped crying at the familiar and firm touch of his grandmother, and gave her a toothless grin.

Satyavati looked at him with forlorn fondness, ruffling his curly hair.

'He is blind, dear, and that most likely disqualifies him from becoming king.'

'No!' said Ambika vehemently. '*Never*! Pandu might be just a day younger, but my son is still the older son and I am the older queen! Dhritrashtra will be king!' she swore, and Satyavati noticed the stubborn line of her mouth.

Ambika had already made him king, and Satyavati felt a sudden unpleasant knotting of her stomach. It was the same expression of words, the same mad ambition she had when her sons were born... She would have to quickly talk Ambika out of her growing obsession, or it would be too late.

'Exactly, you are the older queen. That is why I came to you and not Ambalika,' said Satyavati shrewdly. 'You shut your eyes the first time; maybe this time we can have a healthy child?'

She saw Ambika hesitate.

'Or should I go to Ambalika? She might agree and be the mother of two sons, one of them most likely to be crowned king, rather than a blind one!' she thrust the knife cruelly into Ambika's fluttering heart. She would ensure she got a healthy heir for Hastinapur.

'I'll do it!' muttered Ambika. 'What a paradox it is ... this war of the scions—the virile is a celibate, the impotent was made king, and the widows are made to supply heirs from a stranger-son of the queen mother!'

The small smile of triumph slipped from Satyavati's face. Her eyes widened in shock: Ambika's irreverent words uttered in an undertone, shouted aloud the story of the dynasty.

~

The moment he touched her, he knew the woman in his arms was not Ambika. It was dark, and she had cleverly lit just one oil lamp in the chamber. It was the same chamber, but not the same woman. She was veiled, hiding her face, but she could not hide from him the fact that she was not who she was supposed to be...

She pulled him down to her, as the other two women never had; she kissed him with a fervour that inflamed him, an uncontrollable fire that he was eagerly consumed in; she led him to a world of ecstasy that he did not know existed, and with a thick cry of surrender, he collapsed on the soft swell of her heaving breasts. Exhausted in his sweet bliss, he felt her getting up, still a dark silhouette of desire, and slipping away in the darkness. He stared after her. Who was she?

Vyas could not let go of her, of each and every moment she had lain with him. He could not meet his mother's eye when he said shortly, 'It was not with your daughter-in-law that I spent the night.'

Satyavati was speechless, as she assimilated his words and what they portended.

'Then who was it?' she whispered, bewildered. She received a shake of her son's matted head as a reply.

'Wait!' she pleaded. 'There's been some misunderstanding, Vyas. If not Ambika, I shall convince Ambalika. Please spend tonight with her,' she implored, and noticed the stern look on her son's face. 'Give Ambalika a second chance!'

Vyas shook his head coldly. 'It can't be.'

'Give Hastinapur another chance, Vyas!' she cried.

'Ma, I am a rishi, and I shouldn't be here,' he said, controlling his rising anger. 'I agreed to do this only for you.

And I have done what you asked me to—thrice. The law permits niyog only three times. Besides, I am soon to marry the daughter of Rishi Jabaali. I can't do this to Pinjala, to us,' he said, his voice firm. 'My work here is done, Ma!'

Satyavati barely registered him bowing and touching her feet before taking leave. Her heart contracted painfully. She stared at him with inert eyes, drained of hope, as she watched him walk away from the room, down the corridor, out from the palace, away from Hastinapur forever. She wanted to stop him, but the words stuck in her throat. Would she ever see him again?

She did not know how long she stood there. Then she recalled that he had left behind some unanswered questions. And only one person would have the answers—Ambika.

One look at her, and Satyavati recognized her expression of fearful defiance. The tightness of her mouth, and her glittering eyes told her at once that she had lied to her.

'I could not go through it again,' she stated firmly, before Satyavati could say anything. 'I refuse to be a pawn in your games, Mother, and not for the second time, at least! I have a son now; I have given you the heir you wanted.'

Satyavati regarded her with helpless anger. 'The poor boy is blind, thanks to you. How can he be king of a kingdom? How can he lead an army? My next choice would be Pandu...'

'*No!*' Ambika rounded on her fiercely. 'Not Pandu! He cannot be king. If my son is disqualified because he is blind, neither can Pandu take the throne as he is...'

'Why?' challenged Satyavati, furious. 'Because he is pale-skinned? An albino king is deemed better than a blind king, foolish woman. I gave you a second chance, and you threw it away!'

'To hand you a healthy heir?' barked Ambika. 'God, how I hate that word—heir. It is ironical isn't it, Mother, that for seven years, your son could not give us heirs. But one night with your other son has got what you so desired.'

Satyavati went white. She knew Ambika was implying that Virya had been impotent, and she would have never received a successor to the throne from him.

Smug contempt flitted on Ambika's face. 'I don't want a second child, Ma. I have Dhritrashtra, and he is the rightful king. No one else!'

'We shall see when the time comes,' retorted Satyavati. 'Bhishm and I will be very much there to anoint the next king. But right now, I want to know, you lying coward, whom did you sacrifice for your selfish ambition? Who did you send to Vyas?'

'My maid,' shrugged Ambika. 'Parishrami. I thought she would suit him best. After all, the rishi, too, is a low-born like her, isn't he?' she taunted.

Satyavati was too stunned to register the jibe.

'Do you realize what you have done, fool?' she whispered, horrified. 'Your maid's son, Ambika, will be perfect, unlike yours.'

Nine months later, her words came true. He was the perfect baby, cheerful and smiling, without any physical defect or any imperfection. Satyavati held him close, and instinctively she knew he would be her favourite. Not because he was handsome and healthy, but because he was destiny's unfortunate child. He would have the qualities, yet not be qualified to be king. It was his birth—as a maid's child—and not his worth, that would be his lifetime's burden to carry. Like she had done. But she had managed to clamber and claw her way up. Would he? Could he?

'I can never thank you enough,' Satyavati told Parishrami. The girl smiled wanly. 'Nor can I express regret for what my daughter-in-law did,' she apologized earnestly.

'Please don't ask for my pardon again, Queen Mother; you have said it before,' assured Parishrami, embarrassed. 'The moment you came to know, you asked me if I wanted this baby. You gave me a choice, oh Queen, and I shall forever be thankful for that. I wanted to have the child and you agreed. It is you who have tended to me all these months, given me a new status, wealth and house. I am no longer a maid,' she said gratefully, tears welling up in her eyes. 'I did as I was ordered, but what you have done was not your royal duty. You did it out of compassion, and I shall ever be indebted to you!'

'No, I remain indebted to *you*. You have given me a beautiful grandchild!' smiled Satyavati, pressing the girl's hands.

It was not compassion; it was empathy, Satyavati reflected ... a certain affinity she felt more for this girl than her two daughters-in-law. It was the dilemma that she had faced when she had Vyas: whether she wanted to have the child or not. She had wanted it, and not because Parashar wished for it. She could not inflict the same pain on this poor girl, who had been forced to be with a man when it was neither her duty nor her decision. Parishrami was a slave obeying orders, and Satyavati had freed the girl from the shackles of royal command. She was, after all, the mother of Vyas' son.

'Vidur, the wise, that's your name,' she said softly, gazing down at his wise, warm eyes, just like his father's.

She heard a movement behind her, but she knew who it was before she turned around to look at him, her eyes shining with anguish and joy.

'So I got my heirs, Dev,' she breathed, her lips stiff, finding it difficult to say the words. 'Three of them ... though Vyas had said one would be enough, as more than one often results in rivalry, particularly in royal houses. But I had two, and both died... I wanted to take no chances,' she said, her shoulders slumping. 'Vyas, like you, was openly shocked and refused to obey my orders, warning me that preserving the dynasty by adopting such means was improper. I argued with him that improper orders from elders ought to be obeyed when it comes to royal duties. That such obedience carries no blame. But I am to blame, Dev! I even used the low trick of using sentiments against my son.'

'I am to blame, too; I should have stopped this when I could,' interrupted Bhishm harshly. 'But I urged him as well...'

She threw him a look of utter amazement.

He sighed wretchedly. 'I saw we had no choice, and told him so too. It was then that Rishi Vyas agreed to engage in what he described as "this disgusting task".'

Satyavati's hands tightened into fists. 'Vyas had asked that Ambika and Ambalika live a year of austerity so that they would be cleansed of the last seven years of overindulgence. He meant to purify, not the girls, but *me* so that I came to my senses! I now realize that he was simply trying to defer my decision,' she shook her head in abject despair. 'But I paid no heed; I was in a hurry for an heir and was in no mood to wait. I ordered Vyas to be done with his task at the earliest. And see what happened! I now have three heirs but none are perfect for the throne. Not even this one, my Vidur. Look at him, Dev, he is so tragically perfect!' she cried, placing him gently next to the two princes in the cradle.

'But he can never be king,' Bhishm said sorrowfully.

'Why?' she cried. 'When I place him with the other two princes, he is like them: the son of Vyas. Under you, all three children will train and flourish. Why then should this child be denied, though he is superior to the other two? Just because he is a maid's son? Will he have to suffer that stigma all his life?'

'Yes. He is a reminder of our mistakes and manipulations.'

'But why should he suffer for our transgressions,' she protested.

'As Vyas voiced his doubts and openly wondered whether such progeny could ever be a source of happiness for anyone!'

'They are. However disappointed we may be, Dev, the two mothers are now very happy. They are now mothers, and each have a son they adore. They are both glowing with unbridled happiness.'

Bhishm noticed a slight change in her voice. 'What is it?' he asked quickly.

'There is also unbridled ambition glowing in Ambika's heart,' she looked up into Bhishm's unhappy eyes. 'She is already dreaming of Dhritrashtra as king, as he is the firstborn. But how can it be? I have heard her cooing it to him in his ears. She will poison his mind this way as he grows up,' she cried frantically.

'The glitter of the crown is mightier than the burden of it,' he said bleakly. 'But till we are here, we can look after the throne as we have done until now.'

'Did we really take care of the throne, or ourselves?' Satyavati said wistfully, as if she was speaking to herself. 'Do we have it in us to protect this boy so he will get his rights as a royal?'

'We cannot dispute the thought itself, we are chained by rules,' he hesitated. 'Rules, ironically made by us, often unfair, inconvenient and prejudiced ... making life difficult for others, and of no use to anyone!' he threw open his arms helplessly. 'I made my oath a rule for myself, made it rule me instead. The strength with which I persevered with that oath—I wonder if I have that strength in me to start a new order, make a beginning, pioneer a new path. Yes, I am a coward!' he said, his eyes burning in strange intensity. 'But I hope I do have the strength to fight for this little boy!'

'I shall!' she said fiercely. 'He shall grow up as a Kuru prince, with the other two boys. You will make him fit to be a king! You have to. Dev, you talk about your ancestors; of how they were never ruled by the dictates of society, that the best deserved to be king. And I say it is *this* boy who will be the best amongst the three.'

She recognized the defeat in Bhishm's eyes.

'I did it for myself, Dev; why can't I do it for this boy, too?' she pleaded. 'Who doubts it? I am not advocating revolt, but a change. A good king makes rules, but a great leader is one who knows when to break them. You have done it all along; I am sure you will do it for Vidur, too, and give him the status he deserves as the third Kuru son.'

She glanced at the sleeping infant.

'I shall, I promise,' she vowed. 'But I need your support as well, Dev. We must look into the root, the very cause of all the other causes. I don't want to be like the others—everyone seems to have grown smug and, slack—we fear change, we don't want reforms. We are now a people of fatigued whimperers; we do nothing but talk of war and victory, glory and gold. But why are we not accountable? We fight wars in the battlefield, but what about our internal wars of progress? Why are we so fearful of change? A king is a leader, too, more than just a head who wears the crown; a king has the power to make a change. Then why does he not? Why can we not make new laws, new rules that break shackles, instead of chaining us? If I, a fisher girl, could be queen, I shall see to it that a maid's son gets his rights! Can we not together make it happen?'

Bhishm hesitated, his frown deepening. 'Can we in our arrogant capacity do so? You thought you could make your own future, but it eventually led you to the path you were avoiding for so long. That is the irony; *that* is Fate. This boy and the other boys were meant to be born...' he sighed. 'We are of too little consequence to affect the destiny of a whole generation,' he murmured. 'We thought we could do it, and we tried; but we failed. We must hope for that larger, more general good and better future. But not one wish from our lips is made without the will of Fate—nothing happens by chance or coincidence. Everything has its cause, and is inevitable.'

'That's all very well; you are a fatalist, with a more submissive outlook. I am not,' she retorted, agitated. 'I believe the future will be clearer for the generations to come, and our experience will be at their service.' She threw him a doubtful look. 'But what about our mistakes, Dev? They get carried forward, too, don't they? I don't worry about Fate because I don't believe in it. I am more worried about our mistakes becoming their mayhem?' she said anxiously. 'One wants to live beyond death, to last through the next generation. Life is only given to us once, and I wanted to live it boldly, with full consciousness and beauty and honesty—at least to myself. Often one wishes to play an important, noble part; one wants to make history so that later generations do not dismiss us as non-entities or worse, failures! I want to be remembered not for my errors, but my endeavours. I might agree that what is going on is inevitable and not without a purpose, but then, what do I do with that divine inevitability?' she lifted one elegant shoulder. 'I have power over only myself, and not others.'

Bhishm smiled a hollow smile. 'Do you know what's inevitable about you—you take the bad with as much grace as the good, and move on. You will never give up; your never-say-die spirit will not allow you to surrender. But then, if so, why should we worry and despair for what we cannot escape? We have that much control over the good and the bad. What is cruel? What is unfair?' Bhishm looked weary. 'What is right? Which wrong is right or which right is wrong? There are no clear answers, just questions we need to ask ourselves. The art of righteousness is very subtle, indeed!' he sighed. 'If you observe our family history closely, right from King Bharat till now, see how we perceive and discriminate unconsciously. The reasoning behind our discrimination might make sense, but would it still be right? Stop seeing differences, and you see the truth.'

'What is our truth, Dev?' Her voice faded into a sad whisper. 'That I tried to make a difference in my life, but at your expense. Yet you let go and served us loyally, without rancour or regret. Dev, you are the *prajnamanin*, the wisest, most unselfish and the most revered man in the country, and will be so for generations to come. Possibly your wisdom is the result of the hard life you have endured. Is it your kindness and your selflessness that make me what I am?'

'I do not deserve the glory thrust upon me,' he said, clenching his jaw. 'For my own sense of mission, I have wrought great injustices. I am not noble. I made mistakes, and some died for it,' his voice crumpled in a hoarse whisper, his eyes clouding in sudden anguish. 'And some will live through it...'

Fearfully, her eyes came up slowly to meet his.

They heard a chortle, as if a sound in agreement. Both of them turned to look at the three babies, swaddled in a crimson and gold royal shawl. The babies stared back at them attentively, without blinking, as though they knew their futures were being decided.

EPILOGUE
Satyavati

The reflection she could see of herself in the cold waters of the Ganga was blurred, but Satyavati could see her life clearly...

'They will destroy each other: the sons of Dhritrashtra and the sons of Pandu. It will be annihilation! The seeds of decay have been planted; the harvest will be gruesome. Do you want to live to see the destruction of your grandsons ... the heirs of Hastinapur?'

Vyas' words, condoling Pandu's unforeseen death, rolled over her, stinging more than the icy breeze against her raddled face. Had she planted the seeds of war for that tree of decay to grow and destroy? She remembered how the three princes had been born. 'Disgusting,' Vyas had said. And so all had come to nought. Ambika had a son, Dhritrashtra, born blind and manipulative; Ambalika had Pandu, pale and impotent, who had ironically died, lusting. And Vidur, the maid's son, had been made prime minister–counsellor to his brothers, the kings, but never to be a king himself.

When Satyavati had once asked about her grandchildren's strengths, Bhishm had acknowledged Dhritrashtra's strength, Pandu's military acumen and Vidur's intellect. Vidur amply displayed his knowledge and intellect when it was time to choose the crown prince. It had been his wise suggestion, albeit controversial, which upset Ambika, Dhritrashtra and the assumed primogeniture that, though the eldest, Dhritrashtra's blindness made him an unfit king. He supported Pandu's election to the kingship, much to her secret relief and Bhishm's as well. Though reluctantly agreeing with the verdict, Dhritrashtra had never forgiven Vidur.

Upon Pandu's later abdication and departure for the forest as penance for having killed a rishi, and the blind Dhritrashtra's resultant succession, it had been Vidur—impeccably groomed by Bhishm—who had taken on the reins of the kingdom, steering his brother's reign till a new heir was appointed, a move that would end in a bloody battle, if Vyas' words were to come true.

If only Pandu had not abdicated the throne, Satyavati thought wistfully. She should have been more adamant... And then he had died, killed by that same lustful urge that had killed Shantanu and Virya. His widow, Kunti, had come home with the five sons—the Pandavas—whom she and the dead Madri, Pandu's second wife, had conceived through niyog.

But her family was *not* impotent, Satyavati told herself fiercely. Pandu had five sons, the Pandavas. And Dhritrashtra had a daughter and a hundred sons—the Kauravas—who were the Kuru heirs. She was now the great-grandmother of one hundred and six grandchildren. The Kurus would henceforth rule over the entire nation; now her family and her kingdom would be invincible, invulnerable. It would flourish, not perish...

But Vyas had portended otherwise. *'The green years of the earth are gone. Do not be a witness to the suicide of your own race.'*

The palace was filled with family and laughter. Satyavati had listened to the children's' chatter in the courtyard, filling the corridors, pervading the palace as they played below in the garden—the same garden where Bhishm had taught her sons to string the bow and arrow, where Dhritrashtra, Pandu and Vidur had been groomed to be astute marksmen.

The sound of the children had suffused her heart with hope and happiness. They were her new band of valiant warriors who would take over the nation. They were all together once again, they would all live and love happily ever after; they would conquer, they would marry, they would have more children, and they would be kings.

'No, they will die fighting each other for the throne! Leave before you witness this internecine bloodshed! Use Pandu's death as a pretext to retire to the forest, Ma...'

The ominousness of his words had frightened her then, but the fear had receded to make way for the realization to sink it, drowning in its sorrow. For once, she heeded him, and decided to leave Hastinapur. She could not shed anymore tears, her heart was so broken that she felt like the last piece of her had been wrenched away. She had thought she was unvanquished. She had power, wealth and progeny, but in her heir-yearning, prestige-hungry life, she had witnessed her husband, her two sons and one grandson die. She thought she had succeeded in using authority to achieve and accomplish, but where had it taken her? At this crossroads where her family would be annihilated in a bloodbath? Was her leaving for the forest an escape from an end that was so lost that she could not bear to face it? But she *had* to let Bhishm know why, to warn him about the future as well; Fate, as he called it. He had been her constant companion. He had been the only one who knew that, beneath her strength and ambitions lay her uncertain fears; it was this that made her the ruthless, assertive woman that the world saw. It was only he who had recognized her vulnerabilities and her attempts at self-preservation. How could she leave without him?

Ambika and Ambalika had surprisingly agreed to accompany her. Ambalika had never been the same since

Pandu had left for the forest with his two young wives, but his unexpected death had undone her completely. She now reminded Satyavati of herself when Chitrangad had died those many years ago.

Possibly, Ambika, too, had intuitively observed the beginning of the terrifying truth Vyas had foretold. Dhritrashtra had never forgiven her, blaming her indirectly for his blindness, his resentment churning to hate over the years. He barely tolerated her, as did her grandchildren. All had turned their back on Ambika a long time ago. Though she had fiercely held on to her ambition, her son's hate had completely disarmed her. Shunned by her own family, she now sought her salvation.

Was it acceptance or escape, Satyavati pondered over her decision. Had she, Satyavati, too, lost relevance in this palace? She and Bhishm still ruled the palace and kingdom. But it was time; it was the turn of the new generation of queens of Hastinapur—Madri was dead, Kunti remained the uncrowned queen, now the widowed queen mother. Sulabha, Vidur's sagacious wife, would never be queen, like her doomed husband could never be king. Gandhari, Dhritrashtra's queen, had turned the hurt and anger of having to marry a blind man on herself, and tied a blindfold on her bitter eyes. As the blind queen of a blind king, she shut her eyes to the world, the kingdom, and her hundred, short-sighted sons.

Satyavati had immediately sensed the new tension in the family since the arrival of Kunti and the Pandavas. Duryodhan, the eldest Kaurava, had not welcomed his cousins, displaying his resentment openly. Dhritrashtra had indulged his oldest son far too long, far too lavishly. Dhritrashtra was blind in every way: refusing to see his son's flaws, fortified each day by the poisonous mentoring of Shakuni, his brother-in-law. It was just like Ambika had previously indoctrinated a young Dhritrashtra to believe that he was the rightful heir, not Pandu.

There again, Bhishm and she had erred—to propitiate the piqued Dhritrashtra whom they considered had been unjustly sidestepped, they had been overly accommodating, allowing his unrequited ambition to infect his son. When the weak no longer remain weak, any support to make them strong feeds the natural hunger for power and privilege. To know when to stop is very important, and she had not.

Satyavati had got Kunti back to Hastinapur with the young Pandavas, but she was going to leave the young widow to fight alone for the throne for her sons. She would not be able to fight their battles any more. She was too tired, too crushed.

She shivered as a cold breeze blew, and it seemed like an ominous hurricane blowing over Hastinapur, which would take the city, her family and her people in a bloody storm. She had wanted heirs—she now had more than a hundred, destined to ruin the throne. Was that a future of her own making? She could not put it on the still strong shoulders of Bhishm either, though he had resolutely refused to come with her to the forest.

'How can you leave, especially when you have been told the future?' he had demanded. 'The war which Vyas mentions will not be between the descendants of the great Kuru king Bharat, but your blood; they are *your* descendants! The Kuru bloodline ended with me, Chitrangad and Virya. *You* are the grand matriarch of this new dynasty that you started. You can't forsake them.'

'I have to. I can't bear them killing each other, and that's what Vyas has said...' she pressed her lips together unhappily.

His voice was like a whiplash, cutting her short. 'You pride yourself on having control over your life, crafting your own path, so do it now! Stop this war if you can!'

'No, I can't. We started it, Dev!' she cried. 'I lost! Just a week ago, I thought I had got my world back, that though we had lost Pandu, we had got him back through the Pandavas. All of them together were kings of our future; I thought I had got my reward. But it's an illusion. Everything's undone, and it will end in destruction! My dreams will drown in rivers of blood ... our blood, the blood of our family, the blood of these very children!' she paused, trembling at the terrible truth. 'Your blood as well, Dev. You will perish as well. No, not like this! Whom will you choose? You will be a torn man, wretched and alone, fighting a pointless war within your family whom you have loved and lived for all these years. Dev, come with me, I entreat you. Let's not witness the destruction of our creation,' she implored, her heart sinking, recognizing the unmistakable determined glint in his eyes.

She pleaded again, clutching at his arm. 'Or accept your icchamrityu and go back to Ganga. Your mother is waiting for you!'

He moved away from her. 'For all your faults, I could never accuse you of being a coward,' he gave her an empty smile. 'But now you are leaving the battlefield even before the day has begun...'

'No, Dev, the day has long gone. We started this war, but I won't be there to watch it. No, Dev. Don't ask that of me.'

'But I need you here!' he said thickly. 'Hastinapur needs you, your family needs you, your orphaned Pandavas need you, Kunti needs you!' he faltered, his eyes bleak. '*I* need you!'

Her heart contracted painfully, but she shook her head,

bowing it to hide her grief. 'That is the significance we place on ourselves, bestowing us with self-importance. With me or you gone, the days will pass into years, the Kauravas and Pandavas will grow up. Leave them on their own. They don't need you, they don't need us. If you do believe in Fate, then what is to happen shall occur, with or without you. So, Dev, it's time to leave. Retire gracefully to the forest. You are obsessed, as I once was. I know it; one becomes a slave to one's obsession till it destroys one completely. Don't remain here in Hastinapur. Why do you choose to linger on?'

'I can't; I won't,' he said, that stubborn line on his lips. 'They need me. I have to be here to serve them and protect Hastinapur.'

'By selecting one over the other? Will you have the courage to do it? Why do you want to torture yourself more? Have you not suffered enough?' she cried, tears in her voice. 'Come, Dev, please come with me,' she begged, her pale face turned up towards him, her eyes filled with all her love. 'Let's go, Dev; let go of your oath, your principles, your life. Our work is done here, for good or for worse.'

'You are escaping at the worst hour,' he said viciously. 'You are a queen! You cannot flee when your throne is in danger!'

She shook her head violently, too choked to argue with him. She dropped his warm hand, her heart aching, swelling with unbounded anguish, weeping tears of blood and love. She would have to let go of him, and the thought made her shiver, her eyes closing briefly in horror. He would be alone, with no one to turn to.

She quickly turned away before he saw her tears, before his tormented face made her weak enough to stay back with him, with the throne, with doomed Hastinapur...

'You *are* a coward, you are running away!' he shouted after her, his voice breaking.

She sighed and kept walking; she was too fatigued to argue further with him...

~

She was now in the forest, with its endless trees and the Ganga flowing through the serene greens... Ganga again: always bigger, stronger and more popular than the smaller, darker Yamuna, who, like her, remained neglected and ignored: just as she was, as the fisher girl from the banks of the Yamuna.

Ganga. Would she ever forgive her for what she had done to her son? Each time she had caught sight of the river in the horizon from the palace in Hastinapur, she had been the conscience that pierced her.

She was standing in the river now, the cold waters gurgling at her waist. She had finished her morning ablutions, and she had to go back to the ashram where Ambika and Ambalika would be waiting for her.

And then she saw it. Just a speck, but the orange glow grew larger as she kept staring at it, rooted to the spot. She heard the growing screams and the frightened cries of the animals, the terror-stricken screeching of the wildly flying birds—the forest was on fire, the flames licking hungrily at branches and felling tall trees as it ravaged new paths, swiftly approaching her.

She gazed into the unwelcoming waters, and saw rivulets of blood streaming into it—of Shantanu, of her sons, and of all the heirs of Hastinapur. Even of Amba.

Satyavati caught her reflection in the waters. Parashar's boon was still with her. She looked young, but was so old now that she had lost count of the years she had lived on this earth. It was time to leave this earthly kingdom, too. She took a step deeper into the river and another and another, not faltering, a prayer on her lips. 'Absolve me, oh Ganga, forgive me for what I did. Wash away my sins, give me my salvation...'

She no longer felt the wet gravel under her feet, but the clear waters rushing, swirling gently, closing on her, her submerged face and her eyes which she finally closed in tired surrender. Ganga had accepted her in her arms.